Black River

Richard Cucarese

To Fran and Emilio AND Vinny,
Thanks for the support.
Enjoy the book!

Richard Cucarese

Note for Librarians: a cataloguing record for this book that includes Dewey Classification and US Library of Congress numbers is available from the National Library of Canada. The complete cataloguing record can be obtained from the National Library s online database at: www.nlc-bnc.ca/amicus/index-e.html

ISBN 1-4120-2262-2

TRAFFORD

This book was published on-demand in cooperation with Trafford Publishing. On-demand publishing is a unique process and service of making a book available for retail sale to the public taking advantage of on-demand manufacturing and Internet marketing. On-demand publishing includes promotions, retail sales, manufacturing, order fulfilment, accounting and collecting royalties on behalf of the author.

Suite 6E, 2333 Government St., Victoria, B.C. V8T 4P4, CANADA
Phone   250-383-6864   Toll-free   1-888-232-4444 (Canada & US)
Fax   250-383-6804   E-mail   sales@trafford.com
Web site www.trafford.com   TRAFFORD PUBLISHING IS A DIVISION OF TRAFFORD HOLDINGS LTD.
Trafford Catalogue #04-0090   www.trafford.com/robots/04-0090.html
10 9   8   7   6   5   4   3   2   1

ACKNOWLEDGMENTS...

I would like to begin by thanking family and friends who have been a constant source of support during the writing of this novel. There are so many of you to list, but none of you are forgotten in my thoughts.

Thanks to the members of the NYPD Public Relations Staff for helping me gather facts for the novel. I'm especially grateful, because they did much of this only a few weeks after the September 11th tragedy. Thanks again, and none of us will ever forget the heroism you all displayed in the line of duty.

Thanks to the staff of the Logan Inn, who allowed me to use their great establishment as an integral part of the story.

Thank you also to Scott Edwards, editor of the New Hope Gazette, who took the time to read the manuscript and write an article in his paper about the book, and myself. Your support on this project has been greatly appreciated. I would also like to thank Scott for introducing me to Amanda Eick, who shot the great photographs for this book. Her work ethic and attitude were top-notch.

Lastly, I would like to thank my wife, Jennifer. Her faith in me never wavered while I wrote this book over the past three years. During this time, we've been married, bought a house that we've been remodeling since day one, and in June of 2003, she gave me the best gift of all, my daughter, Giavanna. This book is dedicated to them.

CHAPTER 1

"EVIL HAS COME HERE TO DIE!" The haphazard, scrawled writing on the buildings sidewall was what caught your attention even before your eyes drifted towards the lifeless, bloodied body that lay at the Ferry Landing walkway this morning. The ominous color of death looked as if it bled from the wall. As Police Chief Tom Miller surveyed the crime scene a dull, hammering feeling started to pound his skull. That there was a murder in this quiet town of New Hope was chilling enough. The murder, on the surface, showed all the makings of a hate crime and it was enough to make Tom's skin crawl. "AIDS, DIE FAG, DIE" was written on the blood soaked cloth mercilessly driven through the victims chest with a long knife adorned with a wood and jewel encrusted handle.

"It looks like the knife was plunged almost to his spine," stated Sergeant Al Jeaneau. "We're showing at least ten knife wounds. His skull was split wide open, and his face is so badly beaten we can't even tell if it's a local resident. We're searching for the victim's identification now, Tom. You have to be pure evil to do this, just because someone is a homosexual. And why in this town, of all places Tom, just to prove some sort of sick point?" The Sergeant had seen enough. As he turned to head back to search for any more reasons as to how this despicable display of violence took place, Tom heard the low growl of Al's voice. "Why? Why here?"

The angered, questioning reverberation of Al's voice only made Tom's skull pounding turn thunderous. It was bad enough Tom understood the ramifications of this crime, but for Sergeant Al Jeaneau and many other openly homosexual members of the writers and artists' community of New Hope, this heinous act took on an even more painful and chilling reality. The hatred of the big world had found their small hamlet.

New Hope, Pennsylvania is a truly old time picturesque town nestled in between the hills of Upper Bucks County, and along the banks of the Delaware River. During the cold days leading up to the Christmas holidays, it takes on all the trappings of a scene from a Dickens holiday story.

In its heyday of the 1940-50's, a number of homosexual writers and artists flocked here to revel in its serene and peaceful nature, while at the same time, escaping the fears involved with big city living. It was a great fit for these individuals since the town had many artisans in its mix since the 1800's. The residents of New Hope take great pride in their town, and their ability to have diverse cultures, points of view, and lifestyles mix together in a very homogenous setting.

Now, Chief Miller achingly thought, the fabric of this composed setting was about to be torn apart. Tom had seen this before, while he was a Homicide Detective in New York City. His beat was Greenwich Village, a very openly homosexual community in Manhattan. When there had been a "gay bashing" or even worse, a murder in the Village, Tom knew the uproar and the repercussions that would ensue. The finger always pointed at the police for not being vigilant, or even caring. Then, the demonstrations and rallies would follow. The Mayor, and the other assorted, ass kissing, "need the gay vote" politicians coming out of the woodwork like termites, with their "we feel your pain" speeches. Now, he wondered how a small community such as this would handle such an atrocious crime.

Joining Chief Miller and Sergeant Jeaneau were Officers Robert Pagano, Jenn Gates, and Andrew Rose. While Jeaneau and Pagano had been with the force fifteen and eight years respectively, Gates and Rose had only two years of service under their belts. While they all had been busy in this bustling tourist town writing out speeding tickets, breaking up minor altercations at some of the clubs, or moving along the local teens loitering on some of the street corners at night, none of them could have fathomed that this grisly murder would take place in this quaint borough. The numb feeling gripping all who were involved with the crime scene would pale in comparison to what would soon transpire.

Tom had already sent in the obligatory call to the Pennsylvania State Police barracks, considering the magnitude of the matter at hand. Sergeant Jeaneau took Pagano and Gates to help him search the Ferry Landing area by the river to see if they could find any identification of the brutally beaten victim.

As he moved his hands through his sandy-blonde hair, the rubber sole of his shoe met the Marlboro he'd been inhaling. Damn cigarettes, I'd better give them up soon. Tom possessed the youthful look and physique of a man a good ten years younger than his forty-eight years of age. Today though, his body felt twice as old. The damn banging in his head, damn familiar crime scene. Al was right, why in this town? He looked past the crime scene, and his ice blue eyes met with the equally ice blue water of the frigid Delaware.

Within a few minutes of the dispatch, the unit of State Trooper John Boyle came hurtling into view. He came to a screeching halt at the intersection of Main and Ferry Streets, and some onlookers and a local member of the press came rushing towards him.

"Good morning, and I have no comment to make at this time Miss Mary Mc Guigan!" Boyle yelled in the direction of the well-dressed young woman from the New Hope Gazette.

"Good morning to you too, and I haven't even asked you anything yet Trooper Boyle. But since you're here, what's going on down by the river, John?"

"Why it looks like an investigation is goin' on by the river, Miss Mc Guigan! Now, I'm goin' down to converse with one Chief Tom Miller and assess the situation, if you'll excuse me," and on that note, John Boyle, the barrel-chested Irish immigrant and combat proven Marine, strode off to do just that with the, got-you-again-Mary grin firmly affixed to his face. To anyone who was familiar with the history of these two, it was not unusual for these sparring matches to take place, and John Boyle just landed the first punch.

"God damn you John, what is going on by the river!" the exasperated reporter yelled. From the crimson color shooting up her neck, it looked like an eruption of Vesuvian proportions was about to take place.

"Miss Mc Guigan, for shame! And with Christmas being this Saturday! That's the problem with you Yankee micks, so hot tempered..."

and again with the grin, and off to the scene he went. And the winner, by knockout in the first round.

Tom managed a wry smile as the Irishman approached. "Are we done fucking with Mary this morning, John?" Tom inquired, as he shook John's hand.

"Aye, no I am not! She needs to learn proper protocol. And you, with the mouth too! Forgive them Father," John said as he put his hands together and looked up to the heavens. "Heathens, the whole lot of them Lord, they know not what they do." His eyes caught Tom's and again the leprechaun's smile appeared. "Now Tommy, let's have a look, shall we?"

Trooper Boyle's frame of mind underwent a chameleon like change upon approaching the murder scene. A former Philadelphia Homicide Detective himself, he was all business now. "Do we have an approximate time the victim was discovered, Tommy?"

"Estimated time was around six A.M. Ken Coverdale found him. The poor guy was out for his morning jog before he opens his restaurant, and he comes upon this horror. He ran all the way to the station. He's probably still sitting down there shaking."

Tom's head began to pound even harder while viewing the body. On the victims' badly beaten face, brownish, caked blood had iced up over the eyelids and lips. So brutal, and yet so familiar. Too damn familiar.

Sergeant Jeaneau made his way over to the two men with a very quizzical look on his face. "We found the wallet thrown in the bushes." He paused to catch his breath. "Cripes, Al, you look like you're going to pass out, man! What's wrong?" asked John Boyle.

"You're not going to believe who this is," was all that Al could say. He handed Tom the picture license from the deceased man's wallet. They looked intently at the beaten skull, while a resemblance to the photograph began to transform. "Sweet Lord!" John exclaimed. "That's Luke?"

The victim of this wretched slaying was Lucas Stone, owner of the hottest jazz joint on New Hope's Main Street, 'The "A" Train'. "Why Lucas?" Tom asked in hushed tone. "He was one of the most loved and respected men in this town."

Al stood next to Tom, nodding his head in agreement to Tom's statement. He then began to shake his head copiously. "Oh God! Phil!" exclaimed Al. "This is going to kill him. They were inseparable." Al began walking to the beckoning call of Officer Rose. Tom knelt down next to Luke's body. He began thinking about what Al said. They were inseparable. Phil Antos was Lucas Stone's companion. For all of Luke's Nordic looks and muscular build, Phil was much more diminutive in stature. Phil had the features of a light skinned Pole, the most piercing green eyes and raven black hair.

The two of them had met when Phil moved here twelve years ago. Lucas was already well established in the community, and 'The "A" Train' was drawing in a considerable amount of business. Phil found Lucas very approachable, an equal to Phil in his love and appreciation of jazz. Both of them had dabbled in jazz music in their youth, but with no major success. Lucas discovered his forte existed in promoting area talent at his fledgling club. Soon, word had spread to the big names about this jamming club in the middle of nowhere. In the ensuing years, Cassandra Wilson, the

Marsalis brothers, George Benson, and the late Miles Davis, just to name a few, would be booking for engagements at his intimate club.

Phil found his niche in design. When 'The "A" Train' was in need of expansion, and the inner sanctum needed a makeover, Phil offered his services to Lucas, gratis. What emerged from this dynamic combination of talent were the hottest area and big name jazz talents, playing in the trendiest designed club this side of Miami Beach. The club had all the best elements of New York City resonance, and South Beach Art-Deco style.

The two of them knocked the design and jazz world on its ear. They were a success, a team, in business, but more importantly in each other's lives. They were inseparable and remained that way for years to come. Now they had to tell Phil that love was lost, and it was taken from him in the darkest and cruelest way man had created.

As Tom righted himself, Sergeant Jeaneau again approached the area where he and John Boyle had remained. "Tommy, John, you may want to see this." Al led them further down the Ferry Landing walk. "Gentleman, I've never seen anything like this. This goes beyond a hate crime. This is like a cult or ritual sacrifice." Down on the Landing's stone steps was a small cloth, neatly folded. "Drew found this and unwrapped it. Okay Drew, undo the cloth." As Officer Rose unfolded the cloth, neatly placed in the middle of it were two eyes. As Rose bagged them for evidence, Tom reluctantly picked up the cloth. On the cloth was the same scrawled writing that was on the wall back on Ferry Street. He began reading, "Homosexuals are blind to their sins, but God sees you, and he DAMN'S YOU." The cloth, the eyes, Jesus, it's happening again. The pain in Tom's head was reaching a breaking point. His ears felt like they were sizzling from the pressure.

Tom looked up at Rose and the others. "Did you happen to find the victim's tongue?" The question caught them so off guard that Officer Pagano questioned Tom on everyone's behalf. "Excuse me Chief, but did I hear you right? Did we find his tongue?"

Tom glanced at Pagano and the others almost apologetically. "Yes, Rob you heard me right, his tongue." Pagano glanced at Tom. You could tell he was becoming visibly shaken by Tom's question. "No, Chief. I can definitely tell you we have not found the victim's tongue. Tom, what the hell is going on here? What are we dealing with here, man?"

Tom leaped to his feet, his mind racing too quickly to answer Pagano's question. Al Jeaneau and John Boyle were following Tom, almost on his heels now. He was right beside Lucas' beaten body again. "John, give me some gloves please." His ears were hissing, his mind flashing the darkest images of horror. Somewhere, from the depths of his mind, he could hear the voice. Every second, it was getting clearer. It was right by Tom's shoulder. "You're remembering everything, aren't you Tom? I told you it would happen again. I have come back with a vengeance. I will turn your dreams into nightmares." He expected the knife, but it never came. His head shot up quickly, but no one was directly behind except for Jeaneau and Boyle.

"Tommy, you okay pal? You look like you've seen the devil, himself," said John, with visible concern. "What are you thinkin' lad? Is there something to all of this?"

"I'll tell you soon enough, John." Tom affixed the sterile gloves and knelt down directly next to the head of Lucas Stone. Again, the voice came. "With a vengeance...a vengeance...a vengeance." Tom pried open the blood encrusted mouth, and as he peered in, the town of New Hope became a little colder, a little darker, in Tom Miller's world. He pulled the bloody cloth from the orifice recently housing Luke Stone's tongue. His mind exploded into a kaleidoscope of forbidding thoughts. He was back. Jesus Christ, he was back.

Tom's systems were about ready to overload. He couldn't be back. Get hold of yourself, man. He's been put away for almost fifteen years. He's going to die in seven days. But if not him, then who? Who would want to renew this chain of evil again? Another one, God no! His sick mind, fueling a prophecy through another disciple? But, even the writing on the wall and the note he just read; exactly like the son-of-a-bitches. Seven days, and he'll die. This note, don't open it. Don't open it, and maybe it will all go away. His brain felt like it was hemorrhaging from the pressure.

Al was trying to snap him back to reality. "Tommy, what is it, man? What's on the cloth? Do you want me to look?"

Tom gathered his composure back somewhat, but his hands still trembled a bit. He began to peel open the cloth. "That's all right, Al. This is for me."

"For you? But, how do you know... Who would do this and write to you? Who did this, Tom?" Al was as perplexed as anyone in the vicinity of the murder scene.

You have to look. Tom was still trying to convince himself. He looked down, and there it was, spread out in front of his eyes like the pillager returning home with the spoils of war. "VENGEANCE", was boldly written across the top. "I will come from the wilderness, with a vengeance. This is just the first. In the next seven days, I will make you remember." It has begun, Tom thought. Even if it wasn't him in body, it was his sick handiwork being carried out. He had brought evil back into Tom's house.

"Tommy," John said, looking very concerned. "For the life of me, you look like you've seen the Almighty, or a ghost. What's goin' on lad? Who is this?" He paused for a second and then looked at Tom again quizzically. "Tommy, you're not thinking about.."

Tom got up, and placed the blood soaked "scripture" in John Boyle's gloved hands. "You had it right a while back, John. It's a note from the devil himself, and he's back." Tom lit up another Marlboro and walked to the river's edge to be alone, amongst all this chaos. John Boyle looked, opened up the cloth, and quickly closed it. "Christ, Tommy, the son-of-a-bitch! It can't be him!" Who though, he thought. Who?

While Tom looked out over the Delaware River, a hard, bone chilling rain started from the east; hard enough to wash the blood from the pavement of Ferry Landing. As it rolled down like waves around Tom's shoes and into the cold, black depths of the frigid river, the river now knew what Tom did. Death had seen her waters before, but never with such evil as this. Yes, death had come to her again, but this time it wouldn't leave. Not just yet.

CHAPTER 2

Back at the station house, everyone milled around trying to make sense of a senseless, murderous crime. Chief Miller had his door closed, and was on the phone. Trooper Boyle was close enough to hear fragments of the conversation.

"I may need to call on you again," he heard Tom say in a hushed voice. "Yeah, I know. I can't believe it either. It's a sick, cruel, world. I'll be in touch soon, pal. Best wishes to the wife and kids. Thanks, I'll tell her. Merry Christmas to you too."

When he opened the door, Tom saw an audience had gathered around the station. "Everything okay, pal?"

He looked in John's direction and nodded. "Well, I'm sure you're all trying to get a semblance of what we just witnessed out there. I'm also sure it's safe to say that you've all summed up this murder has a lot more to it than meets the eye."

"You could say that Chief," Officer Pagano piped up. "I mean, this murder borders on the occult."

"Well, Tom," John Boyle added. "You and I know it can't be who we think it is, considering he's locked and ready to die in a few days. It's probably not any of his disciples either, being that most of them were locked up too for their knowledge of his acts. Maybe, it's a copycat, but why now? One last glorious stand, possibly?"

Tom again looked around the room and spotted Mary McGuigan from the New Hope Gazette. "Mary, I need a big favor to ask of you."

"Go ahead."

"I've never asked you not to print a story before, and I'm not specifically asking you not to print this one, but..."

"Tommy, you've probably been the most honest Chief I've reported about in ten years of journalism. If you're asking me to keep quiet on certain things, I'll do my best. But, if you don't mind the nosy part of me asking, I'm kind of curious as to why?"

"Mary, we may have a copycat killer on our hands. I'm again stressing, we may. I don't care if you report that there was a murder. That's a given." His comment gave everyone a well-needed laugh. "You know as well as I do, Mary, a murder in this town is almost unthinkable. The major city print and television news will be all over this story. I already spoke with Ken Coverdale. He has agreed to say nothing more than that he came upon the body during his morning jog. He realizes the magnitude of this murder. He realizes the effect a brutal, hate crime murder would have on this town especially. He also realizes how badly the murder of a much loved member of this town is going to hurt this community, especially happening two days before Christmas."

"Tom, you have my full cooperation. I will report nothing more than the basics of the murder, who was murdered, where he was found, and that the police are exhaustively investigating the case. All I ask, is you keep me abreast of all aspects of the case."

"In other words," John piped in, "Mary wants first dibs on the story when you find the killer. It sounds fair to me, Tom." John looked at Mary and winked.

"Why Trooper Boyle, it's a revelation. You do have a heart in that Neanderthal body of yours after all."

"Please McGuigan, you're makin' me blush," Boyle retorted.

"Okay, if the love fest is over," Tom added. "Mary, thank you for your help in a very touchy situation. I promise you that this department will do everything in its power to get you your story, just please, be patient with me. I've been through cases like this before. I don't want the town turning on itself. It could get to be an ugly case, as I'm sure you can imagine."

"You have my word Tom," Mary replied.

"Okay, well, with that being said, let me pose this question to my officers and you, Mary. Do any of you remember a man named Martin Kane?" Tom inquired. Everyone began to look around, except for Jeaneau and Boyle.

"Maybe this will refresh their memory, Tommy. You mean Martin "Lucifer" Kane, "The Reverend Reaper"? He preached against homosexuality in his World Church in the Soho District of Manhattan. Had a lot of followers, especially for being in that area. He murdered and mutilated how many gay men and women in the Village?"

"Seven all together, five men and two women", added Jeaneau. "He did them sacrificial style."

"Of course, the Kane case," replied Officer Gates. "You worked the case when you were Homicide in New York."

"Yes Jenn, I did. They were grisly murders. Looked very similar to what you all witnessed at Ferry Landing."

"How did Kane come about?" Mary asked.

"It was the summer of 1985, and the city was gripped in a panic. I mean, it was only about seven or eight years after the Son of Sam Murders, and the papers and television news were making the new murderer out to be a modern day, "Jack the Ripper of Homosexuals." You know, appearing out of the fog, committing his crimes and disappearing from where he came, leaving the police baffled. It was all very theatrical for print, but no substance. No offense, Mary."

"None taken, Tom," Mary replied with a wry smile.

"And Kane?" asked Jenn Gates. "Where did he fit in, Tom?"

"Well, at each murder, the murderer would leave us his calling card; a priest's collar always placed on a table in the victim's residence. We had never even really heard that much about Kane until we started questioning residents in the Village. More than a few said we should check out the good reverend's preaching down in his Soho church. So my partner, Stan Tilden went as a perspective parishioner to check him out."

"And what then?" asked Officer Rose. "Well, to say the least Drew, he spewed a lot of hatred. He said gays were sick, sex starved, disease infested scum. He said they deserved AIDS. It was God's way of punishing them for their abnormal behavior."

"You guys followed him for quite a while, didn't you Tom?" asked Officer Pagano.

"Yeah we did Rob, but to no avail in the first days. His alibis were tight, and his followers tightlipped. The toughest predicament we faced was, because of his strong anti-gay stance in such an openly homosexual stronghold, there were always protests in front of his church. The only times he really left was under police protection and private security because, understandably, he received numerous threats against his person. We were only able to question him and see if he thought anyone in his congregation would take his fiery preaching to the next level".

"I can only imagine his answer," added John Boyle.

"He said he didn't know of anyone off hand, but, he added he prayed that in the future some of his flock could act as God's knights and defend the kingdom from the evils of homosexuality. He hoped they could eliminate the homosexuals as the Crusaders had eliminated the evil, Arabian hordes."

"Nice guy, a real charmer," added Mary.

"Yeah, he was all that, Mary. So, he pretty much became a non-factor. Besides, his attorney got Judge Rieger to deny any more search warrants, since we really had no hard evidence linking him to the crimes other than his rhetoric. The crime scenes, for how grisly they were, turned up no fingerprints, skin or blood samples other than the victims."

"Didn't the papers end up finding out that some politicians put the squeeze on the Judge because he had some skeletons in his closet? It was something to do about an adulterous relationship with a seventeen year old girl, right?"

"Good memory, Al," Tom replied. "Plus, they revealed Kane was receiving money from and contributing money to those same politicians. He had some very influential friends in high places who agreed with his twisted teachings. Thankfully, their careers were destroyed when this was uncovered by the police and the media, and Kane was charged with the murders."

Jenn Gates was still intrigued. "But if he was in his residence at the church, how was he getting out if he was under constant surveillance, and how did you end up nailing him?"

"The tunnels, young lass, the tunnels!" exclaimed John Boyle.

"Tunnels?" asked Jenn, curiously. "Yes Jenn, the tunnels." Tom walked over to a blackboard in the conference room. "In many parts of the city, dating as far back as the Revolutionary War days, tunnels were crudely constructed to move everything from goods and munitions, to troops. Soho and Greenwich Village were no exception. Many of the Five Points gangs used them in the 1800's. The tunnels went neglected for many years until Prohibition. Many of the lofts and galleries in today's Soho District were warehouses during Prohibition, and quite a few of those warehouses were owned by the mafia. Well, to move the liquor to the speakeasies located throughout the city, they needed to the store and deliver it through a safe place.

"The tunnels, of course!" Jenn exclaimed. "When my dad grew up in Chicago, he read stories about Capone using the tunnels there for the same thing."

"After Prohibition, the tunnels were never really used again. Many of them were boarded up, or fell into disrepair from neglect. If it hadn't been for one of the old timers telling Stan and I about them in idle conversation, we probably wouldn't have even remembered of their existence. We found our way to the tunnels around Kane's church. We checked them out for three weeks, with no luck. The day our luck turned, Stan went up ahead to check out some of the tributaries located almost directly under the church. All of a sudden I heard a scuffle and a yell. I ran quickly to where the noise had come from, and I was face to face with him. He was standing over top of Stan. He had already stabbed Stan in the back once, and was coming in for the kill. That's when I shot him in the knife hand. He lost two fingers from the shot. I didn't kill him because I wanted him to stand trial. I wanted to know he was the only one."

"You thought there was another?" Rob asked. "Wait a minute, Al said seven. There were eight murdered."

"The Feds found articles of the seven victims in Kane's residence, at the church, but none from the eighth. Kane's going to die in eight days and he still only admits to seven killings. He never says anything of the eighth." The look of pain etched on Tom's face was showing. "The victims, you knew one?" asked Officer Rose.

"The seventh one was my dads' soul mate," Tom replied. "Oh, I'm sorry. I didn't know your dad is a homosexual. I didn't mean to pry," offered Rose.

"No harm done. You couldn't have known my father was homosexual, unless you'd read about the case."

"You said your dad was homosexual, Tom, don't you mean is homosexual?" Drew asked again.

"No, was Drew".

"Your dad…"

"The eighth victim, Drew. They found him the same day we caught Kane," Tom solemnly answered.

CHAPTER 3

Sergeant Jeaneau accompanied Tom to the residence of Phil Antos and the now deceased Lucas Stone. This was the part of being a cop Tom detested. It always conjured up the memory of his father, the memory of his gruesome murder. The memory of Stan Tilden, coming across the police tape, the blocked the stairwell leading to Edgar Miller's loft. The look on Stan's face, how he couldn't even look at Tom, just grabbed him by the shoulders; how he couldn't even grasp the words he was choking on, the tears streaming down Stan's face. Less than two hours ago, they were celebrating the capture of Martin Kane at the precinct house. Now, his father was gone.

Tom and Al made their way down Main Street. He began to think about the man who shaped his life. Tom pulled a cigarette from his coat, and lit it quickly. The deep inhaling of the Marlboro seemed to clear his mind even more. He looked out the window of the patrol car and took in the early morning dreariness for all it was worth. Well dad, he thought, we meet the evil in men's hearts and minds again. The smoke billowed from his mouth like exhaust steam on a chilly day. God, I wish you were here dad.

Edgar Miller was the consummate jazz musician. His inquisitive and free spirited characteristics were displayed throughout his musical repertoire. The sounds emerging from his saxophone could flow through your soul, like a stream gently running its course through a forest. "Smooth," was how John Coltrane described Edgar's sound when he came to visit. Numerous jazz greats came to visit and play with Edgar Miller from the 1950's, until his untimely death, in 1985. The list of names was a "Who's-Who" of jazz performers. Ella Fitzgerald, her melodic voice filling his loft, as he matched her with his sweet sounds rising from that gleaming brass saxophone. Miles Davis, the innovative trumpeter who pushed Edgar's talents, and sometimes his patience, to the limits. The two collaborated on four, well-received albums. Gil Evans, Louis Armstrong, Duke Ellington, and so many more played with him. But, the one that would make the biggest impact in Edgar's already solid career was Gary Johan.

Cut from the same jazz-fusion cloth as Miles Davis, Gary cast his spell on everyone he touched with his music. Edgar would be no exception to this formula. They met at an open jam with Evans and Davis in the summer of 1951, and the rest was history. They proceeded to collaborate on eight albums, two of them winning Grammy Awards. But, aside from the way they approached their musical relationship, their personal relationship blossomed also. It was this commonality that would keep them together until their tragic demise, exactly one week apart, in the sorrow-filled summer of 1985.

No one in the childhood years of Tom Miller would be able to understand the relationship of Edgar Miller and Gary Johan, let alone the relationship between the two of them and Tom when he was growing up. In the 1950's and 1960's, such talk of their relationship was taboo. In some cases, it could physically get you into trouble. At school, Tom's teachers and friends only knew Tom lived alone with his divorced father. It was the only way the situation could be handled. The Village, even with being enveloped by the entire Metropolitan area, was at least a type of safe haven for alternative lifestyles. Safe, until the 'Summer of Hate'.

Tom grew up only knowing his father and Gary. Tom's mother, Mary, moved out to Seattle to start a new life after the realization marriage and a baby could not change who Edgar was. Since he had the most stable career, the raising of Tom fell into his waiting hands. At twenty-two years of age, Edgar never shirked his responsibilities; if anything, he relished in them. He also made it a point to have Mary visit whenever she wanted to. The first year she came back East five times. He traveled out there twice. The second year, after the divorce was finalized, and Gary began living with Edgar full time, the visits from Mary became less frequent. By the third year, she'd moved from her apartment and left no forwarding address or phone number. Mary was gone, never to be heard from again.

Edgar and Gary raised Tom in a home full of learning, kindness, understanding, and most importantly, love. They never pushed their views or opinions on Tom. When Tom lost interest in music and wanted to pursue football and baseball in high school, they encouraged him. Gary, a pretty good athlete in his own right, was the one who taught Tom the powerful pitching style that would, in a few years time, send scouts from various colleges and professional teams, such as the Cardinals and the Mets, scurrying for contracts.

Tom's senior year was plentiful with misfortunes. Tom's dreams of diamond stardom were to be put to and end in the spring of 1969, when he obliterated the rotator cuff on his throwing arm. Because of the injury, he became ineligible for the draft that year, which brought a heavy sigh of relief from both Edgar and Gary, who were staunch and vehement supporters of the Greenwich Village anti-war movement. It was, however, not an opinion shared by Tom, who felt he was obligated to serve his country, and not to have someone less fortunate be placed in peril, instead of himself. Although Tom's decision not to dodge the draft caused considerable friction in the household at times, Gary and Edgar never got in the way of his decision. They also didn't question him two years later when he explained his decision to enter the Police Academy. Police treatment of known homosexuals could be a fairly perilous experience, especially for males in the 1970's, but they both knew Tom's moral convictions of right and wrong would always prevail.

"Chief." Sergeant Jeaneau's voice brought Tom back to the present. "Got a lot on your mind with this one, I can imagine. We're coming up to Phil's house."

"Yeah, Al," Tom replied, as he flicked the spent butt of his cigarette out the window. "It's amazing how much your mind remembers in a five minute drive."

They both took in the incredible beauty of Phil and Lucas' residence when they pulled in the drive. Estates at the Riverwoods, as its name bore out, sat atop one of the numerous rocky and wooded knolls surrounding the borough. From the grounds of their house, the borough of New Hope, the bridge into Lambertville, New Jersey, and the Delaware's waters were laid out below. Its beauty caught your eyes in the same way it must have caught any of the multitudes of artists who'd painted scenes of this serene area. Today, though, the town and the river had a very dark and still look about them. Even the rain and stiff winds couldn't push away the feeling of evil lurking amongst the rolling landscape.

The house itself was a sight to behold. Every detail was taken into account. Phil commissioned one of his well-known architect friends and the builders to turn blueprints, rocks, and brush land into Lucas and Phil's dream house. Phil had designed the house from the pattern of its slate roof, to the highly wrought doorknobs, to the elaborate brickwork for the driveway.

A beautiful evergreen wreath, adorned with a few elegant ribbons on the main door, caught Al and Tom's attention. On a few of the bows, in gold leaf writing, the words, "Lucas And Phil Wish You A Merry Christmas And A Glorious 2000!" brought Al and Tom back to the reality this was not going to be a happy holiday. "Damn it," Al muttered, "I hate this part."

Tom held part of the ribbon in his hand and turned to Al. "This," as he shook the festive ornament, "doesn't make it any easier".

They could hear movement in the house when Tom rang the bell. They could also hear the sounds of Duke Ellington rising from a stereo somewhere in the structure. They heard the sound of footsteps approaching. "Just a minute," they heard Phil say, as the music was lowered to a more appropriate level.

Phil opened the door, greeting the officers with his usual beaming smile. "Well, if it isn't my two favorite Keystone Cops. Do come in!" Phil Antos laughed. His charm and humor was always disarming. Phil could make anyone feel comfortable and at home with his demeanor.

"Good morning, Phil," Tom answered with an awkward grin. It was the best Tom could muster, and Phil's lightheartedness made the situation even more abysmal. Al quietly said hello to Phil as he and Tom entered the luxuriously appointed hallway. Phil had decorated the main stairway and the hall with assorted greens and holly for the holidays. The crystal chandelier sparkled like the North Star. All the brass and silver items in the hall gleamed, and all the mahogany furniture shined as if dust had never permeated this area to rest on their surfaces.

"Gentleman, you look, excuse the expression, like something that the cat dragged in. Please, let me take your coats."

"Phil, that's okay," Tom said. "We have to talk to you."

"Oh nonsense, we have all day to talk. Listen, you caught me right in the middle of baking Christmas cookies. Go in the sitting room, and take a load off. I'm sure you gentleman could use a break, and then we could talk. I'll be back in a minute. Make yourself at home!" he yelled in their direction. "I have an ashtray in there if you'd like to smoke, Tom. Bad habit, though. I wish I could persuade you and Lucas to quit. You know you've got a lovely wife and son who need you around, but again, who am I to meddle?"

Tom and Al moved to the sitting room. The sounds of Ellington still softly wafted from two miniature speakers located in the top corners of the rooms opposing walls. A fire was roaring with Floridian warmth. On top of the Italian marble mantelpiece were more greens and holly, mixed together with a few small ornaments and some deep red colored candles in jars. The candles gave off an aroma of cinnamon and apple. Mixed with the smell of the new logs burning, it presented the physical and mental perception of warmth.

In the one corner of this charming space, behind the two gold upholstered Queen Anne chairs upon which the men now sat, was a freshly cut Frazier Fir tree, which easily reached ten feet in height, and also added to the fragrance in the room. The tree was adorned with everything from modern mechanical ornaments, to blown glass antiques dating back to the late 1800's. In the other corner were two beautifully carved oak tables, which were topped with various shapes, sizes and colors of picture frames, and a few items purchased during trips abroad. Oriental rugs were laid over the parquet flooring in the room, and a beautifully appointed gold upholstered love seat, with burgundy pillows, was across from Al and Tom. The crown molding was painted in a majestic gold leaf. The walls, done in a stylish hunter green, poked out from behind various modern and classically styled paintings produced by local artists. A fair mixture of modern and classic design ran throughout the house, as only Phil Antos could pull it off. It was no small wonder numerous people of influence in the Bucks County and Philadelphia locales utilized Phil's interior designing expertise. The house exuded an air of elegance, warmth, and happiness. Today though, Tom would only bring sadness to it.

Tom extinguished his cigarette and quickly lit another. So much for trying to quit. "You know what? The bows were bad enough, but this," as he motioned to all the festiveness of the sitting room, "is killing me. It's making the situation unbearable."

"I know," replied Al. "I was just thinking the same damn thing." They both could smell the fresh baked cookies now. "You know," Phil said, as he walked down the hall towards the sitting room. "I was just thinking about all of you at the station just a few minutes before you rang the bell. As a matter of fact, some of these cookies were going to be delivered your way, just as soon as Lucas came home".

"Where is Lucas this morning Phil?" asked Tom. "Where else, Tom? He's at 'The "A" Train', Phil said with a smile. "The man is non-stop energy. I don't know how he does it sometimes. He left me a note on the kitchen table. He left about three-thirty this morning to go finish paperwork. You know he is so quiet, I didn't even hear him leave."

"Lucas hasn't mentioned any problems with anyone at the club, has he?"

"None I can think of, Tom."

"Has everything been alright around the house, Phil? No quarrels?" Al asked Phil.

"Yes, everything's been fine. Nothing but bliss, as always is the case here." Phil looked rather puzzled at the line of questioning. "Why do you ask?" He began to shuffle the cookies on the platter.

God, how Tom hated this, especially when it was someone he knew and cared about. He remembered having to tell his father when the police had found Gary murdered at their studio, which was located two blocks away from Edgar and Gary's loft. "Phil, there is no easy way to tell you this."

"What's the matter, Tom?" Again, Phil shuffled the platter.

"We believe we found Lucas' body at Ferry Landing this morning."

"What are you trying to tell me Tom?" Phil's expression reminded Tom of a deer caught in a car's headlights. Unfortunately, the deer was about ready to feel the crushing impact of a direct hit.

"Lucas was murdered, Phil. I'm so sorry".

A tear streamed down Phil's face. "Why...why, that can't be... it just can't be true. I mean he was....". His hands shook so violently, the plate of cookies came crashing to the wooden floor. Shards of red china speared through the soft dough, like a knife through skin. The art of death as portrayed on Phil Antos' floor. "Oh, my!" Phil exclaimed.

Al jumped to his feet and began to help Phil. "Phil, relax. I'll get this." Tom sat Phil down in the wing chair that he previously occupied.

Phil looked up at Tom, the tears flooding from his eyes. "Who would do such a thing?"

Tom knelt down next to Phil. "Al and I were hoping you might know."

Phil tried to calm himself down as best as he could. "Is it why you asked how Lucas and I were getting along?"

"Yes, Phil. I'm sorry, but when someone is murdered, we have to cover all of our bases. Again, I apologize."

"No," Phil began to wipe away some of the tears, and compose himself. His hands were still trembling fiercely, and he began to sigh. "That's okay. The two of you were only doing your job. I wouldn't have expected anything less from either one of you."

"Phil, could you think of anyone?" Al asked when he returned from disposing of the cookies and broken china.

"I don't know Al. I can't think of anyone having a dispute with him, even in his business dealings. He haggled non-stop with his vendors, but they all respected him. Everyone he met was like a friend to him. I mean, who would want to hurt Lucas? Everyone loves him."

"Yeah, I know Phil," Al responded. "They usually seem to be the one's that get hurt."

"Yeah, I guess so," replied Phil solemnly. "I really, honestly, don't know who did this to Lucas, Tom."

"Phil, is there anyone you'd like us to call?"

"No, Tom, I'll be fine......where is he?"

"Excuse me, Phil?"

"Lucas. Where's Lucas, Tom?"

"He's been taken to the Coroners Office."

"I'd like to see him."

"I don't think that would be a good thing for you to see, Phil. His body has been brutalized."

"Tom, I've lived with Lucas for how long? Good times, bad times? I know what I need to do Thomas, and I need to see his body. Please Tom, I understand and appreciate your concern for my emotional well-being, but it's something I have to do." Phil's words echoed with the eerie familiarity of his fathers' upon hearing the news of Gary's demise.

"Okay, Phil. I'll get in touch with the coroner and see how she and John Boyle are coming along with their work. John is going to be helping us investigate the case."

"I appreciate that. John and all of you have always been so gracious to me and Lucas."

The shrill sound of Al's pager caught everyone off guard, and made them jump. Al turned off the alarm, and took note of the number. "It's Trooper Terrant's unit. I'd better take this call. Phil, may I use your phone?"

"Certainly, Al, you can use the one in the kitchen, if that's convenient."

"That would be fine, Phil. Thank you, if you'll excuse me." Phil now faced Tom. His composure was returning in small increments. "I don't know what to do. I should probably call his parents, not that they'll care. I just need some time think," Phil said, as if looking for an answer to an unanswerable dilemma.

"Give yourself some time, Phil." Tom reached into his pocket, and pulled out another cigarette. "God, I've been smoking like a chimney since this morning. Debbie is going to freak. I told her I was going to quit. Well, so much for that idea."

"It's just a good form of stress relief, and since I'm feeling a ton of that right now, I hope you don't mind." Phil reached across to take a cigarette from Tom's pack.

"Be my guest." Tom lit the Marlboro for Phil, and then his own. "I thought you gave up, with the way you were on Luke about quitting."

"I return to the filthy plague every now and then, and this is definitely a now situation." Phil took a long, deep drag and exhaled. "And as far as your wife goes, Debbie is a saint. She'll understand why you're smoking. This all conjures up some pretty horrific images for you, I know."

"Yes Phil, it does. But I can't worry about that now. It's happened to your Lucas, and I have to stop whoever this is. Are you sure Al or I can't call anyone to stay with you for the time being?"

Before Phil could respond to Tom's question, Al appeared in the entranceway. "Excuse me for interrupting, Phil...Tom. Trooper Terrant found Lucas' car. It was ditched at the Holly Edge Bed and Breakfasts' driveway."

"Phil, we're going to have to go. I'm going to call Jenn Gates to come and pick you up, so please don't try going out in your condition. She'll take you to the station. I really hope you change your mind about viewing Lucas..."

"Good times, bad times, Tom," Phil reiterated. "I'll wait for Jenn."

"Thanks, Phil. I do have one favor to ask of you. The print and television media are probably going to jump all over this. Could I ask you to please keep your comments to a minimum. You know, if this turns out to be viewed as a hate crime, passions in the town may really heat up."

"No problem, Tom. Interviews are the furthest thing from my mind, anyway".

"Thanks, Phil." Tom headed from the room with Al. "We'll see you at the station."

"Okay, Tom."

Al turned around before opening the front door and hugged Phil. "I am so sorry, Phil. We'll do our best to catch the animal that did this."

"I know you will, Al. You and Tom have always been good friends to us. I'll be okay, now just do your work. I'll be fine here waiting for Jenn."

"Please, Phil, don't answer the door unless it's Jenn."

"Al, I'll be fine. Really, I will. I'll see you soon." Phil smiled as best as he could muster, waved goodbye, and closed the door.

When they reached the police unit, neither said a word. Upon backing out of the driveway, Tom looked again at the house. The house appeared outwardly very much as it had before they'd invaded it this morning with their sad proclamation. It was like the house became human, exemplifying a quality just as Phil had, almost surreal. An important piece of the puzzle was forever missing, but they were both hiding behind a mask, unwilling to let the true feelings flow. The house had its festive atmosphere. Phil had those impenetrable eyes; house and human, hiding their grief and pain. Nothing would ever be the same in this house, and for that matter, in this small town again. Tom could not escape this thought as he hastily departed Riverview Circle.

Tom looked at Al and proceeded to light the last Marlboro in his pack. The expression on Tom's face said everything you needed to know, but he said it anyway. "I'm getting too old for this shit, Al, too damn old."

CHAPTER 4

Al's patrol car ascended further into the wooded hills surrounding Route 232. Nestled into one of the Route's many valley's, lie the Holly Edge Bed and Breakfast. It was an old manor, built in the late 1700's. The new owners, John and Marge Thorpe, had painstakingly restored the manor to its original grandeur over the past few years. The Bed and Breakfast was located a few hundred yards from the roadway, and only accessible by a steep and winding driveway. At the top of the drive was Trooper Terrant and Rob Pagano's units. A few more feet inwards, towards the woods, lay Lucas Stone's Lexus coupe, with the headlights on and the doors wide open. Al stopped the car a few yards from where Terrant and Pagano were conversing. While Al and Tom stepped out, the two officers approached them.

"So, what do we have, if anything, gentleman?"

"Well Tom, outside of the car itself, not much," replied the visibly disgusted Pagano. "Zoul checked for prints, and so far we've come up empty. There's not even a sign of blood, and the trunk looks spotless. I brought Drew along. He's checking the woods for footprints, the keys for the car, or anything else."

"We've come up clean on weapons of any sort. Whoever did this was good, I mean real good!" replied Trooper Terrant. "I'm wondering if it is someone local. To just vanish into these woods without a trace, you're a good hiker, hunter, or both."

"The skills of both, plus a clean murderer sets up a chilling description."

"Yes, it does Al. I don't think anything will be easy in this case." Tom looked down and saw faces peering from the windows of the Bed and Breakfast. "It looks like we have a captive audience. Were they questioned yet, Rob?"

"Yes, Zoul and I questioned John, Marge, and their six guests. Nobody reported seeing or hearing anything out of the ordinary this morning." Pagano stared into the woods. "I'd better go find the kid, and see what he's up to. He's probably out there collecting old Indian arrow heads or something." Tom smiled and turned his attention towards Officer Terrant.

"So Zoul, what do you make of this?" asked Tom.

"I don't know, Chief. Pagagno was mentioning something about the "Lucifer" Kane case, and that Luke was murdered in the same fashion. Is there any truth to that?"

"Yes, but please keep that under your hat, Zoul," Al replied.

"No problem, Al. Jesus, Tommy!" Zoul exclaimed. "Yins got a lunatic on your hands."

"You and that yins," Tom laughed. "Six years down here Al, and he's still spouting western Pennsylvanian, hayseed vocabulary."

"Yo' Chief, that's my roots you're messing with. Besides, let's not tawk about the New Yawk thing you got goin' on!" Zoul shot back, flashing his toothy grin.

"Alright Zoul, you got me!" Tom chuckled, and began to approach the Lexus.

Razoul Terrant, or Zoul, as his good friends referred to him, was an enigma. He had an athletic physique and a streetwise manner. It gave him an outward aura more befitting a city youth, than that of a child born in the dirty steel town of Clairton, which was located outside of Pittsburgh. Zoul grew into adulthood at a very young age. His mother, Vera, was extremely busy raising him and his four brothers practically on her own.

Maynard Terrant, Razoul's father, was a steelworker in the United States Steel Clairton Works, where he toiled for almost twenty-three years. Clairton Works was a coke plant that belched out filthy black smoke from the coal it utilized in the coke processing. The hardened steel run-off, known as slag, was heaped into piles as tall as buildings. At nighttime, the heat generated from the slag heaps would make them illuminate into a filthy red glow, which almost resembled lava. Maynard used to tell Zoul of the rich people in the mountains surrounding Pittsburgh who could see the glowing heaps from their stately residences. "A monument to American prosperity," Maynard would tell his son.

But prosperity came at a price. Maynard worked an average of sixty to seventy hours a week, when there was work to be had. On the times when there wasn't, young Maynard would take to hunting in the hills or drinking away a portion of his unemployment check at the local watering hole. His father's circumstances gave the young Zoul an abundance of free time, both good and bad. Zoul took an immense interest in his studies and sports. He remained an honor student throughout his grade and high school years, and was a consistent captain of his school basketball and football squads. Unfortunately, he also had an ample amount of time to become associated with the "wild bunch" in town. These young toughs did everything from rolling street bums for beer money, to picking fights with troublemakers from the other sections of town.

This all came to a screeching halt when Maynard Terrant cleaned up his act, and settled into fatherhood. Maynard sat Zoul down and told him he would not let his son waste his athletic, and especially his scholastic talents in a jail cell. "Zoul," he would often reiterate, "you are someone special. You will make a difference in this world someday." On his eighteenth birthday, Razoul was handed a check for ten thousand dollars from his father. "I've been saving this money since I started working at fifteen. Now use it for the good things I know you can do. I know you'll make me even prouder of you than I already am." With his father's check, and scholarship money in hand, Razoul enrolled at the University of Pittsburgh, studying criminology.

During the ensuing years, father and son formed a close bond, doing everything from working on cars, to deer hunting in the thickly wooded hills around Clairton. It was a bond Razoul was forever grateful to have, for his father would not be around to see him achieve the lofty goals Maynard knew he'd accomplish. In the month prior to Zoul's graduation, Maynard Terrant literally worked his life away, fading from the intense heat of American prosperity. He was dead from a heart attack at the age of thirty-eight.

Zoul never forgot the bond they had formed. He made sure his mother and brothers were provided for. While at the university, he'd forgo sports to maintain a full-time job, sending the majority of the money home to supplement the family budget. The rest of his hours were spent pursuing the academic excellence his parents knew he would accomplish. After graduation, Zoul would go on to marry his college girlfriend, Lucinda. A few years later they would have a son of their own, Maynard II. He moved them all away from the black dreariness of Clairton to this beautiful place six years ago, when he took the transfer here.

For the first time in years, Zoul felt the darkness and despair he thought he'd left in Clairton. Unbeknownst to him, his mind began to ask the same question Sergeant Jeaneau asked earlier today; why here? The only quick answer his mind could respond with was the old tale his grandmother used to tell him when he was very young. "Everyone's woods and rivers hold dark secrets, secrets never meant to be discovered."

Zoul and Al followed Tom to the car. When they reached the Lexus' passenger side door, they saw John Boyle's car approaching. "I just heard you boys had found Luke's car. I figured I would swing by and see if you could use some help. Besides, I just wanted to let you know the town's beginning to buzz about Luke's death. Didn't take long, did it?"

"Never does," Tom replied bluntly.

"Car looks clean, eh? Oh, this lad is a good one, isn't he?" John asked.

"Whoever it is, they're doing a damn good job of imitating the prick, aren't they John?"

"Aye, Tommy. It's as if he was out and about again, the dirty bastard!" Like a cannon shot, they could hear yelling off in the vast thickness of the woods. It sounded like a pleading call for help, and it was coming from where Rob Pagano and Andrew Rose had gone to survey the area. "If that's Pagano..." Tom looked around at the assembled officers.

"Let's get goin' gents, it doesn't sound good," John Boyle offered, as he bounded through the woods with Zoul in hot pursuit. Tom looked to Al. "You want to stay here, and call us in some back-up? It looks like show time!"

"Sounds like a plan. Now get a move on Chief, and be careful. This guy's nuts!"

"See you soon, Al. Keep in contact. If you even think you're in shit..."

"I'll fire off three, now get going!!"

Tom flashed him an anxious look and then he was into the woods, full steam ahead. Tom could hear the loud voices getting closer. Up ahead, he could see Zoul and John. He was catching them with each stride, but his lungs were burning like a blowtorch. Goddamned cigarettes.

"Keep your eyes peeled, Zoul. God knows what we're in store for," John yelled, as he pulled his service revolver from its holster.

"No problem, John," Zoul yelled back, his Glock 9MM ready for action, and set on automatic.

Tom Miller had drawn his old, but trusted, .38 revolver. They were getting closer to Pagano's voice. Up ahead, the sound of a stream flowing rapidly slowed them down to a fast walk. The heavy rains this morning had been the first ones' in quite a while, so the leaves and other various array of ground cover were very slick. They were close enough to see Rob and Drew. Rob was kneeling next to Drew, who was moving slowly. Rob saw the three men, and motioned for them to proceed with caution. "I think we've got one of the murder weapons!"

"Jesus Christ! What in the hell happened to Drew?" John bellowed.

"I'm alright, John," Drew replied. He began to awkwardly sit upright. Tom and Zoul grabbed his arms to steady him. "The sonofabicth booby trapped the area. I went to pick up the damn club he must've left here for us to find, and I didn't see it was rigged to a wire. The next thing I know, I see things flying into the air, and then I feel a burning sensation through my leg."

"Lucky kid, a few inches over, and it could've sliced some tendons open. Good thing for you, it just looks like a superficial wound." Rob and John Boyle helped the visibly shaken young officer to his feet.

Tom got on his two-way and contacted Al. "Are you there, Al?"

"Yes Chief, what do we have?"

"Drew caught some metal from a booby trap, but the wound is superficial."

"I copy. Is an ambulance needed?"

"No need. Al, if Jenn Gates is back from getting Phil Antos, tell her and whoever else is available to get down to 'The "A" Train,' cordon off the rest of the area, and check the place from top to bottom."

"Consider it done, Tom."

"Thanks, Al." Tom now turned his attention to the bat. He cut through the thin gauge steel that was slipped around the neck of the bat. The razor sharp edge of Tom's knife made quick work of the wire. Tom looked up at John and smiled. "It came in handy fifteen years ago for this stuff too."

As John holstered his revolver, he smiled back. "I bet it did, Tommy."

Tom began to look over the bat that had been so conveniently left behind. "Sonofabitch is playing us real good." He showed the bat to Boyle. "Exhibit A" was written on the barrel. The writing style was identical to the ones' found on the blood soaked cloths at Ferry Landing.

"That prick! I swear to the Almighty, it's like Kane all over again!" John Boyle spat on the ground. He looked around the woods. The rain, the precise traps. He felt like he had just stepped back into the nightmare jungles of Vietnam. Could there be something to that, he wondered? Could this be the work of a seasoned veteran, utilizing the skills so masterfully used against him almost thirty-five years ago to his advantage? He knew Tom said there were still files available on the backgrounds of Kane's original followers. Maybe some had been Vietnam veterans.

During the Anti-War Movement, the homosexual community was a vocal supporter for removing American troops from Vietnam soil. Some were very militant and venomous in their disdain towards any soldiers involved in the conflict. A disgruntled veteran of a war who had been left with many psychological scars, now meting out his own brand of justice; and at the same time, fulfilling Kane's prophecy? It wasn't far removed from the realm of possibility. John Boyle remembered the airport scene in San Francisco when he returned home from Nam. He remembered how they would spit on you if you wore your uniform. He remembered how their chants of baby killer echoed through his ears. He could never forget them. It took a good two years of drinking, brawling, sobriety and counseling to bury his hatred, but, John thought, maybe somebody still hadn't. He figured he would keep his thoughts to himself, until he took notice of Tom observing the scene. "A case of ghosts from years gone by lad?" he asked.

"Are we thinking alike here?" Tom replied. "The war's been over for a long time."

"Aye, lad. For you and me, it has been. For some others, it's still going on every day. We both know about that."

"From different sides of the ocean we knew about that."

"Hey, Tommy, you didn't have to be there to know what I was feeling. You would've been there too, if you hadn't been injured. Besides, you had to deal with the war at home. Being a cop at that time was no easy task."

"Unfortunately, my friend, you're right. Well, it is a long shot, but do you think you could check the computer files and search out some names?"

"I'll get on it as soon as I get back to the office. I'm always happy to request files from New York's finest. Should I should ask for Stan Tilden?"

"Yes," Tom replied. "You know he'll keep things nice and quiet for us." The sound from Tom's pager pierced through the empty morning air. "Hold on a second John," Tom said as he checked his pager. He reviewed the numbers, shook his head and rolled his eyes. "Well, it's time to get someone up to date on the situation, before he has the papers eating us for lunch." His wry expression said more than words ever could.

"Aye, that one? Better it be you than me, Tommy boy. Better it be you!"

By now, Sergeant Jeaneau had made his way down towards the group.

"Be careful, Al. There might be more traps out here than we bargained for."

"Okay, Tom." He then motioned towards John and Zoul, who had hoisted Drews' arms around their shoulders. "Let me give you guys a hand."

"Thanks, Al. This boy's a handful even for me and Zoul to carry".

They all came back to the top of the driveway where the ominous specter of the Lexus coupe remained. Tom got everyone situated and turned to Rob. "Pags, get Drew back to the station house and get his leg cleaned up. When Jenn gets back with Phil, I'd like the two of you to give 'The "A" Train' the once over."

"No problem, Chief."

"John, could you check out our hunch for results?"

"I sure will, Tommy boy."

"I'll help John out with whatever he needs," Zoul chimed in.

"Great, Zoul. I appreciate it."

"And as for you, Sergeant Jeaneau, you get the dubious distinction of joining me at a meeting,"

"With whom?" Al quickly asked. Upon realizing Tom's mockery, his pained expression answered his own question.

"Why, with our illustrious Mayor, of course, Al."

CHAPTER 5

"The crowds," he said aloud. "Nothing good ever comes of a crowd filled with inquiring rabble." Mayor Jerry Ward looked from the confines of his office window, and viewed the faces of disgust, pain and sadness. Jerry Ward was used to commanding a crowd, captivating them, holding them in the palm of his hand. In many an address since his high school forensic days, he dazzled throngs of his colleagues and peers with the brilliance of his eloquent verbiage and charm. As he grew in years, wisdom and cynicism, he became attuned to the fact that baffling them with bullshit could also be an equally resourceful tool.

Jerry was never short on words. A sharp, and sometimes scathing wit, crept into his conversations. Sometimes it would make you laugh, and you would adore having his company. Other times you felt as if throttling him within an inch of his life would be the honorable thing to have done.

Jerry grew up in the historic and well-heeled town of Yardley, which is within a fifteen to twenty minute drive from New Hope. His parents owned a very spacious house looking towards the Delaware River. His father was the CEO of a steel conglomerate, and his mother stayed at home to raise their only son.

One of the few reasons Jerry would venture out of this comfortable domain was to pursue academics. Although diminutive in size, it never inhibited him from becoming fully engrossed in athletics, either. This led him to the near manic worship of the sport, ice hockey. The speed, the precise measure of skill it took to send a hard, rubberized sphere between the goal pipes, absolutely fascinated this young man who was filled with a need for perfection. The hard charging, hard hitting, the drive and determination required to excel at the game definitely had a spill-over effect on what was already an ambitious individual.

In the life of Jerry Ward, this hard charging drive would lead him to the doors of Harvard University, more forensics championships, a law degree and eventually, a stab at the political realm. After delivering what many insiders viewed as the preeminent speech of an otherwise blasé 1996 Democratic National Convention, the then twenty-nine year old Mayor of New Hope was moving in the right direction, but not fast enough for Jerry Ward. The young man had bigger fish to fry. A trip to the state house as Governor would be the next step in achieving his legacy, or, so he thought. In the mind of the voter, stability is a big key. For all his command of the English language, ability and civic minded nature to do the right thing, or to at least make it look that way in the press, Jerry was missing the key ingredient to becoming a proper politician; a wife.

With the push of these many years centered on achieving his goals, he dismissed paying attention towards cultivating any meaningful relationships. From high school until the present, this fueled speculation Jerry was a homosexual. Unremitting denunciations of this claim did nothing to detract from this image.

Jerry's alleged off color, and supposedly off-the-record remarks in 1998 to Harrisburg Globe reporter Bev Johnson about the First Lady's handling of her husbands' infidelities, and the insinuation of truth to rumors of her sexual preferences, led to a firestorm of controversy and almost derailed whatever future he thought of having. Jerry managed to alienate everyone on both sides of the political spectrum in town and for a brief time, in the nation. He offended liberals and homosexuals because rumors, true or not, they viewed the First Lady as champion of gay rights. He also managed to offend the conservative factions because even though she was vilified by most of them, she was, after all was said and done, still the First Lady of the United States. If not for his commanding verbal skills, and a meeting with President Clinton and his wife where he basically pled his innocence on being raked over the coals and thoroughly misquoted by a right-wing writer with a grudge, and them believing it, his career would have been a footnote in political history. After the President, the First Lady and Jerry held a press conference to show support for the Mayor and denigrate the Globe reporter for tabloid journalism, Jerry was again sailing in somewhat less turbulent seas. It still did nothing, however, to close the lid on a can of worms re-opened. Jerry was still being labeled a homosexual.

It was at this time, Jerry Ward, the first, but not truly known homosexual Mayor of New Hope made a silent pact with himself. If a wife is what these fools needed to satisfy what they perceived as political stability in this land, then a wife he would have. Maybe even a child, he thought. He would play the loving husband/father role in public, but, in reality, probably never care for either outside of financially. He would polish up his somewhat tarnished image and this town would love the now thirty-three year old, brash "kid" again. The state would learn to love him again also, with his wife and child by his side, supposed comments forgiven, if not totally forgotten. He would have his day in the sun. Everything was working smoothly towards that goal.

Now, he had this fiasco. Lucas Stone, a pillar of the community, brutally murdered. Whispers of a ritual murderer targeting homosexuals were starting to swirl around only a few hours after Stone's body was discovered. In no way would this damn murder derail his dreams. His desire would not let this happen. All he wanted was Chief Tom Miller to tell him who, what, why, and would they catch the bastard. Just have your damn force make an arrest, get me my photo op, and in a years' time I'll roll up to the State House.

Somewhere from inside of him, he saw the little boy again. He heard him screaming like before. The beatings, the embarrassing, painful beatings taken at the hands of a father who had no time for failure. A father who had no time to understand why he caught his teenage son cross-dressing and almost hospitalized the boy. He heard the pleading screams of the boy, except now, the boy was screaming at Jerry. Where did all of this go wrong? When did love become replaced by the blind ambition to win at any cost, to please an abusive father and a somewhat distant mother? He saw the patrol cars lights approaching. Miller and probably Jeaneau were here. He turned towards where he thought the pleading boys screams had come. "Deal with you later," he said in a hushed voice. "I'm on to bigger things." He stepped forward and through the doors of his office to meet Miller, Jeaneau, and a sea of questions and flashes.

"Mister Mayor, do you have any evidence leading towards who committed this dreadful act?" asked Mary McGuigan.

"Mary, it would be very premature to relay any evidentiary matter at this time."

"But, Mayor Ward..."

Jesus, Channel 6 news is here already. Even the big boys from Philly deemed this all newsworthy. Lucas Stone was, after all, a pretty prominent figure in this town, and he was betting that by now every one of these vultures knew it was Stone that was murdered. It's time to put on the charm, boy. "Yes, Dan", he said as he faced Channel 6 newsman, Dan Kway.

"Mayor Ward, is it true this may be viewed as a hate crime?"

"We're viewing all avenues of this tragedy, Dan. We're....

"Are you also viewing the option of a ritual or serial murder?"

You sons-of-bitches. Stirring the public into a wave of panic to sell papers and get people to watch your damn newscasts.

"Mister Mayor?"

"Any truth to this?" he was asked again.

Okay, you pricks. You want the answers, you'll get them when I'm damn well ready to. Until then let's play some run around. "I have unequivocal proof from my law enforcement officers that, as of this time, this crime is being viewed as nothing more than a murder case. Now, there is always the possibility such an act of violence could sway our opinions and emotions towards the more dramatic conclusions, but this is a murder case. Grisly, barbaric? Yes, it was all of that. But, no, this is not a serial or ritualistic murder, nor should our clearly concerned citizens view it as such". Nothing like a simple yes or no answer, isn't that right you jackals?

Your editors will be kicking your ass for wasting ad space on the garbage you just got handed.

He glanced towards Tom Miller and Al. The press bit the cue. No more answers from the long winded one. Oh well, next victims. "Chief Miller!" shouted Ian Thomas of the Philadelphia Daily Eagle. "You were on the Lucifer Kane case. Any similarities?"

Oh, you're a good one, Ian Thomas. Nothing like soft-soaping the last question you guys just asked. "None that I can see from our preliminary investigations, Ian".

"Chief Miller?" Thomas inquired. "Any comments on Kane's impending execution on New Year's Eve? Do you think he'll receive a stay from the Governor of New York?"

"I have always said, I'll leave those decisions for the politicians and their last approval ratings to decide," Tom said with a wry smile as he turned to Mayor Ward. Ward returned the smile in kind, which led to a few chuckles from the gallery.

"Do we have the victims' name, Chief?" Thomas asked in a rather smug fashion.

Oh, Ian. Did you really think I was going to hide it from your carnivorous bunch? Two could play the shock game. "Lucas Stone has been identified as the victim". This drew a mixture of real and contrived gasps from many of the assembled. "The identity, as Sergeant Jeaneau and I were en route to update Mayor Ward about, was also confirmed by a family member."

"Would that be Mister Antos, Chief?" asked Kway.

"There's no need to elaborate, Dan, although I will add that at this somber time, we'd ask you to please refrain from visiting the Stone and Antos household. Mister Antos does not wish to take any questions at this time and hopes you'll honor his request for privacy at this tragic time."

"And, folks of the press," Sergeant Jeaneau piped up. "If you do not choose to honor Mister Antos' request, Chief Miller, his officers or the State Police would be glad to escort you to some cozier accommodations." Al broke into his trademark grin, as the members of the press who knew his wry wit began to again chuckle. "Seriously though, folks. Hear me out. Let the man have some time to grieve."

All of them nodded in approval. Phil Antos would be off limits, for now. "Thanks again," Al replied.

Mayor Ward again stepped to the forefront. "Ladies and gentlemen, and the citizens of our beloved New Hope. Luke Stone's loss is as tragic a blow as this community has had to face. It is hard to fathom the effect his loss will have on our town, or to the jazz world. Everyone who knew Luke loved him. I counted Luke as a close, personal friend. It will break my heart to not see his smiling face at 'The "A" Train' again. I also mourn Phil's loss as he comes to grips with the passing of a loved one."

"Our grief will firm our resolve to apprehend this evildoer. Evil may have come today to New Hope, but mark my words, evil will be caught. I have the utmost confidence in the capabilities of my officers and the State Troopers. Their vigilance will prevail, and I believe they will act swiftly and without malice to quell any fears our residents may have. Go about your lives, worship on Christmas Day, and prepare for our Millennium New Years Gala. There will be sorrow in our hearts, but we will conquer this trouble. Now, I must go to confer with my very capable agents of law enforcement. Thank you ladies and gentlemen, and have a blessed Holiday season."

Upon saying his piece, Mayor Ward headed in the direction of Miller and Jeaneau, leaving the flashes of cameras and the barrage of questions behind him.

"Gentleman," he said as he passed them. "Would you care to join me?"

As he proceeded to put a small amount of distance between them, Al rolled his eyes and looked at Tom. "Jesus, Tommy, if that wasn't flagrant, photo op bullshit. Does this guy think he's the President making these kinds of speeches?"

"One day," Tom chuckled, "he may be. Besides, the press just eats up the way he speaks."

When they entered Mayor Ward's office, Tom began to pull the Marlboro pack from his jacket pocket. "I know we're not supposed to, but…"

"Not to worry Chief, you're in my humble abode now. The rules need not apply, so long as you send one a good, old friends way."

"How about I send one the way of a wet behind the ears' kid? I have only one friend in this room today."

The mayor shot Tom a nasty glance as he went to search his office for an ashtray. In the meanwhile, the two officers could not help but notice the office in which they sat had all the trappings found in a big city politicians reside, and definitely not that of a small hamlet such as New Hope. But, Jerry Ward always thought big. He sat in a big, Italian made, leather chair.

The ostentatious desk was made of solid oak, apparently ordered from the upper echelon of North Carolina's furniture mills. Pictures of himself and such political luminaries as Presidents Clinton and Carter, Senators Kennedy and Glenn were placed on the oversized desk. Other pictures of himself and hockey stars such as Gretzky, Mario Lemieux, Mark Messier, and Gordie Howe, to name a few, were strategically placed on other tables and around the walls, not to mention the diplomas. You couldn't miss the diplomas. They hit you right smack in the face as soon as you sat down in the smaller, but equally grand leather chairs in front of the mayors' desk. It was Jerry's not so subtle way of saying, "here is my pedigree. What do you bring to the table?"

The lavish interior was designed by Phil Antos' firm, and not a penny of taxpayer money was reportedly used. Jerry supposedly paid for it all, and would leave it as a gift to the future mayor of New Hope. This room was like home to him, his own personal comfort zone. But today, there was no comfort here. As he flung the thick, glass ashtray onto his desk, he felt backed into a corner. It made him feel like a caged animal, and remarks like Tom Miller's had just made gave him an ample reason to lash out.

"Oh Tom, thou dost protest too much. Please save your grandstanding for the press outside."

"Me? Grandstanding?" Tom shot upright in his chair, looking every bit like he would leap across the obnoxious hunk of wood separating himself from Ward, and beat him from one end of his office to the other. "Well," Jerry snorted, "what would you call that garbage statement that you made on the Kane verdict just before?"

"It wasn't garbage, Mayor," Tom laughed sarcastically. "It was the truth."

"You know, Chief, you've just had a sour disposition ever since I spoke out against you wanting to shut down the tattoo parlors in the town."

"They are drug dens!"

"No Tom, they are money making establishments that entertain all the little college aged snobs of Bucks County. They want their little ink drawings on them to look cool."

"Yeah, and then they buy their drugs there, they get high, and they harass the honest tourists who then in turn, don't come back to enjoy the town."

"It's not a proven fact, and you are just espousing the views of a few, crotchety old timers, who think they can return this town to one hundred years ago."

"No, it's just a hard issue to prove when your mayor is unwilling to have the courage to back his police chief!"

"You are trying to use strong arm tactics to conduct your police business!" Jerry's eyes were so honed in on Tom, it looked as if they were burning as black as coal.

"No, Mayor. I'm not utilizing any methods of brutality," Tom shot back. "All I'm trying to do is return this town to what it was all about. If I need to jog your memory Jerry, it was a musicians and artists colony for over one hundred years. Yes, there has always been some semblance of drug use in this community, but it used to just be happy, grass smokers, who did it in their own homes and apartments. It wasn't a bunch of spoiled, rich kids, who drive in from their big suburban homes, to get jacked up on cocaine and Ecstasy, and then roll some tourist for their cash to get some more."

"Return the town?" Jerry howled with laughter. "Please get off your soapbox, Tom. You are far from being a politician."

"You're finally right about one thing, Jerry. I'm definitely not a politician. I'm not a big enough asshole to be one of them."

Sergeant Jeaneau had seen enough of this verbal sparring over the past year to know it was reaching the boiling point. "Gentleman!" he yelled, as he stepped in between the two of them. "Gentleman, please," he said in a much calmer tone, "the issue at hand."

Tom felt himself cooling down just enough to glance at Al. "I'm sorry, Al. Jerry, Al is right. This is not the time to dredge up our quarrels. Let's say we agree to disagree, and call a truce."

"A truce sounds plausible," Jerry retorted as he extended his hand. "I think we can do this, ay, Tom?"

"We've done it before Jerry", Tom replied, as he took a firm grip of the mayor's hand. "Now, let's get down to the heart of the matter." My chance to deal with your wrong doings will come soon enough, you little prick.

"Do we have any damn idea as to who perpetrated this crime?" Jerry asked bluntly.

"No, we don't. Whoever this person or person's are, they're good. In fact, almost as good as…"

"Kane?" asked the mayor, sheepishly.

"Yes, Kane," replied Tom, gravely. "It's like they have the whole M.O. down to a science. The ritualistic mutilation of Lucas' body, the immaculate cleanliness of his car, which was left at the murder scene. Kane's death sites were always clean of any hair, skin, clothing fibers, and blood. The only time you saw blood was when it served him a purpose to utilize it."

"Do you mean like with the wall, or the cloths that we found in Lucas' body, Chief?"

"Exactly, Al." Mayor Ward was about to ask another question when Tom's cell phone rang.

"Excuse me, gentleman. Hello?"

"Yes hon, I'm ok."

"Yes, all the other officers too. Drew had some minor cuts, but he'll be fine."

"I know, it's horrible about Luke."

"No, nothing yet. Listen, Deb, I'm getting another ring."

"Yeah, I'll see you soon, hon."

"I love you too."

"Hello?"

"You did a complete search?"

"You did find one? Where was it?"

"Good spot. Everything was spotless?"

"I figured as much."

"Did we find any traces of other foreign materials?"

"Damn, they're good."

Tom lit another cigarette. "Okay, thanks Pags. Jenn and you hit the streets, for now. We still have a town to protect."

Tom hung up and began to wince. That damn sharp pain was crushing his skull again. The laughing in his head was getting louder. "I've come back," he heard him chuckling. "Back, for you!"

"Chief?" The mayor was standing in front of him. "Are you okay? Do you need some air?"

"No, Jerry, I'm fine." Tom quickly righted himself in the chair.

"Well, is there any breaking news to be aware of?" Mayor Ward asked.

"Well, the fit of the M.O. is consistent. Pagano and Gates and two of our other uniforms did a thorough search of 'The "A" Train'."

"Was anything turned up?" Al inquired as he shifted agitatedly in his chair.

"Spotless was the one word that kept getting volleyed about. They also found a priests collar on the kitchen-cutting table. They are also dusting for prints, but I guarantee that it'll turn up nothing. Hopefully, the Luminol will turn up some blood type besides Luke's."

"Well, it is beginning to look as if we have a master imitator on our hands gentleman."

"Indeed we do Mister Mayor, indeed we do," replied Tom.

"Do you think that you and your officers can handle this, Tom?"

"Is that a round about way of asking me that we should have the federal agencies involved Jerry?" This question made the mayor shrug sheepishly with a half-smile. "I say we don't. You have the final say, Mister Mayor. I know you have a lot of pull with people on the national level, but I'll tell you, when I was in New York working on the Kane case, they hindered our investigation a lot more than they helped us. If you feel that we should tender their services then I will acquiesce."

"Al?" asked the mayor. "Any thoughts?"

"Well, I think we can catch this animal. I personally think the feds will stir up emotions in this community that shouldn't be touched. I think they'll drive this person further away and will help fulfill Kane's sick prophecy."

"I see," mused Jerry. "So, we agree that as of right now the feds are a headache that none of us need." There was a knock at the mayors' door. Jerry's personal secretary, Emily Pfister, came in. "What is it, Emily?" His quirky, politicians' smile was quickly affixed again, as if he had something to hide.

"Excuse me gentleman, but Trooper Terrant would like to speak with you."

"By all means!" Jerry bellowed. "Show him in, Emily."

There were the sounds of shuffling and muffled voices from the hallway, and then Trooper Terrant appeared. He nodded in Mayor Ward's direction. "Mister Mayor, begging your pardon, but I wanted to talk to the Chief and Sergeant Jeaneau for a moment."

"Please do then," the mayor replied.

"What's up, Zoul?" asked Tom.

"Well, when I was leaving from the bed and breakfast this morning, I did remember seeing someone during my area patrol. I guess it just lapsed in my memory because it didn't and still doesn't seem as if it will have any bearing on the case."

"Go ahead Zoul. What do you have for us?" asked Al.

"Well, I did see a jogger on my route this morning."

"Description?" inquired Tom.

"Female, Caucasian, very slender. Well built though. She had blonde hair tucked up under a ball cap, a bright yellow running jacket with a yellow and black back pack."

"Color coordinated little thing, wasn't she?" chided Al.

"She also had on a bright yellow, tight running pant. I would guess it was like a Spandex material. Again," Zoul said with a grin affixed this time, "a very good body on her."

"Did you happen to get a look at the eye color?"

"Not really, Chief. It was still around five or so, maybe even earlier. Like I said guys, there is probably nothing to it. I see joggers around here all the time, mostly the same ones day in, and day out. Some of them are so used to my patrol times, they wave or stop to say hello, but this girl was new. Still though, she seemed rather friendly. She smiled and waved as I was passing her. It's probably nothing, but I figured I'd fill you in just the same."

"Thanks Zoul, I appreciate it nonetheless."

"No problem Chief. Well gentlemen, good day to you. If you'll excuse me, I have some matches to look up on my computer."

"Happy Holidays to you, Trooper Terrant," said Mayor Ward. Zoul, again nodded in reply.

Oh, Zoul!" Tom shouted towards the now vacant doorway.

Razoul appeared again. "Yes, Chief?"

"Just out of curiosity..."

Al started to laugh. "Oh God, here we go folks! The master detective is on overload again."

"As I was saying, before 'Sergeant Jester' interrupted, did you happen to take notice of the jogging shoes? I'm just curious because you said she had on a backpack. Did the shoes happen to look like they were hiking runners or jogging shoes?"

"I would definitely say jogging shoes and not all terrains. I think I know where you are going with this, and no, they weren't the type of shoe that would support your feet in the woods we ran through this morning."

"Thanks again Zoul'," Tom replied. "It still gives us something to think about, nonetheless."

"No problem Tom. Good day gentlemen."

"Well, if that is all Mayor, we'd better get going ourselves."

"Yes Tom, that's fine," replied Mayor Ward. "Listen, Tom, no hard feelings about before?"

"None at all Jerry. I will keep you in constant contact with our ongoing proceedings."

"That is fine, thank you. Goodbye and good luck, gentlemen."

The men exchanged their pleasantries and left the office. Tom and Al made their way quickly to the front of the building and as they got into the unit, Tom scornfully looked at Al. "Insufferable little jerk, isn't he?" he said with a smile.

"Without a doubt, Chief," Al replied with a belly laugh that rocked the unit.

"Listen," Tom said still catching his breath after a well needed laugh. "I'm going to drop you and the car at the station."

"Going to make a house call, are we?"

"I think it would be well advised, after I tie up some odds and ends along the way."

"Agreed, Chief. Tell Debbie that I said hello. I'll keep you alerted to any new developments. Otherwise, I'll see you in the morning. Hell, it's almost quitting time anyway. We haven't even stopped for lunch today, but I'm assuming you've got no appetite either."

"None whatsoever."

"I'll be back in, Al. Don't even.."

"Tom, call me at my house tonight. We're getting close to the station."

"Okay, into your capable hands I will leave the situation."

"Good riddance, Chief Miller! I knew you'd see it my way."

When they returned to the station, Tom jumped into his Ford Explorer and rushed onto Main Street. He smiled to himself. Home, he thought. It was only this morning, but it seemed like it was almost a year ago since he had seen her. Debbie.....

CHAPTER 6

There was a solitary figure in the tall windows of 5937 Chapel Road. On cold, bitter days like this one, the eight-foot windows and the twelve-foot ceilings of this grand old house made the figure seem somewhat dwarfed, but this was home. "Oh Tom," sighed the figure. "We've been down this lonely road before, haven't we?"

Indeed they had. Almost fifteen years ago, Debbie Miller thought. And yet, here she was in a house and not a loft apartment, still staring through the windows like she had back then. These were the windows viewing the woods and the deer that occasionally frolicked on the front lawn, and not the view of the dramatic World Trade Center and the imposing West End skyline in the distance from their Soho loft. Murders aren't supposed to happen in small towns like New Hope. It just goes to show you really aren't safe no matter where you are.

Debbie sat in the Queen Anne wing chair, with a coffee in one hand and a cigarette in the other. She hardly ever smoked, but like Tom, she fell back into the habit whenever a crisis struck. She looked out the window again into the long expanse of their beautifully landscaped front yard, and into the dense woods across the street. What a piece of heaven this house has always been, she thought.

They bought the house in 1987, after the Kane murders had been put to rest. Tom and Debbie still loved New York, but when a mutual friend informed Tom that the position of police chief had become available in the peaceful town of New Hope they decided to make the move. They both viewed it as the perfect situation to leave the city, but not leave it too far behind. They both agreed the change was for the better. It would be a healthier environment for them to raise their son, Edward. It was also considered a beneficial move into soothing surroundings so Debbie could continue writing her well-received line of children's stories. It was a career affording them a comfortable living and hopefully, one that would give Tommy the opportunity to retire within the next year or two. It was a hard sell on Debbie's part to talk Tom into this, but with all the talk of Kane's pending execution it was getting easier for him to take into consideration.

Her heart began to ache at the thought of Luke Stone being murdered. The call that she had received from John Boyle made her freeze in her tracks this morning. John had hated to call Debbie to fill her in on the grisly details, but he was worried sick about Tom. He knew all the feelings of Gary and Edgar's murders would come flooding back into his head. He asked if there was anything Debbie needed, but all she could tell John was to pray for Tom. She asked John to be Tom's strength when he needed it.

She also began to weep for Phil, who had become such a close friend to Debbie over the years. Phil was a regular at the Miller household. Lucas and he attended so many of their parties and barbeques. He was also almost totally instrumental in helping her to transform this old, drab house into a place that was warm, elegant, full of country charm, and with some modern accents for flair. Phil and Debbie's touches were spread throughout the

Miller domain, from the grand oak stairway in the front hall, to the magnificent sitting room with all of its 18th century maple pieces. The bright and airy peach colored walls that made the living room just glow with brilliance. The gray washed walls that surrounded the stunning deep cherry antique dining room set which seated twelve comfortably, not to mention the glorious matching china cabinet. A kitchen with all the most modern appliances clad in stainless steel and bordered by luxurious light cherry cabinetry. The bedrooms, with an old world French style, to the sports oriented room housing Edward until he went to college and again until his subsequent move to California. Debbie could feel all the good memories in every room of this wonderful old domain.

She picked up her coffee and went into the room that she always thought of as her and Phil Antos' crowning achievement to the house, Tom's den. Tom had let her have free reign to do the house to her liking and in return, a few years ago she finally created, with Phil's assistance, a spare room into something special that was kept under wraps until its completion.

When it was finally unveiled, she brought Tom into the room blindfolded and sat him down in the leather chair behind his father's ball and claw mahogany desk she had lovingly restored. When the blindfold was removed, his eyes took in with amazement what she had accomplished. His eyes filled with tears when he saw the desk. His face beamed with delight when he saw the inlaid cherry bookcases filled with the restored leather-bound classics from Edgar and Gary's Greenwich Village flat. Tom was equally in astonishment when he observed one of his old Lionel model train sets laid out on an elevated track near the ceiling, running effortlessly around the perimeter of the den. Debbie then took him over to the large picture window at the back of the room to let him observe how it was placed in perfect proximity of the cherry blossom that Tom, Debbie and the teenage Edward had planted in the park like setting of Tom's pride and joy contribution to the house, the backyard.

While he was taking this all in, an explosion of noise filled the room from behind. "Surprise!!" everyone exclaimed. "Happy 45th birthday. Tom!" Tom was getting hugged and kissed by faces both old and new. John Boyle, Razoul, his wife and his son, Al, Rob Pagano and his family, and many more from the New Hope area were there to join the celebration. Of course, Luke and Phil were there to witness Debbie and Phil's labor of love and friendship come to fruition. Debbie's mother and father, who thought of Tom as their own son and not an in-law, were there after driving from upstate New York.

Even more of a surprise was the New York bunch who came to take part in the joyous occasion. The veteran cops from Tom's old Precinct Six in the Village, and especially his partner and Edward's godfather, Stan Tilden, were there. The big surprise of the day came when in the den's entrance way appeared Edward, his wife of two years Sara, and their newborn son, Thomas II. They had flown into Philadelphia International that morning, and John Boyle delivered them directly to 5937 Chapel Road via police escort. Debbie decided to take a picture of Stan, Tom, Edward and little Tom. All the generations together, plus one, just like in 1974 when she had taken a picture of Stan and Tom, both in uniform, proudly holding Edward in between them. Standing behind them was the proud and beaming grandfather, Edgar. She would eventually put the new photograph next to the other one that she had already placed in Tom's new den.

What a day it had been for Tom. She remembered how happy he was as he sat amongst new and old friends, all watching his beloved Yankees on the big screen television that Debbie had purchased for his special day.

She looked at both of the pictures again and then at the wedding picture Tom and Debbie had taken in Central Park. She laughed quietly at how young they looked. They were two headstrong youngsters who thought they could save the world, but in differing ways. She walked over to the bookcases and saw one of Tom's favorite pictures of her. It was a picture of her taken on the Empire State Building's observation deck. Her long hair was flowing freely from the winds up there. She was wearing a camouflage bandana, a jean jacket with a peace symbol tee shirt underneath, tight jeans with the big bell-bottoms, and the cumbersome, clunky platform shoes that were all the rage in the early seventies. The cop and the hippie-chick she laughed to herself. What a pair we were. Debbie began to smile remembering how they had met in that tumultuous summer of 1971.

Debbie was a literature major at the New York University, and a vehement supporter of the anti-war movement. They had first encountered each other at a protest in Washington Square Park. Tom had told Debbie later, her long, curly, sandy blonde hair and the gleam in her almost hazel eyes caught his attention first. He later joked with her the tight shorts and the stars and stripes bikini top didn't hurt his eyesight either. But it was the courage of her conviction making him take post right in front of where she was passionately espousing her views. Tom was fresh from his four months of academy training and was now doing his three-month stint of field service. She saw the handsome, clean cut, and athletically built Tom and smiled. She then proceeded to spew out her anti-war rhetoric in his direction. He calmly asked her to please quiet down. She told him where he could go. He tried to disarm her with his charm and ask her if she would like to discuss their differences of opinion over dinner in a much more calm setting. "If f nothing else, you could tell your NYU friends the enemy truly is an asshole." She began to laugh and took him up on his offer.

After a few months of agreeing to disagree on many issues, she began to feel herself falling in love with him. After she met Gary and Edgar she was intrigued by Tom even more. A pure renaissance man, she thought. He was a man who would fight and die for his country, but would also fight for the right that his father had to lead life in a fashion considered by a vast population of the country to be an abnormal existence.

Edgar and Gary adored Debbie, as she did them. The same type of caring and love that they had for Tom, existed with her as well. It led to a very special relationship, existing until their tragic demise.

As for Tom, she had found her soul mate. She found the person whom she would love forever, the person for whom she would lay down her life to spare his. She thought again about the magical day of their wedding. She remembered the exchange of their vows in the church, and how she started to sob when she got to the line "until death do us part." She remembered how she screamed with delight when Tom and the boys from Precinct Six tossed her, wedding gown and all, up in the air after the bride and groom were announced at the reception. She always told Tom, every day of their married life reminded her of that day.

Debbie began to sob quietly as she thought again about Gary and Edgar, and then Lucas and Phil. She then started to weep openly for Tom.

"Oh God, Tom!" she yelled out. "Oh God, what you must be going through. Oh, Tommy!" She felt the two strong arms wrap around her and was about ready to scream, but Tom's quick, reassuring voice made her melt into him.

"I'm okay, Debbie. I'll be okay." Tom laid her down on the carpet in front of the warmth of the fireplace. He knelt at her side, put a throw blanket around her shoulders and began to caress her neck and run his fingers through her long, blonde curls. She turned towards him, and began to kiss his neck as he lay down beside her and hold her in his arms for what would feel like an eternity.

"Be with me, Tom," she said in a hushed tone. "Be with me."

As the fires light began to dim, and they became enveloped into each other under the blanket, for one brief moment in this day of grief, all seemed right in this cold, cruel world.

CHAPTER 7

Tom awakened to the sounds of a stiff breeze hitting the house. He lit up a cigarette and walked to the den window. Although it was about five in the morning, the timers had taken care of illuminating the inner and outer areas of the Miller household. He looked out at the cherry blossom in particular, which was aglow with bright white Christmas bulbs. He smiled as he thought back in time to the day that father, mother, and son planted that tree. He remembered his son, dirt from head to toe saying, "Dad, I'm going to watch this tree grow. When I have children they'll watch it become an old tree. As long as there are Miller's, this tree will live on." Such prophetic words from such a young man. Isn't it funny, how the simple things in life matter the most? Isn't it funny, how when we face tragedy, it's these things we hold dearest to our hearts and revere the most?

He promised himself that he would try and keep these memories to uplift his spirits. God knows, he'll need them to. If there really was a chance for Kane's prophecy to be fulfilled, it meant six more ritual murders and the possibility of a seventh. That damn Kane, he thought. I'll make the bastard talk. I'll make him admit to my father's murder if I have to jump on the table and take the needle with him. He's either going to admit to it, or tell me who did it.

He put more logs on the fireplace and set them ablaze to warm this place of solitude. Debbie felt this warmth and snuggled in the blanket again. Tom gave her another kiss and walked into the kitchen to make some hot chocolate. His shift would begin in another hour, so he decided to give Al his usual morning call. He let it ring until the customary third time, when Al would always pick up the receiver.

"Might this be the one and only Thomas Miller callin' my residence?" Al asked in a dead ringer imitation of John Boyle. Tom started to laugh and said, "I can always rely on you Jeaneau, to disarm an otherwise tense situation."

"Why thank you for those kind words. I think we'll need a bit of humor considering the events that are unfolding." Tom did not take too well to the last comment, so he took the bait. "Another one?" he asked calmly.

"Yes, but not in New Hope," Al replied stoically. "Where and when, Al?" Tom finished the cocoa, and started making a quick breakfast of eggs and bacon. He had no appetite, but food was needed. He knew without it he would drop from the exhaustion the next few days would bring. He was talking to Al on the speakerphone.

"You remember Robert Pond?" Al's voice crackled on the unit.

"Oh God", Tom replied, "not him too."

"Unfortunately Tommy, I got the call about a half hour ago. He was murdered in his house in the Mill Hill section of Trenton. There is only one difference though, and it means one of two possibilities."

"What would those be Al?" Tom asked in between bites of his breakfast.

"Well, one is that our murderer got very sloppy, very quickly, or we have two murderers."

"Two murderers!" Tom exclaimed. "This is the last thing that we needed, Al. Does the Trenton Police Department have any leads?"

"Thomas, do you not know me by now? I've already called my contacts and we'll be meeting Chief Townsend. Mayor Palmer will be there also."

"Boy, you worked quickly, as usual," Tom replied.

"I know. Thank you very much," Al answered. "Towny already filled me in briefly on the crime scene, which he would like us to tour. The murder was conducted in the same ritual fashion. The collar was left behind, but here's the difference. There were definitely signs of a struggle, and the labs are reporting two different blood types. They also have prints and they're not just of Pond's."

"Damn!" Tom exclaimed. "A copy-cat who's thorough, to a point. The labs worked quickly."

"They had some time. Reports have the murder taking place at approximately one in the morning. Merry Christmas Eve!" Al snorted.

"So when do we meet our Trenton partners?"

"They would like us at the crime scene by seven," Al said.

"Okay, buddy let me roll then. I'm going to hit the shower and then I'll be down your way. Call up Pags and let him know..."

"Already taken care of Tommy. I told him he'd be running the show here for a few hours and to keep us informed if anything arises."

"What would I do without you, Jeaneau?"

"Why, you'd be doing it all by yourself," Al said with a smattering of sarcasm.

"Okay, okay, I get your point. I'm assuming Towny and the Mayor are expecting our presence in Trenton to not include us being in unit or uniform?"

"They did happen to mention that, yes." Al sounded like he was gulping down some breakfast also.

"Okay pal, finish your breakfast and I'll see you in about thirty minutes."

"I'll be here Tommy. See ya' then buddy."

"Bye, Al." Tom was already done eating and was proceeding to clean up his mess when he heard footsteps lightly approaching. He turned around to see Debbie standing there, trying to muster a smile. She still had the blanket wrapped around her. "Good morning," she said.

"It is, now that you're up."

"I heard you talking to Al. Was there another murder?"

"Yes, and another person that we knew. Robert Pond was found murdered in his Mill Hill row house."

"No!" Debbie exclaimed. "First Lucas, and now Robert. Do they think that there is any connection to them both being high profile jazz club owners?"

"I'm sure they'll look into it, but I think they'll find that as purely coincidental," Tom said stoically.

"Listen, go and take your shower and get to Al's. I'll take care of cleaning up."

"Thanks, honey. I love you," he said as he gave her a quick kiss.

"Love you too, Tommy." As she heard the shower water running, Debbie sat at the kitchen table and lit up a cigarette. Fifteen years later and it will just be the painful experience of watching good people die again, and the dredging up of deaths from the past. She had to put in her head that she would be strong for Tom. She would have no choice but to be bulletproof, just as she had been back then. Within a matter of minutes, Tom was down from the shower and already dressed to leave. He grabbed his keys, his badge and his service revolver. He then grabbed Debbie and pulled her close to himself. She could feel Tom's heart beating. She heard his breath getting ready to escape, but cut him off before he could say anything.

"Don't say a word. Go get Al, get to the scene and find this maniac. Tommy, you did it before, I know you'll do it again." She kissed him on the forehead, and gave that smile of hers that said everything would be just fine. He kissed her and proceeded to the front door.

Tom left down the drive and onto the road to start anew the hunt for a madman. She began to shed a tear but she composed herself quickly. "And now, it does begin again," she said as she approached the tall windows of 5937 Chapel Drive. A small, solitary figure amongst giants.

CHAPTER 8

Tom made quick work of getting to Al's house, which was approximately three miles up from the Miller residence, on Sugan Road. Al was already standing in front of the long drive leading to his modest and tidy Cape house. With all the new, gigantic dwellings sprouting up around him, his house looked out of place. His residence sat on quite a sizeable acreage of land but he never expanded the home. A major developer from Maryland had offered a large sum to buy the land, but Al refused. "Those crazy New Yorkers," he laughed when the man told him the amount. "They can't buy a shoebox loft in Midtown Manhattan for under a half-million dollars, but out here they can live in a mansion. Well, they can have their mansions, but not on my land. This is home for me, and it will remain this way until the day I die." He gracefully turned down an offer that could have made Al Jeaneau a millionaire cop.

"Good morning, Chief," Al said, as they made haste towards New Hope Borough, and across the Free Bridge into Lambertville, New Jersey. In another twenty minutes they would be through the hills and the rural lands, and into the city of Trenton.

"How's Debbie holding up? Strong as usual, I suppose?"

"You know her, Al. Just like a rock."

"And you, Chief?"

"As well as could be expected, pal. Nothing more and nothing less."

Al unfolded the morning papers he'd brought along for the ride. "HATE CRIME? SADISTIC COPY-CAT MURDERER? PURE EVIL!!" screamed the New Hope Gazette. "HATE MURDER IN A SMALL TOWN, JAZZ NOTABLE SLAIN" said the Philadelphia Daily Eagle. "Enough said, don't you think Thomas? Both of them alluded to the Kane murders and his prophecy, although I will admit that Mary toned her article down. She said, as of now, this all was merely unfounded speculation."

"Well that's good to hear. How about the pot-stirring prick in Philadelphia? I'm sure he's figuring that this is his fast track to a Pulitzer, if he plays his cards right."

"Ah yes, my perceptive Chief! That's why you get paid the big bucks," Al retorted with a sarcastic grin affixed to his face for good measure. "Dickhead Ian's angle figures that you are tried and true when it came to the Kane murders, but now you are a "past it" small town police chief. Basically, you should move over, be retired to the glue farm, and let the technological whiz kids at the Fed take over the case."

"He said that?" Miller asked laughingly.

"Not in as many words, but you get the gist, my commandant."

"I kind of figured that. I didn't think he could spin an eloquent thought like that one together. Well," Tom said as he handed Al his revolver, "that's it, Al. Put an old man out of his misery. Useless to all I am, Sergeant Jeaneau."

"Sorry, Chief. I'll use my Glock. Your old .38 is a rust bucket. It would probably jam on me anyway."

The two men began to laugh hysterically as Tom re-holstered the gun.

"More better we laugh, Sarge."

"Yes Tom, more better we do. On a more somber note, I saw Phil at the station yesterday."

"Phil? Wasn't that a few hours after we had Jenn take him home?"

"Yes it was. Apparently he came back to the station asking for me. The dispatcher told him we were out on an investigation, and Phil said he would wait."

"So, what happened?"

"Well, after we parked at the station, I went inside and I see Phil sitting inside my office. I go in, say hello, give him a hug, and ask him if everything is okay. You know, the usual. So, he tells me about how after Jenn dropped him off, he started to think about what happened and he starts feeling a rage inside himself. You know, the type that you only get once or twice in a lifetime?"

"Oh, I know the type well, Al."

Al nodded in agreement. "Well, Phil tells me that the only person he could tell about this was me. So I say fine, let's talk. I tell him that it is understandable to feel what he is feeling, especially with the way in which Luke was murdered."

"So, what does he say?" Tom asked, as he pulled out a cigarette.

"Well, Phil says that's all well and fine, but that's not at all what I am looking for. I proceed to ask him what is he looking for, and he says payback."

Tom glances in Al's direction with a look of surprise.

"That's exactly how I looked at Phil" Al replied. "So I continue the conversation and ask him, how exactly do you mean payback? Do you mean to exact revenge? Phil says, I think you're right on target Al. When you find Luke's murderer, I want you to kill them. No arrests, no trial, no convictions, just kill the bastard. I don't care how you do it, Al. Make it look like they struggled with you, whatever. Hell, get Tommy and John to help, they probably would. What this person did to Luke is barbarism. They don't deserve a life, even if it's life behind bars. Just kill the damn animal, Al. Just fucking kill them!"

Tom extinguished the spent cigarette and looked again towards the winding roads that lie ahead. "The grieving and the anguish begins, ay' Al?" Tom sighed heavily. "Boy, we've been there before. Haven't we, pal?"

"Damn right we have," Al reflected solemnly.

"Were you able to calm Phil down?"

"It took some time, just like it always does, Tommy. Phil broke down and cried, and then he would start to vent again. When he had calmed down enough, I sat next to him. I told him that I could relate to his anger and pain. It was the same way I felt when Roger was taken from me. I cursed the person that had given him the sickness. I damned them and the physicians who I thought weren't trying hard enough to horrible deaths. It was then, I began to realize, all this hate would never bring Roger back. Phil, I said, vengefully taking this person's life will never bring Lucas back either. I told him, two wrongs just don't make this situation right."

"What did he have to say to that?" asked Tom who was already fueling his lungs with another blast of nicotine.

"He eventually agreed with me. He said he felt really foolish now because he had never felt that way about hurting someone. He said it just hurt so much because Lucas was his life and now he was gone."

"Was he okay when he finally left?"

"I asked him if he was too shaken to drive. He replied he was fine, but I followed in the patrol car to make he got home in one piece. I was also quite curious to see if our beloved members of the press had kept their word on not harassing Phil."

"No press?"

"None to be seen, Tom."

"Good."

The scenery on Route 29 had started to take on a much different appearance. Gone were the lush fields and forests separating the hamlets from the city. Trenton had definitely seen its share of better days. It was always a working class town during the early and mid-20th century. During its heyday, it had boasted notable industrial giants such as Roebling Steel, Lenox China, American Standard, and quite a few others.

Following the riots in 1968 that had escalated after Martin Luther King's assassination, many of the mainly white owned big and small businesses pulled up their stakes, never to return. Those that had stayed would barely survive at times. Dealing narcotics had become the main industry of income in certain Wards of the city, and unemployment was running rampant. It was then, the capitol city of Trenton began to collapse on itself. From the row home neighborhoods of the blue-collar workers, to the more expansive domains housing the professional set located by the city's river regions, Trenton had reeled into a state of ruin. These once tidy neighborhoods were now abandoned and decaying, and were becoming homes to crack houses and dumping areas for murderers.

In the 1990's though, a young, eager, and much needed African-American mayor, Doug Palmer, was trying to change his city's tarnished image. Mayor Palmer had brought minor league baseball back to Trenton, housed in a state-of-the-art facility, and he had been instrumental in the completion of a glitzy new ice hockey and concert arena in what used to be a branch of the old Roebling Steel mill. He also got the funds to refurbish and modernize the Trenton War Memorial, so theater and classical music could again flourish in the capitol city.

The rejuvenation of Trenton brought an influx of entrepreneurial spirit from as close quarters as Lambertville, and as far as the West Side of Manhattan. The lure of inexpensive real estate, government subsidies, and the chance to revive the city into a crowning achievement that other small cities could use as a rebuilding blueprint, gave the mayor and this band of mostly young, eclectic pioneers the energy needed to forge ahead. They felt they had a chance to make Trenton a new spot on the map to enjoy a day of culture, cuisine, and the arts.

One of Palmer's shining stars was a young man named Robert Pond from Greenwich Village. A new inhabitant to Trenton in 1997, he quickly fell in love with the quaintness and historical value of the Mill Hill District. He and a few West Side acquaintances purchased a dilapidated, Federal style row home in the section and began to return the luster and grand living of years gone by to the residence. The hardwood pine floors were replaced from top to bottom. New wiring and phone lines were added to bring the relic into the high tech dawn of the 21st century. The kitchen and the bathrooms were gutted and rebuilt to include the modern conveniences and style the three men were seeking.

Soon after he'd settled into the area, a mutual associate introduced him to the older in age, but not in savvy, Luke Stone and Phil Antos. He traveled to New Hope to view the famous "A" Train, and to pick the brains of its founders. What Rob came away with were new friendships and a plan for his new club, City Sounds.

Rob had bought a ramshackle electric supply warehouse on South Broad Street, directly across from the arena, which was still under construction. He proceeded to gut the premises and altered the spot into a hip, eclectic domain that featured a range in tastes from jazz and acid jazz, to hip-hop or spoken word poetry. After a few weeks he would bring in a West Side chef who made a knockout array of dining pleasures. It was not unusual to see a menu that included Thai dishes mixed right in with a more staid Continental fare. Robbie, as he was referred to by his close friends, and his living partners then acquired a three floor abandoned factory next door to City Sounds, and created 'Buzz', which was an independent, avant-garde movie house on the bottom, and a nightclub on the top two floors. The two businesses floundered at first, but once the arena was up, running and drawing crowds in the latter part of 1998, both enterprises shot off the charts. Rave reviews were flowing in from patrons, the local presses music and food critics, and the mayor's office. Robert Pond, his partners, and Mayor Doug Palmer were beginning to see their dreams come to fruition. They envisioned their revitalization as a small-scale version of what had taken place on the Avenue of the Arts, located on the more famous Broad Street in Philadelphia.

Today though, as Chief Tom Miller and Sergeant Al Jeaneau walked up the steps of Pond's Mill Hill home, they saw a shaken mayor. It wasn't that the mayor hadn't been witness to these tragic murders which had plagued the town, but a murder of this magnitude, with this type of ferocity, looked as if it had shaken even the rock solid Doug Palmer right down to his very core.

He gazed up to see Tom and Al approaching, and did the best he could to regain his composure. "Thanks for coming on such a short notice, Tom. I know you have your hands full in New Hope with Luke's murder."

"No problem, Doug. I wish we were meeting under our usually less serious circumstances," Tom said as he shook the mayor's hand.

"Me too", replied Palmer. "Al, it's been a long time, brother. How's the task master treating you New Hope boys?"

"Like gold, Doug, like gold."

"So Doug, where is Towny? I thought he'd be out here before we'd even hit the steps."

"He's by the victim, Tom. I don't know what kind of madness could go through this persons mind to commit such an act. I can't imagine hating a person's sexuality that much to do what was unleashed on Robert. Worst of all, we may know who this animal is. He's an elusive one and the Fed's can't even find him. He's been on their hit list for a while."

"Speaking of which," Tom said in between drags of his Marlboro, "are our little friends getting involved in your neck of the woods?"

"Not yet guys. All this Y2K scare and the possibility of terrorist strikes are making this a small time deal, for now. If the press keeps expressing its opinions, it could blow up real big. You know, hate crimes are a touchy situation to avoid."

"We know," Al replied. "Believe us, we do!"

"Speaking of blowing up", Mayor Palmer countered. "Has your boy seen fit to ask for their assistance?"

"Not yet Doug, but you know Ward. If he gets pressured from his ties in Washington, especially the White House, we could have Feds coming out the ass", Tom said.

"Oh, I know Ward," Palmer laughed. "Sometimes, I wish I didn't know him. He's a loose cannon."

"Very loose", replied Tom.

At that point, Trenton Police Chief Artis Townsend entered the doorway. He shook both of the officer's hands, and cracked a smile. "Tommy, you're looking good, you old war horse. Hey Al, you keeping this man in line, I hope?"

"Tryin' Art, tryin.' It's all a man can do."

Tom smiled in Al's direction, and looked towards Townsend. "Towny, in answer to your statement, thanks. You look like you've been enjoying your wife's cooking."

"Round muscle, my good man," Arits replied as he slapped his stomach.

"So I hear we have an idea on who murdered Rob Pond?"

"More than an idea, Tommy. We know who it is. I think you'll recognize the face and the name. Here's the printout." Artis handed Tom the sheet and awaited a reaction.

"Jerome Jones? Jesus, are we still trying to catch that guy?"

"Ten years later he's hopping from here, to Newark, to New York, and maybe back here again. Who knows? He could be roaming around in your neck of the woods."

Tom looked at the picture of Jerome. Man, he thought, he still looked the same. Jerome had handsome features, in certain ways quite feminine, but the pretty face was attached to a muscular frame and a vicious temper. "This doesn't follow his usual gig. I thought he was a straight up dealer who rolled junkies with debts and murdered his competition."

"Oh, he still does all that," a distinct Irish brogue chortled from behind the door. "But, Tommy my boy, he also leads another life. Jerome Jones, also known as Jessie Johnson, Robert Wilkes and Reverend Malcom Xavier, pastor of the Newark and Trenton "shadow" parishes of Martin Kane's thought to be defunct World Church."

"John, my friend, somehow I knew you'd would be joining us."

"What, and miss out on all this fun? Of course I'd be here, Tommy boy," John snorted. "Seriously though, Towny called me too, and asked if I could find some more information. He figured if we were all going after the same guy, then we could pool our resources. In the worst case scenario, which I think this is, that we have two crazy dickheads, at least we all know who one of them is."

"So, Malcom Xavier?" Tom asked snidely, as he lit another cigarette.

"Yeah, Malcom X! Cute, isn't he?" chided Artis.

John started to speak again. "Well, gentlemen, as if that weren't bad enough, Jones likes to roll gays now. He evidently targets certain ones, chats em' up in the bars, goes home with them and then beats them senseless.

Apparently, he does this trick on lesbians when he dolls himself up as a body building dyke named Roberta."

"Great. A big, elusive guy, with a bad temper, who beats up gays and lesbians, occasionally cross dresses and is a reverend?" asked an exasperated Tom.

"Talk about split personalities, eh Tommy boy?" John asked.

"Well," Artis inquired, "are you gents ready to tour the scene?"

"Yes," Tom replied in between puffs of his nearly spent smoke.

"It's not pretty, Tom," Mayor Palmer offered.

"Never is, Doug," replied Tom.

"Some of my homicide boys have been checking it out, but I'm sure they'll be happy to get an experts opinion since you've dealt with this before."

"Towny, it's an expertise I wish I'd never had."

"You've got that right," John added.

The two young detectives turned from the body of Robert Pond, to meet the approaching entourage. "Detectives Canty and Pruett, this is Sergeant Al Jeaneau and Chief Tom Miller from New Hope. I assume that you have already met Trooper Boyle."

"Yes Chief Townsend, we have met Trooper Boyle. Sergeant Jeaneau, Chief Miller, it's a pleasure to have you working with us", said Detective Ronald Canty. He, in turn with Pruett shook hands with the two men.

"I hope that you don't mind if we pick your brain, sir. We've never had to deal with a murder of this magnitude," chimed in Pruett.

"Any help that I can give is yours. Well gents, what have we uncovered so far?"

"Well, Chief, as you can see, the victim took a pretty thorough beating about the face and chest area. His face was swollen severely, and his chest and rib area had a number of black and blue marks," answered Canty. Pruett showed the men the stab wounds.

"Its pattern is identical to Luke's," Al replied.

"Same as all of the murders," Tom said with remorse.

"The stabbings seem to go from front to back in a very smooth fashion," Pruett added.

"Too smooth for the knife stabs I am used to seeing. The eyes were removed I assume?"

"Yes, Chief. Pru and I found them placed in a bowl with a note partially tucked under it."

"Shall we go see the note?"

"Yes sir."

"Then lead the way, Detective Canty." As they moved towards the kitchen, Tom took in all the mayhem that had taken place in the Pond house. Blood was splattered in every direction. The heavy oak furniture in the living room had been toppled. The smell of alcohol and blood mixed into a nauseating aroma and the Oriental rugs throughout the lower floors were saturated with both. The walls of the dining room had slash marks in them and were splattered red. What looked like precious antique china and crystal goblets had been shattered. The kitchen had received much of the same abuse.

"It looks like he used a chainsaw rather than a knife."

"I don't know about a knife in this case, Towny, but I think this note may give an explanation for the mess we have been left with," Tom replied. Tom opened the note and that old sensation from 1985 began to run its course through his veins. He started to read aloud. "These eyes have been witness to the glorious resurrection. Christ Jesus has shown the sodomized his displeasure meted out with his vengeance. With sword in hand, I will decide their punishments with his blessings." He put down the letter and became quiet, almost contemplative.

"With God's blessings!" John Boyle exclaimed. "Jesus, he really does think he's Kane!"

"With my sword I shall deliver God's justice," Tom muttered.

"What was that you said, Tom?" asked Al.

"With my sword I shall deliver God's justice. Stan Tilden said Kane used to cite a verse quite similar to that one in his homilies. He also used to say that with his sword in hand he would strike down his enemy like the crusaders had done to the heathen hordes."

"That's why the marks through Pond's body and the wall look so clean. The son of a bitch is using a sword. We took the sword reference as being rhetorical."

"I agree Detective Canty." Tom looked at the men. "Some things, it seems, gentlemen, our murderer does put to literal usage. I think, unfortunately, we are going to find, this time we are dealing with two killers. Do you have surgical gloves that I can use Detective Canty?"

"Yes sir, I have a pair I can give you."

Tom put on the gloves and proceeded to the victim's mouth. "I am assuming that you did not look in Mister Pond's mouth yet?" Canty and

Pruett looked at Tom quizzically. "His mouth?" asked Pruett. "No, what for sir?"

"Well, another little ritual that our good Reverend used, and our New Hope murderer kept alive, was the removal of the victim's tongue. A note was usually left in its place."

"Jesus," Canty exclaimed. "This is nuts. What kind of mind thinks this shit up?"

"A very sick one", Al added. "Your boys may want to check outside, or in the trash cans for that body part."

Detective Pruett started to walk away, shaking his head as he did. "I'll tell them to start looking."

"Detective Canty?" asked Tom. "Would you want to do the honors? It is, after all, your crime scene."

"Sir, I have no problems with you stepping in on my turf. You can do the honors," replied the young detective who was looking rather queasy.

Tom knelt over Pond's head. He very gently began to open the deceased's blood soaked mouth. As he put his hand inside Pond's mouth, he could hear Canty gasping for air. Welcome to the world of homicide kid, better get used to it. Tom probed a little deeper past where the victims tongue used to be, and grabbed what felt like a plastic baggy. It felt about the size of the ones the pushers used to peddle their wares. He pulled the blood soaked bag out and began to wipe it off. Tom extracted the clean, white piece of paper that had remained untouched by the waves of blood that had flooded the house. He unfolded the note and began to read it.

Tom shook his head and smirked slightly. "Well folks, if he is to be believed, Mister Jones is not the only killer. The note reads, I do not know who my disciple in New Hope is, but their work will be rewarded. They have implemented a swift and just execution upon the purveyor's of sodomy. The evil land of Sodom has not yet seen the end of our reign of righteous terror." Tom gave the note to Canty. "I think you will need this."

"Does it follow the usual pattern?" Canty asked as he pocketed the note.

"Your man follows it, but just to a certain degree. He is more brazen in his actions. Kane and the New Hope murderer were much more meticulous. They show no blood, no prints, no anything, except the victims. Your man Jones wants us to know who he is."

"Yeah, we know who he is, and we still can't catch the elusive asshole though, can we?"

"He'll stumble, Towny. Sooner or later, they both will."

"I hope you're right, Thomas. I really hope you are." The officers began hear a commotion out in the backyard. They moved swiftly towards the back doorway.

"Do you think that they found some of our missing evidence?" Al inquired.

"By the sound of the hacking and the heavin' out there, I would say so", added John Boyle.

"What did you find Pru?" Canty asked as his partner looked at him in bewilderment.

"A tongue Canty! We found a freaking tongue!"

"That would be Pond's tongue," Canty answered.

"Where was it found, Detective Pruett?"

"In the trash cans back there, Chief Miller." Pruett pointed to the cans located in the furthest corner of the yard. "The tongue is over where Detective Rashard is losing his breakfast."

"Is this the first homicide for him?"

"Nah, Chief Miller. He's a transfer from the Traffic Division. He passed the test, but I don't think he got the stomach for it, dog. No pun intended."

"But of course, Detective," Tom answered with a chuckle. "Have we made any contact with Pond's live-ins?"

"Affirmative," Chief Townsend replied. "They're both on their way back from the Apple."

"So, we have two on our hands. A sword swinger who isn't afraid to let us know who he is, and the other one is trying to be a throwback to the master. Well gents, we shall be in touch," Tom said as he lit another cigarette. All the men proceeded to the front of the house where Mayor Palmer was now fielding some random questions from a few media types. Tom nodded in the mayor's direction and then made haste towards his Explorer. Mayor Palmer nodded in return, all the while looking quite pleased that Tom, Al and John hadn't compromised their identities. Townsend, Canty, and Pruett followed the men to their vehicles so their conversations would remain a private issue, and not fodder for the morning papers.

"As I was saying before guys, we'll make sure to keep a very open line of communication. If anything goes down, let us, or Trooper Boyle know. Consequently, if we come across anything Artis, we'll let either you, or Detectives Pruett and Canty be the first to know. Artis, it was a pleasure, as always. Detectives, I look forward to working with you young bucks again."

"The pleasure was all ours," Canty said. "Any information that you could supply we would greatly appreciate."

"No problem, lad," John Boyle chimed in. "Trooper Terrant is working on compiling some pertinent information as we speak on just that matter. It will be hand delivered to you this afternoon."

"Now there is a young dog you brothers can learn something from," Artis offered to Canty and Pruett. "Zoul is the man."

"Well, if Towny says that he's the man, then we look forward to meeting him," Canty replied.

"Hey John Boy," Arits said in a hushed tone. "I know that Zoul don't mind doing this, but aren't your boys getting heat? I know how the Staties are."

"Towny, ye' of little faith. They shoulda' thought of that before they gave me command. My command, my watch, my say, it will get done. If the brass don't like it, hell, retire me. I could use the rest." All the men began to laugh as they went their separate ways.

"Boyle, you are one tough Mick!"

"Why, thank you Chief Townsend," Boyle said as he bowed. Tom and Al jumped in the Ford and John into his Silverado. The men were out of Trenton and onto Route 29 in a flash. As the scenery became more lush, daybreak had begun to show Tom and Al all of God's glory in his creations. The sunlight skipped along the ripples on the river. They saw the deer running through Washington Crossing Park. As they drove further into the countryside, back towards New Hope, the early morning sun gave way to thick, dark clouds. Tom lit up another cigarette and shook his head. The men had not said much of anything until now.

"A penny for your thoughts, Chief."

"I'm just thinking," Tom said in between drags of his Marlboro. "Out here, somewhere in all the splendor of our surroundings, of our town, an unthinkable evil is here." Al went to speak, but Tom politely cut him off. "Just hear me out buddy. I'm not saying that it shouldn't be peaceful in the city, but you expect it there. I expected it in New York too. Man and his plotting, deceitful ways are all about you in the big towns. Out here, though? Out here is where you come to escape all of that. Out here is where you come to live your life to its fullest. It's just hard to accept, Al."

"I understand where you are coming from Tom, but it's like Zoul used to say about his grandmother. She used to say that even out in the hills and the rivers that they inhabited, tales were told of the evil secrets that still remain hidden in those "pristine" areas. Tom, you know as well as I do, evil will exist wherever man touches, but God always creates people with righteous hearts to conquer them. We have to fight evil, always. Sometimes the good guys win, sometimes they will lose. People like John, you, and me? Guys like us will fight until there are none of us left. Good will win here Tom. Good will win."

Tom just nodded and smiled in Al's direction. His good friend had just said all that needed to be conveyed. They would have to fight to win. He just wished the sun would shine. It sounded stupid, but he just wished that it would shine like how it always did in those sappy, old movies when people really needed a sign of hope. But, the sun was gone. As they drove across the bridge into New Hope, the Delaware River looked so dark, so inhospitable and evil to Tom. He could almost see the deep red of blood rising to its surface. It had become, Tom thought as he had another cigarette, his black river. He would have to fight harder than he had ever fought before to make it shine again. Good will win, he said to himself as the smoke billowed from his mouth. Good will win.

CHAPTER 9

The remainder of Sergeant Al Jeaneau and Chief Tom Miller's day was spent at police headquarters, searching through files, crime reports, and anything else possibly aiding them in their quest.

"I'm making printouts of anything that may help us down the road," Al said to Tom. "Who knows? If all this Y2K crap is true, we may lose our whole information base. I read that in New York they are taking all sorts of precautions to make sure the lights stay on in the Apple to avoid any chaos."

"Isn't that a laugh? Chaos? New York? New York will survive just fine if the lights go out. They had better worry about Los Angeles and all of their Silicon Valley, Nostradamus reading, "Oh my God, we're going to break off into the Pacific Ocean!" Californians my son is surrounded by."

"Okay," Al laughed. "What about the terror threats on Times Square, the subway system, and the bridges and tunnels surrounding it? That's not reality? I mean, in Times Square alone, they're welding down the manhole covers and stopping subway service to that area. Pretty serious shit, my friend."

"I agree with you Al," Tom said as he ran through some more files. "A bombing by terrorists is the real deal. I mean we've known just in the past few years that we're not susceptible form the rest of the worlds problems. You've had the White House nearly hit by an airplane, the Oval

Office shot at by a maniac in the street with an automatic rifle. We had the Trade Center get bombed in 93'. Mc Veigh in Oklahoma in 95'. I mean, we're far from being immune, but I don't fear for New York. Giuliani is a good, tough, no-nonsense mayor. If anybody could handle this Y2K garbage, it will be him. Remember, I saw what he did as a prosecutor against the mafia, and saw firsthand what he did to land Kane on Death Row."

"He did prosecute the Kane case. How the time flies anymore. I had totally forgotten about that. No wonder Kane went to the "Row" so quickly."

"You've got that right, my friend. He put Kane away, and then he went after all the politicians and judges that had a vested interest in Kane's well being."

"Well buddy," Al said as he shut down his computer terminal, "why don't we call it a day? The rookie has the desk, and we've got a full crew on that already knows to call me or you if anything out of the ordinary comes to pass. Besides, tomorrow is Christmas Day. You and I both have off, and your incredibly beautiful wife is preparing our usual December 25th feast."

Tom tried to muster a smile. He knew Al was hurting as badly as he was over the loss of their good friend Luke, but that he was trying his best to get through Christmas. "You're right, Al. Let's close up shop here and head home. I'll see you tonight after mass."

"Yeah, Trinity has an 8 o'clock mass too. I think I may just go this year."

"Well, then I'll see you at our house. Let's say, 10 o'clock?"

"As always, I'll be there. Who is going to be there tomorrow?"

"Well, besides the three of us, it will be John and gal of the moment, Rachel."

"The young, redhead singer from the Havana? You go, cradle robbing John!"

"Now, now, she is almost thirty."

"Oh, a mature woman this time. He's starting to settle. When is he just going to give in and ask McGuigan out? Everybody knows they've got the "hots" for each other. They're so pigheaded, that's why they're always fighting."

"I know it. You know it, and so do they," Tom chuckled. "Anyway, after dinner it will be the previously mentioned, Razoul, Lucinda, and little May. Pags and his wife, and with your help, I'm thinking we get Phil over. We need to get him out of the house. Being alone in his mourning is unpleasant enough, but on Christmas? He has never missed one of our Christmas events since we've had them, and he needs to be around life even if it is just two days after Luke's death."

"It's agreed then! We'll go over and get him for dinner."

"Great, Debbie will be thrilled."

"No Edward this year?"

"Not this year, Al. His wife and he are stuck out in Silicon Valley trying to make sure this Y2Kproblem doesn't wreck the computer industry."

"Well, I'm sorry to hear that, Tommy. Listen, I'm going to run. I'll see you at your place tonight."

"Later, Al."

"See you, pal."

CHAPTER 10

It was Christmas Eve in New Hope, and all was quiet. All the shops had closed early and the streets were practically empty, save for the people heading to church services in the town. Tom and Debbie headed into St. Mark's Roman Catholic Church for the early Christmas services. The service was packed, which anyone outside of the town would have found quite peculiar considering the church's stance on homosexuality. There was a portion of the parish of Saint Mark's that led an active homosexual lifestyle. This could have led to friction in the parish, but Father Michael Brown always managed to maintain a delicate balancing act between the teachings of the church and the special needs of an equally special community.

It was a balancing act that Tom Miller knew all too well, and thus became one of Father Michael's strongest supporters. Tom had been Baptized into the Catholic religion by his mother and father, who were both of the faith. Even when Edgar went through the trials and tribulations of his realizations, he wanted young Tom to be brought up with a strong formative background and belief in the Catholic faith. As Tom became older, Edgar told him that his and Gary's lifestyle was too radical for the Church to accept, but he wanted Tom to follow the teachings of the Bible and come to his own conclusions and judgments. Edgar even went as far as to tell Tom, if his son came to the decision that his father's lifestyle was wrong, he would accept his sons' thoughts. The only thing he asked his son, was they respect and love each other. Edgar's willingness to hear his own son could possibly disagree with his father's way of life led to an honest and open relationship between the two. Many hours were spent conversing, and quite a few debating every subject known to mankind. Gary also entered into the fray many a time, to add another set of views. It made for quite an interesting and informative maturing process for Tom. As the mass proceeded, Tom sat in the pew and thought back to something he never forgot his father telling him when he was in his late teens. "The great thing about God, the church, and this incredible country we live in, is that we have the right to think with our own free will." Edgar went on to tell him the three of these institutions may not agree with your final decision, but you won't be jailed for a lifetime or condemned to death for espousing your beliefs. "You may be frowned upon Tommy, for going against the norm, but you'll always be a free man."

As Father Michael finished the gospel passage, he stepped down from the altar. He glanced towards the front pew, and saw Tom and Debbie seated there. He smiled peacefully in recognition. The viciousness of Luke Stone's murder had shaken him to his very core. Father Michael had, as did many in town, considered Luke a very dear friend. Although Luke was not Catholic, he ran quite a few charity events to which all the proceeds benefited organizations dealing with Father Michael's church. Luke Stone had always thought Father Michael was quite a unique character. Luke used to laugh as he would tell his patrons of the young priest. "He even comes to the club, toe taps to the old jazz, and indulges in a few beers and a couple of cigarettes. Any priest who could do that and hang out in a club run by gays, I've got to get to know him!"

Father Michael gathered his thoughts and began to compose himself. The parishioners of Saint Mark's had, for the past ten years, looked towards him to be their guidance, to be their rock. Damn it, he thought to himself, I am not about to let them down now.

"I am glad to see that so many of you are attending the mass tonight." He then pondered, "if only it were Christmas every week." His wry sense of humor had made many laugh, and tonight was no exception. "I'm just kidding folks. I am really glad so many of you are here. Christmas should be a time of rejoicing in Christ's birth. On our greatest day of gift giving, God sends us the greatest gift of all, his only son. His only child. Yet, so many of us, including myself, feel so empty this Christmas. We feel so hurt. A good many of us here tonight knew Luke Stone. Very many of us could count ourselves as his friend. It is so hard to fathom someone committing this sort of hateful brutality around a time of year that is so much focused on peace on earth and good will towards mankind.

When we see something like this happen to such a good person, we may ask ourselves how can God permit such evil to exist? How could he let an individual exist who could hate another person so much, just because of their race, their religion...their lifestyle? Part of the answer is free will. God gives us this ability, and lets us be able to base our decisions on what is right and what is wrong in life. Some of us will choose the path of the righteous man, others will not. It is what we do with this ability and many others that God will judge us on when we finally meet him, and be in a place of blissful happiness.

I am not expecting people to not be angry or resentful as to what has happened to our friend and our town in the past day. I must beg of you though, to please firm your resolve and bury your hatred. Remember, my friends, if God as powerful as he is was truly a being of vengeance, he could have easily destroyed man and his world for the murder of his son. He let's us learn from our mistakes.

I am not going to get into the politics or policies of what man considers right or wrong. God knows," he said with head arching skyward, "we deal with that more than enough in this particular parish." The last remark brought about more laughter, this time with a little more emphasis.

"So, my friends if I could ask a favor of you, please bring love into your hearts this Christmas. Say a special prayer of thanks for having your loved ones here, and say one for those who are not. I would also like to ask you to do one more thing. Please say a prayer for the men and women of our towns' police force. I know it is very easy to be critical, to think that they look the other way because it is a crime against homosexuals. This town of New Hope has a very dedicated group of men and women from very diverse cultural backgrounds who go out of their way to make all feel important. Pray for them, because this tragedy hurts them maybe even more than it does us.

Merry Christmas, everyone."

Tom was very grateful to Father Michael for the prophetic, considerate words of his homily, and made sure to say as much to him when he and Debbie sought him out after the service.

"It was easy to say Tom. It is how most of us in this town feel."

"Well thank you for being the one to say them, Father Michael," said John Boyle who was also in attendance, and made it a point to visit with the three of them.

"I know I appreciated those words too," said an all too familiar voice that approached from behind them.

"Al Jeaneau," Tom laughed as he gave his partner a hug. "I was unaware of your recent conversion."

"Saints and angels take me away, the end is near!" John bellowed as he placed his hand across his forehead.

"Oh, they're a laugh. Your husband and his leprechaun counterpart are regular comedians, Debbie. For your information big time detectives, I come to St. Mark's from time to time. I also come here to pick Michael's mind about questions I have on theology, morality, and the teachings of your church. Besides, tonight I knew this was the place to be. If anyone in New Hope could be a true voice of reason, it would be you Michael."

"Thank you, Al," Father Michael replied sheepishly. "Let's just hope that it lasts folks."

"Amen to that, Father!" Al exclaimed in his best imitation of a Southern preacher. As Father Michael, Tom, Debbie and John burst into laughter, Al waved goodbye. "I'll see ya'll at the house," Al said with an exaggerated drawl.

"Aye, if you two lovebirds don't mind, I think I could partake in a wee bit of liquid to remedy this parched throat."

"Come on over then," Debbie said as she smiled.

"Hey Boyle, no girlfriend tonight?" Al inquired as he walked down the path from Saint Mark's. "What's the matter, is it past her curfew?"

"Oh! Oh, so you're a good one yourself for comedy are you Jeaneau? Maybe you and I should start a stand-up act, ay'?" John asked as he quickly strode down the path to catch up with Al.

"It would never work, Boyle."

"And why would this be, Jeaneau?"

"Nobody would think you're the least bit funny."

"Why, you!"

Tom and Debbie heard the two men's voices and laughter trailing into the distance. "We'd better go, Father," Tom said as he shook his head. "Apparently, we're babysitting tonight," he said as he smiled and gestured down the path.

Father Michael brought his hands together and looked skyward. "Bless them both, Lord. They'll need your help tonight."

"Merry Christmas to you too", Debbie chuckled. As they made their way to the car, Debbie gave Tom a kiss.

"What was that for?"

"It's just nice to see you smiling again."

"Well, it's nice to be smiling again. Thankfully, I am surrounded with people who handle a crisis with some laughter, although tonight I think you'd better keep the glasses full, honey. I think we're all going to need to blow off some steam."

"Agreed."

When they returned home, it was exactly as Tom had figured. An abundance of drinking and cigarette smoking, mixed in with good amounts of laughter, crying, venting, and reflection. When all was said and done, the three men came to the conclusion that no man, no force, would shake their resolve. Evil may have come to their beloved town, but they would not let it leave here and bring its devastation elsewhere, and they certainly would not let it win. The evil shattering their peaceful existence would be destroyed, even if it meant with their lives.

"To the good guys!" John Boyle toasted.

"To the good guys!" Al and Tom said in unison.

CHAPTER 11

Christmas day had come and was almost a memory in New Hope. Although the murder of Luke Stone was still fresh in everyone's mind, the townspeople were doing their best to get on with life as normal. Therefore, Christmastime this year had become a welcome distraction.

Sergeant Al Jeaneau was trying not to be the exception to this rule. He was mourning the loss of an old, close friend in Luke, and the loss of a newer acquaintance in Robert Pond. Even with those two cataclysmic events in his mind, Al was using Christmas to fight off something even worse, the ghosts of the past.

Al was doing such a good job of it too. He had gone to Phil Antos' house this morning, and persuaded him to join the entourage that was assembling at Tom and Debbie's home. When they arrived, warm greetings were given by the cheerful host and hostess, along with John Boyle and his date. Everything had gone off without a hitch. The table was a visual feast for the eyes in itself. The tablecloth was made of white Irish linen. The gold rimmed Lenox plates were the ones Debbie's mother had used for many a Christmas dinner. The napkins were spun with a fine, silver thread and placed in round, gold plated holders. To top off the display were the hand-blown, Irish crystal candlesticks and goblets, surrounded by an array of cut greens, and bright ribbons and bows.

The ham, mashed potatoes, candied yams and all the other assorted goodies Debbie served for their early dinner were exceptional, and enough to feed ten more people. After dinner, everyone sat around the warmth of the living room fireplace and exchanged their gifts. After the gifts were opened and the drinks were passed around, all the participants seem to loosen up more. Everyone began telling stories about everything from family events, to hilarious things that had taken place just between this small band of friends. Even Phil, with his heavy heart, had started to chuckle and spin some of his own hysterical tales about Luke and himself. He also had them in stitches reliving the events of certain times when Al, John, Tom or anyone else in this tight knit group had come to 'The "A" Train.'

By four-thirty in the afternoon, Razoul and Rob Pagano, along with their families had joined the crowd. Debbie put out her vast array of desserts and coffee, and after everyone had their fill, more presents were exchanged. The obligatory calls were made to wish Jenn Gates, Drew and the other officers who were keeping the town safe, a very merry Christmas. Debbie and Tom then called California to wish Edward and his family the same, and was soon followed by a call to her parents.

The gentlemen then retired to the den to enjoy some cognac and cigars, and of course, to tune into Sports Center and check out the results of the NBA Christmas game. This left the women to enjoy the expanse of the living room and discuss everything and anything.

Around six-thirty, Phil asked Al if he'd mind taking him home since the next few days would be quite harried. Everyone knew exactly what Phil meant, and he began to sense this. "Please, everyone!" Phil exclaimed. "Today has been great. It has been a non-stop cry for me until I came over today. In two days, I'm laying Lucas to rest and I don't need a somber event. I want it to be a celebration of his incredible life. If you can make that happen, I would be forever grateful. Please, enjoy the rest of the evening. I know for me, it was a blast."

Phil then proceeded to give everyone a hug and kiss, as did Al. As they drove away from the Miller's residence, Al and Phil kept up a constant, jovial dialogue until reaching Phil's driveway. Phil asked Al if he'd like to come in for a drink, but Al thought better of the situation. Tonight, Al wanted to escape to the comfort of his own domain. He thanked Phil for the offer, but he said he hoped Phil would understand that he just needed to be home. Phil replied he could definitely understand, and they both embraced.

Phil got out of Al's Accord and turned to close the door. As he stooped down to do so, he impeded the door's progress. He knelt down by the opening and looked at his friend. "I know why you're going home, my friend. I also know I'm being a demanding little jerk by saying this, but I only say it because I care, Al. I have to fight to go on. I can't live in the past. Please Al, don't live in the past anymore. Think about the good things. Celebrate Roger's life as I will Luke's."

Al turned to Phil, shook his head and began to smile. "Ah, Antos. You are a smart one. Don't worry bro', I'll be fine tonight."

Phil shut the car door and turned around again towards Al. "Celebrate life Al, and have a merry Christmas."

"I'll be fine, and the same to you." Al waited until Phil entered the house and then took off. Since he was basically the only car on Main Street, he darted through the town. How he loved this town, especially at Christmas time. He slowed down long enough to glance at the town

Christmas tree, located directly across from Ferry Landing. How cheerful the tree looked with its multi-colored lights, and festive ornaments and bows. It was hard to imagine, in a serene a setting such as this, a vicious murder had taken place.

After he left New Hope Borough, he sped up the pace again, and the small town was soon history. As he turned into his driveway, he stopped to look at his modest domicile which was nestled another quarter-mile in from the roadway. He breathed deep as if it were a relief to be in his place of solitude.

As he exited his car and approached the front door, he heard a frantic, rustling noise from behind him. The blood was coursing through his veins at breakneck speed as he shot around quickly to confront his menace. When he saw his confronters, he emitted a burst of laughter. Over in the distance, near the woods that bordered his property were his attackers. Two deer, that had been his "neighbors" for as long as he could remember, were frolicking about through the trees.

Al caught his breath, calmed his nerves, and began to laugh again. He turned on his porch lights to bring the pair into clearer view. "Hey you two!" he yelled in their direction. "It's Christmas time, man! Chill out and go find Rudolph, or something." The deer looked at him for a few seconds and bounded for the safety of their woods. Al smiled as he turned around to go in the house. He thought to himself, as he put the keys on the kitchen table, people have to be crazy to think he would sell this land. There is no way he would be able to live without his woods, the deer, or to plant his gardens and vegatables every year. He also had something becoming a rare commodity in these ever, encroaching environs. Al Jeaneau had privacy.

Al had seen what had happened to the farmlands and the wooded areas of Newtown and Yardley, and he'd hoped this area would hold out also. He didn't mind having neighbors, but he liked the fact there was some distance between them. It was an inclusive feeling, one of solitude.

Al made his way to the refrigerator, pulled out a bottle of beer, and ventured towards the living room. He sat down in a taupe colored, overstuffed chair, and grabbed his remote from the antique maple end table. A compact disc of Coltrane began to play, and the smooth, dreamy sounds of his saxophone slowly enveloped the room.

Al began to think again about his reaction to the disturbance made by the deer a few minutes ago. The last few days had unquestionably placed everyone's nerves on edge, and he surmised he'd been no different. He tried to gain some concise thoughts about the case. It was becoming more obvious by the minute there were two murderers this time. He was just trying to understand the logistics.

The Trenton murderer was a pretty elementary character. Jerome Jones would have murdered in Trenton, Newark, or anywhere else he ended up. Jones, Reverend Malcom Xavier, or whatever he was calling himself these days, was a stone cold, elusive killer. Al narrowed Jones persona down to that of a person trying to become infamous. Jones was going to ride the Kane prophecy for all that it was worth. Jerome Jones was going to ritually murder gays to produce his fifteen minutes of fame. Nice guy, I ought to have him over for dinner sometime. We could discuss what went wrong with his inner child. The biggest problem in getting to Jones was the same one that had dogged any cop or Federal agent trying to apprehend him over the last few years.

The first of these was his already mentioned elusiveness. The other was the fear of the repercussions facing an individual who could enlighten the authorities of Jones' whereabouts. Most of these people were either dependent on him for their high, or they owed him quite a substantial sum of money.

Al had read Jones' profile when he accessed the FBI's criminal log. Jones was part of the "Most Wanted" list. Al guessed this was not enough of an accomplishment to soothe Jones' ego. He read about the man who in one breath could be quite charming, and in the next one could produce a rage so vicious, that the "Sword of Vengeance" could hit its mark with devastating accuracy. Robert Pond found this out in a very harsh manner. Finding an individual with such fearlessness would be a tough task, but if they could get lucky, his murderous ways could soon end.

The murderer of Luke Stone was another story all together. This was a calculated killer. A profiler might label this individual as an organized serial killer. The New Hope murderer was so thorough, it almost made Al shudder. It was like reading Oswald Jeffords best selling, "The Reverend Reaper (The Kane Murders and The Summer Of Hate)," all over again. Jeffords had collaborated with then Detective Tom Miller, to put the accounts of the murders into words. Tom had recounted to Al about how reluctant he was at first to do the book. It was only when he saw that Jeffords angle was not to smear the New York Police Department or to glorify the murders with cheap, tabloid journalism, he felt at ease and jumped in. He had mentioned to Al, in some ways, it became a very therapeutic process. It kept the good memories of Gary and his father constantly in his mind. It also helped to keep his sights on the fact that if

Kane really did not murder Tom's father, and even if it took him years to do so, he would find out who did.

Al began to feel Tom, this town, and he were in a book of their own, with a new and more gruesome chapter unfolding every day and night. It was happening right before their eyes.

He also thought of the possibility that this murderer could be living in New Hope, or somewhere in the vicinity. Allentown was only an hour away, and most everyone in this neck of the woods knew there were quite a few "hate groups" operating on its outskirts. Just a year ago, Mayor Ward and John Boyle received word from a credible Fed source that a splinter group of Kane's, World Church, had opened shop there. The group called themselves, "The Defenders of the Faith." The source said no hostile movements had been noted from the so-called church's compound, but with the agency's recent record in Ruby Ridge, Montana, and Waco, Texas, this didn't exactly give Al, Tom or anyone else involved a total sense of security.

Now, with the Trenton murder surfacing, it cast more speculation and doubt that the New Hope case would stay solely in their hands. Like it or not, and with Mayor being the catalyst or not, Al, Tom and John had all agreed just last night that the FBI would soon be here. They all knew the President would start hearing the complaints from homosexual and civil rights groups that the Y2K and terrorism issues had taken precedence over a few gays being ritually massacred by a Kane copy-cat.

None of them disagreed the groups complaints wouldn't be well intentioned. What they did agree on was the Fed's involvement usually turned a rationalized effort into a case eventually becoming nothing short of a major catastrophic event.

The disc of Coltrane was starting to replay itself as Al got up to get another beer. Kane and these murders were starting to weigh Al down tonight. He sat again and tried to look around the room to distract his train of thought for just a while. That's when his eyes fell upon another distraction no less jarring for this time of year. Al's eyes had locked on the picture of Roger and himself, set on top of the coffee table.

It was ten years ago on the week before Christmas, Al had buried his companion of nearly ten years. Al had met Roger in 1979. Al had been with the New Hope Police force for almost three years by then. Roger had just moved in from Omaha, Nebraska, and had taken up residence in a small apartment on Main Street. Roger had read about the scene in New Hope and thought it would be much more relaxed to live in than the jarring, overwhelming metropolis of New York City. "Omaha was not exactly a hotbed of activity for the arts, or the gay community," Roger joked with Al when they first met. "New Hope sounded like the perfect fit to become creative and socially active."

Al could relate to Roger all too well. Both of them had been completely shunned by their families. Roger's father was a big cattle man in town, and his mother basically lived in the church. Neither of them had time for a son who was aloof to their way of life. "I have no time in my life to be supportive of a son who sculpts things, sees plays, wants nothing to do with females, and doesn't have an ounce of respect for the law's of God." This is what Roger was told by his father upon his graduation from the University of San Francisco. "You are a queer, boy, and queers have no place in mine or your mother's house." The response prompted Roger to stay in San Francisco until 1976. In 1977, he moved back to Omaha, and tried to muster up the courage to see his parents. A year later, he went to see them on Easter Sunday, and was promptly shown the door.

Al's situation was about as cut-and-dry as Roger's. Al grew up in Wheeling, West Virginia, in a family of two older brothers, and one younger sister. Wheeling was a gritty, blue-collar town, located not too far from Pittsburgh, Pennsylvania. Steel and coal were king in this territory, and it was also the only job a black man such as his father or brothers could obtain. Al Jeaneau wanted neither of them. A very aloof youngster, Al put his efforts towards his schoolwork and his horn playing. He did hang around with girls in social settings, but just to converse with them. Dating did not enter the equation. By the end of high school, Al had just two ambitions. One was attending the University of West Virginia. He planned to go there and get a criminology degree. This would give him a chance to become a policeman or, better yet, a federal agent. The other ambition was to keep up with his horn playing and possibly become an accomplished jazz musician.

A month before graduation, he received his first wish and was accepted to the University of West Virginia. A week before graduation, however, his life would be changed forever.

One night while Al was in his room playing the horn, his father knocked on the door and asked if he could come in. When Al said yes, he entered and sat down across from him. He proceeded to tell Al, he'd like to have a talk with him.

"I know your mom tries to deny things, says I'm bein' foolish, but I want to know what's up with you?" The tone of his voice was very edgy.

"What do you mean, pop?" Al asked in a worrisome way. He couldn't remember doing anything wrong, but usually when the boys got a "talkin' to" from dad, it was usually followed with a "whuppin".

"What's up is, I want to know a little about the odd ways you been keepin'. I mean, boy, you're always in the room readin' about art, and playing jazz. When you go out, you don't date with no girls, and when you're with them, I hear from your brothers it's always just talking girl talk. They say you're always hanging 'round them at the diner chattin', gossipin', or some such foolishness. I mean, son, you don't play no sports. Hell, I don't even know if you like sports. Do you even like girls, son?"

"I guess so". Al began to tap his fingers on the horn, which was perched on his lap.

"But y'all just likes to talk with 'em?

"I guess so, sir." He was tapping Davis. He was tapping Gillespie. He was tapping anything. Just stop dad, I know where this is going.

"Well, MisterGuess So, I guess I want to know something before you and my hard earned money gets to stepping to college. I feel I've earned that right. Your brothers were never interested in all this college silliness, but you, you different, son. You're soft. This brain work seems to fit you. I'm givin' you what money I can, but you need to tell me somethin'."

Tapping Davis, Gillespie, Armstrong, anyone. "What, dad? Just ask me."

"Are you gay, boy?"

He knew the question was coming but it was still impossible to prepare for. "What did you just ask, dad?"

"You heard me, boy. All them things you do, nobody's boy 'round here acts or think like you do. Not even the boys that do go to college! So, are you?"

"Well, gee dad, I never thought about all of my "qualities" being equated to becoming a homosexual."

"Boy, don't sass me! This ain't the time or the place to be jokin'! Now, answer me honestly. Are you gay?"

Al was becoming livid and nervous. How dare his father strong-arm him into an answer. Who gave him the right to judge his son? Who cared if his father's premonitions were correct, no one, absolutely no one, had the right to look askance at Al. At the same instance though, he realized how much his whole world would change with one word to the affirmative. It scared the hell out of Al, but he had always been honest, and he'd be damned if he would change now just to appease his old man.

"Honestly dad", Al said squaring off eye-to-eye with his father, "it isn't that I don't find girls attractive, just not in the way you do. So, in answer to your question, yes, I think I am homosexual."

It took everything in Jefferson Jeaneau's being not to kill his son, but he ended up knocking the young man hard to the floor. He then stood over the groggy boy, pulled him up by the neck, and slammed him hard into the wall. His blood was boiling, and his grip became strong enough to cut off Al's air intake.

"Do you know what we are, boy? Do you know what we are?" Jefferson bellowed. "We are black! We are descendants of French trappers and Cherokee Indians! None of 'em believes in what you say you are, boy." His voice was simmering now. "Being gay is through for you, boy. College is through for you. After graduation, it's either the mill with me, or to the mines with your brothers. Either one, that's your life. You will work there and become a man. You will go with girls. You'll fuck'em, and when you're done playin' with 'em, you settle down, get married, and have kids. Fag talk has ended. Keep two feet in one shoe, boy. Play my way and maybe you will be my son again. Until then," he snarled, " you just a nigga."

Jefferson took the vise grip that he had around Al's neck and let him drop to the floor. Al had nearly blacked out, but little by little, he regained his breath. The next week was pure hell for Al. His whole family ignored him completely. Even his mother, who adored him so much, did not dare to go against Jefferson Jeaneau's word. None of them even came to watch him graduate. The day after graduation, his father broke the silence long enough to inform his son he had decided Al would work at the mill with him. "You start next Monday at three A.M. with me. Be up at two and don't make me wait, boy."

Al went to sleep early Saturday night, but he wouldn't be asleep for long. When his father left for work at midnight, Al was up ten minutes later, with a flashlight in his hand. He had grabbed his father's old army duffel bag and was packing it with as many clothes and necessities as he could carry. He then put on a camouflage jacket, his West Virginia University ball cap, and proceeded to his dresser drawer. He took out the envelope holding his college acceptance. He then grabbed another one containing approximately eight hundred in cash he'd earned from the odd jobs that he worked. Al slowly opened the bedroom window and placed the duffel bag, and then himself through the opening. When he had made it across the street, he turned to take what would be his last look at the house he'd grown up in. He thought about what leaving this way would mean. He'd probably never see his family again. His father would treat Al's disrespectfulness towards him as grounds for disowning his son. Al looked at the house for a few minutes while he pondered the ramifications of his actions. As he continued to look at the house he began to flash his trademark smile. He opened his mouth to speak, if only to hear the words so that he knew this was for real. "Forget you. Forget you all", he said as he turned from the house. With his confident smile still affixed, Al Jeaneau began his journey.

As planned, Al would make his way to the University of West Virginia. It would take seven years of sometimes working two or three jobs to live and pay tuition, but when he graduated, he was in the top five percentile of his class. A friend in his class had informed Al of his intentions to enlist in the Philadelphia Police Academy. He asked Al if he would like to try. Al quickly packed his meager belongings, and at twenty-five years of age he was ready for another of life's adventures.

Al made it through the Academy and was ready to join the force. He was in Philadelphia for a year when he heard of the job opening in New Hope for a police officer. He knew of the New Hope scene, and had visited the area quite a few times since he'd moved to the city. He thought New Hope would be the perfect fit for him. Even as he had become savvy and matured to the ways of the world, and how many individuals dealt with the topic of homosexuality, Al had become tired of covering his tracks. New Hope would be a place where he could finally be who he really was.

Al's life was finally falling into place. He had received word of his hiring in New Hope. He gave the Philadelphia Police Department his notice, and was out of the city like a flash. The small amount of money he had saved over the last few years was put towards the down payment of the modest, and, at the time, dilapidated Cape style house in which he now resided. Al became a fast learner at how to repair the house, and what he didn't know about was taken care of by one of the many friends he was making in town.

Al's charming personality and wicked sense of humor quickly won over his fellow officers and many of the residents he came into contact with. Not too long after meeting Roger in 1979, Al asked if he would like to move in. They had become very close companions, and as Al noted, it was rather ridiculous for Roger to pay a rent when Al had a more than big enough house to accommodate both of them. In time, Al would turn the house into a very livable and cozy dwelling, and Roger filled it with many of his sculpted treasures. They would live in the house in much happiness for many years to come, or so Al thought.

In 1986, Roger started to have numerous bouts with fever, and he began to lose weight. His sculpting work had slowed down to a crawl so much that Al and he decided to sell his Main Street studio. Rogers' hands had become so wracked with pain, it was nearly impossible for him to create his beautiful pieces of work. Quite a few friends in the community had begun to see these symptoms creeping like the plague into their small hamlet. Al knew what their fears were and it was his also. He talked to Roger who had basically come to his own conclusions, and they made an appointment with their doctor. When the test results were returned all their worst fears had been founded. Roger was diagnosed with AIDS.

Neither of them knew how long he had to live, but they made a pact to remain happy for as long as they were together. Al did the best he could to keep up with his police work and give the adequate time and attention that was needed to care for Roger. All of this began to give Al an even stronger hold on his own life, and at times, when Roger's care seem to sap even his boundless energy, new fiends such as Luke Stone would help to lighten his load. A few years later, when Phil Antos entered the picture, the young man also helped in numerous ways, right until Roger's last hours.

Two other events in 1985 and 1986 would change Al's life. In 1985, the State Police had announced they had a new man coming in from Philadelphia who would soon run the barracks post on the outskirts of town. His name was John Boyle. Al had heard a bit of John's bio from a few of the officers in their station. He then read it for himself.

Boyle had been born in the County Cork section of Ireland. He had immigrated to the United States in 1963, and in the winter of 1964, he enlisted in the Marine Corps to fight for his new country. While in Vietnam, he had received medals for uncommon valor in combat. He re-upped for a second tour of duty, and then came home. He then became a Detective in the Philadelphia Homicide unit, where more awards were given for heroism in the line of duty. He left Philadelphia, and became a decorated and highly regarded member of the Pennsylvania State Police.

Al had the chance to meet John early on in his stay. They worked on some cases together and the men's chemistry soon clicked. Their intellect towards a crime scene, mental toughness, and their quick, sometimes rapier wit made them a perfect match when the state and borough police needed to collaborate.

In 1986, Al's career was already solid. He had been moved to the rank of Sergeant in 1983. When Chief Gideon announced his retirement in

1986, Al breathed a sigh of relief. He liked Chief Gideon, but the man was older and out of touch with the needs of a community that had such a large homosexual population.

Many in the community thought Al would be the perfect replacement, but due to Roger's ever weakening condition, Al felt the need to be flexible to accommodate his situation. When Al, the strongest candidate at the time opted out, Mayor Sam Exton asked his opinion of who he should look for. Al didn't have a specific name, but he did ask the mayor to get someone who was very open and sensitive to the needs of this special community.

A few weeks later, Al was summoned to Exton's office again. The mayor told Al, he had his man, Detective Tom Miller from the NYPD. Al had read enough about Tom in the past year to realize that this was as good a pick as you could find without hiring a homosexual. Being somewhat of a jazz historian, he also realized who Tom's father had been, and what a strong voice Edgar had been in the gay community. Al thought if Tom's strength of character had half the impact his father's had in the gay community, it was a great choice for New Hope.

When Al told John Boyle the news, he was equally enthusiastic. The former detective couldn't wait to meet the man who almost single-handedly captured Kane. When the three men finally got the chance to meet informally at one of the local pubs, the chemistry that would last for years to come began to click. Tom's dry wit was a perfect match to Al and John's sarcastic humor. They all began to tell stories of their lives, their loves, and much more. By the time they had closed the pub down and crawled off their barstools, it felt like they had been friends for years. This tight bond they had formed would help Al immeasurably in the next few years.

By the fall of 1989, Roger's health had deteriorated to a catastrophic level. The doctors told Al that at this point that nothing was working. They began to tell Al as calmly as possible, the news he had expected to hear. Roger, they told him, would probably only live out the next few months.

Tom and Debbie, John Boyle, Luke and Phil, had all helped out Al and Roger as much as they could in the last few years. Anything this tight knit band of friends could do, from shopping, cleaning the house, or cooking dinners which they would all attend to afford Roger the company that he'd become so used to, they would do.

When they could all tell that Roger's last days were upon them, they stayed in vigil at his bedside. On the night of December 18th, they all kissed Roger good night, hugged Al, and said they would see them both tomorrow. When they had all departed, Al tried to give Roger his medication. Roger looked at him peacefully, and in what little breath he had said, "I don't need them Al. I need strength, and I need courage."

Al knew exactly what Roger had meant. He laid down the cup of water and the pills on the nightstand. He sat down next to Roger, kissed his forehead, and put his head on the corner of the pillow to sleep. Roger smiled as he watched Al drift off into a serene sleep. Roger would drift away soon after, never to awaken from the blissful state of solitude his ravaged body had entered.

Two days later at the eulogy, Al read from a letter he had written the night before. He told his usual funny stories about the events in his and Roger's lives. He prayed he would again see the friend and life partner that had become his family, and he thanked everyone for joining him to, "not grieve, but celebrate the life of a great friend, and a great man." After the funeral, he invited his five closest friends to the house for a meal. When they had all seated themselves at the dining room table, Al raised his wine glass for a toast. "You know, neither one of our blood families remained in our lives after we made our revelations to them. For many a year, Roger and I remained distant from making close friendships. We are very glad faith and love for our fellow man reentered our lives when you all came into the picture. I would never have traded a day with all of you to be with my blood relations again. You have become my family. Tom, John, Luke and Phil, you have become my brothers." As he lovingly looked at Debbie he added, "and you, my beautiful woman, have been my little sister. I know Roger felt the same way about all of you. I know he will also look forward to the day that he will meet all of his new family again. To Roger."

"To Roger!" they all shouted. Those last words snapped him back to the present. The smooth Coltrane sound had been replaced in the disc changer by the sultry voice of Sade. He went to grab another beer and as he came back, he saw another picture.

It was one of him hamming it up with a young Edward Miller at a local amusement park. Family, he thought again. This is my family. Heck, Edward has been calling me Uncle Al for years. Even Pags' kids and Zoul's little one call me that. He thought again about his new family, and the even newer additions that had become such an integral part of his life. Sadly, he thought again of how viciously Luke had been ripped from this tight-knit group. He could now understand, as a tear began to fall from his cheek, the pain and sorrow that Tom still felt from time to time. His drifting off in thought was this time cut extremely short by the telephone's jarring ring. He ran over to get the cordless.

"Hello?" he answered frog throated.

"Did I wake you, pal?" the familiar voice asked.

"No, Tommy. Not at all."

"Are you feeling okay? You sound kind of down, man."

"Nah, I'm alright, bro. I'm just chillin', and thinking about the past."

"Good thoughts I hope?"

"I'm trying to make them that way," Al replied.

"That's good to hear. I don't need my sidekick going manic on me. Then I would only have Boyle to tell me his stupid jokes."

"Oh God, no. I mean, how funny could that be?"

"Scary thought, isn't it?"

"It's enough to make me depressed, Miller."

Tom began to laugh. "Listen buddy, I need a favor of you."

"I didn't imagine it would stay a social call for long," Al sighed.

"Ha, ha! You're a real riot. I'm not going to be able to pick you up in the morning. Jenn is going to come and get you."

"That's fine. You know I like the company on the drive in. Besides, I'd much rather look at her fine body and pretty face, rather than some middle aged, married...."

"You may want to stop right there, Sergeant Jeaneau. Remember, this is your superior officer you're about to disrespect."

"Define your use of superior?"

"A riot you are tonight!"

"So, enough making fun of you. What's up, Tom?"

"Stan Tilden just called. He had some news for me."

"This doesn't sound good."

"Not really. Apparently, the New York press has caught wind of the murders. The networks have also been alerted to the news and they are very close to making our case become a very national media event."

"Great! Public exposure to make two possible murderers disappear until the opportune media moment causes them to strike again."

"Oh, it gets better, Al. Stan tells me the word filtering around the Village is that Kane is pulling the strings on these murders from his Death Row cell. Now, Stan and I don't know how much truth exists in the gossip, but..."

"It is Kane we're talking about, bro'."

"We're on the same page, my friend."

"As is the norm, Chief."

"We also got the word, our Trenton boy was apparently seen in Newark again."

"On the move again, is he?"

"Well, Stan's sources sure think it was him. A woman with facial features and a physique that closely resembled his showed up at a club that he frequents to do his drug sales."

"Oh, so he is in his fem, bodybuilder phase again?"

"Well, the description that Stan received was that of a muscular, black female, approximately six feet in height, or taller. The woman also has long, dark brown hair, possibly extensions. She was also wearing a short, black minidress and thigh-high, stiletto heeled black boots."

"Nothing like going for that porn star look, ay?"

"Yeah, well this female was spotted in the presence of people whom Jerome usually peddles his wares through."

"Are the Feds closing in on him?"

"No. Unfortunately, from all accounts he has vanished again. Listen, let's get back to Kane, because I need a favor."

"Fire away, Tommy."

"I'm calling Stan early tomorrow morning, and then I'm filling our favorite Mayor in on my itinerary for the next few days."

"Lucky you."

"Yeah, thanks for the optimism, buddy. I need you to run the show while I'm talking with Stan tomorrow."

"No problem, Tom. Is that all?"

"No. I know the twenty-seventh is Luke's funeral, but I won't be able to attend. I'm going to need you to hold down the fort that day too."

"Do I want to know why?"

"I'm sure that you won't, but I need to tell you. Stan is getting everything in order for me to visit Clinton Correctional on Monday."

"Clinton Correctional? That's where..." The nerves in Al's body began to sizzle. He didn't want to, but he knew he would have to ask Tom if this was the best thing to do. "Whoa, hold on!" he heard himself yell. "You're not thinking..."

"I figured that fourteen years between talks is long enough. It's time, Al. This evil has got to be stopped."

Al began to feel the sweat pouring from his face. It felt cold against his body. The thought of the man that he'd regarded as his brother, going into a room with Kane, made his skin crawl. "Tommy, are you ready for this? I mean, you do realize you'll be opening up Pandora's box when you see him again, right?"

"Yes, I do realize what wounds it will re-open, Al. If it is true about Kane pulling the strings to make his prophecy become a reality, it is our duty to question him." Tom paused to catch his breath. He began to think about Kane sitting across from him with a manic look of enjoyment in his eyes. It was making him sick. He took another drag from his cigarette and began to say what he knew was true in his heart. "Al, it's also my duty to make him break and admit to a lot of things he's never brought to the forefront." Tom began to chuckle. "Who knows, buddy? By then it will be four days until he dies. Maybe he'll have an epiphany."

Al chuckled at the thought, also. "You're hoping, Tommy."

"Isn't it all we really have to go on, sometimes?"

"True," Al mused. "Does Debbie know about this decision?"

"Yes, and to say the least, she's not thrilled with it. Even with that being said, she also knows I need to do this if there is a chance we can stop these murders now."

" I agree, but let's talk about it again tomorrow. I'm sure you do, but for my edification, I'd like to know you have a clear head going into this."

"Thanks, pal. We'll do just that when I come to the station."

Al paused for a moment. He thought again about what his good friend was about to face. The words came out effortlessly. "You are a brave man, Tom Miller. The bravest man I've ever known."

Tom was not expecting such words. He was honored that Al would think so much about him, but it was not Tom's style to acknowledge such praise. "Thanks, Al. I appreciate the compliment, but I just look at this as doing my job, and this has to be done," he said emphatically.

"You're a brave man," Al said with just as much emphasis. "I am proud to know the man who would face the devil in his own pit."

Tom could feel his emotions welling up. He figured it was time to make the conversation short. The two men had been through hell the past few days and he didn't need to compound it with his feelings about this whole fiasco. It would, as he took another drag of nicotine, be better for everyone to think Tom Miller's coat of armor was with no cracks. "Thanks, Al. Listen, I won't keep you."

"Okay, good night pal. I will see you tomorrow."

"You can count on that," Tom Miller replied. "Good night."

Al hung up the phone and looked around. It was getting onwards of ten o' clock. Luke's funeral on Monday would be mentally and physically exhausting in its own right, but Sunday was becoming quite hectic also. Daylight would be coming soon for the lawmen.

Al began to collect the spent beer bottles and placed them in the kitchen's overflowing recycle bin. He tied the bag and grabbed the other trash that needed to go outside. He opened his door, grabbed the bags, and started his journey. This night was pretty mild for Christmas time in Bucks County, so he didn't even bother to put on a jacket. He was just about towards the base of the drive when he turned to open the fence and place the bags in the cans. As he closed the fence, he stopped quickly in the drive to hear the sound of lightly running footsteps approaching from the desolate roadway. The darkness made it difficult for Al's view to be clear, but after a few seconds he began to make out an image.

Approaching from the direction he faced, on the opposite side of the street, appeared a shape in a fluorescent orange jacket. He also made out a fluorescent orange ball cap, and what looked to be bright blonde hair tucked under it and neatly pulled through the caps back opening. When the figure was nearer to him, Al noticed the skin tight orange Spandex and the backpack. Well, fancy this, it was the jogger that Zoul saw. It's quite a long shot, but maybe she witnessed something out of the ordinary that morning. As she glanced over, Al smiled and called out to her. "Good evening! Merry Christmas!"

"Hello" the young woman replied as she smiled in kind. "The same to you."

"Are you new in town?" Al asked.

"Yes, I am. I moved here a few weeks ago," she replied as she jogged in place. "I'm sorry. I'm not trying to be rude by not coming closer, but once I kick into gear it's hard to turn off the motor."

Al laughed from the driveway. "I totally understand. My name is Al Jeaneau. I'm the Sergeant in New Hope Borough."

"Nice to meet you, Sergeant Jeaneau. My name is Sandy Jones."

She had a sweet voice, almost too sweet, like it was put on. She did sound nice though, and the view, even from a distance was not hurting Al's eyes either. "Well Sandy, be careful tonight. Aren't you nervous jogging by yourself, especially after what happened the other night?"

"Oh, you mean the murder? I'm from Manhattan. Unfortunately, you get used to this sort of thing. It is rather sad, though, for it to happen in such a nice place."

"Yes, it is sad. Listen Sandy, I don't mean to be nosy. One of our local State Troopers gave a description of a young female jogger, and it resembles your features and attire. She was said to be jogging within the vicinity where we found the late Mister Stone's car. You didn't happen to notice anything out of the ordinary that morning did you?"

"It was me jogging, because I did see your State Trooper. I'm sorry, though. Aside from seeing the officer, everything else was quite routine."

"Well Sandy, I figured it might be a long shot, but I figured I'd ask, anyway. Mister Stone was like family to many of us. We'd like to see the murderer caught soon.

"Nothing to lose by asking," the young woman replied, still keeping her pace. "It is a shame about Mister Stone. He seemed like he was a much loved man from the way the papers described him."

"He was, and a good friend also."

"Listen, Sergeant Jeaneau...."

"Please, call me Al."

"Okay", she laughed. "Listen, Al. I should go. It's getting rather late and I have a little more running to do. It was a pleasure to meet you and I am truly sorry about your friend."

"Same here, and thanks", Al replied. Upon ending the conversation, she smiled, turned, and continued down the dark road. Al watched as her brightly colored, shapely physique disappeared into the night. As he made his way up the driveway, he chuckled. His head was still buzzing a little from the alcohol he'd consumed, but it was clear enough to make a quick assumption. "I know why Zoul was checking her out," he said to himself. "The boy was right, though. She's just a good looking girl out for a jog."

As Al began to approach his porch, he heard a thunderous commotion from the woods. He quickly turned to his right and witnessed his neighbors, the deer, still running about. This time though, they ran alongside of him. They were so close, he could smell the musky odor of their fur, and feel the breeze from the speed at which they passed him. "Hey you two!" he yelled happily as they bounded by. "Mating season is over! Go to bed!" With all of the calamity the two animals had caused, Al could not hear the sounds he needed to. It was the sounds of footsteps quickly approaching. By the time he came to the realization that the deer were startled and not playing, it was too late.

The hot, searing pain in his back felled him by the door. He tried to yell but he felt the pain again. This time, it was lower. He tried to crawl towards the door, but he just kept feeling the searing, burning pain, over and over. Al tried in vain to muster some strength and turn to fight his assailant. His brain sent the signals, but his body could not react quickly enough. Al was rendered helpless against everything happening to him. He tried in vain to reach the door again, but the door swung open. He felt some tinges of movement. He wasn't giving up. Lord, he thought, I won't give up. It was the last hope Al had, and it slipped away in an instant. He heard the grunts of his attackers' voice. It was a strange, garbled voice, and it was hard to decipher. All Al knew was it was getting harder to breathe. He started to see blood and it was everywhere. He felt very warm from it around his head, but he felt cold everywhere else. Al was choking and it was on his own blood. The evil menace that had attacked Al cut him so quickly and with such proficiency he hadn't even felt the knife-edge come across his neck.

Everything was a blur. He was going in and out of consciousness, and it felt at times as if his brain impulses were shutting down. He felt his body moving through the house, but it was not under his own power. He heard the door slam and the garbled chanting again. It was such a malevolent and vicious sound. Al felt himself going out again, when something kicked his brain on, even if just for a minute. A wisp of blonde hair appeared over his shoulder. He could also see flashes of orange. The chants were becoming a little clearer. The voice was shrill. It was the jogger, Al's brain screamed.

How was this possible? How could she have this kind of ferocious strength? Al must have outweighed his assailant by at least one hundred pounds, but her force was maniacal. He started to go in and out again, when he felt himself being rolled over. He could see a bright, white sky. It was so bright. He must be dead, because he couldn't hear anything. He didn't hear the chants anymore, his breath, anything. It was like he was in a vacuum. He thought in flashes of his adopted family. Tom, Debbie, the kids, John, Zoul and his brood. Just for a moment he felt his hand reach out and touch Roger. Sometimes, it seemed as if they flashed by so fast, Al couldn't even tell who they were.

Just when Al had thought his peace had come, he saw the orange color again. His senses were almost shut down, but he had enough of them left to know that he wasn't gone yet. She was standing over him as if she was pondering a new plan of attack. She stalked around him just as a lion would its prey. She knelt over him and his vision soon became murky. He blinked his eyes, but the murkiness grew even more. Al was drowning in a sea of his own blood. With what power he had left, he blinked furiously until he saw his light again. He saw Tom and told him to be strong. He saw Roger and told him how much he'd missed him. He saw shades of orange moving quickly towards him, but he did not feel the knife plunge into him as evil tried to extract his final breath.

Al Jeaneau looked towards the heavens above, and as he prayed to God, his bright light slowly faded away.

CHAPTER 12

Tom was already awake for an hour speaking with Stan Tilden about tomorrows meeting with Kane when he received a frantic phone call. Jenn Gates, his usually calm, cool and collected officer called in a panic not even a minute after he had hung up with Stan.

"Tom? Tom!". Jenn was yelling into her cell phone.

"Jenn, I hear you. Where are you? It sounds like quite a commotion in the background."

"Tom," Jenn sobbed. "You have to get here. You just have to."

The hair on the back of Tom's neck began to stand up. He tried to remain calm. "Jenn, what's wrong? Where are you and why are you so upset?" As calm as he tried to stay, he began to click up and down on the button of the pen he was holding. Tom had never seen or heard Jenn Gates lose her cool since he had hired her a few years ago.

"I'm here!" she yelled. "I'm at Al's! You've got to come!" She was in total loss of her emotions. Tom heard the cell phone drop, and then heard the light sounds of Jenn sobbing. He could also hear a male's voice and what sounded like his morning dispatcher in the chatter. He then heard the phone being picked up again.

"Jenn? Jenn? What's going on? What about Al?" The force of his fingers snapped the pen in half as ink pooled on his notepad like blood at a murder scene. Murder; the pounding in his skull had returned.

"Tommy," the Irish voice answered solemnly.

"John? What the hell is going on?"

"Tommy, let me come getcha'. I don't want you driving down here."

Tom had never heard John Boyle ever speak so somberly. "Driving to where?" Tom asked. He didn't know why he asked. He knew what the answer was going to be.

"To Al's place." Deafening silence filled John's end of the line.

Tom Miller had always tried to prepare himself for the worst since his father's murder, but he was feeling the pain again. Al was like his brother. He was trying not to flash back to the day of his father's murder. Stan Tilden held him back then from seeing how badly his father had been mutilated. John Boyle was trying to fill the role now, but Tom knew he had to see this one. "I'll be ready," he said quietly as he hung up the phone. He went upstairs and sat at the foot of the bed. He looked at Debbie turning over to wake out of her slumber.

"Good morning, Tommy," she said but there was no reply. "Did you talk to Stan?" Tom just nodded. "Are you still going tomorrow?"

"Yes, I am Deb," Tom responded quietly.

"Then, what is wrong?"

He turned to face her. Tears were streaming down his face. "John Boyle is coming to get me," he choked out. "He's coming to take me to Al's home."

Debbie's eyes grew wide as her sleepy demeanor changed quickly to one of horror. "No, Tom! I know that you are not going to tell me this. I just know you're not." She jumped from the bed and quickly walked towards the master bathroom. Tom tried to grab her, to hold her tightly, but she avoided his reach. "No! No, damn it! Don't do it, just let me go! Damn it!" She ran to the door and slammed it shut.

Tom could hear Debbie's cries from behind the bathroom door. Inside the large room, Debbie was a wreck. She knocked down some small, rose-colored crystal vases from the shelf that was over the commode. As they exploded into many small fragments on the bathroom floor, she yelled again. The fine, pink color of the tiny shards, when mixed in with the water from the flowers, looked like blood. In her own small piece of this world, Debbie Miller was surrounded again by blood. She was so tired of seeing blood spilled by her loved ones. "Damn it! Damn it!" She was screaming at the top of her lungs. She could her Tom banging on the door, asking if she was all right, or had been hurt. "I'm fine honey," she said in between the sobs. She started to collect her emotions and began to pick up some of the glass fragments.

She had to be his rock, she thought, but the rock had crumbled badly. All the pain of these vicious murders came crashing in like a tidal wave. She unlocked the door and Tom came rushing in. He held her tightly as she tried desperately to compose herself. They both could hear John's car bolting into the driveway.

Tom was already dressed, but he did not want to leave Debbie. "I know what you are going to say Tom, but please don't. Don't apologize for what Kane did then, or for what these animals are doing now." Debbie's hazel eyes pierced right through Tom's being. "I have faith in you. John has faith in you. This whole town needs you and Al would tell you this if he was standing here instead of me. Do what you have to do to bring them in. I know you can do it."

John Boyle was standing at the door that led into the bedroom. "Sorry for intrudin', but the front door was open." Tom and Debbie both nodded as if to say it was okay for him to be there. As John slowly approached them, they could see the redness in the big man's eyes.

"I would just like to reiterate what your lovely wife just said. I do have faith in you, as do my men and yours. So does this town have faith in you, Tom Miller. We all know there is not a better man alive to handle this situation, and we're proud of that fact." John hugged his two friends tightly. He then put his arms on Tom's shoulders. "Now look pal, what they did to Al is definitely worse than how Luke appeared. Christ, I haven't gotten the shakes in my belly this badly since the war. I don't even know if the scene will conjure up the memories of your father's mate. All I'm going to tell you, Tommy boy is I'll be right by your side."

"Oh, by the way, Al had called me last night after you two had conversed. He was tellin' me of your intentions to visit the Reverend Kane." Tom slowly nodded his head in the affirmative. "Are ya' still going tomorrow Tommy?"

"Now more than ever, John. Yes, I am going."

"Then I agree," John said as his voice trembled with emotion, "with what my good friend Al Jeaneau had said to you just last evening. You are the bravest man I've ever known. Now lets get going brother."

Tom gave Debbie a quick peck on the cheek and headed down the stairway. John embraced her, pulled back and gave a wink. "I'll take care of him Debbie."

Debbie held back the tears and smiled peacefully towards the burly Irishman with a heart of gold. "I know you will John Boyle. I've always known that you would."

Neither one of the men said much of anything during the short drive, but as they approached the melee' beginning at the foot of Al's driveway, Tom looked at John. "It's just like New York all over again."

"Aye, Thomas. I couldn't even have imagined it, if not for seeing it with my own eyes this day."

The front property of Al's house was total pandemonium. It almost bore a striking resemblance to a three-ring circus. News vans, reporters, curiosity seekers and God knows who else were vying for position up by the police lines. Mary McGuigan was the first one to spot Tom and John. She made haste towards their vantage point.

"Tom, John, I am so devastated about Al", she said as a tear rolled down her face. Her pink complexion was more of a sick pale today. Tom and John figured she'd seen the body. "I hate to ask this but..."

"We know McGuigan," John Boyle said with an understanding smile. "It's your job."

"Go ahead, Mary," Tom added.

"Thanks guys. Are there any ideas of who the killer is yet?"

"No," Tom replied to Mary and the other reporters who'd since congregated around the two lawmen. "We all know who our Trenton man is. Even with all the information that we have on him, please, let's not take him lightly. He's a stone cold murderer whose eluded the police and the Federal agencies trying to apprehend him over many a year. Jerome Jones is a man of many names, faces, and talents. This time, he has hopped on the Kane bandwagon."

"But, Chief Miller, what about your New Hope murderer?" asked John Royce of the New York Reporter.

"John, nice to see you again. I'm sorry it had to be under the usual circumstances upon which we tend cross paths. I will tell you the same thing I've told my officers. We do not yet have an identity. Even with our more advanced methods of detection, we are finding no blood and no fingerprints. We also have no hair or skin samples. This is a very smooth and vicious killer we unfortunately are dealing with."

"It's almost as if you were dealing with Kane again, Chief," Royce intoned.

"Yes John, it is like that, to a point. Mark my words though, ladies and gentlemen. We did find Kane. We will find this one too. Now, if you will excuse me, I have a crime scene to investigate." As Tom strode off, he could hear the shouts from the reporters who were still trying to ask questions. He also made out the voice of John Boyle telling them after the crime scene was investigated, he and Tom would make themselves available to answer some more questions.

Tom peered into the distance and saw his officers and some of John's troopers crowding one particular area of Al's property. For years, Al had planted corn and other assorted vegetables in this farmed area of the field. They were milling around where Al had a post in the ground to hold his scarecrows. As he approached the site, Tom cringed. He took out a

Marlboro and inhaled quickly. He knew this would not be a scarecrow hanging from the thick, steel pole. John Boyle made haste in catching up to his friend. He glanced over at Tom.

"You realize what you are about to see, don't you?"

"Oh, I know very well what I am about to witness, John Boyle. I am about to view the devils handiwork so he can laugh at me one more time."

As they reached the spot where Al was, Tom noticed how still the scene was around Al's body. None of the officers uttered a sound. Many of them just stood around the body in various states of what amounted to shock and wonder. Tom looked over his shoulder and saw Jenn Gates who had called him just minutes ago in such a panic. All she was able to do now was kick at the hardened dirt in front of her and look down at her hands. Tom heard her murmuring something softly and saw the rosary beads rolling through her clenched hands.

Andrew Rose and Zoul stood frozen. They appeared, understandably, too shocked to fathom what had taken place at this house. Tom knew the look all to well. It was the same look that he had in 1985 when he saw the first of Kane's victims. It was also the same look he had when he discovered Gary's mutilated body, and when he heard about the death of his father.

Tom knew this time, he would have to keep his composure. He could not lose any of these fine officers to the horror they had witnessed in just the past few days. If that was to happen, John Boyle and Tom Miller would truly be on their own. When he looked up and saw Al's badly beaten and mutilated body, he just wanted to scream or to cry. He would not, and could not let Al's death phase him. Chief Tom Miller put it into his head and his heart, when all of this had ended, then would be his time to cry. At the present time though, he needed to be strong for himself and his people. It was the only way he could hold this tight knit squad together.

In the only way he knew how to, Tom marched up to Al's body with John at his side. He viewed Al's badly beaten and mangled face. He could feel the tears and the desperation of the situation welling up inside of him, but he held them back. He could feel his throat tightening but he swallowed hard. When he spoke, Tom's words came out clearly and to the point. "I will see you again, my good friend. I have to stop this person from hurting anyone else, so until then, go to heaven and be reunited with your family. I promise, we will talk soon."

"Amen to that, Tommy. Amen," John Boyle said in a stern but solemn tone. As they turned to face their officers, John snapped them back to reality. "Well, you heard the man! We have a job to do! Now let's get to it!" he bellowed. Upon hearing the words of their two leaders, the officers started to dart about, making the crime scene alive with activity.

Al's body had been hooked to the pole when Jenn Gates spotted it in the field, six this morning. Andrew Rose and Zoul carefully removed it now and lay Al's body on the ground, as Tom waited to do his work. Tom quickly noticed that Al's body wounds were very similar to the ones Luke Stone had received. This definitely was their killer and not Jerome Jones. The only thing different was the beating Al's face had received.

The eyes had been taken out, and Tom was already checking his mouth area. Al's tongue had been removed and in its place was left the obligatory note. Tom did not want to read the note just yet. He was still fascinated with why the killer had deviated from the Kane method of murder and beaten Al's skull so severely. Tom tried to understand why such rage was inflicted to this part of Al's body since these were not the blows killing his friend. In fact, Tom surmised, these blows may have been delivered a few hours after Al was dead.

John Boyle had been looking over the corpse also. He took notice of Tom's reaction and stopped what he was doing to stand by his side. "This," he said as pointed to the skull area, "must have been done long after Al had expired."

"Are you reading my mind again, Boyle?"

"I was just thinking about it myself, lad."

Tom lit up another cigarette and pointed down at Al's face. "Look at how around the eyes, the mouth and the slit across his neck, the blood is caked and solidifying."

"Right you are lad, but in the skull area they are quite a bit fresher."

"Yes, John. In fact, the wounds around there are still seeping in some areas," Tom said as he pointed to a spot above Al's crushed left ear.

"We have to realize that head wounds may bleed for a long time Tommy, but still, bein' the majority of his facial wounds have congealed, there is a chance this damage was inflicted long after Al expired."

"But why, John? I mean, it doesn't fit into the Kane style the killer followed to the letter with Lucas. Those murders were all done in such a meticulous nature. This one was too..."

"Until they crushed in the skull after the fact."

"Exactly, it more resembled how Jones had desecrated the corpse."

"Maybe," John said as he raised up his hand to push back his lid, "he thought by doing that he would throw us off a bit. Mixing the two styles of murder together."

"That could be a possibility until you see the notes." A slight breeze was kicking up, so Tom used his hand to hold the paper down while they perused the writing. It had been pierced by the knife, and, as in the past murders, was plunged into the victims chest. As before, the knife was thrust almost through Al's body. "Exhibit B" was scrawled into the wood of the finely crafted, jewel-encrusted handle. Tom shook off the temptation to explode as he read the words...

"I have made SADNESS in your life again, Thomas. I AM BACK!"

"As you can see John, the handwriting is exactly the same as the one we found at Luke's crime scene." John peered at the note and stood back up. "Right you are, Tommy," he scowled as he took in the sadistic weight of the words he'd read.

"I'm sure the one I have in my glove is no different."

"I'm sure you are right, Thomas," John said. You could still hear the irritation in his voice. "So, what does our little literature major have to say in the second one?"

Tom began to speak and then froze. The words hit him like a ton of bricks.

"Are you all right Tommy?" John went to grab the paper, but Tom waved him off.

"I WILL KILL EVERYTHING THAT YOU HOLD DEAR TO YOU, JUST LIKE I DID YEARS EARLIER! Beware of the wolf in sheep's clothing, Thomas....."

"Sweet Jesus!" Boyle exploded. "This sonofabitch thinks he is the real deal! Tommy, he's playing with us. He wants us to believe he's like the spirit of a soon-to-be dead man."

Tom placed the note into a baggy, just as he had done with the previous one. "It's possible, using the head games to try and frazzle us. I'm just beginning to think there is something more to this. I think Al's murder has opened up a plethora of possibilities."

"Go on then, lad."

"Well, there is the rage factor, John. There is a rage of a different kind that has entered the picture with Al's murder. Luke's killing stuck much more to the calculated ways of Kane's."

"Are you thinking the killer knew Al, Tommy?"

"I am starting to think that the killer knew both of our victims. Maybe they didn't know this individual on a close, personal level, but the killer knew them enough to maybe try to reach me through these murders."

"To reach you? I am not quite following you, pal."

"Think about it, John. Two close personal and influential members of the New Hope homosexual community are murdered. Both of them just happen to be close friends of mine. Both of them are murdered in the same ritualistic style taking the lives of eight people in Greenwich Village, my dad and his companion included."

"Go on, Tommy."

"The notes we just found with Al, listen to the words again. I have made sadness in your life again. I am back, Thomas. I will kill everything that you hold dear to you, just like I did years earlier." Tom lit up another cigarette and looked again at John Boyle. "The last line is almost like he is alluding to my fathers death. It's as if he is taking credit for the murder of my father, and not Kane."

John took it all in and glanced down at Al's body. He sighed and brought his eyes back up to meet Tom's. "Your dad's killer is here in New Hope. Kane didn't commit the last murder, and the person who did is picking up from where he left off almost fifteen years later?" Saints and angels, if he's right about this, we've got problems.

"I know it sounds crazy, John. Look at it this way, though. The murderer is back to fulfill a prophecy and maybe hurt Kane's apprehender in the process."

"Oh, I'm not disagreeing with you pal. It's definitely a possibility, but God, where to start looking?"

"I know John," Tom said as he took a long drag from his cigarette.

"I mean, Zoul and I scoured through the archives trying to find a link to what we witnessed out there in the woods a few days ago. We came up dry with that."

"That's why I need to see Kane. If he's got a clue as to what has been going on here, I have to try and get it out of him."

"It's gonna' be a right tough thing to do, lad."

"I know, but I have to try. We have a funeral tomorrow, and we'll be having one soon after. This town is resilient John, but if these conditions persist, its breaking point will come and it could be real soon."

The men paused and tried to fathom the possibility that fifteen years ago Kane knowingly, or unknowingly had help in his murderous spree. It was frightening to imagine the willpower the New Hope murderer possessed. Could he really have turned off the rage from almost fifteen years ago when he killed Edgar Miller, only to turn it back on in the present? What an incredible amount of patience and a frighteningly calculated mind this person had, Tom thought.

He looked at the knife they'd removed from Al's corpse. Identical to the one we found in Luke. "John."

"Yeah, buddy?"

"Have Zoul search around and see if he comes up with anything about the knife type."

"Aye, I noticed too. Exact to the one used on Luke. I'll get him on it right away."

The rustling of leaves from behind them broke both of the officers' train of thought. Razoul was already approaching. "Zoul could you do some searching on the maker of this knife?"

Zoul took the knife and bagged it. "Sure, Troop," the young man replied in an agitated tone.

"Zoul, I know more than Al's death is eatin' at ya' with that tone. What gives with the sour disposition, lad?" Boyle asked.

"Well guys, I would just like to fill you in before he does." Razoul's head made a quick turn towards the field behind him. There, Mayor Ward stood talking with a few members of the local and national press. "Apparently a very high-up in Washington called him on his way over here. The Feds will be coming, and they will be here soon." Zoul looked at his two fellow officers. "The man didn't even give us a chance. He didn't even us a goddamn chance at all." Zoul started to walk away. Within a few feet, he stopped to turn and glance at Tom and John again. "I'm sorry guys, so sorry."

The men watched Zoul depart and John looked at Tom. "It begins again, brother," John said woefully as he patted Tom's back.

"John, did it ever really end?"

"No, I guess it never did Tom. I guess it never will."

Mayor Ward passed Zoul on his way to speak with Chief Miller. "Trooper Terrant," the mayor said with a slight smile.

Zoul could only muster a nod and a tip of his lid as he muttered, " Mayor," before walking on. God, I'd like to deck that bitch.

As the mayor started to put in his mind that he would soon be approaching hostile territory, he tried to stay calm. "They act like I want to railroad them," he garbled to no one in particular. "It's my ass first if the killer gets away." He walked a little further to reach the two officers. "Gentlemen!" he bellowed as he reached their position.

"Mister Mayor," Tom replied in a low voice.

"Mayor," answered John in a guttural tone.

"Well gentleman, I have some tough news to break. Washington is beginning to feel some heat from these murders and they want this nipped in the bud. The President and his team have their hands full trying to quell all the Y2K rumors and the chance of the impending chaos that may result from them. They do not need to add a serial killer of homosexuals to the mix."

"We figured as much Jerry," Tom said brusquely. "When will they be coming?"

"The lead man and a few of his agents will be arriving here tomorrow afternoon. He expects to be fully briefed on your findings soon afterwards."

"That's fine, but he will probably have to meet with me tomorrow evening or early the following morning."

"Why the delay?" Ward asked in an irritated manner.

"Well, I was going to update you this morning, but obviously with Al being murdered, the update took a back seat."

"Update? About what? Did we get some new evidence?"

"Mayor, there's a possibility that Martin Kane could know who the other killer is. We have it on some good information, Kane could be pulling the strings on this debacle right from his jail cell."

"A good lead, or just a rumor?"

"It seems like a good one but we're not one hundred percent positive yet. That is why I have arranged, through Detective Stan Tilden of the N.Y.P.D., to take a flight from the Mercer County Airport to the Clinton Correctional Facility in New York. The meet with Kane has been set. I'll be back in New Hope later that evening. I will hopefully be able to give your agent some more information."

"So, let me get this straight," Ward said tersely. "You are planning to desert this town while a murderer runs amok, to go on a wild goose chase and meet with a man who is going to be dead in five days because there's a chance...."

"A damn good chance," Tom interrupted.

"A chance," the mayor snapped, "that he knows who it is?"

"First of all, I never desert my post. But, Mayor, I am obligated as the Chief of Police in this town to cover ALL the bases in an ongoing murder investigation. Secondly, my officers and the local state troopers are very capable of handling any situations that arise."

"I really don't care about their so-called capabilities. If there is a lead up there, then let the Feds go up there!" Ward snapped.

"The Feds? Do you think a bunch of computer kids with degrees are going to walk in and be able to shake down a masterful criminal such as Kane?" Tom snidely inquired.

"No, but I am sure the man who caught him could, right?" Ward asked sarcastically.

"A damn sight better than they could," John Boyle piped in as he stared down the mayor. Ward just glowered in Boyle's direction and then looked back at Tom. "Let me ask you something, Tom. Is this a chance to catch a killer, or is it a chance to chase down some ghosts for you, eh'?"

Tom's face immediately flushed to a volcanic red. John Boyle saw this and jumped in. "Are you trying to insinuate that a decorated officer, with more commendations than some entire police forces put together, is going to question a murderer for personal gain?" John was exasperated.

"What I am saying is, I see a police chief who has no clue who the local killer is. His father was murdered and there was always speculation Kane was not the one who killed him. Kane has always denied killing him, and now the chief has heard Kane may be conducting these murders straight from his death row cell. I am starting to think that I'm dealing with a burnt out cop who just lost a good friend, and today, his partner." The mayor looked at them both with a sadistic expression. "It may almost lead a mayor to believe that he needs to ask if his chief could use a rest."

"Are you threatening my badge?" Tom asked. His fists balled up tightly.

"Go tomorrow and it could happen," the mayor replied with a tinge of enjoyment to his voice.

Tom was ready to pounce, but a flash detonated in front of him. The flash was John Boyle, and he had heard enough. "You little shit!" Boyle yelled as his beefy hands encircled the mayors' neck. Tom yelled for John to stop, but it was to no avail. Trooper Boyle grabbed Ward so hard that the mayors' feet were nowhere near the ground. He proceeded towards the crime scene where Al's body lay on the ground.

"Let go of me this instant." The mayor was probably screaming, but through John's vise grip, it came out like a whisper.

"Look at him! Look at him!" John bellowed towards Al's lifeless body. "Who did this Ward?"

"I don't know," the mayor strained out. His face was beginning to go very pale from the grip of John's hands.

"Louder, you little prick!"

"I don't know!" Ward gasped.

Tom rushed towards Boyle. "Let him go John. He's not worth it!" Tom yelled.

"Leave me be, pal!" John snapped. Everyone else around the site by now had dropped whatever it was they were doing to witness this spectacle, especially the out of town press. "Get me away from him. Get me away from that body!" Ward screeched as he was face to face with Al's flattened skull.

"Shut up!" John hollered. "Look at Sergeant Al Jeaneau, 'cause he's not coming back to us. You see, Mayor Ward, we have a madman on our hands. There is one man my troopers, this police force, and the townsfolk believe in to apprehend this animal, and that man is Tom Miller. No one, I repeat no one, not you, not the Feds, no Congressman will interfere with him performing his duties. There is a damn good chance the same individual who killed Edgar Miller is the one performing these acts. Fifteen years later, and this devil may be killin' again! If he has to go to the moon to find out what kind o' maniac can turn their killing drive on and off like a light switch, you Mister Mayor will help Tom Miller. Do I make myself clear?" John asked as he loosened his grip and dropped the mayor to his knees.

As he regained his balance and gasped for his breath, the mayor walked past John Boyle and hissed, "I'll have your ass for this Boyle."

John gripped Ward's shoulder and in a low growl said, "I don't think so, boy. For your information, I'll be retiring in March so get your big shots to pull my badge. I'll still collect my pension. See, I am starting to get a good read on why some of those clubs and ink parlors stay in business, and why it seems like they freely peddle their shit out the back door. See, Tom Miller has been finding out why too, and you are looking for any way you can to dump him. It won't happen, Ward. I've got a case building up, and it shows where the money trail leads to, and I'm looking right at him."

The mayor's eyes widened to the size of silver dollars. "Ah yes, Mayor Ward," John crowed. "Don't look so surprised, me boy. You pull Miller off this murder investigation and this town will be in chaos, and when I break this story to our dear Miss McGuigan, you will never work again. Shit on you ever becoming Governor. Heh, the hell with even bein' the mayor, buddy. By the time they're done raking your butt over the coals, you won't be able to shovel shit as a job in this state. Now, Jerry boy, don't fuck with me or Tom." John Boyle's tone would have sent the shivers through a cadaver. "Are we clear?"

"Yes" said the mayor brusquely.

"Ah, Mayor Ward," said John with a smile. "I think we need some happiness in your tone of voice, don't you? Now, let's try again. Are we clear?"

"Why yes Trooper Boyle, we are perfectly clear", the mayor said while gritting his teeth.

"Thank you, Mayor Ward," John said with a grin. "Now, be on with ya'. I'm sure the press has many a question for you now."

Mayor Ward stroked his neck gently and glared at the Chief. "You've still got your job Miller. You'd better catch this individual."

"Oh I will, Mayor Ward", Tom said with a grin. "You can count on that." As the mayor tried to push by, Tom gently grabbed his arm. "Now, be a good sport and give your most diplomatic politician excuse about what just happened. Are you getting my vibe, Jerry?"

"Loud and clear, Miller. Now, let go." Jerry broke free of Tom's grip, ambled down the driveway and towards the gaggle of news reporters. Jerry Ward could be heard loudly explaining away what had just taken place. The big story of Al Jeaneau's horrific death had taken a back seat to the melee everyone had just witnessed. The head of the local State Police throttling the stuffing out of New Hope's controversial mayor was the juicy news of the moment.

Ward, probably still flashing back to the loss of air from Boyle's grip and both of the lawmen's warnings, decided to take the high road. He said it was nothing more than a case of consummate professionals who were passionate about catching the animal letting their emotions get the best of them. As far as the mayor was concerned, the matter was a moot point. While it may have sounded good to the press, Jerry Ward was still smoldering inside about being publicly humiliated. *I'm not done with you yet, Boyle and Miller. By the time I am, you may wish it was either one of you on that pole instead of Jeaneau.*

Tom and John had canvassed the crime scene and were starting to walk towards Al's house. "John, thanks for your emotional support, but I can handle my own battles without you getting yourself in the wringer."

John looked at him with that trademark leprechaun grin. "No shit you can fight your own battles, but why lose your badge beating on an asshole like Ward?"

"Oh, and you won't?" Tom queried with a chuckle.

"Number one, you know I'm this close to having the ace up my sleeve with that prick, Tommy my boy. And number two..."

"What would that be John?"

"I don't really care."

CHAPTER 13

John Boyle returned with Tom to the station house. The initial investigation of the crime scene had turned up nothing new. The priests collar was found in Al's kitchen. The house, as usual, was spotless. No signs of blood were to be found in the domicile. Tom ordered Luminol tests just like he had for the "A" Train, but he expected to hear the only blood the lab techs discovered would be that of the victim.

It gave Tom the sinking feeling he'd felt in the fateful summer of 1985. He started to think back to when Gary was found. The Feds and Tom's group had been keeping a close eye on Kane, but nobody knew even at that point if he was the killer. They weren't even sure until he was apprehended, if Kane was the only one. He remembered the anguish of having to tell his father that his soul mate was gone. "He can't go now son," Tom remembered his father pleading. "We had so much more to do, so much life left to live. Outside of you, he was the only one who could understand me and understand my love." Little could Tom or his father have known, but in a matter of time, Edgar would soon be joining the person he'd loved for so long.

"Tommy. Hey, Tommy my boy." John was trying to easily coax Tom back into reality. "Tom, I know things look bad for us, but I know, and I think you do too, that somewhere out there is our break. I know this sounds like a lot of like high school, rah-rah crap, but I'm serious. Somewhere out there is our break."

Tom smiled as he took a drag from his cigarette. "Thanks John. I'm trying to keep the faith also. It's all we have in our favor right now." Tom began to look around his office, just to get his mind off the happenings of the day. John saw what Tom was doing and followed suit. Tom walked towards the wall closest to his desk. There, numerous commendations and medals were displayed. Dispersed amongst them were pictures of events from his career. The one his sights had locked onto also caught the interest of John. "Is that you with Mayor Giuliani? I'd never taken notice of that picture before."

"Yeah, I only hung it there about a month ago, John. Debbie unearthed it while she was rummaging through some photos we'd stored in the attic. She thought it would be a good photo to remind me of the triumphs of the Kane case."

"That's a mighty fine lady that you have there, my friend. Always thinkin' about her man."

"Yes she does, my friend." He glanced at the picture again. "Mayor Giuliani was still the lead prosecutor back then. All the New York and national papers ran this picture. I even heard some international bureaus ran it too. It was taken right after the jury had handed Kane the death penalty. Needless to say, the mayor and I were all smiles while the press interviewed us on the courthouse steps."

"So I can see. You know, I do vaguely remember this shot. That's a tough customer, one Rudolph Giuliani."

"Tough guy, yeah John, he definitely fits the description. I wish I had a guy like him running this town. Ward is always too worried about his political maneuverings, press reactions, and his bloated image. Even if we caught that creep red-handed, taking the hush money we think he's receiving from some of the ink parlors and the clubs, he'd probably still walk."

"True, slime such as Ward usually do, but bide your time Tommy. Egomaniacal fellows like him slip up, and when this one does I'm putting the squeeze on his nads like I did 'round his throat today."

"God willing that you are right, John Boyle. Hell, you ought to run for mayor when you retire. You'd be just as good as Mayor Giuliani."

"Normally I'd laugh at such platitudes being thrown my way, but I may just fancy the idea a little more than you think, Thomas. Indeed, I fancy that. Besides, Ward and McGuigan would shit a brick at that news conference, ay?"

Tom began to laugh. "Boyle, leave Mary alone. I know that deep down you have got a soft spot for that pretty gal'. You two definitely have that sexual tension thing down to a science."

"I don't know what you are talking about, Chief Miller," Boyle replied in a flustered manner.

"Besides, the young one's are right up your alley."

"Hush boy!" Boyle shot back. "Even if you are right, and I'm certainly not implying that you are, I'll handle her in my own way."

"Oh, I bet that you'd handle her real well, Boyle. You'd handle your arms right around her waist and.."

"Miller!"

"Is it getting a wee bit hot in here fer ya', O' Johnny boy?"

"Miller!!" John bellowed even louder. The two men looked at each other and burst into a fit of laughter. They quieted down to a chuckle when there was a rap at Tom's office door.

"Come in!" Tom exclaimed as he attempted to catch his breath. Officer Gates and Trooper Terrant entered the room. "What, was there a party going on in here and we weren't invited?" Gates inquired of the two men.

"No, not at all Jenn. You and Zoul come right in. We were talking about the case and somehow slipped into John's love life."

"Miller, it's none of the young folks concern!" John protested.

"What's the big deal, John? They are both topics bordering on the insane."

"Gates!!"

"How far did you delve into the Boyle case, Chief? Were you discussing the point about how the whole town knows that John and Mary have the hots for each other, but they are both too bull-headed to admit it? Heck," Jenn chuckled, "even your gal pal singer from the Havana knows that."

"Gates!!" John roared again as his eyes shot beams through her.

"Oh, pipe down John Boyle. Good work, Jenn. You are, as I've told you before, great detective material," Tom said smugly as he turned towards Boyle.

"Yer' great detective material," John mimicked in his sarcastic and animated way. "Ah, mularkey!! She's a nosy young woman, is what she is." Hearing John's diatribe caused Zoul to chuckle.

"Oh!" John said wryly. "Do we have something to add to this nonsense, Trooper Giggles?"

Zoul shot straight up in his chair. "Oh no, not me sir. I have nothing at all to add."

"Good answer, Trooper Terrant. Answers like that will you get you far under my command," John said triumphantly.

"In retrospect, though, Jenn is correct in her assumption that you have the "hots" for Mary and you just don't have the guts to do anything about it," Zoul mumbled.

"Bedad! The hell with you all!" John helplessly exclaimed as his arms flailed frantically. "Let's talk about the case!" he blurted in the direction of the conspirators. After hearing his exclamation, all in the room, including Boyle, burst into laughter.

When they began to catch their breath, Tom looked at everyone and smiled. "Thanks for the well needed laugh guys. I'm sure Al is looking down at us all, and he's grinning right now. If there is one gift he left to all of us, it was the ability to find the laughter through all of the tears."

"Amen to that statement," John said as Jenn and Zoul nodded their heads in approval.

"Well, let's try to get back to business," Tom said. "Am I correct in assuming our two young officers have come here to tell us something?"

Zoul looked towards Jenn and replied, "it's your show, girl." It was a moment the twenty-five year old officer had relished. It could possibly be a chance for her to make a major impact in a very important case.

Jenn Gates was born up the river in the blue-collar town of Easton, Pennsylvania. Although she had her father's last name, she definitely had the features of her Italian-American mother. Easton was a town priding itself on a having a hard work ethic. This work ethic, handed down from her parents, propelled the attractive brown eyed, sandy blonde haired youngster through her high school years.

Her excellence in academics spilled over into sports, cheerleading, and other activities. When she chose to attend her hometown college, Lafayette, many people thought she would pursue a career in the arts due to her love of the theater. Others thought she would delve into the field of child psychology because of the duty she felt towards helping young people find their way in life.

What no one expected was the choice she eventually made. With her zeal to solve a problem and dig deeper to attain results, she chose criminology. She felt becoming a detective would be the best of both worlds. She would need the good communication skills of a performer and the analytical prowess of a psychologist to probe the criminal mind and become an exemplary detective. The decision, in her mind, was a no-brainer.

Upon completion of her studies, she heard of the position for a police officer in New Hope. She took the entrance exam and passed with flying colors. Tom and Al took a special interest in Jenn's progression on the force after hearing of her ambition to become a detective. A recent discussion between the mentors and their prodigy had alluded to the fact that when Tom would retire, he would need a good detective to run the show. Even though Al's rank was Sergeant, he performed many duties of a full time detective, and he, in all probability would become the new Chief. By seniority, Rob Pagano would have been the next in line, but Rob confided in Tom and Al that he had no interest for the position.

Jenn would now have the chance to prove herself worthy. She would be ready for any task facing her. She was ready to find the person who had killed her mentor, Al Jeaneau. She took a deep breath and began to speak. "Well, we may have a break in our case." Tom and John's eyes lit up. "That's pretty much the reaction that Zoul and I had." She reached into her jacket pocket and produced a baggie containing a few long strands of blonde hair. "Here you go, Chief," she said as she held out the baggie. Tom took the bag and looked it over. "We have a start," Tom said. "John, have your lab buddy DNA test the hair strands. It looks as if we may have traces of someone's blood here." He pointed out the spots to John who was now observing the strands.

"Beware of a wolf in sheep's clothing," John said softly as he lifted the bag towards the bright lights above Tom's desk. "Someone who we wouldn't fathom accomplishing such a brutal act, of course."

"Like a woman?"

"That's a distinct possibility, my young Gates. Finally, we may have a break," John sighed. "I'll be happy to oblige with the test, Tommy."

"Don't get too excited just yet, gentlemen. There's more."

"More! Why, you're just full of surprises Gates!" John exclaimed.

"We would have told you at the crime scene. When the Mayor pulled all of his insanity and the press was milling about, we figured waiting would be the most prudent course of action."

"Prudent indeed, Jenn. Well, what else do we have?" asked the Chief.

"I'll go get it from the unit, Jenn, while you fill them in on the details," Zoul said.

Jenn looked again towards her superiors. "Not too far from where we found those hair strands, we also found one footprint. The killer's left foot must have gone through the minute patch of mud located in Al's otherwise hard or frozen field. Zoul and I grabbed shovels from Al's shed and carefully dug around the print. Luckily, the ground under it was still hard, so it held together very well."

Zoul entered the room slowly, carefully carrying the piece of earth they'd placed in a large, black trash bag. "Good Lord, we have an archaeological team too, I see", quipped John. Zoul placed the bag on the floor and pulled the flaps of the bag down to reveal the earthen mass. He then took out a pen and pointed down to the print as everyone else gathered around him. "It looks like a jogging shoe. The person has a small foot. I don't think I'd be off base in saying it's a woman's shoe print."

"Blonde hair, a woman's jogging shoe. It sure makes you think, doesn't it folks?" Tom mused.

"Zoul and I were talking about the jogger on the way over here, but she seems like a waif from her description, Chief," Jenn added.

"That's true, Jenn. Remember though, as far as her size is concerned, when rage enters the picture, the size of our killer doesn't always matter."

"Especially, if she was attacking them from behind. Less confrontation to deal with," John chimed in.

"Yeah, it is pretty coincidental too that she is not too far away from either murder on the days they occurred, don't you think?"

"True again, Jenn, but it could be purely coincidental. John, let's get a read on the blood and let's get a cast made of the shoeprint before we build up our hopes."

"No problem, Tom. Zoul, would you do the honor of taking care of the evidence for us? I think the Chief and I need to pay a social visit to a dubious member of our community. He may be able to help us fill in some blanks."

"Yes sir, I'll get on it immediately. I gather whatever we discover we'll be sharing with the F.B.I.?" Zoul asked as he pocketed the hair samples and gingerly picked up the bag containing the print. "Let's see how they act when they arrive. If they behave, we will use them to our advantage. If they try to run the case and run us out, let them find their own clues," Tom said. "Are we in agreement?" Jenn, Zoul, and John all nodded in approval. "Well then, we know what we have to do. Thanks, Zoul."

"No problem, Tom. I'll get this evidence moving immediately."

"I know you will Zoul. Oh, and Officer Gates?"

"Yes, Chief?"

"Would you care to take your own unit and follow Trooper Boyle and myself into town? I'd like you to help us pay a visit to an old friend of yours."

"Sure thing. Who?"

Tom smiled. "Why, the 'Inkman', of course."

CHAPTER 14

The pulsating tone of the needle hitting flesh was music to his ears and dollars in his pockets. The day after Christmas was always a boom for his business. College kids home for their Christmas break, and a smattering of local kids in their late teens filled his shop. All of them had an overabundance of cash and credit at their fingertips, thanks to mom and dad. Occasionally, a biker from the local chapter of the Warlords or the Brethren would stop by, but most of them stayed away when the yuppie set invaded town for the holidays.

The news of the towns' second murder was the hot topic of discussion this afternoon, but it did nothing to deter the masses flocking to the popular locale. As he glanced up from the intricate dragon coming to life on the back of his female customer, George Rossini ran his hand through his black, spiked hair, breathed in deep and exhaled for what seemed like an eternity. Murder or not, the much anticipated cash flow continued at his shop. Thankfully, it was just another day at the 'Den of Inkniquity.'

George Rossini, or the 'Inkman' as he was known by many, had crafted a tattoo parlor renowned for having the best art and needlework for miles. Scattered amongst the photos of Ink's famous designs were posters of the many punk, alternative, and death metal musicians whose sounds invaded your ears as you entered his underworld.

Another thing catching your attention immediately was the cleanliness of Ink's lair. Hospital clean was the description given to it by his workers and his patrons. No spent ink vials or bloody tissues were thrown on the floors of this world. There was also no needle sharing in the Den, a practice commonly used in the trade to achieve ridiculously inexpensive prices in some tattoo parlors.

The 'Inkman' would be damned if a hepatitis or, God forbid, an AIDS case would be caused by his shop, so every needle that was used was disposed of in the proper manner. The needles would then be sent out to be autoclaved and sterilized, or they would simply be destroyed. If you were lax in following this procedure, you would summarily be dismissed from being an artist in his parlor, no questions asked. This extreme cleanliness drove the Den's prices up, but ask anyone who had a 'Den of Ink' tattoo if they minded the extravagance and they would answer with a resounding "no". As far as the 'Inkman' was concerned, it was a small price to pay to be considered a respectable young entrepreneur in this community.

It was far more than could be said about the ink and piercing parlors invading Main Street in the past few years. Everyone, including the police, knew these establishments were the peddling houses for the "club drug", Ecstasy. It was the newest rage in the designer drug market, and it was sweeping the area with dangerous results for the predominantly young crowd using it. Everyone knew these shops peddled it, but catching them in the act had been difficult. It didn't help that every time one was raided by Tom Miller and his police force, the mayor would push hard for the town council to re-open these "shit house parlors," as George referred to them. The mayor always said his sole intention, even while they were under investigation, was to keep a positive cash flow in town because they attracted so much business.

George Rossini was extremely savvy about what went on within the confines of this small Borough, and everyone from the bikers to the police respected the young man's opinion. If you needed the lowdown in town, the 'Inkman' was the person to see. This made Ink come to his own conclusions about the mayor. He was thoroughly convinced Mayor Ward had other motives, none being of the legitimate nature. George trusted the mayor about as much as he did the Ecstasy peddling shops that were giving honest, working stiffs like him a bad reputation. Needless to say with his personal opinions on drugs, if you were caught taking or peddling any on the Den's premises, God help you. Expect to receive the literal heave-ho from the Nob Alley shop, either by the stocky, tattoo laden George Rossini, or by one of his equally menacing looking employees.

George looked down at his female patron and smiled. "Denise," he said in his gravel- toned voice, "I've been working on you for almost an hour. How about we give your back and my arm a short break and catch a smoke outside?" The girl nodded in the affirmative as she rolled down her sweatshirt and put on her leather jacket. As the two of them ambled outdoors, George pulled his trademark Macanudo cigar from the pocket of his black leather jacket and lit the tip. The smoke billowed and rolled effortlessly from his mouth while his thoughts wandered to the insane events transpiring over the past few days. He had lost a respected mentor and colleague in Luke Stone, and a good buddy in Sergeant Al Jeaneau. His thoughts lasted for only a fleeting moment. His attention was now drawn to the sounds of footsteps in the alley and he soon spotted Tom Miller, John Boyle and Jenn Gates approaching. "Denise, I'm gonna' need some private time here, if you don't mind." The young girl smiled, extinguished her cigarette, and departed into the Den.

"Ink, how goes it?" John Boyle asked as he grabbed the young man's shoulder.

"As well as could be expected, Irish," George responded with a somber expression. He took another puff of the cigar and continued to speak. "Listen guys, I am at a loss for words as to what happened to Al. It hurts, man, does it hurt. I'm going to miss the 'Smiler'. I'm sorry."

"We are at a loss too, Ink," replied Tom. "We know how good a pal you were to Al and Luke."

"Yeah man, I feel like I've lost family. How is Philly coping with all of this insanity?"

"Okay, I guess. I don't know if he's heard about Al yet."

"Oh, be assured that he has heard about it, Tommy", Ink replied emphatically. "This town is just buzzing about the 'Smiler' getting killed. I bet Philly is sure enough shaken up about Luke, and then their friend Pond getting knocked off. He's got to be wondering just how close he could have been to Jones whacking him."

Tom, in the midst of inhaling his Marlboro, nearly choked. "Close to Jones whacking whom?" he inquired.

"Phil and Luke, man," Ink responded nonchalantly. "The word was going around about Jones trying to get the 'Train' to be a prime Ecstasy peddling location a few months back. Luke and Phil naturally told Jerome to get lost with that drug crap. Things got a little heated between Luke and

Jerome, but Jones went on his way. I heard he was trying to push his way into the new ink shop on Main Street, 'Fantasy Tats', but that's Warlord turf. Old biker, Tim Ottis, owns the place. I know for a fact he doesn't peddle, but if he receives static from anyone, all it'll take is one call to his old Warlord buddies and they'll settle the score. If they didn't settle it, the Brethren will. But with Jones, it is a different scenario. Both of those groups know he's crazy, you know, a loose cannon. They keep him out of here, but they let him be when he runs his mouth. I've heard they figure, they waste him, the Feds will turn the heat up on their operations. You know as well as I do, the boys don't want that to happen." Ink took another puff from the Macanudo and winked in the direction of the officers.

"Christ, we had Jones right under our noses and we didn't even know it," John lamented. This "X" peddling makes you wonder if there is just a little bit more to these murders than just ritual killings to fulfill a prophecy."

"It sure does," Tom added. "Think about it. Jones, and maybe this second individual use the ritual murders of prominent homosexuals to scare the community."

Jenn looked at the three gentlemen, and was very eager to add her voice to the mix. "Sure, then you peddle your product and if you meet any resistance subtly inform the person they could find themselves victims of the same fate that had befallen Luke, Pond, and Al." She looked up towards the sky, and to no one in particular said Al's name again.

"You're wondering why him?" Ink questioned. "That's easy enough, Italy. New York, Irish, and the Smiler have been trying to rid this town of narcotics. Everybody, including the suppliers knows you guys were making inroads."

"Bedad, Ink! Is there anything that you don't know about?"

"Hey Irish, isn't that the reason you have all graced my presence on such a dreary afternoon?" Ink asked wisely.

"Yes, you are right about that, young one."

"I do have to thank you and Tom," Ink said as he billowed more smoke from his prized stogie. "It's always a pleasure to converse with you gentlemen, but bringing along young Miss Italy was a nice touch. You have got to love a girl with brains and the beauty to match, man." Ink smiled and winked in the direction of Jenn Gates who was blushing ever so slightly.

"Don't forget to add, a girl who can knock you off your pins if you misbehave," she replied and winked in kind.

John and Tom started to laugh as Ink tried to defend himself. "Italy, I have nothing but respect for you, girl. Listen Jenn, that new band, Krane, is playing tonight at John and Peter's. Why don't you join me for some talk and some brew?" he asked while trying to look chivalrous.

"Who knows? Maybe, I'll take you up on that, Georgie. Will that be all gentlemen?" she asked her superiors.

"Actually, I would like you to follow us again. You like the investigative end of this work, so why don't you tag along?"

"Fine, Chief. I'll be waiting in my unit. Goodbye George, maybe I'll see you tonight." Officer Gates turned quickly and proceeded towards her patrol car while John Boyle glanced over to observe Ink following her every move down the cobblestone path.

"Pathetic, Georgie! " he sarcastically exclaimed to Ink.

The Inkman quickly turned to face his comedic nemesis. "Hey Irish, just because you don't have the balls to get a groove on with McGuigan, don't take it out on me." The remark sparked uproarious laughter from Tom, but only exasperation from the Irishman.

"Cripes! Is this town turning into the dating game?" John asked as he threw his arms into the air. "Can we go now, Miller?"

"Yes John, I'll save you again. Let's go," Tom said with a chuckle. As he lit another Marlboro, he turned towards the 'Inkman.' "Ink, thanks for the word. We'll be in touch."

"New York, Irish, the pleasure was all mine. Call on me anytime." As Ink traveled up the path towards the Den, he turned and shouted to the departing officers. "Guys, do me a solid?"

"What would that be, Ink?" Tom inquired.

"Get the town back to normal, man. Nail these creeps. We've all got faith in you."

"Sure thing!" Tom bellowed as he turned to walk with John again. As the two of them approached the car, Tom glanced in John's direction. "Ink said to get the town back to normal. Do you think we're ever going to see normal again, John?"

"As optimistic as I try to be, my friend, I truly don't know the answer to that question," John remarked woefully. "God in heaven, I wish I did."

CHAPTER 15

The three officers were on the move again as Tom quickly turned from Main Street. To his surprise, the town was quite busy despite the news of Al's murder. Tonight, he thought, it will be a ghost town except for the nightclubs. He wondered how much business they would drum up anyway, but it was always hard to judge the mindset of the younger set. They seemed to always spit in the face of adversity, just as much of Tom's generation had done in the 1960's.

Tom turned the patrol car into the Estates at the Riverwoods. He felt that after hearing Ink's spin on the chain of events, it would be a good idea to ask Phil what had transpired at 'The "A" Train.' He knew that Phil's psyche would be in a fragile state, and the news of Al's death would throw his friend into even more grief. He also knew though, if he could jog Phil's memories of the day in question, he might just be able to narrow down the ever- growing list of theories. Tom's experience had shown throughout the years, one minute piece of evidence could change the landscape of the whole investigative process.

As the officers approached the magnificent residence, Phil opened the front door to greet them. "I saw you coming up the drive from the sitting room windows, so I figured I'd save you from ringing the bell."

"How are you doing, Phil?" Jenn asked as she gave Phil a warm embrace.

"I'm still quite shaken, but I am the one who should be asking how you are coping?" A tear quickly raced down his face. "I've heard about Al," he said as his voice became quite graveled.

"We're fine, pal. No need to worry about us. Would it be a bother if we were to join you for a few minutes?"

"No bother at all, John. Please, all of you, come in," Phil said as he cleared his throat. "Can I interest any of you in some coffee or something to eat?" he asked as they all made their way to the sitting room. "Coffee would be fine, Phil. Thank you," Tom responded as he sat down near the fireplace.

"Same here," John retorted.

"Jenn, would you be so kind as to help me bring everything out, hon'? Besides," Phil said as he tried his best to smile, "I know you all love those Christmas cookies. I'll bring a tray of them out, also." Jenn alighted from the plush wing chair and made her way towards Phil. "Come on Phil, let's go." John and Tom noticed Jenn had put her arm around Phil's shoulders while they walked in the hallway.

Tom leaned over and conversed with John in a mild tone. "She is a very compassionate girl. That is a breath of fresh air. Most of the young cops these days are so robotic in their approach."

"Aye, I agree, Miller. She needs to disassociate herself from the personal feelings at times, though. If she really wants to be a good detective, those feelings could come back to bite her."

"They could, but people are so much more apt to display their emotions these days. It could actually be an attribute to have such a level of caring. I agree, you can't utilize it on every case. Letting your emotions guide you instead of instincts could tear you to pieces and leave you vulnerable. God knows, John, we have worked the cases to observe that firsthand."

"We have done that, indeed, my friend, me with Einhorn, and you with Kane. Now, we both have this calamity. I think you may have something with Gates. Maybe with a case such as this one, her compassion and energy could be a vital resource."

"She is a tough kid. Give her some time and she may be better than the two of us combined. Who knows, maybe she'll save both of our carcasses on this case."

"Miller my friend, I pray you are correct. If you are, we can finally retire."

"Amen to that, Boyle," Tom replied mimicking his good friend. John winked in kind as Phil and Jenn approached.

"What were you two murmuring about?" Jenn inquired.

"Nothing to worry about, lass."

"Oh, I see. It's guy talk, is it, Trooper Boyle? You are right I have nothing to worry about, because I'll find out anyway. I have a gift that neither of you gentlemen will ever acquire."

"And that being what?" asked Boyle coyly.

"A woman's intuition." Her quick retort brought a smile to Phil's face.

"That is why Luke and I always adored you, honey. You are not afraid to speak your mind. It's so refreshing."

"Thank you, Phil," Jenn said as she returned to the comfort of the plush chair.

"Well, what is it you have come to inquire of me, my friends, as I am sure this is not purely a social visit?"

"You are correct about that," Tom said as he took a sip of coffee from the fine antique china in which it was served. "We've received information from a reliable source, Jerome Jones had visited the Train a few months ago. Do you mind telling me what took place?"

"It was probably nothing more than what you've already heard. I think it was right after our Columbus Day bash. One of the waitresses informed us there was a real ominous looking fellow who was asking for the owners. I told Lucas I would go and see what he wanted."

"That's when I saw him. He was a muscular, African-American. He stood about six feet and three inches tall. He had thick, black dreadlocks, pulled into a ponytail. He also wore a long, black leather trench coat. As a matter of fact, I would have to say all of his attire was black. He was quite an imposing figure, although he looked quite stylish. He had a fair, light brown complexion and possibly hazel eyes. His eyes, I must say, were quite frightening."

"What do you mean by frightening, Phil?" John asked while pouring himself another cup of coffee.

"They were angry looking, John. It was the kind of piercing look that would just strike some fear into you. I tried not to be intimidated, so I quickly introduced myself and he did likewise. He said his name was Jerome Jones and he smiled, but even as he did, his eyes were filled with such… hate. Yes, I think hate would be the best way to describe them."

Cocky son of a bitch went by his real name. Cocky, or calculated, Tom surmised. "What did he talk about?"

"Well Tom, he asked if there was somewhere we could sit and talk without being interrupted. I suggested one of the tables in the Ellington Room, since it wasn't being utilized at the time." Tom picked up another cookie. "Were you nervous at that point?"

"Very much so, Tom. I mean, this man looked as if he could snap me in two, if he so desired. I motioned over to another of our staff to have Luke keep his eyes and ears open. I think they all had an idea this fellow was shady. Anyway, we sat down and I asked what it was I could do for him. He said it wasn't a matter of what I could do for him. On the contrary, it was more a matter of what he could do for me. He asked me if I had ever heard of Ecstasy. I said yes and then quickly asked him what does Ecstasy have to do with the conversation?"

"He began to chuckle in a somewhat evil tone. He very calmly explained to me that he had a very lucrative "distribution service" running out of clubs in New York City and various cities in New Jersey. He said he'd also made some inroads in clubs outside of New Hope. He thought a high-end club catering to the "beautiful people" such as the Train would fit perfectly into his plans."

"For peddling "X"?"

"Yes Jenn, but I think Ecstasy was just the tip of the iceberg. He tried to add in hastily that this "business deal" would make Luke and I wealthy beyond reason. I went on to tell him that Lucas and I, under no circumstances, would ever have his business fit into the Train's plans. I went on to tell him Luke and I would never sully our good reputation in this community to make a profit on drugs. I also told him we were good friends with the local police department, and that maybe they'd be interested in his business dealings."

Tom lit up a cigarette and looked straight at Phil. "Did he say anything at this point, Phil?"

"He just looked amused, but in an almost frightening way. I swallowed hard, and repeated the comment about informing the police. It was about that time his eyes grew colder and deeply set. He still was smiling and said it definitely wouldn't be in my best interests to pursue such a line of thinking. I asked him why and he replied if I did pursue it, my cop friends may find my little faggot ass floating in the river the next day."

"Did anyone hear the conversation at that point?"

"Yes Tom, Lucas heard all of it. He came charging in and I think for a moment he startled Jones. Lucas told him it would be a good idea if he were to leave. Jones became very belligerent and asked Lucas if he was going to nail Jones in the ass if he didn't go. Luke replied no, but added that he just may kick his ass if he didn't."

The officers started to chuckle. "That sounds like Luke to me," John replied.

"It sure does," added Tom. "Now Phil, what took place afterwards?"

"Well, Luke asked him again to leave. Jones smiled, got up, looked at us and said we "girls" weren't done dealing with him. Luke said that we were more than done and if Jones had any sense, he'd never step foot in here again. If he decided he couldn't obey our wishes, the police would be called."

"Did he reply?"

"No, Tom. He just smiled again, and then he left. He never came back after that. Luke and I were talking to Ink, and when he heard Jones' name he nearly fell over. He told Lucas and I to watch our backs. He also said we should call you."

"Why didn't you?" Tom asked in a pleading tone.

"Luke said to just wait and see what happened, so we did, and he never returned."

"Phil, I asked you the other day if Luke or you had experienced any problems with anyone at the club. I understand you were in shock over Lucas. Could it be why you didn't recall a situation clearly remaining quite vivid in your memory?"

Phil looked at them all as a tear trickled down his cheek. "I'm..so sorry, guys. When Al and you told me about Lucas, I just went numb. Now, Al is gone, and my mind is such a jumble."

"That's alright, Phil. I don't think it would have prevented any of the events from taking place. Our killers are going to be very elusive."

"Thanks for understanding anyway, Tom."

"Well, we've taken up enough of your time," Tom said as he extinguished his cigarette. "We'd better leave."

"I'm sorry that I couldn't be of more help to you."

"Aye, don't worry about it, lad. Get yourself some sleep, you are going to need it."

"Thanks John, I'll try. I suppose I will see all of you tomorrow?"

"You'll see John and Jenn. I'm sorry that I can't attend, Phil, but there is an urgent trip I must take."

"Don't worry Tom, I understand. This trip you're taking, could it help find Lucas' killer?"

"Quite possibly."

"Then go. Luke and I would have expected nothing less from you. He'll know you're there in spirit."

"I'll see you soon, pal. We'll show ourselves out," Tom said as they made their way to the front door. "Oh Phil, one more question for you!" Tom exclaimed as he proceeded to turn the doorknob.

"Sure, Tom," Phil replied as he hastily returned to the hallway.

"Have you happened to have noticed a jogger around the Borough lately? Female, I would guess in her mid-twenties. She has a very slender, athletic build. She's about five-eight in height, and she usually wears her blonde hair tucked up in a ball cap and pony-tailed through the back. She usually wears a back pack and brightly colored jogging shoes too."

Phil thought for a moment. "She doesn't sound familiar. Does she have something to do with these murders also?"

"We're not sure yet," John chimed in.

"We're putting out a poster including a rough sketch and a description of her. If you see anyone fitting the mold, please, give us a call. We'd like to talk to her."

"I will certainly do my best to keep an eye out for her."

As the officers left the festively decorated entrance, they remained silent. As they approached their vehicles, Jenn Gates piped up. "Guys, I may be totally overanalyzing this, but why do I fell that Phil knows more than he is letting on to?"

"Your premonition may be correct, Jenn. I feel that way also. How about you, John?"

"Well folks, I think there is going to be a whole lot more to this case than just copy-cat, ritual killings. I think this town is going to be in for some surprises. Now, of course, that is just my vibes."

"Why don't we talk about it over an early dinner at the Logan? It will be my treat."

"Miller, you sure do know how to keep a brain energized! I'll never turn down a free dinner, especially at the Logan. How about you, young lady?"

"Thanks, Chief." Jenn looked at him mischievously and added, "you know, after all that garbage this morning, you should charge this to the Mayor's business account."

Tom and John howled in their approval. "Hey Tommy, I think we just found your replacement when you retire."

"I agree, unequivocally. Well, "Chief" Gates, do you care to follow us to the Logan?"

"As long as the "new" Chief isn't footing the bill, why not?"

CHAPTER 16

The Logan Inn. For many a century, it had been a place to eat, lodge and enjoy the ambiance of New Hope. The founder of New Hope, John Wells, had originally established the inn as a tavern, in 1727. The Logan was a throwback to the towns more pristine times, and many people felt it was the focal point of the area.

Tom, John and Jenn crossed Main Street and stepped back in time. The Logan was festively decorated for the holidays. Christmas trees, filled with every type of ornament graced the lobby. As the hostess greeted the officers, she led them past the warmth of the fireplace in The Cottage dining area, and sat them at Tom's favorite table in the Garden Room. The tables were still decorated with green and red candles and pine wreaths were hung above the French period furniture. Tom and Debbie were regulars at the Logan, and they loved the view the windows in the wraparound dining porch afforded them. Debbie also liked the room because it featured an imposing stained glass wall, which was created by a friend of hers. Tom also used to frequent the most fabled part of the inn with Al, The Tavern, when they needed to blow off some steam. The colonial fireplace, the antique woodwork and the coziness of the spot used to make the two of them forget about the hazards of the job.

The three officers settled in and looked over their menus. They could feel the eyes of the locals upon them. "The funeral procession begins, lad," John quipped in a hushed tone while a few of them approached the table. The first of them was the man who discovered Luke's body, Ken Coverdale. Feeling awkward about what to say, he quickly offered his condolences for their fallen comrade. Before he would turn to leave, he bent down near Tom and John. "Just catch the bastard. We are all behind you." A few more reiterated Coverdale's statement, if not in as callous a tone.

"It's going to be quite some time before this town heals," Tom uttered while he quickly lit a cigarette. Only after they had ordered their food did a discussion of the past days events ensue. Tom decided to begin the dialogue.

"So, do my partners have a take on anything? Would you like me to start?" John and Jenn both nodded their approval. "I think there is something more to this than just a rehash of the Kane prophecy. I am really starting to feel as if the motives for the killings themselves are the same, but that somehow, the Ecstasy peddling ties in on both fronts. The only way they seem to differ is our New Hope friend, I think, depicts a rage that makes his or her murders' a bit more personal. The individual really seems to think what they are committing is performed with righteous motive. Jones, on the other hand, for lack of a better term, commits his for the hell of it."

"Jones is a walking contradiction," said Boyle. "I mean, he gets off on doing the deed, and then he fronts himself as the "reverend" of the revamped World Church. At the same time though, much of his personal behavior is of a nature that Martin Kane would find absolutely abhorrent."

"You mean the dope peddling and the cross dressing?"

"Absolutely, Officer Gates. You are learning the game quite nicely."

"I've got a way to go to, but I'm trying."

"Keep at it, and you'll be the next Miller or Boyle," Tom chuckled.

"Heaven forbid," Jenn replied as she rolled her eyes. As their dinner was served, Tom and John dove into their steaks with a relentless abandon, while Jenn slowly ate her salad and broiled salmon.

John took a few breaths and glanced at Jenn. "Eat up, young Gates. Food powers the brain, and Lord knows, we have a lot to deduct today."

They remained quite silent as they enjoyed the cuisine. After a few more minutes, they all rested their full stomachs. It was at this point that Tom decided to speak again. "I think the New Hope killer is the same individual who took my fathers' life."

Gates looked like a deer caught in a vehicles headlights, but John Boyle remained quite stoic. "I think you and I always had a premonition it wasn't Kane, lad. You really think it could be the same one after all these years?"

"Yes John, I really do."

"Why Chief?"

"Jenn, at social times you can refer to me as Tom. You have served around me long enough to realize the protocol crap is out the window when we are not around the higher-ups," Tom said, smiling at his young charge.

"Okay...Tom, why do you think it's the same person?"

"Well Jenn, our killer follows Kane's murderous ways to a tee. The only thing seeming to differ is the strength and the depth of the knife plunges."

"I noticed at Al's crime scene that you seemed to be measuring something on his body."

"I eventually did the same thing to Lucas' body when I saw it at the morgue, Jenn. I had always kept records of the stab depths of Kane's victims. When my father was killed, Stan followed suit and measured the wounds for me. The results were different than that of Kane's victims."

"Do our new victims match with your father's?"

"Yes," Tom said as he lit a Marlboro. "Luke's did, and I'm sure that Al's will when I investigate it some more."

"Now," Tom continued, "both of the initial plunges made by Kane and the New Hope killer have the same disabling quality, but Kane's remaining plunges have a slow, almost intricate quality about them."

"It's as if he took pleasure in watching them die a slow and painful death."

"Absolutely, John. Now, our killer seems to increase their ferocity with the remaining plunges. There is an anger, some kind of a sadistic passion within our killer."

"It's like the victim has done something to personally hurt this individual."

"Yes, Jenn. All seven of the murders Kane admitted to were done in this precise, crafted manner. My father, on the other hand, was murdered with a much harder and meaningful animosity."

"It's akin to the method used now."

"Yes, John. The forensic labs showed it in my fathers' death, also. Another similarity I discovered in my old notes and Luke's, and, I'm assuming Al's murder, is upon extraction of the knife."

"The extraction? How so?"

"Upon extraction of the subsequent wounds, the knife seems to have been twisted back and forth."

"Sweet Jesus, as if the murderer was adding insult to injury."

"Yes, John. I believe that when the full lab reports come back, they will contain a method that is consistent with that type of ferocious precision. I also took into account the handwriting on the new notes. The one's from my father's murder were strikingly similar to Kane's writing. The killer had some help imitating the writing style when the press printed photographs of the notes. At first, we figured Kane's hand may have been a little shaky, but now, I see the new writing as similar to the one's found at my dad's crime scene. I sent them to our handwriting analyst."

"Christ, Tommy. Awakened from the dead to fulfill a prophecy, monetary gains, or both. It makes you shudder to think, this individual could be more dangerous than Kane."

"Yes it does, John Boyle. I believe that when we lay our hands on Mr. Jones or our local suspect, this will open us up to a whole new and frightening world. For some warped reason, I also believe that Reverend Kane may willing or unwillingly provide us with some revelations."

"We can only hope so."

"Yes we can, Jenn."

After their dinner plates were cleared, they all ordered dessert and coffee. Tom lit another cigarette and fell silent again. "Tom, are you afraid to see Kane again?" Jenn asked nervously.

"Very much so, Jenn. It's going to be hard, after all these years, to see the man who was solely responsible for Gary's death, and was also instrumental in my father's demise. I would like to think that I could heal the wounds the visit may re-open, but I have to be prepared that the hurt will be there."

When they finished their cake and coffee, the waitress proceeded to hand Tom the bill. "Och, no. Jessie, bring that bill over here. Miller, Gates, this one is on me." This brought a look of amusement from the two officers and a look of confusion from the young waitress. John Boyle became aware of these looks and responded. "What, like I've never paid before? And you, Miss Jessie, are ya' looking to get a bad tip?" John looked over the bill and quickly handed her the money. "Now, be gone with ya', and happy holidays, Jess."

"Thank you, Trooper Boyle," the still flustered but smiling waitress replied as she turned to wait on another table. He turned around to see Tom and Jenn still with a look of bewilderment frozen on their faces. "Oh, enough from the two of you. Let's just say I'm felling as if the Chief has sprung enough times."

"Well, thanks John. Now Gates, don't fall for this. He's just trying to impress another young woman that he's an old softie at heart."

"Aye, some gratitude. Besides, I can't impress Gates anyway. She's got eyes for the 'Inkman,' John said snidely. "Mister Eight-Thousand Tattoos. What do you see in a character like him anyway?"

"He's a nice guy," Jenn responded quickly. "He shares in a lot of the same music tastes I have, and he also makes me laugh."

"Gates, chimpanzees at the zoo make me laugh, but it doesn't mean I need to hang out with them socially."

"Ha, ha, you are hysterical, John," Jenn replied wryly. "Since we're on the subject," she said as her voice became very sultry, "when do we plan on asking Mary McGuigan on a date?"

"Gates, now don't make me be yellin' at you in a public place."

Tom could only chuckle before he polished off the last of the coffee. "Well dating contestants, I need to go and prepare myself for tomorrow. I'm going to walk to the station, grab some notes, take my unit and head for home."

"Good luck tomorrow, Tommy boy," John said as he bear-hugged his good friend.

"Same here," Jenn added as she kissed his cheek. "We're all pulling for you."

"Thanks guys, I'll be seeing you soon."

Jenn watched Tom leave and was overcome with emotion. "I hope he'll be okay," she said as she wiped a tear from her cheek.

"Ah, don't worry about Tommy, young Jennifer. He's a strong man. The strongest I've probably ever known." As the two of them left the Logan Inn, Jenn asked John if he'd mind crossing Main and Ferry Streets' to walk with her to the Landing. As they made their way to the low, wrought iron fence separating them from the river below, Jenn turned around. She found herself gazing towards the wall that had been cleaned of its evil writing. It was just a few days ago Lucas Stone was murdered, but it felt in many ways as if it had occurred a year ago.

She turned around again and pushed the soft, wind swept curls of her hair, away from her face. She stared at the river and began to speak. "This has always been my favorite spot in the Borough. I always used to come down here on my lunch break and just watch the currents of the water carelessly go by." She looked at John and continued. "I always used to think of this water as being so serene, so much a part of me. Now I look at it and it seems so cold, so unforgiving."

John nodded and looked out towards the ominous Delaware. "The river looks mad indeed, young Gates. Blood has been spilled into her, and she is angry. She is trying to tell us something."

"Do you really believe that?" Jenn asked as she took in the vastness of the river that lay in front of her. "Do you really believe in signs?"

"I do, Jenn. I do, and so does Zoul. We were talking just the other day about the river's signs."

"What do you think it is trying to tell us?"

"I think it is telling us with its darkness that the evil we are hunting is right here among us. I think the swirling of its currents is telling us the sorrow is far from over. We will feel more pain in the days to come."

"Do you really believe that, John?" asked a somewhat pensive Gates, who again moved the soft curls from her pretty face.

"Unfortunately, I do lass, but I also believe something else. I think my friend the river does too."

"What would that be, John?"

"We believe no matter what kind of adversity we face in the near future, as long as we have God and a man named Tom Miller on our side, we will win."

"Amen to that, John!"

"You took the words right from my mouth, young one."

Tom picked up some files from his office, got into his police unit and made a hasty departure from the station. As he drove down Main Street, he started thinking about his impending meeting with Kane. He wondered if any good would come from all of this, or if it would just push close to fifteen years of quelled emotions to the forefront. Next August would be fifteen years without Gary or his father. God, where does the time go?

Fortunately, when he reached his homestead, he had too many things to do, so he didn't have the time to dwell on the last question. Debbie was not home yet, so Tom took advantage of the time alone. He began to pack a small bag with a change of clothes, his notes, and some files.

Tom took a short respite and watched some of the evening news. The national press was so engrossed with the Y2K furor, talk of any ritual killings was not even mentioned. Aside from the Gazette, Philadelphia Daily Eagle and a few blurbs in the Trenton papers, the press coverage was almost non-existent.

It made Tom wonder if nationally the White House was trying to keep a lid on this story. With all the other fears they had to calm the public about, a serial killer on the loose would probably make it appear that the country was falling into an anarchistic state. It always amused Tom how the government could sugarcoat, or just make their unpleasant news disappear when it was convenient.

Tom turned off the television, put on a pot of coffee, and picked up the telephone. He spoke with Rob Pagano for upwards of an hour. They coordinated the events of the day and were able to be in constant contact if an emergency were to arise.

Tom was confident in Rob's ability to handle a situation, but this is where he missed having Al. Al Jeaneau could have been New Hope's Police Chief. Al could do the detective work, the paper work, and everything else required of the position. He also had a very amicable personality to deal with people and their various problems.

Rob, on the other hand, did not have the same passion for the position. He was a very good street cop, but he wanted nothing to do with the rigors of being a cop, detective, goodwill ambassador for the city, and delegate the authority required to run a sound ship. Tom also factored in Rob's heart attack of three years ago. It had taken much of the fight out of Rob, and had increased the discussion of his retirement. Rob seemed as if he was just counting down the days until it happened.

Pagano would be a satisfactory stop-gap measure, but Tom needed to groom someone from within. If he did not, he would have to revert to the Mayor hiring an out of town cop when Tom was prepared to retire. Leaving it in Ward's hands made Tom shudder, but he come to the realization that he was getting older and this case was already beginning to take its toll on him, physically and mentally. Boy, did he miss Al Jeaneau.

By the time Tom had settled in front of the television again, Debbie had come home. As she had always done, she put the best face on in a tough situation and gave Tom a kiss. "I heard about the garbage "Mayor Toad" pulled at Al's house this morning."

"Oh, did you?" asked Tom with a sly grin.

"Yes. I also heard John just about broke the jerks neck. Good, he needed a butt kicking to bring him back down to earth. Did you find out anything, evidence wise?" she asked as she sat down close to her husband. Tom moved closer and snuggled Debbie tightly.

"Well, our Miss Gates and Zoul found some hair samples that looked like it may be from a blonde wig. They also found a sneaker print that may be from our infamous jogger. Apparently, she was in Al's yard the night it happened."

"Really?" Debbie asked looking quite shocked. "Well, good for Jenn and Zoul. The young ones are making some inroads. Did you hear anything else about Jones?"

"Yes. We found out that he was in town a few months ago trying to push his Ecstasy business into 'The "A" Train.' Luke and Phil apparently told him to get lost and he did not resurface."

"This looks as if it bothers you."

"It does Deb. It just sounds too coincidental to Pond in Trenton. I just have a gut feeling that the Ecstasy will tie into the club murders, somehow."

"How so? Like a cover for the peddling?"

"I don't know if it's a total cover, but I think it definitely coincides somehow with the murders. I think that both of the killers' want the ritual killings to take place, but they also get the best of both worlds. They murder homosexuals, and at the same time, rid themselves of the individuals who are resisting to comply and peddle their wares." Tom stopped for a moment to look at Debbie. He didn't know if he wanted to discuss the other topic weighing on his mind.

"Say what you are thinking about, Tommy. I've seen that look for long enough to know this isn't the only thing you are having issues with." Debbie came close to him again, her eyes gazing directly at his.

Tom took a deep breath. The searing, head pounding that had occurred at both murder sites seemed to be returning. Just say it, the voice inside told him. "I have a very strong feeling the New Hope killer also murdered my father."

Debbie did not even blink. In fact no look of distress registered on her face at all. "I was afraid of this," she said quietly. "I think you and I always had a fleeting suspicion that someone else had killed your father."

"Yes, well, I think our hunch has unfortunately come true. It would have been nice, as weird as it sounds, to find out Kane had committed the murder. So much for convenience."

"Tom, if there is anything you and I have learned, life is very rarely convenient. That is what makes us stronger as people when we need to deal with adversity."

Tom smiled. He knew Debbie was correct. "Well, 'Miss Optimistic', do you feel like making an early night of it?" Tom asked while extending his hands towards Debbie. She grabbed them and pulled herself from the couch.

"I think we could both use the rest." Debbie followed Tom upstairs and into their bedroom. After they had changed and retreated under the covers, they held each other tightly. As they kissed for what seemed like an eternity, Tom tried to savor every moment of the night.

Debbie soon fell into a deep slumber and Tom looked around the room that was dimly lit from a hallway sconce. The antique, Victorian-era, cherry furniture, placed with such thought around the large master suite, shimmered even in this low light. Debbie takes such pride and care of this house. As with the other rooms, Debbie made sure to provide ample amounts of framed photographs, scattered to and fro, in this one also. Giant begonias exploded in vibrant tones of yellow, pink, and white on various stands and end tables.

In all this warmth and coziness, Tom Miller settled in, and began to fall asleep. While doing so, he thought about the murders, he thought about tomorrow, and how the events of the next few days, weeks or months could again alter his life.

It made his pattern of sleep become quite restless in nature, especially when the face appeared, and even more so when the laughter followed. The devil himself even had to shudder when he heard the sadistic, evil laughter, of Kane.

CHAPTER 17

The winds howled long and hard in this mountain region of the Adirondacks. Ask anyone about how they would describe the seasons in Dannemora, New York, and they would tell you, "July and winter." Nestled into this environment and built into the side of one of these mountains was the Clinton Correctional Facility.

"Little Siberia", as Clinton was nicknamed, started as a mining prison over one hundred and fifty years ago. It was where New York City, over three hundred and twenty miles away, sent their worst prisoners. Back in the 1800's, the prison was the only spot inhabited by humans. Otherwise, it was a vast wilderness out past the prison structures. The initial prison was built from the sweat and blood of inmate labor. Clinton was notorious for taking only the most physically capable prisoners to labor in these harsh climates.

As the years went on, certain wardens reformed the prison and updated many of its services. The prisoners still crafted much of the housing and workshops, but they were made to feel more like they were in a communal setting and not a death camp.

For all of the well- intentioned reforms that had taken place, the next few days at Clinton would be tense, for something would be happening on these grounds that hadn't occurred in almost half a century.

Chief Tom Miller passed through the gates and entered the administrative wing. He immediately caught site of a familiar face. The crew cut, graying gentleman smiled, and began his approach. The loose, civilian clothes he wore hid the many years of greasy diner food encircling his waist. He held out his arms and hugged Tom as if they had not seen each other for years. "What do you say, partner?" the man asked, with his thick, Brooklyn accent.

"Stan," Tom replied with a warm smile. "Thanks for your help in making this happen."

"No problem, buddy. Hey, if this asshole knows anything at all, I figured it was worth a shot to see if he'd talk. Hell, in four days the animal will be in the ground, where he belongs." Let the devil deal with ya' after that.

Tom nodded. "It's hard to believe, isn't it? All these years have passed and he's finally leaving us. It's like reading the last part of a well written mystery novel, and asking yourself if it's really over."

"Tommy," Stan said as he pat his good friend on the back, "this is the last chapter of a book that I'll be glad to put down."

As they followed the labyrinth of corridors leading to the wardens' office, Stan asked Tom how Debbie was holding up. For the most part, Tom replied, she was her usual, rock of an individual, but he thought this go-round was going to take a toll on her. "The older we get, the harder it is, Tommy," Stan replied. "Now, how are you holding up? I heard about Al." Tom glanced up quickly as they walked. "I'd called the station to see if you'd left yet, and I got your Officer Gates on the line. She informed me of all the latest happenings. It's a damn shame about Al, Tommy. He seemed like a really nice guy from the occasions I had to meet or speak with him. I'm sorry."

"Thanks for the words, Stan. I am doing as well as I can. It's hard to stay focused, but if I don't, it will turn into pure chaos around me. Did Gates mention to you about the Feds coming today?"

"Yeah, but it don't surprise me. They are trying their best to keep a lid on the murders being picked up by the national or worldwide press. They are trying to make them seem like a local problem down by you. Word out of the Bureau is they are worried about the press glamorizing the killings. You know, they think it'll turn Kane into some kind of cult hero. The only problem is, some Internet sites caught wind of the murders and they are swirling around stories about Kane's prophecies being fulfilled."

"So it will eventually surface anyway."

"People will start to scream about another cover-up by a government who don't give a shit about specific groups of people."

"Which leaves us with the potential of protests, chaos, and riots days before this Millennium garbage which already has enough people in a panic."

"Ah, you gotta' love their thinking in these situations."

"The press will leak it, you just watch," Stan said matter-of-factly. Tom and Stan approached the door of Warden Jack Smith's outer office. Stan took a deep breath and looked in Tom's direction. "Are you ready for this, partner?" Tom gazed at the ceiling, and then met Stan's eyes. "I'm as ready as I'll ever be." Stan put his hand over the doorknob and began to turn it. "Then let's do this, pal."

Warden Jack Smith was staring out of the massive windows located directly behind his equally impressive desk. He peered into the distance of the prison yards that lay below them. A good layer of snow had fallen and it made the environs look pristine. You got used to the snow up here. No problems so far today, Jack thought. Jack had taken great strides in producing an even more model prison for his 2, 900 inmates than the one he had received. Jack was very progressive in the methods he used to take care of the prison population.

The prisoners were given their usual state perks, but Jack made sure they all knew they were to be a productive member of this prison society. That meant everything from cleaning the heads and the sinks, to learning how to read and write, and even taking courses improving their chances of obtaining a job, if or when they were released from prison. Jack was serious in his efforts to make them become a productive member of the outside world. Jack rewarded their efforts by giving them some type of a communal existence behind the wire. The sloped hills the prison was built into resembled an outdoor type of condominium. The inmates planted gardens in them in the short, summer months, and they also used them as a social area. The class structure that evolved in these short hills resembled a type of "hobo paradise" as one reporter referred to them. Jack also encouraged athletics. Since the weather dictated the sports, Jack introduced skiing and bobsledding classes on the prison grounds. Many critics shook their heads when told of the goings-on, but it seemed to be working.

Jack's rewards were also given with a level of stern lessons on how the prisoners transition would be back into the real world. He pulled no punches. "If you come away with nothing learned from the lessons learned here, I am assured of seeing you again. If I have to see you again, you may as well contemplate you've made a fairly shitty mess out of your life. Be smart, and learn from your previous mistakes. Try hard not to make them again."

Jack Smith had worked his way up from the grunt ranks of the system. Still an imposing figure at the age of sixty, Jack commanded and received respect from guard and inmate alike. Put forth your best effort, and he would do whatever was in his power to help you. Likewise, screw up on him, and your tour at Clinton Correctional could be a hard one.

One individual who fit this latter description was the Reverend Martin Kane. He had his run-ins with Smith from early on, when Jack had taken the Clinton post in 1992. Even though Kane was on the Death Row bloc, his limited, solitary visits to the inner yard made him a cult hero with certain groups. As Kane walked the paths flanked by an army of guards, he would preach the fiery rhetoric as he had in his Soho church, to any inmate who was on the other side of the fence.

Various members of the Arians, Panthers, and the Hispanic gangs began to form an odd alliance known throughout Clinton as The Tribe. Their main objective was to put Kane's speeches into action, and purify the prison of the homosexual population. It gave Kane exactly what he had long waited for. He now had a formidable army of miscreants who would perform his will at his beck and call. "It worked in the civilized world, it will work like a charm in here," he eerily told Jack when Smith had tried to stifle his plans.

Jack soon stopped Kane's tour of the yard, which is exactly what Kane had hoped for. Word of Smith's efforts were carefully filtered throughout The Tribe and their branches of allies. The silence around the prison put Jack Smith's nose for sniffing out a disaster into high gear. When he began to hear rumors of what was about to transpire, Jack deployed various groups of his "Strike Team" into the bowels of the prison, just in case the threat of Kane's words turned into a reality.

The "Strike Team" was Jack's baby. They were a crack unit, personally trained by the warden to quell just these types of incidents, with the loss of life to be minimal to none. Jack Smith was firm on this last order. No loss of life was to be permitted unless the threat of death was imminent to any member of the team.

Kane's plan would become reality just a few days later. It started in the yard and filtered into the mess hall. Jack swiftly led his group in to corral The Tribe, and after the dust had settled, no one had died and only fifteen inmates were injured. Though some prison activist groups questioned the injuries resulting at all, most of them quickly retracted their opposition when they were informed of the uprisings scale. Jack Smith's quick and decisive action had probably saved many lives.

He was also applauded by these groups when he mended the wounds caused by the schism, and formed his own alliance with all of the groups that Kane had utilized. The wardens actions has basically left Kane exactly where Jack wanted him, alone on Death Row, with little to no allies. Kane never saw the outside world again, only from a small window in his cell. He had become an endangered species, so to speak. For the past six and half years of the wardens tenure, Kane had become an increasingly insignificant member of the prison population, but upon hearing the rumors of Kane's prophecy, Jack still viewed him as a potentially dangerous individual. "Four more days, Kane," Jack said as he glared at the Death Row bloc. "I'll be so glad when you are gone."

The sharp tone resonating from the buzzer on Jack's desk quickly brought him back to the present. "Warden Smith?" asked the hushed, female voice.

"What is it, Marie?" Jack asked as he tightened his necktie a bit.

"Detective Tilden and Chief Miller are here to see you."

"Great, Marie. Please send them right in."

"Well if it isn't the two guys that gave me a seven year headache!" Jack bellowed while stepping from behind his desk.

"Howda' hell are you, Jack?" Stan asked as he took hold of the wardens' shoulder.

"I'm doing well, thanks. Hell, I'll be even better when someone departs our graces in four days."

"What are you talking about, Jack? Heck, we made you a famous warden when you got to watch over Kane," Tom chortled.

"Yeah, thanks...for nothing."

"You are very welcome, Jack," Tom laughed.

"Have a seat guys, it's been a while", Jack said as he sat down and kicked his feet up on his desk. The two officers settled into the plush, velour chairs, and Jack gazed at Tom.

"You are giving me that look of yours," Tom said as he pulled some papers from the small portfolio he'd brought with him.

"Are you sure you want to do this, Tom. I mean, almost fifteen years is a lot of hate to have bottled up. Why not get someone with no ghosts from this to go and stir up the asshole? Let someone else go and feel out if he knows who the killer is."

Tom shook his head. "Thanks for the offer Jack, but like I have told Stan and everyone else for that matter, it's my job to do. If I can't handle this, I should have never become a cop."

"True, but Kane is such a venomous piece of garbage. It's hard to imagine him not getting off on the scenario of you coming to him four days before his demise and," as Jack put his fingers into the symbols of quote marks, "asking for his assistance. Besides, you know he's going to throw your dad and his mates' murder in your face. That's a lot of emotions to relive."

"I'll say it again Jack, it's my job to do. If I can't handle it, I should retire." Jack and Stan looked at each other and nodded their heads. "We're sorry we keep asking you, but just take it as two buddies who are concerned with your well being," Stan replied.

"No hassle gents, I appreciate the concern."

Jack pulled himself up straight in his chair, and stood again. "Enough said, then. Let's pay a visit to the demon."

"On your lead," Tom replied. The three men left the office, proceeded down the hall, and remained in silence until they came closer to the meeting area. Jack slowed to a snails pace. "I have placed Kane in a high security meeting cell. They'll be a plexiglass partition between the two of you. Stan and I will be in the monitoring room directly next door. I've also kept two guards to be with him at all times. Call me cautious, but I don't trust this guy until he is pronounced dead."

"I understand Jack, and I appreciate it. Believe me, I do."

"Good luck in there, Tom," Jack replied as he patted the Chief on the back. "God bless you for what you are about to face."

"Tom, you need us, remember, we're right in this room," Stan added as he pointed towards the adjacent steel door.

"Thanks guys." Tom took a deep breath. On the other side of this door sat the man who had altered a good portion of Tom's adult life. A flood of emotions rushed in on Tom as he grabbed the doorknob. He thought of his father, and then Gary. Visions of all the New York victims, Rob Pond, his good friend Luke, and the man who'd been a brother to him, Al Jeaneau, came in flashes. He opened the door, and as fast as the memories had been there, they disappeared, and there sat Kane.

Even behind the glass and dressed in his orange prison garb, he struck the same frightening aura surrounding him fifteen years earlier, when he used to walk the streets of Soho and the Village in his all black attire. It was the black attire that gave him the look of a western, modern day version of Jack the Ripper. His menacing look included the long, past shoulder length black hair, the long, black trench coat, the black boots, and a wide brimmed black hat. Stan Tilden used to tell Tom that he looked like "a Wild West, gunslinger from hell in that get-up. He scares the hell out people with that look, and then there's his eyes."

Ah, the eyes. Tom remembered the first time his eyes locked onto Kane's. They were cold and dark, almost the color of coal. No matter how you tried to avoid them, they followed your every move, and sent shivers down your spine. Not that Kane was unattractive, quite the contrary. It was this attractive nature he deployed so brilliantly when he was in the presence of people with influence. Flashing his perfect smile, getting a twinkle into those eyes, and displaying an excellent taste for the finer things in life, Kane's ranging knowledge and vocabulary sealed the favorable impression he left with many important people.

It was when Kane was in the World Church, you got your chance to see the real man in his dark, dismal world. It was as if the devil himself threw a ring of fire around his preacher when Kane began to disgorge his rhetoric of hatred. When Kane delivered his homilies, it was with such venom it felt like the man could end the world with one word from his lips. Needless to say, he was a very persuasive serpent when he had you in his clutches.

Kane looked a bit more bulked up than the rangy frame he had years ago. Solitary hours could do that to a man. A few push-ups and sit-ups can turn into thousands. Your cell and the few accessories with which it was equipped could transform into a gym quickly, when you had nothing but time on your hands. His forearms were quite muscular, but they were scarred with self-inflicted bite wounds. Tom heard that Kane went into this masochistic activity when he was confined solely to his Death Row cell after the failed uprising. It was Kane's punishment for being caught and failing to execute what he thought was God's master plan. He had failed to save the planet from the abnormal.

His hair was still long, but it was now peppered with streaks of gray. When he looked up to observe Tom standing at the door, he broke into his handsome grin, but as Tom noticed, the eyes remained dark as death. Tom surmised that Kane was going to hang on to every ounce of hate his body could store. There would be no repentant soul in Martin "Lucifer" Kane. The reaper would die, damning the earth to hell for not heeding his words.

"Detective Miller, or should I say, Chief Miller? You have gone far. Please, sit down." The eyes narrowed in on Tom. "The years have been well to you, Thomas." Tom nodded in acknowledgement, but still did not say a word. "So, I hear that you are visiting with the Reverend to confer about my prophecy becoming fulfilled. It's glorious, isn't it? The Millennium will start off with a cleansing spirit, ridding God's planet of the infidels."

"It's quite interesting to hear you say that Martin, because many God fearing people feel the same way about you leaving us."

Kane began to laugh mightily. "Touché, Thomas, touché. So good to see all the latest sacrifices to our Lord have not dampened your humorous side."

"Is that what we call them? Sacrifices?"

"Why, absolutely Thomas. My disciples are sacrificing the Millennium infidels so God will spare your planet. The good people of God's land deserve that much."

"So, tell me about your disciples."

"What is there to know?"

"Well, I hear a certain Reverend Kane is pulling the string on the "sacrifices" from his Death Row cell. So, let's talk. Is it a possibility?"

"Thomas, people give me way too much credit. It's just like when they tried giving me credit for killing your father."

"Didn't you?"

"I think we have both known the answer to that one, don't we? Your father, talented, but flawed in his lifestyle as he was, would have been such a trophy to rest my laurels upon. But, alas I was not so lucky to reach him first. You see, Thomas, in some cases I am just God's messenger to the flock." Kane then leaned lose to the glass separating the two men. "But, on other occasions, I am his executioner," he added in a low growl.

He's still trying to put the fear in me. Take your best shot, Martin. "The line separating them is a very thin one, isn't it Reverend?"

"As it is with many things in life. I am sure you are finding that out again. I hear my disciple in New Hope is very precise in their manner. My compliments to this talented individual."

"You are not as satisfied with your Trenton disciple?"

"My disciple? Jerome Jones is a freak of nature!" Kane scoffed. "I applaud his murderous side towards homosexuals, but his morals, in general, are questionable."

"A lesson in ethics from a ritual murderer? Isn't that a twist? Next, they'll be sending me to Rome to be trained by the Pope in the fine art of terrorism."

"You never know," Kane replied as a smile creased his face. "Anyway, Jones is a warped individual. He is unsure of his sexuality. He is also unsure of his responsibility to God. He pollutes the streets of poor areas with his narcotics."

"Alas, one thing he is sure of, Thomas, is the notoriety and infamy he'll receive from these killings. He craves fame from these actions, and in the same breath he mocks God with his lust for fame. I knew this seventeen years ago when he appeared on the steps of my Soho church. I knew back then he would have to depart, but apparently he still has the charm to make the sheep follow."

"It seems as if you think capturing Jones will prove insignificant compared to our other individual."

"Jones is a perfectly engineered creature of all that is wrong with modern society. He will just jump on the next big thing coming along. It is why I cannot admire someone like him. Besides, Jones will not be of this life for long."

"Really? Do we know this, or are we speculating?"

"Thomas," Kane laughed, "when your life is spent behind bars and in between cinderblocks, everything becomes speculation."

"Point well taken."

"Jones will die soon, but not at your hands. He will self-destruct from his own insanity. He will die a glorious death because all he knows in life is to live for notoriety."

"What about your disciple? No thoughts on the outcome of this individual?"

"It's not as easy to decipher as Jones' because I do not know this person."

"I'd like to show you some photographs of the unknown murderers victims."

"By all means," Kane replied, relishing the thought of viewing the deeds. Tom walked over to the window slot, where a guard took the envelope from him and examined its contents. The guard then placed the pictures in front of Kane. Kane viewed the pictures with an almost sadistic pleasure. "Fabulous, unbelievable. This is sheer perfection. The black one, is that your gay, cop friend?"

"Oh, so you know about that?" Tom asked, trying not to look shocked.

"I know much about everything," Kane said slyly.

"Fill me in, then."

"I know he was in a great deal of pain and anguish. That's enough to please me." The vicious smile appeared again, and he began to chuckle, but Tom did not even blink. He would be damned if he would let Kane get to him. "I'm glad to see your are enjoying this so much, Reverend."

"Now Thomas, there is no need to be sarcastic. I am just overwhelmed at the likeness to my work. Why, it's as if they had been in the rooms with me taking notes while I performed my sacrifices."

"Maybe they were, Reverend."

"Oh Thomas, I wouldn't be careless enough to leave a witness. Why, if you and Detective Tilden hadn't been so savvy as to peruse the tunnels, I may still be executing the heathen hordes as we speak."

"Well, all I can say is thank God for being savvy."

"Yes, thank God indeed," Kane said coldly as he looked down at the hand missing the two fingers. "Well, the pictures are fascinating, but I don't know who's doing this. I would love to meet them before I perish."

"Why, so you could compare notes?"

"Thomas, again with that wit of yours. Let me ask you something now? Did all of this bring back memories for you?"

"Yes, it did," Tom replied gravely.

"Did you notice anything was amiss with the sacrifices of the New Hope disciple?"

"As a matter of fact, yes. The depth of the knife wounds seemed to be deeper and more forceful."

"More than mine were?" Kane asked with a tone of slight indignation. "Well, someone's hatred of homosexuals runs deeper than mine."

"I would gather so."

"What conclusion does that bring you to, Thomas?"

"One is, you have a very willing disciple who exacts your so called mercy even better than you do."

"But, why?"

"Years of built up hatred, I suppose. Now, they have an outlet to release it."

"If my prophecy could have such an effect on individuals, than I am truly impressed by my power over people."

"Or, your power over their vulnerabilities," Tom said low, and more to himself than Kane. It sparked a thought that had not seriously crossed his mind yet.

"What was that, Thomas?"

"You have power over their vulnerabilities. If the individual was a homosexual, and they hated themselves for it, wouldn't they hate other homosexuals even more?"

"An awe inspiring thought, Thomas. What better way to relieve the guilt of dishonoring God? Sacrifice the ones who made you what you are. Brilliant deduction, if you are correct. Now comes the problematic part of your assumption. You reside in a town that has an abundant homosexual community!" This amused Kane to the point of hysterics.

"Thomas," Kane mused as he regained his composure, "you realize, of course, almost every homosexual has had this kind of rage against one's self."

"Or so you say."

"No, I think we both can acknowledge its existence. It's a hatred of knowing that all they stand for is physically, and most important, morally wrong in the eyes of God fearing souls, and God himself."

"In your mind, I guess this made them an easy target?"

"In theory, I suppose it makes sense. What made them easy was their susceptible nature to being manipulated."

"Really? I would think that because of the abuse they faced from their lifestyle you would find them hard to manipulate." Tom could sense his last comment hit a nerve with Kane.

"What garbage. Many of them take on the mantra of it won't happen to them. Whether it's with the gay bashing, transmitting their perverted virus."

"AIDS kills more heterosexuals per year, Reverend."

"Please, go ahead and believe your decadent government. We of the cross and the way know the truth. Homosexual loving liberals like this President and his sick, bitch of a wife parade around their statistics. They make it all sound so correct to be queer."

"You make it sound as if the whole world will become homosexual, Reverend." Tom was hoping engaging in this conversation might loosen some information out of Kane. It was a long shot, but one worth pursuing.

"Hasn't it already started, Thomas? Politicians condone their behavior. Television and the movies glamorize their lifestyles to impressionable children whom are not monitored by the parents. Some churches even perform same-sex marriages. How quaint. It is such a useless society that we live in. I wish I were amongst the populous now. I would be glorified and vilified in this cult-of-personality society."

"Hell, Kane, they would probably give you your own show," Tom said with a degree of contempt.

"Couldn't you imagine it, Thomas? Then you could have all been witness to the brilliant mapping out of my seven sacrifices. The whole world could have seen me lurking through the dark alleys of the Village. The background music they could have played while building up to the crescendo, why, it would have been beautiful. I always had incredible music running through my mind while I did God's work."

"You should have seen me peering inside the windows of their domiciles, perching on their fire escapes, or standing outside their doorways at four in the morning. I used to watch them making phone calls, or doing their daily chores. I used to watch them making love in their sick, disgusting ways. It was horrific to view, but it built up my hatred inside. That, and the music."

He looked at Tom with those deep-set, dark eyes. The sadistic grin appeared again. "You should have witnessed the expression on the face of your father's lover when I sacrificed him in their recording studio. I believe Hector Berlioz's, 'Symphony Fantastique', was running through my mind. Have you ever heard Berlioz, Thomas?"

"Yes, I have heard his work. I cannot say that if he were alive, he would appreciate the way in which you've perverted his beautiful music."

"On the contrary, I think any artist would take pleasure in watching the emotions their music could evoke. His dark, forbidding sounds for death, or his triumphant finale, which makes you think of God winning the battle against evil. What a beautiful synchronization of sound it created when I plunged the knife into Gary Johan's spine." This thought made Kane start to laugh hysterically. "Imagine it, Thomas," he seethed.

Tom could feel his blood boiling. He could imagine it all.

"You should have witnessed the fear, the pleading in his eyes, right before I slit his throat. I used to love watching them choke on their own blood. It was so empowering."

Tom decided it was a good time to shift the direction of the conversation. No one in the viewing room could believe the composure Tom was commanding over his emotions. Most men would have been broken by Kane's sadistic nature, but Tom never strayed from his plan of attack. He took a breath and continued. "Did you have any homosexuals in your congregation years ago, Reverend?"

"Yes, quite a few, actually." His eyes lit up at the thought of it. "They came to repent. You could see they despised who they were so much. You see, Thomas, you may be on the right track with your theory. That is why I liked you and Tilden so much, such great intellect. No hard feelings about the knife wound, Stanley!" Kane exclaimed as he waved towards the mirrored glass. Tom looked at Kane in wonderment. "As I conveyed before, Thomas, there are a multitude of things I just happen to know."

Tom stared straight into the face of darkness. "Why stir things up with your prophecy? Why not repent, and pray the Millennium will be a peaceful time of existence for mankind?"

The reaper looked ready to become hysterical at the talk of such naiveté on Tom's part, but his eyes quickly grew cold again. "Do you think it will end with my prophecy, Thomas? This is the only the beginning of what I refer to as 'The Whole Prophecy'. Would you like to hear more?"

"Color me curious, Reverend. Preach on."

"Much of this, your Detective Tilden heard fifteen years ago, when he came to my church under the guise of being a possible parishioner. Thomas, my first prophecy is a small taste of what its to come. What is taking place now will end when I die the death of man's world. A small semblance of peace will come to your world for the next few years. Then, the 'Whole Prophecy' will take its hold."

"Take heed Thomas, in your beloved city of New York, will such horror take place. The skies over the city will grow dark, and death, so swift and sudden, will take place. The river called Hudson will overflow with the blood of the dead." Kane's voice began to boom as it had when he was master of the pulpit. "Lucifer" was back.

"Panic in the free world shall occur. Needing someone to blame, we will allow the Hebrew flock to annihilate the Arab devils, and then we will witness the area be engulfed by flame from Russia!"

"It sounds like Nostradamus, revisited," Tom chimed in.

"Oh, Thomas, Nostradamus did not have a clue. If Russia had turned their cold, inhumane hearts back to the Blessed Virgin, they may have been spared. Instead, the encircled camps of the Mongols will turn on them, and tens of millions between both lands will perish instantly. Europe, and its alliances on other continents, will lie in blood soaked ruins, and your beloved America will not be spared either. God is tired of your self-righteousness. You bastardize his name so easily. He has given you a land of plenty, and you have polluted it with your greed and sick behavior. Los Angeles, and other major port cities will be annihilated. New York will grow dark again. Famine and diseases will spread worldwide."

"When the dust has settled and God feels at one with the earth again, one from this land, in your beloved city, will rise from the ashes like a phoenix, to continue my work. He will rid the planet of the remaining infidels and heathen hordes. The world will be in awe of his eloquence and the power he wields. The good people left will flock to him, and then they will aid him in this elimination. The new world will live in peace with the remnants of his city at the epicenter of world power." Upon saying this, Kane lowered his head, and began to pray.

Tom took a minute to let the gravity of Kane's words take hold before he spoke. "Reverend, you are a brilliant but very sick man," Tom said as Kane looked up again. "You have too much time to contemplate things which will not happen."

"You may be right, Thomas. I assume you are still a God-fearing man?" Tom nodded in response. "Pray it does happen. Good, but misguided people such as yourself, will have a place in the new world."

"In your version of the world? Count me out. I'll continue to keep my faith in God. Eventually, we will all find a way to coexist."

Kane began to sigh. "Thomas, I grow tired. If there is nothing more?"

"No, nothing more, Reverend. I think you have been helpful in your own, unusual way."

Kane chuckled. "I guess that I will say thanks for the compliment." When Kane stood up, he continued looking at Tom. "I know you won't believe this, but I did feel sorry for the loss of your father. He was a brilliant, but misguided man. I pray for his soul every now and then. I can tell you this much, that, in my vision, you'll find his murderer and the new disciple are one in the same."

"I guess I will thank you again for your words. I can't say that I fully understand you. You are exceptionally gifted, but to me, you used those gifts for evil. In a few days, you will pass on. Aren't you sorry at all?"

Kane turned and walked towards the partition again. "As you said, in a few days, I will die at the hands of man. Are you at all apologetic for that?"

"You were judged by a panel of your peers to meet your fate. They were people who respected the life God gave them, and they mourned the lives you took away."

"Judge, jury, executioner."

"Yes, I think they chose the right course of action, Reverend."

"Thomas, I think you just answered for the both of us. I am not in the least bit repentant for smiting the heathen hordes. You are bound by the laws of man, but for one, glorious year, I was directly bound by the law of God."

Kane leaned near the glass again, face to face with his captor. He looked very much like the wild- eyed man of fifteen years prior. "For a year, I was judge, jury, and executioner."

As Kane walked away, he turned again to smile at Tom, and then he was gone. In a few days, he'd be gone for good, Tom thought. He stood up and entered the viewing room. Sweat was pouring from his body while Stan and Jack looked on.

"Are you alright, buddy?" Stan asked.

Tom lit a Marlboro, and deeply inhaled the tobacco smoke. "I'm fine, pal."

Jack looked shell-shocked. "Stan, that prophecy crap. Did he really say all of that?"

"Word for creepy word. The only thing changed was the year amounts, but it's right on the money from when he said it would still occur. It still gives me the shakes hearing it because that animal makes it sound so believable." Tom looked at both gentlemen. "He makes it sound believable because it isn't so far fetched."

"Whoa', bud. You, of all people, are not buying into Kane's shit, are you?"

"Not buying into it Stan, but I'm just coming to the unfortunate realization there are a multitude of bitter and wayward people out there, who are easily swayed by all their anger. Kane, in a perverse way, is giving them that hope."

"Gents, I'll stick with my faith in the Almighty!" Jack Smith exclaimed.

"Me too," said Stan.

"Same here. I just pray for one thing."

"What would that be, Tom?" Jack asked.

"That on the stroke of midnight, January 1, 2000, God has mercy on our souls for killing a madman."

CHAPTER 18

Tom said goodbye to Stan at the airport. It was the kind of goodbye making you believe you'd be seeing each other again very soon. On the plane ride back, Tom started jotting down some mental notes. He began by surmising the possibility of the murderer being a homosexual individual was not that far fetched a prospect. He'd have John and Zoul run some random profiles of the towns inhabitants through the states Criminal Data Base. This would have to be done with the utmost secrecy. If Ward ever found out what they were up to, he could turn the whole of the borough against Tom and his officers in a heartbeat.

He also thought about the Ecstasy connection. He didn't know if Ink was totally on target, but some of his previous tip-off's were of solid quality. Maybe, he could get the Fed boys to follow that trail. Tom figured if he could keep the mayor and the Feds happy and informed, they would leave him to his own devices. That would alleviate Tom of two problematic situations.

With as much turmoil as his town was in, he was happy to be going home. New Hope felt like a safe haven after being exposed again to the likes of Martin Kane. Could the madman be correct in his assumptions of the world's future, or was it just the sick ranting of a delusional man? Close to fifteen years in prison had done nothing to bury his hatred. Tom thought for a moment of how sad it all was. Kane could at times show what an incredibly intelligent individual he was capable of being, but somewhere in his thought patterns, the evil rotting away his soul started to take control. It was a jolt to the senses of anyone who had encountered the two sides of Reverend Kane, because it made you realize exactly what the man was and what he had been capable of accomplishing.

He started to think about how Kane had all but dismissed Jerome Jones as nothing more than a glory hound. Jones would have been quite perturbed to find out the master was not impressed with him one iota. The master was, however, impressed with the New Hope murderer, and this made Tom worrisome. If this person was as crafty as Kane had been, Tom, the Feds, and the town could be in for a long, hard winter.

He began to think about Debbie, his son Edward, his friends, and the townspeople of this beloved burgh'. He thought again of the prophecy. Could anyone really predict what was to happen? It was hard for Tom to imagine everything he'd known in life could disappear in an instant. What could make someone think of such deep, dark horrors? When he was a young man, Tom enjoyed reading books about prophecies. He always found them much more amusing than they were alarming. Why, then, could he not shake off the possibility that Kane may be correct?

It began to make Tom question God for an instant. Why would you allow such evil to happen, Lord? Haven't we seen enough horror in the past hundred years? He caught himself before his questioning turned into doubting. It also gave Tom a chance to reflect on his questions. God, he contemplated, always has a master plan for everything. We may not agree with it or like it, but if we truly trust in good over evil, we tried to believe in it. As always, Tom would place his faith in this higher power, and not in the likes of charlatans such as Martin Kane.

The internalizing made a somewhat boring flight turn into a quick one. Tom hustled from the plane, and made haste to his vehicle. He made equally quick work of leaving the Trenton-Mercer Airport far behind. He was soon hustling down Route 29, making all the scenery and small towns between Trenton and Lambertville but a memory. The sight of Lambertville, and the Free Bridge into New Hope made Tom Miller smile. For all of its recent tragedies, he was still happy to be here.

A compact disc of Billie Holliday pulsed through the Explorers' sound system. As he bounded through the curves along River and Sugan Road, he was soon on Chapel Road. He lurched the vehicle into the driveway and his smile grew wider when he saw Debbie pull back the curtains to see who was approaching. Upon entering the house, Tom could smell the wood burning in the den fireplace, and he could hear the kettle whistling atop the kitchen stove. When he entered the brightly lit eating area, he saw Debbie removing the kettle from the burner, and pouring the hot beverage into two mugs. His senses soon became aroused by the smell of his favorite lemon square cookies baking in the oven.

Debbie ran over and greeted Tom with a warm hug and kiss when she turned to see him standing there. Tom reciprocated, and they walked over to the table to settle in for a warm drink and some dessert. As they did so, Debbie cautiously asked Tom how the meeting went.

Tom began to fill her in on everything from Kane's appearance, to his fiery rhetoric. He also told her of Kane's views about the new killers, about having no remorse for the murders that he'd committed, and finally, he told her about Kane's prophecies. When he told her of Kane's insane predictions, Tom noticed tears in Debbie's eyes, especially when he recanted the 'Whole Prophecy'. A few times, he stopped and asked her if she wanted Tom to continue. Debbie said she wanted to hear it all. She wanted to hear all the insanity and gore filled details Kane could deliver. It was the least she could do. After all, this madman had put Tom, Debbie and their family through so much pain. Fifteen years later, Kane's words of hatred were now inflicting that same hurt to their extended family.

When Tom was finished, Debbie just stared and shook her head. "Do you know something, Tommy? I almost feel sorry for Kane. I mean, a mind so intelligent, but so warped by evil. You start to think of all the good things a mind like his could have accomplished if it had not been tainted, and it just makes you become so disheartened. So much of his time was wasted on hate."

"I felt the same way quite a few times as I spoke to him."

"Did you get any feel on who may have killed your father?"

Tom looked at his wife, and with a slightly disgusted tone replied in the negative. "I think, for the present time we should go with the belief that someone from Kane's Soho church committed the deed. In fact, after what little bites Kane did offer up, I'm positive that our New Hope murderer and my father's are one in the same."

"After all this time? What kind of mind could possibly work like that?" Debbie asked with a degree of disgust in her voice.

"Some serial, or ritual killers, are very methodical, honey. Ritual killers are a little more disorganized in their thought patterns. They are more apt to begin leaving evidence behind at each crime scene. Kane was much more like a serial killer. He only left what he wanted you to find. This individual seems to be a mixture of both categories. That could be a very hard combination to track down. Anything is possible to trigger this ones' dormant aggressions. They could strike again in days, or maybe, not for years."

"Well, call me the eternal optimist, but I have faith you will find this one and Jones. You will bring both of them to justice."

"Thanks, honey," Tom said as he took another sip of tea. "Let's change the subject a little. How did Phil hold up today?"

"Remarkably well, Tommy. There were a few times that he began to well up with tears, or cry out, but he would regain his composure rather quickly." She then began to tell Tom about the jazz musicians that had showed up for the funeral. The Marsalis brothers, Chuck Mangione, Cassandra Wilson, and many other notables in the business had traveled to pay respect to their fallen friend and Phil Antos. Rob Pagano and the rest of the force had done an admirable job of dealing with the throngs of mourners and curiosity seekers that had assembled outside of the Old Stone Church, and the rest of Main Street.

After the burial, Phil opened up the "A" Train for a few hours, and held a private, impromptu jam session being held in Luke's honor. John Boyle had given Phil the go ahead, since the investigation of the Train was now completed. The only part of the building John did keep sealed and guarded was the kitchen where Luke had been murdered. Phil had the food catered for the event, and it soon became a glorious testimonial to the love people had for Lucas Stone when the musicians began to play.

Debbie and everyone else had said it was a much-needed diversion from all the events occurring in the town recently, and Tom agreed wholeheartedly. "I only wish I had been there to support Phil."

"Everyone understood. They knew where you were." Debbie said many of the musicians had asked for him. Quite a number of them remembered Tom being a permanent fixture at Edgar and Gary's studio in New York.

"In all honesty, I'd have rather not have been at either place today, Deb." He paused for a moment to light a cigarette. "I don't know how many more people we can lose this way before I break," he said as he exhaled the smoke. "I another day, I am burying a man who was like a brother to me. This is really starting to wear me down, hon."

"I know it is, Tom", Debbie said as she held his strong hands. "You will find the strength to endure this. You always have, and you always will."

Tom's eyes met with Debbie's and they began to kiss each other softly. As Tom began to caress her body slowly, he began to think about how much he loved her and needed her. Through the years, she had been a major part of Tom's ability to have a strong will. She was his rock.

Debbie pulled slowly away and smiled at her husband. "You'd better get some rest, Tommy. You have a big day tomorrow with the 'G-man'."

"The 'G-man'?" Tom laughed out loud. "I haven't heard that since the seventies!"

"Well, you know us old hippies die hard. Do you have any idea what this fellow is like?"

"John rousted up some information on his background. I was reading the file on the plane trip. It sounds like he's an old timer. He came up the ranks through the Kennedy era. You know, very idealistic, very principled. He apparently became a bit jaded with the Bureaus' tactics during the Civil Rights period."

"He supposedly cracked a big case involving the murder of a black rights activist in Levittown during the early sixties. After the case, he apparently voiced his distaste of their policies, and the Bureau kind of bounced him around. John wrote that the FBI kept him on, but it was with a lot of coaxing from some very influential friends up on Capitol Hill. The Bureau was starting to be cautious of him because he had a nose for pinpointing corruption."

"And, this is a bad thing?"

"Apparently, it is when you are pointing the finger at your bosses," Tom responded coyly.

"Ah, I see. This sounds like your kind of guy."

"I hope so, Deb. I really do."

CHAPTER 19

The morning sun peeked over the horizon and made the rippled water of the Delaware River glisten like diamonds. As Agent Sam Tunney peered out from the windows of the Logan Inn's dining room and viewed the pleasant scenery, he sighed.

"Is everything to your liking, sir?" the young waitress asked the elder gentleman.

"Yes, very much so," replied Sam. "The meal was just perfect."

"Would you like some more coffee?"

"Ah, that would hit the spot, young lady. Could you also get me another bowl of your fresh fruit, please?"

"No problem, sir."

"Could you also have Chief Miller and Trooper Boyle seated here when they arrive? I am waiting to meet with them."

"Yes sir, I will. I am sure they'll be here soon", the young woman replied with a radiant smile. "They do love our breakfasts."

"As well they should," Sam replied in kind. Sam brought his attention back to the morning paper. The big news in the Gazette was, of course, Lucas Stone's funeral and the musician get-together taking place afterwards. The columnist, Mary McGuigan, wrote a retrospect on the life and accomplishments of the much-loved resident. From all that was written throughout the front pages, Sam Tunney could tell Luke's death was a bitter pill for this town to swallow.

Mary McGuigan had also written an article on the upcoming funeral of the town's other favorite son, Sergeant Al Jeaneau. Editorials were also written about how the town needed to keep supporting the police and the state troopers in their efforts to apprehend this evil murderer. Quite a few of them especially endorsed the individual efforts of Tom Miller and John Boyle, for keeping the town on an even keel. The editors knew the recent events could have easily turned New Hope into a volatile tinderbox of emotions if not for the work of these two men.

If there were any detractors or rabble-rousers, it was hard to get a good read of their existence. Because it was only his first day in town yesterday, Sam believed his observations over the next few days would show if any of them did. He began to think about how diverse this area had become, and also how people were much more tolerant of lifestyles not particularly conforming to societies "norms". Thirty-seven years ago, and just a half-hour removed from the winding roads of Route 32, a prominent gay businessman, a black, homosexual officer, and a police chief who's father was a well known, homosexual musician, would have probably all been hung from the highest trees in town. The gray haired, well dressed man of sixty-two, knew all too well the Bucks County of his younger days.

In the early sixties, President John Kennedy called on America's youth to perform a service for their country. The highly idealistic Sam Tunney was already doing just that, and his superiors were taking notice of the young man's skills. At the age of twenty-five, and into his second year of service with the FBI, Sam would make many strides with his ambitious nature.

Sam had just settled in behind his desk one early July morning in 1962, when his superiors paid him a visit. Sam was told none other than J. Edgar Hoover wanted to meet the young agent. Sam was astonished. He had never dreamed of seeing Hoover, let alone conversing with the famed lawman. Yet, there he was in Hoover's office, being told by probably the most powerful man in America, that Sam's country needed him. Hoover told Sam of how the Bureau was keeping a watchful eye on the black rights movement. He also told Sam of the Bryant family.

Steve Bryant was a black laborer in the blast furnaces of the United States Steel Company's, Fairless Works. Bryant, it seemed, was quite a rarity in many ways. He was one of the only blacks to be hired into the massive steel mill encompassing six thousand acres of land alongside the Delaware River. He also made it a point to visit the poor, black neighborhoods, in the lower end of the county. It was there he could be seen, by friend or by foe, spreading the word of the movement to achieve equality for black people. He and his family also became the only blacks to reside in the new, suburban community of Levittown, which was located but a few miles from the steel plant. None of these accomplishments made Steve Bryant a very well liked man in the rural, and vastly white populated area of Bucks County, Pennsylvania.

Levittown was a suburban community built in the early 1950's by William Levitt. The premise of Levitt's dream was to giving returning GI's and their families an affordable home of their own, instead of moving back to crowded city apartments. The easily maintained, cookie-cutter homes and the desire for their children growing up in a better, suburban environment, was an easy sell for the masses flocking to this locale. It was the pristine, dream community to live in, if you were white. Levitt, did not go out of his way to attract black home ownership. For the next ten years, neither, for that matter, did the towns' residents.

It helped explain why two months after moving into their home, the Bryant's awoke to the sound of breaking glass, and the smell of smoke. They had been the victims of bottles being smashed in their yard, the mailmen refusing to deliver any letters there, and many times, the sanitation department would not remove their garbage. A few neighbors did try to help the Bryant's in any way they could, but they were soon victims of the same hooligan acts. Anything and everything was tried, including a cross burning taking place in their yard, to rid the town of this family. None of these actions would deter Steve Bryant. He fought valiantly for his country in World War II, and nobody gave a damn when he returned. He fought hard to get his job in the blast furnaces of U.S. Steel. It was one of the best paying jobs in the area at the time, and it made people hate him even more. He endured all the indignities being thrown his way. He endured all the threats he received for just wanting to be treated as an equal, a human being. This was his last stand. Steve Bryant would be damned if these individuals would run him out of his piece of the 'American Dream'.

On the night of July 21, 1962, Steve Bryant's dream would become a nightmare. As the fire from the liquid inside the broken glass began to rage throughout the residence, Steve bravely gathered up his family. While he opened the carport door and led them towards safety, rifle shots rang out. Steve lay motionless as his family and a few neighbors looked on in horror.

Steve Bryant, combat veteran, mill worker, Civil Rights advocate, and father
of three was dead from a gunshot wound to the head, at the age of thirty-
two. The assailants fled and Alicia Bryant held her husband looking on as
the flames engulfed Steve's small piece of the 'American Dream'.

Sam Tunney was about to be thrust into the belly of the beast. He
was handed a no-win situation, and he knew why. No veteran agent would
even want to touch a case having such volatile implications if the killers
were caught. It could mean following a trail leading them straight to the
doorsteps of some very prominent Pennsylvanians, if they were not careful.

Sam Tunney was a young agent whose ambition had apparently
made him a threat to some people in the Bureau. His bosses figured the best
way to sour his disposition would be to give him a case such as this one.
They surmised that if the townspeople, the crooked cops, or the Klan didn't
sour him on being too ambitious, the politics of the case certainly would.
Sam was a man cut from the same mold as Steve Bryant, though. The moral
conviction to achieve some semblance of justice for the Bryant family would
not make him bow out easily. Sam would get these killers.

During the ensuing summer months, he would triumphantly close
the case. He received commendations from a thrilled Attorney General,
Robert Kennedy, and his brother, President John F. Kennedy. He also
received them from a much less enthralled J. Edgar Hoover.

Levittown in the present day was a much more diverse community,
and was still a very good place to bring up a family. It was what Sam had
hoped the whole country would become in his earlier, idealistic days. Much
had changed with the world since 1962, and with Sam's views as well. Even
with all of the progress made, much had not changed with the Millennium

approaching. Sam had been jaded by enough years of the Bureau's bullshit to know protecting certain races and lifestyles from harm still didn't mean a damn thing to the government, which is why Sam was back in Bucks County again.

Like many agents from his time period, he was close to retiring. He had no patience with the Bureau's policies anymore. In Sam's mind, since Reagan had left office, the FBI and the CIA had become a joke. Both of them had the bite of a toothless tiger. The Bureau had botched so many times under Clinton's reign, and the CIA had just as tarnished a record since the collapse of the former Soviet Union. It worried Sam, because he thought the agency needed to be even more vigilant without a strong Russia.

On more than one occasion, Sam told his superiors that the lax attitude towards terrorist organizations "will come back to bite us in the ass. Satellite countries inside the old Soviet Union are selling their nuclear material to anyone who can put bread on their tables." His superiors weren't unaware of this problem. They just didn't need some rabble rouser from the Cold War era being the ringleader of the crusade to save the world. To them, Tunney was a problem they needed to finally phase out. For this reason, they figured the Kane copycats were the perfect assignment to send him on. Their rationale was one of, out of sight, out of mind. The case would probably turn into a wild goose chase which would keep Agent Tunney very busy, and out of the Bureau's hair. Sam was keen to many things, and he knew the Bureau's motives. He would either retire from it in glory, or he'd blunder the case and not apprehend anyone. He would then be replaced by a young computer geek with no street smarts. It was how Sam referred to many of the new agents.

Sam had just started to eat again, when he saw Chief Miller and Trooper Boyle enter the dining room. Sam had always prided himself on his ability to measure a person upon his first glance. Trooper Boyle definitely looked like a no-nonsense guy to him. The way he walked showed an air of supreme confidence. Tom Miller, he noticed, had a fire in his eyes. It was the kind of look that made Sam realize this man would not rest until justice had been served. My kind of guys, he thought.

When they approached the table, Sam stood up and smiled. "Trooper Boyle, Chief Miller, it's a pleasure to meet you. Please, sit and enjoy some breakfast."

Both men smiled in turn, and sat down. "I see you've already been witness to the Logan's great breakfasts?"

"Ah, yes I have Chief. I was lucky enough to enjoy a fine dinner across the bridge at the Lambertville Station last night. Fine food there also, gents."

"I think you'll enjoy them here as well," John added.

"I'm sure I will." The waitress had returned by now, and she looked in Tom and John's direction. "The usual, gentlemen?" she asked with her glistening smile still intact.

"Yes Vicki, the usual," John piped up.

"Vicki, may we have an ashtray here also, as long as you don't mind, Agent Tunney?"

Sam put up his hands. "I don't mind at all, Chief. Actually, I could use one myself, if you don't mind."

"Breakfast and an ashtray. You've got it, Chief," Vicki replied as she turned from the table.

As Tom handed him a cigarette, Sam looked at the two officers. "No need to be formal. From now on, please call me Sam, gentlemen." As Tom lit the Marlboro for Sam, and one for himself, he replied. "Well, since you're going on a first name basis, please, call me Tom. I'm sure John won't mind being called by his first name, either. Will you, buddy?"

"No, not at all, Tommy. Please do, Sam."

As Agent Tunney inhaled the smoke, he seemed to settle in to his chair more comfortably. "Nothing better than a good smoke after you finish a good meal." He glanced over to see Tom and John sitting patiently and waiting for Sam to speak again.

"I see the ball has been placed in my end of the court, as well it should be. Well, enough talk of food and tobacco. You want to know what kind of roadblocks the old Fed agent is going to place in your way. Is that a fair assumption?"

"You could say that, Sam," John replied.

"Fair enough, guys. I know you've done your homework on me as well as I've done mine on you." Sam took another drag from the cigarette as the waitress approached with an ashtray and the officers' meals. "I've spent a lot of years within the Bureau. I have consistently told the high command, the local force is usually the most dedicated group you will find to correct problems within their own community. They know the citizenry and their backgrounds. They know the lay of the land. I have always been an ardent believer, the Bureau serves everyone's purpose better when they become a support vehicle for the local authorities."

"I think the only time the Bureau should come to the forefront is when the local authorities have proven their gross inability to handle a case, or the local force is under suspicion of being involved in any wrongdoing. Knowing both of your gentlemen's track records, I don't believe either of these situations will arise."

Tom and John looked at each other in astonishment. "So, basically Sam, you are at our beck and call?" John asked.

"At your service, John Boyle," Sam chirped. "My two freckle faced, college boys and I will support you with manpower, firepower, or brainpower. All you need to do is ask."

"Well Sam, if our working relationship remains this way, I think we'll get along just fine," Tom replied as he extended his hand across the table.

"Gentlemen, you and I are a dying breed," Sam said with a serious look. "We are men with book smarts, and a keen, natural instinct for problem solving. The new breed definitely has the book knowledge, but overall, they don't have a lick of common sense. Put them in front of a computer, they are geniuses. Put them into the field, and they wander around like sheep without the shepherd. I would not, for this reason especially, want to lose your trust. I'm too damn old to take a bullet because some zit faced kid has his head up his ass out there."

Tom and John began to chuckle. "We can relate, Sam", John said while draining the last drops from his coffee cup. "We've been there."

"I'm sure you have, gents, but I understand you have a rarity under your command, John. I've heard about one, Trooper Razoul Terrant."

"What about him, Sam?" John asked.

"I've heard he's a computer whiz kid, and his field skills are exceptional. A rare find, indeed. I think from what I've heard, the kid may help us immeasurably with this case."

"Aye, he is a natural. He's one of those Pitt whiz kids."

"Ah, a Pittsburgh boy?"

"Clairton, actually," Tom added.

"Clairton. He's from big steel country and the Mon Valley. He must have done a good share of hunting out there when he was young."

"I have heard he did a fine share of it, Sam," John remarked.

"I hear you are also employing an up-and-comer, Tom. I believe her name is Officer Gates?"

Tom and John both began to shake their heads. "You really have done your homework, Sam."

"Tom, I do like to make a point of knowing exactly who I am dealing with."

"Well, to answer your question, Officer Jenn Gates is a very smart and capable individual. She possesses many of the qualities Sergeant Jeaneau had."

"She sounds like a keeper. Well, it sounds like you have two naturals, gentlemen. Maybe they could teach my bookworms a thing or two in the field."

"Um, maybe they could", John surmised.

"Well good, because they may get their chance tonight."

Tom and John gawked at the agent quizzically. "Tonight, Sam?"

"Yes, Tom. I mean, besides meeting your acquaintance, I wanted to include the both of you and Chief Townsend in on the possible apprehension of our man in Trenton."

"Jones!" Tom blurted. "Do you think you've finally got a lead on his whereabouts? No offense, but he's been eluding you fellows for quite a few years. What makes you think you'll get him now?"

"Can I be brutally honest, Tom?" Sam inquired as he extinguished the cigarette.

"Go ahead."

"Before Jones was acknowledged as one of the Kane copycats, the Bureau didn't exactly break their backs to catch this nut. They were too busy checking him out for other reasons."

"Ah, I see. Only after a few gays turn up dead, the Feds decide to pursue this? If they got caught sleeping on this it would be bad P.R. for the Bureau, ay' Sam?"

"Extremely bad, Tom. You know how much the Bureau worries now about bad publicity. They've been blemished on their record just a bit, lately."

"Oh, we know how much they worry about their image, believe me!" Tom replied snidely.

Agent Tunney smirked in response to Tom's criticism, but his demeanor quickly became more serious. "Gentlemen, now you can see why I want nothing more to do with the Bureau. This Administration worries more about damage control than it does about getting to the root of the problem. If we would go back to doing that, there's a damn good chance the subway under the Trade Center wouldn't have been bombed. There is also a chance Waco or Oklahoma City would have never happened, either. But, who is this old man to say, right?"

"No, Sam. I'd have to say I can't disagree with your assumptions," John replied as he downed another cup of coffee and polished of his eggs.

"Excuse me, but would you gentlemen care for anything else?" the young waitress inquired of three men. All shook their heads in the negative, and Tom told Vicki to just send him the check.

"Excuse me, young lady," Sam chimed in. "The check won't be necessary. Just add the tab to my room bill, and here is something for being such a wonderful hostess," Sam said as he slipped her a thirty dollar tip.

"Thank you, Agent Tunney!" she beamed as she turned and walked away.

"Don't get used to that when I'm buying, Victoria!" John wisecracked.

The waitress turned towards John, and frowned. "Believe me, Trooper Boyle. I know I will never get used to either you or your tips. Good day, gents," she replied as her glowing smile reappeared.

She turned on her heels and headed towards another busy table while the three men laughed. "You'll have to excuse Vicki, Sam. John's cheapness is legendary."

"Och, no! Don't listen to this bamboozler over here, Sam," John said as he pointed the accusatory finger at Tom. "Sam, it is not cheapness, it is frugality."

"Okay, Boyle. So, you are the cheapest, frugal person that I've ever met. All anyone has to do is ask any of your past dates," Tom added slyly. John pensively looked around for someone to come to his aid. He glanced at

Sam, but the agent pulled away from the table. "John, I usually put in a hand to help save a drowning man, but, as Tom said, it sounds as if your reputation precedes you. Sorry, my friend," Sam replied with a smirk. "Shall we go for a walk?"

"Oh, so I see how it is! We get up, we change the subject, and then we leave! Is that it, Sam? Bedad, isn't that just like a Bureau man?"

"Why, thank you for those words of kindness, John Boyle."

Tom lit another cigarette while the men walked down Main Street. The December wind was rather biting, but it did not deter the men from their pending discussion. Sam asked if he might partake of another cigarette, and Tom complied. They turned the corner from Main and headed towards Bridge Street. Sam stopped and looked at the two men before they all walked across the bridge and into Lambertville. "I have some information about Jones, but let's get to him later. Do we know anything about this New Hope killer?"

Tom took another drag from the Marlboro, and began to walk. "We don't know much, Sam. The prints from the "A" Train came back with no results. Same goes for the Luminol testing. We tried using the states DNA testing equipment, but the only blood we're finding is Luke's. The spatter patterns that the Luminol found indicated nothing more than what we'd already surmised from the stab wounds. This individual is as thorough as Kane was."

"That's a frightening thought."

"Yes it is, Sam. Al's place seems to have turned up the same results. The only difference is we found a shoe print in the mud, and a strand of long, blonde hair. We've been told it was synthetic, and from what we've heard this morning about the blood, it's Al's."

John shot Tom a look of reluctance to proceed, but Tom just nodded as if to say, relax. "Trooper Terrant had reported a very svelte, shapely female jogger on his rounds during the morning Luke was murdered. It was a harmless enough encounter, until the small jogging shoe print, and the strand of blonde hair showed up at Al's residence. We're having a cast made of the mud print to see if we can get an exact description of the shoe model. The faux hair isn't as simple to pinpoint. We have Zoul's description of her physical features. When the fliers are put out tomorrow with a sketch of her likeness, we are going to hopefully have information on the shoe type and the possibility she has darker, natural hair under a wig."

"We'll also put in that the blonde hair may be extensions blended in with her natural, blonde coloring," John added.

"A female? Boy, that could push the case wide open."

"To a point. We're still not sure whether she's anything more than just a coincidental suspect. Of course, it is the main reason why we'd like her to come forward and offer any information she may have, if she's innocent."

"You see, Sam we're not cocksure that she could be the killer. The knife plunges into Luke and Al were deep. They were done with a vicious precision. Tom seems to think even more than what Kane inflicted on his victims." Tom nodded in response to John's last statement.

Sam began to walk a little slower. "But, and gentlemen, you could attest to this, especially since the fitness craze of the past twenty years.

There are some women, of slight frame, whose strength may be equal to, or stronger than that of an equally sized male."

"We've taken the possibility into consideration. I mean, there is a chance it's her, Sam, but the strength of the plunges and the vicious behavior is more akin to the type of rage exacted by a male." Tom stopped and looked down at the forbidding darkness of the river. In the summer, the playful winds would carry a rainbow plethora of seabirds around the bridges concrete stanchions. The winds of December brought a much different greeting, and they hit his face like a block of ice smashing his skull. Tom pulled up his collar, flicked his cigarette over the railing and started to walk with the two men again.

"Okay, you haven't ruled out the female or the possibility she's an accomplice to a male murderer. You know, she scopes out the territory and makes sure he's in the clear to do his work." When the men reached the Lambertville side and turned to head back, Sam paused briefly. "Gentlemen, have we overlooked the thought of our murderer being both sexes, per say?"

Tom glanced at John as they both caught wind of what Sam was alluding to. "Sweet Jesus, Tommy! We've been so damned focused on finding a carbon copy of Kane or the minute possibility that it was the jogger, we didn't even think of it. A cross-dresser!"

"It's very plausible, Sam. It's actually more believable than a woman, and it would be a very good way for the killer to conceal their identity. The only problem we'd run into there, is the open cross-dressers in town would be too obvious a choice. I don't think any of them fall into that body description. So, if there is a chance the cross-dresser is from this town, this part of their life is still very much in the closet, so to speak."

"I would agree with you there, Tom. It's going to be someone who is not a known cross-dresser."

"It's getting us back to the needle in a haystack mode again, but we really weren't far from there to begin with. This idea of a cross-dresser may ring true, though. I think I'll have Ink keep his ear to the pavement."

Sam glanced strangely at Tom. "Ink?"

"Yeah. The 'Inkman', real name, George Rossini, owns the 'Den of Inkniquity.' It's the most popular tattoo joint for many a mile. We formed our bond with Ink a few years ago, when we were trying to keep the drug scene from hitting us hard. Ink knows folks from all different walks of life, and he has helped us on a few cases with some vital information. He almost single-handedly helped John and I form and alliance with the areas biker groups to keep drugs from hitting the streets of New Hope."

"If they don't peddle it here, then we don't bust them."

"Sometimes, we have to do these things to keep the peace, John", Sam knowingly replied. "Okay, is there any chance I could have a quick meeting with the 'Inkman'? I'd like him to know who I am, if I'm going to be sniffing around town for awhile."

"Sure, I don't think he'd balk."

"Good, Tom. Now, lets the three of discuss things needing to be addressed."

"Such as?"

"The media crunch that will probably invade your town. I have it, on good authority, a story about the Kane copycats will be printed in the largest New York paper. They'll also discuss the local police and the Bureau's efforts to have any major story squashed before it reaches the media."

"Aye, that could mean protestors." Great, Saint Patrick, this is not what I asked for when I prayed to ya' the other day.

"Yes, quite a few, I would imagine," Tom added.

"Listen gents, I'll put in a call to Harrisburg and make sure we have more than adequate manpower."

"Good, John. I'll let Ward know of the possibility of protests also."

"Not a bad idea, Tom. Your mayor is quite an interesting fellow."

"I could think of a few more choice words to describe him."

"I'm sure you could, Tom. I think my men will be keeping an eye on Mayor Jerry Ward. For some reason, I think he has some idea of what's taken place in this town." Tom and John looked at Sam and waited eagerly for him to continue. The old lawman saw this and began to crack a smile. "And, we know this how, Mister FBI?" John asked with a grin.

"Let's just say, all was not totally forgiven with the First Lady comments of a few years ago. His actions have been watched from time to time."

Sam's statement amused John and Tom to no end. "So the idiot painted himself into a corner with a statement against a very powerful person. Well folks, I can't say I feel sorry for the little prick. May I inquire if this sporadic investigation has turned up any evidence of our beloved mayor being involved in the Ecstasy trade?"

"Well Tom, this is a Bureau case." Sam looked at the officers and winked. "Off the record, I could say, you may be correct."

Aye', Bureau man, you've got my curiosity peaked. "Off the record, Sam, has our little snot rag had any contact with one Jerome Jones?"

"Again, off the record, it's possible. We're tying to make sure that the information is correct."

"Interesting, isn't it, Tommy boy?"

"Interesting, but not surprising, buddy. Nothing surprises me when it comes to Jerry Ward."

"Would this be the crux of the reasoning to go to Trenton and apprehend Jones?"

"I think you already knew the answer to that, Chief."

As the men headed from the bridge's walkway, Sam stopped and turned again towards the two officers. "Look, I'm not going to beat around the bush, gentlemen. I want to be in Trenton, tonight. I think Jones is too volatile to lay low for long. My source says Jones has been spotted at the World Church on Rosell Avenue. He says Jones seems to be acting quite erratically, like he's getting ready to blow Trenton soon."

When they reached Ferry's Landing, Sam started to speak again. Don't pull any punches with these two. They can definitely handle whatever it is you need to convey. "Listen, tonight may be our best chance to catch this animal and blow the case wide open. I have a gut feeling, and I think the two of you do also, that Jones knows exactly who the New Hope killer is. If you catch him, I don't care how you go about getting the information from him, either. This is not a politically correct run operation on my end. My young boys know this also. This is from the old farm. You do what it takes, if you get him tonight."

Tom gave the agent a knowing glance. "Well Sam, I think I can say it will be good to work with you. Somehow, I think we'll not only avenge our friends deaths, but also my father's when this case is solved."

"Stranger things have happened, Thomas. Gentlemen, let's meet to discuss our plans at the "A" Train, tonight. Would seven be a good time?"

"I think that would work for us, Sam."

"Good, Tom. You and John bring along your young charges, also. We'll need some good young folks to help us out. Until then, I will see you at Sergeant Jeaneau's funeral. It's so damn sad he had to be taken like this."

Tom and John both looked choked up. Al's funeral hadn't registered this way until Agent Tunney mentioned it. In a few hours, the nightmare of Al's demise would become a reality. "If you only knew how sad, Sam," Tom replied as he fought back the tears. Agent Tunney shook the officers hands and went on his way, leaving the men to contemplate their discussion. Tom and John tried to bring their emotions back in check.

"Well lad, what did you think of our Federal Agent Tunney?"

"I wish they still made men like that at the agency, instead of today's breed."

"I agree. I've always worked well with the no-nonsense approach."

"I don't think we need to, but let's keep just a small degree of caution with him."

"Aye', as I'm sure he'll do with us, for now." Just then, John's cell phone began to ring. "Hello? Yes Zoul, go ahead."

"I see. Well, I'll let him know." John hung up the phone and looked at Tom. "Zoul found out about the knives. They were made in Newark,

New Jersey by Adams and Sons, who have been out of business for almost fifteen years."

"Newark, New Jersey. How strange that it would be one of Jerome Jones' dealing areas."

"Aye, strange indeed. The plot thickens, ay' Tommy?"

"Yes, John. It seems we have another needle to add to a growing haystack."

As the men looked out towards the Delaware, the orange, morning sun glistened playfully over the rivers rippling currents. It was hard to believe the ground on which they now stood, was the spot where all this madness had occurred just a few days before. Tom observed the charming Christmas displays adorning the windows of the nearby shops. There was every kind of ornament and lighted, animated object in them the mind could possibly fathom. New, fiber optic trees were in pots in front of some of the stores, with their branches glowing a rainbow of bright colors. There were also plenty of displays in this old town including the Victorian dolls and decorations of Christmas past. The locals and the tourists just adored them. Tom figured it reminded them all of a time so much simpler, so pure, and so innocent. It was easy to wax of the nostalgic times. Everybody always spoke of how things were so much better back then.

Tom knew this was a version of innocent escapism. Everyone was guilty of doing it from time to time. Tom did it plenty of times, but his strong, analytical side did not let him delve into the past for too long. Tom knew evil had existed in men from the earliest of times. It was just, in these so-called, civilized and modern times, the violence seemed to be rammed down your throat. No matter how hard you tried to avoid it, the violence turned up in the papers, magazines, on the television, the movies, even on your computer, if you dug deep enough. People today seemed to be anesthetized to the violence.

Perhaps, it was the modern humans way of not showing how their emotions were affected. Maybe if they showed them, it would display a sign of weakness. Men and women were so preoccupied these days with not displaying any feelings to be construed as a weakness. For now, as the crowds of people indicated, life went on in New Hope. A few days from now, or especially if there were to be another murder, the townspeople may be more apt to show a crack in their facade.

Tom knew this. He knew John Boyle and the rest of their group would have to move swiftly to apprehend these madmen. Maybe if they could catch them soon, it would give people a glimmer of hope that the world in the new Millennium could be a better place to live. Tom turned towards John and put his arm around the man's thick shoulders. "Buddy, we need a miracle to happen soon. I have faith in all of us that we'll have this miracle occur. I need to believe it will be so."

John looked at his good friend, and smiled. "Brother, we'll get them, and when we do, I know you'll be leading the charge. John put his beefy hand on Tom's shoulder. "Everyone has faith in you, Tommy. Now, c'mon lad," he said as he winked. "It's going to be a long, hard day. We need to have our wits about us. Go to your wife and relax for a while. The station and my barracks are on alert. They'll inform us if anything suspicious arises."

"You're right," Tom said quietly. "Let's get a move on."

"Relax today. This afternoon, we'll let out many an emotion for our good friend and brother. Tonight, we'll need to be razor sharp in the face of adversity."

"Adversity? Is that how we're referring to acts of the bastards who caused all this sorrow?"

"I could think of a few better ones, but it will do, for now." John patted Tom on the back and said he'd see him later. Tom watched John disappear into the masses of the holiday crowds, and then he quickly turned back towards the water. He thought again about Zoul's stories of the black river. It would not happen here. This would be Tom's silent pact with God. For all he knew, or cared, right now it could have been a pact with the devil. All Tom did know was this madness would be stopped soon, and it would be by him.

As he flicked his cigarette into the depths of the water, he could hear his voice aloud. "It won't happen here, Zoul, my friend. No one will make this a black river". No one."

CHAPTER 20

The crowds lining Main Street this afternoon, and the procession filling its center were overwhelming. Nobody from town could remember seeing such a massive congregation of people. The only one to come close may have been for the Bicentennial parade in 1976. Of course, those crowds were in a festive mood. The one appearing today was in anguish. Just a few days earlier, New Hope buried one of its most prominent and treasured citizens, Lucas Stone. Today, it would lay to rest its favorite son, Sergeant Al Jeaneau.

The locals were bewildered as to how fast these funerals had occurred after the victims' deaths. Most had figured the autopsies would take quite some time, but they found out through the town gossips, much of the evidence the police had found were from the crime scenes, and not from the brutalized bodies. Meanwhile, John and Tom's technicians, along with Tunney's whiz kids, were working at a feverish pace to make something out of the minute evidence they did have.

As the lab techs went about their business, the rest of the town began their slow procession towards the Old Stone Church. Although Reverend Bennett Edwards was its pastor, he would leave the eulogy in the capable hands of his good friend, Father Michael Brown, from Saint Mark's.

Reverend Bennett knew of the bond that had grown between Al and Father Michael, so he felt this was the appropriate thing to do.

Police officers from many parts of the eastern seaboard came to be a part of the Honor Guard. The Philadelphia Police Department brought along their bagpipers, as had New York City's, and Al's hometown of Wheeling, West Virginia.

While everyone made their way into church and found a place to sit, they were soon rising to the sounds of the choir singing, "Be Not Afraid." When the time came for the homily, Father Michael approached the lectern. The mourners in the front pews could observe beads of sweat falling from his forehead. Father Michael also made a few, quick swipes past his eyes. Obviously, Al Jeaneau had made an impact in this good man's life, and his horrific death, as well as Luke's, was again taking its toll on the good shepherd.

Like any good shepherd though, Father Michael needed to tend to the remainder of the flock. If there was anyone in town who could soothe the citizenry and their frayed nerves, besides Tom Miller, this was their man.

Father Michael breathed in deep, and began to speak. "I did not expect, and certainly, I did not hope after Luke's untimely death, to be thrust into this ghastly situation so soon. I would have hoped to never see such evil again. Man's wishes do not always follow the path of what is to take place in the grand scheme of things.

Evil does not follow a timeline. It doesn't give us the chance to take a breath, or to take a long look so as to contemplate what has happened. It strikes the hardest, when we are at our weakest. Evil does this for many reasons. It does it to make us feel helpless. It strikes swift and hard to anger us, so that we lash out in a vindictive nature to thwart its progress. We usually accomplish this in a haphazard fashion, and when the dust settles, we have usually laid blame or hurt everyone that we can. Unfortunately, the perpetrator of these heinous acts never really shows up in our crosshairs. Therefore, evil happily walks away unscathed, leaving everyone else to pick up the pieces of the irrational behavior it has caused.

I mention this to you because it is very easy right now to feel helpless, live in fear, and point the finger of blame. It is very easy for us to say the homosexual community has again become the target of some psychopaths sick whims. It is very easy to blame the authorities, whom some think are not doing their wholehearted best to capture the person, or persons involved. Again, I've heard this said because both victims are homosexual.

I will not mention the word coming from my mouth in response to those accusations. Lord knows, I'll be seeing the confessional tonight." Father Michael's remark brought a desperately needed chuckle from the tense and somber congregation.

"The word I'll use now is hogwash, my friends. It is pure hogwash. You are blessed to have a police chief in this town who is passionate about making sure every member of this town, and every tourist who visits who visits here, is in a safe haven. This man has lost family to the man who started this insanity nearly fifteen years ago.

You are blessed to have a barracks commander with the Pennsylvania State Police, who is just as caring and vigilant. Both of these men have lost two close friends. They were like family to Tom and John. If anyone, outside of the grieving family members, wants justice more than they or their respective forces do, I would like to meet them.

With this being said, I pray the good, level headed people of this and the outlying communities continue to give these brave men and women your unequivocal support." Father Michael grew silent for a moment to let his last request sink into the minds of the populous. He then smiled towards his audience, and again spoke.

"Let's dramatically switch gears and speak of a man many of us here knew and loved. I had the pleasure of knowing Al for quite a few years. I got the chance to really know him through the many deep, philosophical talks we would have when he paid his visits to Saint Mark's. I also got to know well the side of him many of you knew and loved, his splendidly humorous nature. A more good natured man I don't think I will ever find again. You almost knew when Al was going to get you with that sharp, rapier wit of his. No one was spared, but nobody really seemed to mind. It was almost expected to happen. I see by the way many of you are smiling, you too are remembering falling victim to Al's tactics." This again brought light laughter from the mourners.

"Likewise, I would also say many of you were witness to he incredible wisdom of Al Jeaneau. Al had so much passion towards any subject of which he spoke, it became increasingly difficult to argue your point to him. It was not that he wouldn't entertain your viewpoint. On the contrary, he loved a differing opinion he could joust with intellectually. The problem became, Al would fill your head with so much food for thought, you would begin to think more about his statements than you would of your rebuttal.

Al was a caring, loving man who would take to his friends children as if they were his own. It was not uncommon to hear the voices of children yelling hello to "Uncle Al" as they saw him patrol the streets of our town.

He was a man who never flinched at taking care of the soul mate who he knew was going to die a sad and painful death.

He was a man who had the courage of his convictions. His love for God was so much, he had spoken many times of converting to Catholicism, even though he knew Rome's stance towards homosexuality. He and I wrestled through the subject of theology on many occasions. He was one of the most selfless, Christian men I've met.

Trooper John Boyle, Chief Tom Miller, and myself spoke on quite a few occasions about this character, Al Jeaneau. We spoke briefly before mass about how Al would best be remembered. It was not an easy decision.

We laughed, we cried, and we shuffled through our many memories of Al. We came up with a short, but concise synopsis of the man. Al loved many, and was loved by many. He wouldn't back down from a fight. He was protective of everyone around him, especially his close friends. But, most importantly, he was a man who loved God and the life God had given him.

God bless you, Al Jeaneau. You were so loved, and will be eternally missed."

The church was so silent when Father Michael turned to sit down, you could hear a pin drop. Everybody was letting Father Michael's words absorb into their consciousness. There were, however, two men who let the words be absorbed, but remained stoic in appearance. Tom Miller and John

Boyle looked at each other and nodded. They were not going to let their emotions get the best of them. Their focus would remain solid.

They went to the gravesite, which was located a few miles in between Al and Tom's house, on Chapel Road. They said a few silent prayers and offered a few, brief words about the close friendships they'd had with the man they both referred to as brother. Tom spoke of Al's tenacious manner when a crime needed to be solved. He also spoke of a man whose compassion and kindness towards everyone he met was so genuine, it was as if you'd been touched by an angel.

John Boyle spoke of his friend who could find try to find humor in almost any situation. "Al pulled pranks that would probably have had the Pope himself swearing at him. No matter how aggravated he would try to get you, he'd always have you laughing at him, yourself, or both by the end of a long and grueling day."

Everyone made their way towards the casket to say a brief prayer and lay a rose by the plot. For many, it was a hard walk to make. Debbie Miller was in a daze. Her eyes were filled with tears, and she could be heard asking herself why this had to happen in a very soft voice. Jenn Gates and Phil Antos did their best to keep Debbie calm, but they too were inconsolable from time to time.

Since John and Tom were both pallbearers, they ended up being the last two people at the gravesite. John placed a rose on the casket, and said a prayer in the native tongue of his Irish birthplace. Tom felt himself getting ready to break down and let his emotions come pouring out, but the strength and willpower, getting him through many a tragedy in his life, catapulted forward. As he lay down the red rose on his good friends' casket, he looked out towards the throng of mourners.

"I thank you for coming and paying your respects to a much loved man. I know somewhere his spirit must be looking down on all of us, and flashing us that loveable grin God blessed him with.

I know this has been a hard day for all of us. I also know the days that lie ahead could be filled with more sadness, anger, and fear." Tom's eyes began to narrow, and his voice grew stronger. While many around him anguished over the loss of life, Tom's resolve held firm. "I will vow to you, on this day, if it takes the lifeblood from me, justice will be served. I promise this as your Chief, fellow New Hope resident, but most importantly, as your friend. Lucas Stone and Sergeant Al Jeaneau will not have died in vain. Justice for them will be done."

Not another word was spoken. The mourners saw their Chief as the man to bring this evil to an end. The critics, who had quietly spoken of the need to replace him with a younger man, now saw the Tom Miller of fifteen years ago. Age had not made him tired or weak. Age had instead made him wise, and he was still a pillar of strength to latch onto. They now saw what the rest of the town had already known. Tom Miller would find whoever was committing these murders.

As he made his way through the crowd, many nodded and smiled in Tom's direction. Their silent confidence was exactly what the police, troopers, and the FBI needed to get their job completed. John proudly matched Tom stride for stride, until they reached Debbie, Jenn, and Phil.

Debbie kissed Tom on the cheek softly. "Did you think we ever doubted you?" she asked with a smirk.

"I just think some of our friends needed reassurance."

"I think you definitely gave it to them, Thomas," said a voice from behind them. Agent Tunney extended his hand towards Tom. "You are a great communicator."

"Thank you, Sam. May I introduce you to Officer Gates and Phil Antos, Agent Tunney?"

"The pleasure is mine, Officer Gates. Mister Antos, you have my condolences. Mister Stone sounded like a great man."

"Thank you, Agent Tunney. He was a great man, as was Al," Phil responded mournfully.

"Sam, you already know John, of course, and finally, but certainly not the least, my wife De.."

"Oh, Tom", Agent Tunney politely interrupted. "There's no need to introduce me to Debbie Miller." Sam had a twinkle in his eyes as he conversed with Debbie. "My granddaughter is a big fan of your "Flatguy's Follies" books. She gets a kick out of that Siberian husky and the historical adventures he has with his other stuffed animal friends." Debbie laughed and thanked Sam for the kind words. "If none of you would mind, I need to speak briefly to the Chief and Trooper Boyle."

When Debbie, Phil, and Jenn politely departed, Sam turned towards the two men. "We're in Trenton tonight. Our source confirms the presence of Jerome Jones at the World Church. He usually preaches until about ten in the evening. We have my boys, your two charges, and Chief Townsends' top units at our disposal. I also spoke with your friend, the Inkman. Thanks for calling him earlier, Tom. A very intriguing young man, isn't he?" Tom and John grinned and nodded in agreement. "He gave me some information backing up what some of our field agents had already confirmed, but we can discuss that when we meet at the Train later. Let's still shoot for seven tonight, okay?" Tom and John both agreed in earnest.

Tom could feel those old senses coming back to full preparedness. A few days ago, the rush through the woods was the primer. Tonight would be old times again, and he was ready. He peered into John's eyes and saw the look staring back at him. The feeling never does leave you. God, I'll need it tonight. Give me strength.

Agent Sam Tunney witnessed his counterparts silent reaction and realized they needed no coaxing. "Well then, assemble your troops, and I'll see you later. Let's turn this from a day of sorrow into a night of triumph."

As Sam walked away, he could feel it again. The thrill of the chase. The move in for the kill. Nearly forty years of service had not taken away those vital instincts from the lawman. Tonight, they would be tested again, in the lands of his first big case.

CHAPTER 21

The inevitable had happened. Tom was making his preparations for the meet, when he heard the familiar voice of national news anchor, Paul Jenkins. When he began to speak of Kane's impending execution, Tom knew the next topic of discussion would be of the copycat murders. Sam had said to expect it tonight, but it still unnerved Tom to hear the story broadcast on the national scene.

The station had set a news hookup directly in front of tonight's meeting place. Tom immediately called Rob Pagano and told him to disperse some uniformed officers around 'The 'A' Train.' He then spoke to Jenn Gates and asked her to do the job of being the New Hope Police Departments official spokesperson. It was a position she knew Al used to handle, so she was honored that Tom would choose her to fill the void. "Pack your heat, Jenn, but show up in civilian clothes. I want them to see you as a representative, not a uniformed officer."

"No problem, Chief," she said as Tom hung up his cell phone.

It immediately rang again, as he answered it. "Are you watching this shite?" bellowed the voice.

"We knew it was inevitable, pal."

"It looks like it made all the major networks. I sent some of my troopers down there. You sent a few of your boys down there too, I'm sure?"

"Great minds think alike," Tom quipped. "I sent Jenn down in her civvies to be our goodwill ambassador for the press."

"Excellent choice. Well lad, I presume we'll be ducking in the back way?"

"Park in the Bucks County Playhouse's lot. If we decide to venture towards the Train, we go via the creek and behind the buildings on Mechanic Street."

"Ah, a little back alley diversion. I've got you, my friend. Zoul and I are departing shortly."

"I'll call Sam and make him aware of our new plan of attack."

"See you soon, Tommy boy."

Tom made a quick call to Agent Tunney and filled him in on the revamped plans. Sam had just seen the news report. He'd also just taken a call from his Bureau Chief who was boiling about the press leaking the story to the major networks. He thought Tom's plan sounded reasonable, all things considered.

Everything was in place. Tom looked at himself in the bedroom mirror. He was ready. Nothing had changed from fifteen years ago. All the senses were still reacting like a well-tuned instruments' would. He thought very briefly about how Al would have helped out in this case. He made it a point to have the thought become a quick memory. He wanted to focus on Jones and the possibility his apprehension would lead to a quick arrest of the New Hope murderer.

He made his way downstairs and saw Debbie sitting on the living room sofa. When cases such as this one came up, they did their best not to go through a big theatrical production when Tom departed. Tonight would be no different. Debbie met Tom at the front door with a long thermos filled with hot chocolate. "Just a little something to keep you and the boys warm," she said as she smiled. Tom thanked her, gave her a kiss, and opened the door. "I'll see you tonight."

"You can count on that, Deb," Tom replied. As the door closed and Tom made his way down the drive, Debbie Miller broke the one habit she'd always followed. When Tom would leave for a big case, she would normally go back to her chores, or her writing. She would not go near the windows of their home to wave goodbye to her husband.

It was their way of feeling life went on. "No waving goodbye to me when I leave," Tom told her when they were first married. "Goodbye means I may not return." Debbie took those words to heart for all these years, but not tonight. She would make sure Tom didn't see her when she turned off the living room lights. The only illumination in the room was from the fireplaces mellow flame, and the small, clear Christmas lights nestled in the greens over the mantelpiece. She knelt behind the draperies hanging from the large, living room windows, and watched Tom's Explorer hurtle down the driveway and into the street. "God be with you, Tom", Debbie said as she held back her tears. "God be with you all."

With the speed of a champion horse rounding the home stretch, Tom reached the Playhouse parking lot in minutes. The other members of this modern version of the round table were already there to meet him. Tom made a quick call to Gates' cell phone and informed her of the group location. Sam introduced his young bucks, Agents Troy Ackerman and David Vincent to the local contingent.

"Saints and angels, they look like twelfth graders!" John guffawed. "Is that how we used to look, Tommy boy?"

"Yeah, back in Neanderthal times. Ah, the sweet memories of a long gone youth," Zoul cracked.

"Aye, and you. Some thanks I get for slogging yer' ignorant self along. Ackerman and Vincent, Trooper Terrant also responds to the code name, "Wise Ass."

Their faces, brightened only by the red-hot flame from Tom's lighter made for an eerie setting. "Well, now that we have the gentlemanly formalities out of the way, let's briefly discuss what you boys have conjured up?"

"We scoured the photo files of our beloved DEA, and came up with some beauty pics their surveillance team took this summer. They'd been keeping an eye on Jones due to the rumor he was peddling massive amounts of Ecstasy through Trenton, Camden, Newark, and some high profile clubs in Manhattan. I'm sure they were pissed we infiltrated their shots, but, they'll have to live with it. The Bureau can jump their train when a peddler is wanted for murder. Anyway, while our boy was carousing Trenton, he made a stop to Pond's club. Take a look at who they were being cozy with."

Sam handed the photographs to Tom and John. The first one showed Jones dressed as a woman, and sitting with the late Robert Pond. Standing in between the seated twosome, was a very svelte blonde, dressed in a tight jogging suit and wearing a ball cap. The next set of pictures, taken a few days afterwards, displays Jones wearing a super short minidress and thigh-high, stiletto heeled boots. In the photo, he is again conversing with a smiling Robert Pond. A few snapshots later, Jones is accompanied back to the table, arm in arm, with a thin blonde who this time was dressed in a skin-tight body suit. Her hair was again neatly pulled through the caps opening and into a ponytail.

John and Tom were speechless for a moment. Tom turned in Zoul's direction. "Zoul, come here and look over these photographs, please?"

The young trooper approached the group and proceeded to peruse the sets of pictures. *Damn, yins got em'.* He looked up at the three men. "Jones knows her. That freakin' asshole knew her all along!" *If he'd only known on that gray morning of December twenty-third he would be staring at the possible murderer of his friend Al Jeaneau, he could have stopped it all. But, how could he have known?*

"Don't let it eat at you, lad. You couldn'ta known. Nobody coulda'." John Boyle knew the look all too well. *He'd had it years ago when he was a homicide detective in Philadelphia. These are the kinds o' things can eat a lad up. I've got to get him back in the right frame of mind. I need him to be sharp tonight.* "So, it's definitely our jogger?"

"Yeah Troop, it has to be. The body frame alone is a perfect match. Damn!"

"Let it go, lad. Just let it go. We'll get them all, Zoul."

"Damn straight we will, Troop. It's hunting time now," Zoul said as he checked over his firearm.

That's my boy. Just keep thinking like that, and you just may bag the prick tonight. "So, Jones and jogger look like they've been quite the cozy pair for a while, ay' Sam?"

"Unfortunately so."

"Well, Sam, I think it's in our interest to proceed to Trenton with haste, and find out just how cozy Jones has been with our suspected New Hope murderer, don't you?"

"Indeed I do, Tom. Let's get going. The agent team's vehicle will follow the officers. Tom, keep in contact on your cell phone. We'll go over some logistics during the ride, and we'll confer with Townsend upon our arrival."

"Sounds good, Sam."

"Let's roll, lads!" John bellowed as he locked eyes with Ackerman and Vincent. "Sharp thinkin' on the part of you two high schoolers' to look back through yer' archives. Damn fine work, young ones!"

The agents thanked John for the accolades as they gathered some of their gear. Everyone was now packed up and ready to move in on Jerome Jones. Tom quickly held up his hand. "One moment, gentlemen. I need to call my secret weapon."

"Officer Gates!" Tom bellowed into the two-way.

"Yes, Chief?"

"The media circus is now officially over. Tell the reporters we are taking no more questions at this time. Refer them to the mayor's office if they need any more clarification on the case."

"Okay, anything else?"

"Yes, have the troopers and our uniforms cordon off the area, and have them kindly tell the onlookers to disperse."

"Fine, Chief. Is that all?"

"No, Officer Gates, it isn't. I need you to meet us in the Playhouse parking lot as soon as you can."

Silence came over the air. "Oh, Gates? Are you there?"

"I'm on my way, Chief," the rushed voice replied.

Within a matter of minutes, Jenn was quickly maneuvering her way along the creek side. As she approached the group she looked in the direction of the two young agents.

"Agents Ackerman and Vincent, this is Officer Jenn Gates," Tom said as the young men nodded in response.

"Agents, I'm pleased to meet you." As she pulled her curls back into a scrunchie, Tom glanced over at his young understudy. Something about her always reminded him of how Al had approached the job. She had the same exuberance, the same need to know every small detail of a crime. It was what separated the good cops from the one's just collecting a paycheck, Tom thought. "Officer Gates, is your weapon loaded?"

"Yes, Chief."

"Do you have reserves?"

"Yes, I have two clips, and a .22 Ladyfinger in my ankle holster."

"Well, come and join us," Tom replied as he put his hand into his jacket pocket. "I wouldn't want my new Sergeant to feel left out in the cold."

As Tom handed her the shiny shield, Jenn didn't know whether to scream with joy, or to cry. Oh God, Al. I never wanted to fill your shoes this way, but I swear I'll make you so proud of me. She put the shield in her pocket and glanced up to see the agents give her a quick "thumbs up", before departing into their SUV. Zoul gave her a quick hug, and offered his congratulations.

"You deserve it, lass. Come, and fight the good fight with us," John Boyle said after giving her a bear hug.

Tom put his arm around her shoulders. "Welcome to the big time, Jenn." Jeaneau, you know this was the best decision to make in your absence. Help her out as much as we will.

Sergeant Jenn Gates wiped away a tear from her cheek, and followed the men to the vehicle. She was thinking about Al, but she knew she'd have to come back to these feelings later. Al would have expected that much from her. She needed to be on her game, now, more than ever. As she reached the front passenger door of Tom's Explorer, she turned towards her friends. "Gentlemen, let's go catch our murderer."

CHAPTER 22

The Delaware River and the leafless trees along its banks were eerily bathed in the full moons glow. Tom zipped along Route 29 and everyone was so involved in animated conversation, no one took notice of how strange the night sky looked for this time of year. Soon, Tom was into the city limits, and pulling into Trenton's police headquarters. Chief Artis Townsend, along with Detectives Canty and Pruett, came bounding down the limestone steps of the old building to meet with the group. "Towny, Detectives, are we ready for the show?"

"Yeah Tommy, we are. I want this bitch bad, bro'. He's been polluting this town for too damn long."

"Let me up your distaste level one more rung on the ladder, Artis."

"If you think you could accomplish that, Agent Tunney, go ahead."

"Jones knows the girl, or cross dressed jogger whom we suspect perpetrated the New Hope murders of Stone and Jeaneau."

Towny raised his eyebrows and bit down hard on his bottom lip. Well, if that just ain't like getting' bitch slapped, I don't know what is. Yeah, you accomplished raising my blood pressure a notch, Tunney. Towny breathed in deep and honed in on the officers. "Many of us here are familiar with the area in which the World Church is located. Now, I ain't going to shine ya'. It's a goddamn war zone down there. It's in a dark location, and there are many abandoned buildings surrounding it, both industrial and residential. We also have a lot of juiced up creatures wandering about in the nighttime, and they wouldn't give a damn 'bout helping a fellow brother escape from the clutches of "The Man." Believe me, this rings true even more for a freak like Jerome Jones.

The church itself, is a dangerous maze. Follow your instincts, folks. If you are chasin' him, call for backup. He could be leading you into an ambush if you decide to fly solo. We still don't have a report of how many troops are surrounding the man. He could be holed up by himself. Either way, be prepared for a firefight. Well, nuff' said, people. Tommy, John, and Agent Tunney know the drill. We need to try and take Jones alive. Do not shoot to kill, unless you are in imminent danger of having your lights snuffed out, and believe me, you'll know when that is with a nut like Jones. You have the right to do this in my jurisdiction. Now, let's go catch this cock."

The groups bounded towards their vehicles and were swiftly onto the mean streets of the states' capitol. The area surrounding Rosell Avenue and Calhoun Street was indicative of the urban blight plaguing Trenton for decades. Many working class row, and single family homes sprouted up between the multitude of factories which kept the town humming for a long time.

The big factories had been shuttered for years, leaving in their wake the abandoned death traps now taking their place in this landscape. The factories which had been demolished by the wrecking ball, created another detriment. Acres of rubble remained on the lots, and over the years, had been strewn to and fro. The extensive size of these abandoned lots created an ideal spot for the homeless, addicts, and also wanton criminals to be able to hide from the law. Occasionally, the police would sweep the areas, but the groups always returned within a few days.

The housing in the area fared no better. Some houses were missing roofs as the result of cave-ins from years of neglect and water damage. The walls of the rooms within were almost non-existent. Rats wandered aimlessly through the trash infested domiciles. Some of the attached homes had gaping holes through their common walls. The holes were crudely constructed by the drug dealers now occupying the homes and provided an easy access from building to building so addicts could hastily make their purchases. They also provided an escape route for everyone when the Narcotics Division performed monthly raids. Needless to say, boring out the common walls made the buildings dangerous and a prime candidate for collapsing, but it deterred no one from using them.

In between all of this chaotic setting was the World Church. At one time the factory was used to make steel cable, and was probably built in the mid-1800's. Over the years, the company added two, Federal style row homes to either end of the factory. The common walls of the two houses and the factory were bored out, thus truly connecting all three of the ramshackle buildings.

Behind the church was a debris filled lot where one of Trenton's famed ceramic works from yesteryear had once stood. Towny's men heard stories of Jones having an easily accessible escape route to this field of hazards, but it was neither confirmed nor denied by informants. They were probably too worried about the NARC squad raiding the World Church and apprehending the states biggest supplier of drugs, Jerome Jones.

It was conceivable to think there was an escape route for Jones to reach. One rumor quickly filtered out about Jones being holed up in an office behind the churches altar. Supposedly, there was a makeshift stairway connected to an equally patchwork catwalk near the offices door. It gave Jones a quick route to all three buildings, where he could check on his lucrative business or indulge in some of his chemists' wares. He could also journey into one of the "private" scum and syringe infested rooms to perform his sexual fetishes involving both men and women at the same time. The rumor was stopped after the supposed leak of it was found with his throat slit, and his body dumped in a dilapidated row just down the street. It led Towny to believe this possibility was more fact than fiction.

So, on this cold December night, these were the obstacles standing between the publics' protectors and one of its most wanted criminals. The groups of officers and agents made sure to disembark well away from the World Church's vantage point.

Towny walked towards John, Tom, and Sam with some old papers in his hands. "I know these are crude blueprints of the place, but it's the best my underfunded, broke ass department could come through with." He laid out the papers and it became apparent to all involved why Jones could be so elusive from within his lair. Towny pointed at the center of the structure. "This is our good, Mister Jones's lair. The main part of the church is right in front of him. His office is behind it on the ground floor. We've heard rumors of the office being filled with motion sensing electronic equipment. Supposedly, it also picks up any movement on the outer perimeter of the building. There is also talk he recently installed video surveillance equipment throughout the church's first level and by the outside doorways.

This is one reason we will need to be careful, but decisive in our maneuvers. People, he will, from all accounts, know we are encroaching on his house of worship. He pointed towards a door located in the rear of the factory. We will have our teams go by code names. As corny as it may sound to the young one's, it will save a lot of confusion when we communicate on our headsets." The elder officers nodded in agreement. "Tom, you, John and your 'Backyarders' will come in here. We are not too concerned with the building behind you. It is very rarely utilized. If any calamity arises, I'll call in our Strike Unit. We are going under the assumption that the catwalk and stairway exist. If they don't, you still have some quick routes to meet us in the center, if you're needed. Do your business with what, or whoever gets in your way.

Sam, you and your agents, the 'Capitol Gang' will contain the right side of the building. Be careful while you're in there. There have been reports he uses some rooms over there as his mixing area. Be aware, we could be dealing with some flammable agents in there. No pun intended, of course." Towny's comment gave the group a well needed chuckle. "Same goes for you gentlemen as to how you conduct your business. Whoever gets past your ranks will be met out front by some of the capitol city's finest uniformed officers.

Canty, Pruett, two of my Strike Unit officers, and myself will come in dead center. I'm suspecting our 'Heroes and Zeroes' squad will deal with the brunt of whomever does not want us to capture Jones.

Let's not be mislead, my people. None of us will have it easy once we breach this compound. This may be the closest many of you come to seeing how our military boys have to deal with urban warfare. Make sure you are wearing your Kevlar vests."

Towny also knew enough to include the next statement. "This includes you too, Johnny Boyle. I don't need no cowboy, hero shit out of you, okay?"

John Boyle had the look of an innocent Irish choirboy on his face as he looked towards his accuser. "Och no, Towny! I'm gettn' too old for that crap, my friend. Don't worry about me," he said with a grin.

"Yeah, right. I start to worry when you tell me not to, buddy."

"Anyway, the electric company is on alert to give some outside light if Jones decides to cut the juice. Do we have any questions or concerns, my young bucks?" None of the younger officers replied. By the looks on their faces, Towny saw they were ready to bring the battle straight to Jones's doorstep. They were ready to stop any more blood from being shed by this animal. Damn impressive, bucks. Damn impressive.

"Sam, this is your ballgame after we catch him. Anything to add?"

Sam looked straight at the young one's in the group, just as Artis had done. "We all know what we're here for. This man has been elusive for many a year. He's crafty, cunning, and vicious. He won't come easily.

On the other hand, we have seen him display a level of hubris. He's cocky enough to foul up his own master plan. Let's make him think he has the upper hand. His false bravado may lead him right into our clutches. The biggest objective is to keep him alive. The good officers and troopers from New Hope need him alive. I am convinced he knows who the other killer is. Do your best to keep Jones in one piece. Do you have anything to add, Trooper Boyle or Chief Miller?"

John Boyle looked over towards Tom. "Ball's in your court, Tommy."

"Thanks, John. I've nothing to add, Sam, except be quick on your draw. Call for backup immediately if you corner Jones. As displayed so far, he's as swift as lightening with that sword. Don't try and be heroic. I look around and see a very determined group of young men and women. I'm confident none of you will shy away from your duty tonight. All I ask of you is to be smart, and be safe. If you do this, we'll catch him, and we'll all make it home safely to our loved one's."

After speaking, Tom began loading his revolver. John spoke up briefly. "These were all good points, lads and lasses. Now, let's get a move on and bring this prick to justice."

As they ambled down Rosell Avenue, John stopped the group and pointed towards the compound. "This is our home now."

CHAPTER 23

The four officers adeptly maneuvered through the rubble of the open field and made haste to the rear of the World Church headquarters. John Boyle reached in his coat and handed Razoul a pair of Night Vision Goggles. "Christ, Troop! Does the state h.q. know we have these babies?" the astonished young man asked his mentor.

"Och! What Harrisburg don't know, won't hurt 'em, now will it? Besides, Zoul, these are going to save someone's life tonight. I've just got a premonition, lad."

Tom moved quietly to the beaten steel door, just like a snake slithering towards its unassuming prey. The patchwork accumulation of metal and rust was held shut by a padlock. Tom reached into a small, leather case, and produced some fine tools of his trade and his headset. "Towny," he whispered. "Can you copy?"

"Yes I can, Thomas. Got your set on already, that's a good sign. Does it mean we're in yet?"

"Negative, Towny. We have a lock to pick." The nimble fingers used in his youth for making hitters scratch their heads at the slew of pitches he'd mastered had not failed him in his later years. Tom placed the tool into the locks cylinder. With a couple of twists and some swift movements, the only shiny piece of steel on the door popped open.

"Remind me to call you when I lock my keys in my house," John whispered. Tom gave him a quick thumbs-up, and slowly lifted the padlock through the metal loop. For how decrepit the door seemed it did not create the expected cacophony of sounds when it was opened.

"Thomas, how is our lock situation coming along, brother?"

"The 'Backyarders' have landed. We're inside the premises and holding our position. We're awaiting your response, Towny."

"Samuel, how's the 'Capitol Gang' making out?"

"We have breached the entrance. No signs of life here, Artis. Likewise, we are holding on your command."

They're in! The juices are coming back, Townsend. This is your night to give Jerome Jones some payback. He's been pissin' in my yard way too long. "All right then. The 'Heroes and Zeroes' are on the move. Let's bring some justice back to my home, officers." The members of Towny's group broke into a slow trot and navigated their way through the alleys of the abandoned row homes across the street from the compound. They started to pick up speed, heading up the stairs and towards the front entrance of the World Church.

Two of the Strike Unit officers grabbed the ramming bar they'd brought along. As they pulled the device back for the impending blow, Towny lifted his hand to hold them. "Yarders and Gang, H and Z have arrived. We're getting ready to bring the noise. Get ready to see the cockroaches scatter."

"Gang is ready," Sam whispered.

"Same for the Yarders," Tom replied.

Towny swung around and faced his squad. "Raise the roof!"

The two officers hit the heavy wooden doors with such a force, splinters and locking devices were flung in every direction. "We're in!" Towny bellowed over the ruckus and commotion of the scene. "Capitol Gang, make your inroads. Backyarders, hold tight."

"Copy that," Tom replied.

"On our way!" Sam exclaimed.

Tom listened to the sounds of what sounded like the whole church being overturned. It was the sounds typical of the initial phases of a sweep. The usual sounds would not last for long. Everyone heard the gun blasts echo through the complex and also on their headsets. "Police! Put it down muthafucka! I said, put the gun down!" they heard Towny bellow. It would be followed by two quick gun bursts. "We've got one down! They're starting to get scattered! Gang, make some inroads!"

"We're on our way!" Sam loaded his weapon and looked over at Ackerman and Vincent. "Well, this is what you signed on for boys, let's get moving." Sam quickly got back on his headset, and they ventured out. "We're moving. We have a sighting on some runners! Proceeding cautiously! Ceiling beams look fragile, and we're encountering lots of old machinery in our path!"

"Okay, Gang! Kick some ass, now! I know you'll do your best! Backyarders, do you copy?"

"We do Towny!"

"We got one comin' in your direction, Tommy. He's carrying, and he's got a shield!"

"A female shield?"

"No other for a chickenshit brother! You know the routine!"

"Yeah, I do!"

Towny and his detectives made haste towards the church's inner sanctum. "Yarders, we are at the chapel doors! Get ready to move, and fast!"

"We're on our way!" Tom said as he beckoned the rest of the group to move forward. "Still no sign of our runner!"

Towny and his boys kicked in the doors and hunkered down quickly behind some pews. It turned out to be a wise maneuver as sawed-off shotgun blasts splattered the chapel walls where they'd entered. "Gang, make haste!" Fragments of drywall and concrete were starting to litter the floor around Towny. "We're encountering some mad resistance!" He could hear a low rumble over the gunfire. It sounded as if it came from Sam's vantage point. "Sam! Get back to me! What the hell was that?"

"We're okay, Towny! Runners have been apprehended and subdued!" Sam growled. "We're caught up in some heavy rubble from a ceiling collapse! Runners must have detonated a device when they heard us coming! Hang in there, Artis. We're moving as quick as we can!"

"Alright, Gang! We're returning fire! Still no signs of Jones! Be watching, people!"

Tom and his group were making good headway to assist Towny's team, but it would have to be put on hold, when the light bulbs directly above Tom's head exploded into millions of pieces. "Get down!" he yelled as he grabbed Jenn Gates and pulled her to the ground. Zoul and John darted behind some boxes not too far away from Tom's position. "Police! Drop the gun, now! There is no way out of here, son!"

"Yeah, there's a way out!" the voice boomed within the dimly lit expanse. "The way is straight through you! I gotta' hostage. You gonna' let met me go, man!"

"Drop the gun, and we have a deal," Tom said calmly. "No need for a standoff." He then turned to Jenn. "Any chance of bringing him down if he doesn't comply?" She peered over the barrels and into the distance. She tucked herself down again and shook her head in disappointment. "No chance, Chief. You can't even see who's who from this distance."

Tom looked back into the darkness. "Son, do we have a deal?"

"Hell no!" the voice boomed again. "I ain't playin', man! Scream, bitch! Let em' know I'm for real!"

They all heard the hammer of the pistol cock back followed by the girls' shriek. "Please, don't let him kill me!" the voice pleaded.

"Damn it!" Tom snarled into his headset.

"What's going on there, Tommy?"

"Towny, we've got a bog down here. We have a non-compliant male, with a female hostage. We're in a low-lit environment, and with no clear shot. I'm going to need Zoul to take a shot from his vantage."

"Does he have NVG's?"

"Affirmative."

"Let me take a guess, Boyle's toy? Then again, don't even answer. I don't want to know." Gun bursts began to fly around Towny and his men again. "Shit, Tommy, use them! Take the dude out! We're encountering heavy fire and Tunney's boys are still sifting through the collapse!"

"Hang in there, Artis. The cavalry is coming," Tom replied. "No sign of Jones?"

"None yet! He's not getting out of here, Thomas! Don't you worry!"

"Okay, Towny."

"Tommy, it's Boyle. I heard Towny's dilemma. Zoul is operational. Let's do the chatter, and keep our shooter occupied."

"Got you, John." Tom turned towards his Sergeant again. "Are you nervous?"

"No, not at all. Even if I were, I wouldn't admit it now."

"Good answer. You ready to chat with our shooter?"

"Let's do it."

"Son, why won't you deal?" asked John Boyle. "We'll let you walk, if you drop the gun. What's so wrong with that?"

"First off, bitch, I ain't none of your sons! Secondly, you shut us down, my livelihood is fucked. Ain't nobody in this town takin' on a dealer who let Jones get took down!"

"So, it's about respect, then?" Jenn asked.

"Damn straight it is, girl, and I've got none the minute you take down Jones without me puttin' up a fight."

"What's your name?" No answer came back. "Come on, now. We may be here for a while," she said sweetly. "Can't you tell me your name?"

"Durrell!" the young man hollered.

"Durrell, my name is Sergeant Jenn Gates. I'm here with Chief Tom Miller, and State Trooper John Boyle. You can call me Jenn, if you'd like to."

"Awwright," he replied in a much softer tone. "Screw them other two, though! I'll talk to you!"

Tom winked at Jenn. "Excellent, keep him going," Tom whispered. He got back on his headset. "Zoul, any progress yet?"

"I found the catwalk, Chief. I'm moving in closer to his voice. Tell Jenn to keep up the chatter."

"Will do. Work your magic, Sergeant."

"Durrell, may I ask you something?"

"Go ahead, young thing," he cockily replied.

"Is the girl okay?"

"Yeah, she fine."

"Is it okay if I hear her respond?"

"Yeah, hold on." Durrell nudged the young woman with the gun's barrel.

"I...I'm okay," the girl said sheepishly. Jenn felt the anguish in the girl's voice, but she tried not feeling too emotionally attached towards the girl's plight. If she hadn't been looking to make a score or hooking, she wouldn't be here in the first place. Nonetheless, she did feel bad the girl was now realizing she may not get out of this alive.

"Awwright, lady cop! You heard the girl! Now, be smart and let me blow outta' here!"

"I'll let you go, if you drop the gun and let her leave by herself."

"No can do, girlfriend."

"Why not, Durrell? Don't you realize Jones would leave you for dead in a heartbeat? He could replace you tomorrow!"

"No way, baby! He calls us his Warriors For the Cause!"

"The Cause, you say? What cause, Durrell? Dealing drugs? Slaughtering gays?"

"You think that's what this is about? Fucking up gays? Nigga' would've rolled the bitch if he was straight. Faggot stopped lettin' us use his place for a dealing spot. Yeah, Jones, he believe in the Kane prophecy, but he mainly doin' it to protect his investments. It gets hard to have a profitable business in the "X" trade, when the rich white boys from across the bridge think the police'll be bustin' them. So he does a couple killin's, cops go lookin' for him, takes the heat off us sellin' product."

"So, he kills for pleasure and for profit?"

"Don't everybody?"

"You ever murder anyone, Durrell?" Jenn calmly asked.

"Why you askin', girl? Think I'm afraid to? Hell yeah I've killed, and I'll do it again if I got to! There ain't nuthin' else for a nigga' to do around here 'cept deal and take care of his own!"

Tom turned to Jenn. "Hang in there. He's about to blow." He got back on the headset. "Zoul, do we have a bead on him?"

In a ghostlike fashion, he crept across the catwalk. It was very reminiscent of the days he spent in the woods with his father. Maynard Terrant was able to stalk so swiftly through the underbrush of those Clairton hills, he could almost touch the deer with his hands. Zoul followed the ways of his father as much as he could. The young man learned very young how to be quick with your eye, and accurate with your shot. In the darkness of this new territory, he slithered towards his target. As he set up his goggles, he answered quietly. "This boy is getting uptight, Chief. It's your call." Zoul could see Durrell's arms were now flailing wildly.

"You've got the go-ahead, Zoul."

"Durrell, can't we end this peacefully? Is it worth having someone die?" Jenn pleaded.

"Enough talk, cops! This is gonna' end! On my terms!"

They all heard the girl scream, as Jenn cried out. "No, Durrell! No!"

The room became illuminated from the barrels flash, but it came from the catwalk. Trooper Razoul Terrant had hit the young man directly in the head. In a split second, the perfect "kill shot" had made Durrell just another victim of the drug trade. The girl was under the slain young man, and was screaming for help.

"Zoul, we need lights!"

"Hang on, Troop. I just passed a switchbox on the way up here." When he located it, he snapped the handle upwards, and the space was alighted.

"John, you and Jenn usher the girl out of harms way. Catch up with Zoul and I as fast as you can."

"You got it, Tommy."

Tom hastily made his way to Zoul's location. "Good shot, kid. You ready to roll?" Zoul gave him a thumbs up, and reaffixed his headset. "Towny, we're on it!" Tom felt the juices of old flowing again. Hopefully, tonight's outcome would be the same as the tunnels of fifteen years ago. Maybe, they could end this madness right here, right now. "Towny, we're on it!"

"Get here quick, Thomas! We're making inroads! One more down, two more apprehended and the Strike Unit is leading the way!"

"We'll be there, Towny!"

Chief Townsend and his men converged on the door behind the altar. As they got closer, they could hear quite a commotion from behind the enclosure. "Get to it," he ordered his Strike Unit duo. As the one rammed the door, and the other followed him, brandishing an assault rifle, wood splintered in every direction. Much to everyone's horror, the debris blew out and not in. The door had been rigged, and by the time everyone regained their senses, Chief Townsend's two Strikers lie dead amongst the rubble.

"Towny, what the hell happened?" Tom barked into his microphone. "Artis, can you hear me?"

"Talk to us, Artis!" Sam yelled nervously, as his agents and he moved through the last of the rubble.

"Gang, we're in deep shit here! I've got two Strikers down! Where are you?"

"We're through the collapse and on our way! Hang tight, Artis!" Sam's heart was pounding furiously. He knew the Bureau dropped the ball long ago by not making Jones' apprehension a priority, and now two cops had paid for the decision with their lives. It was just another reason added to why Sam wanted out.

The smoke was still billowing around the three remaining Heroes and Zeroes. From out of the plumes, Artis saw the outline of a fast moving figure. While moving forward, he could see the individual wore a long coat. He also caught a glimpse of what looked to be dreadlocks moving to and fro. "Jones!" Towny exploded. Canty and Pruett starting firing rounds towards the shadowy outline. "Hold your fire, boys! Let's follow him. Remember, we need him alive," Towny said as he pried the assault rifle from his dead officers' hands. "Tommy, we've spotted Jones, and he's on the move. He's heading in the direction of the dope dens. Be alerted, Yarders, he may have more doors rigged. I've got two DOA's 'cause of that dick. I don't need any more."

Tom's senses hightened rapidly. "This is it, Yarders. You heard the man. Be on alert. John, where are you and Jenn?"

"We're on the catwalk and headed your way, lad."

"Okay, pal. Zoul and I are off the catwalk, and are proceeding in the direction of the shooting galleries. Proceed with caution. The doors may be rigged. Towny's down two."

"I know, I heard," John replied as he bit down on his cheek.

"Be prepared with your flashlights. I think Jones will be the one cutting the lights off, and soon. It will be to his advantage."

"Got you, Tommy. The lass and I are torch ready."

"Ditto for the Gang," Sam huffed. He was still irritated about losing the two men while he was helplessly blocked off from aiding them. "Same for the H and Z's, Tommy. We're ready." Towny was moving, but it was labored. He was still smarting from the debris which had slammed into everyone.

The corridor through which they went was dimly lit. Only the eerie glow from the NV's illuminated this dank structure. Tom held Zoul up before they went any further into the belly of the beast. "If we get split up for any reason, try to maintain contact on the headsets. This guy is not going down solo."

"I know, Chief. We just need to keep our wits about us, right?"

"You said it, kid. Let's just be cautious in the rooms. God knows, besides the doors being rigged, the place in general looks like it could go at any moment." The long hallway was illuminated by only a solitary, dim bulb. Tom began to inch down the tomblike pathway. Zoul stayed back a few paces and on the opposite side of Tom. Tom put his hand up to hold

Zoul's position. "Zoul, I think I hear something coming. Get by an entrance and be prepared to dive in."

"No problem, Chief. I'm just a few feet in back of you."

Tom got on his set again. "John boy, I think we have company coming. How close are you?"

"Tommy, we're entering the hallway and are com...."

Tom could not hear the rest of John's communication. The light bulb blew out, as the concussion from a distant explosion enveloped the hallway.

"Jesus Christ! Zoul, Tom, are you okay up there?" Boyle barked into his set.

"We're good, John! Towny, are you and the H and Z's reading? Come back!"

"Yes, Thomas, we're all right," came the disgusted reply. "Get ready for that prick. Sam and his boys are here with us. The cocksucker just caved in the floor ahead of us with a detonation. We're all totally cut off from you, and have to retreat. There is smoke everywhere. We'll have to come through the back and catch up with you. It's going to take some time to trace our way back. All the power is out."

"We'll be okay, Towny. Take your time, and be careful."

"I'll try and get some uniforms to reinforce you."

"We'll hang in. Don't spread yourself thin, Artis. If he gets past us.."

"Don't sweat it, Thomas. We're covered outside."

"Okay, Artis. I gotta' go, brother. We'll see you soon."

"We'll be there, Thomas." Towny tried to exude an air of confidence in his voice, but deep inside he knew the situation was tough. Sam and he would have to do their best to keep the morale high for their younger counterparts. We will get to you, Tom. We will.

Tom and Zoul put their flashlights on. Even though the blast had been a good distance away from them, a fair amount of dust and other airborne particles began to filter into the hallway. Tom looked back to see two more beams of light approaching their position. "I see you and Jenn approaching. Be careful, troops."

"Aye, we're okay, Tommy. We're having a bit of a time making out your beam, but we'll be there soon."

Tom called back to Zoul to find out if his headset was operational.

"I've got my ears on, Chief. Hearing you loud and clear."

"How are the NVG's working in this muck?"

"Very well, so far. I see you clearly, and I see Troop and Jenn in the distance."

"Good to hear. We're probably relying on them quite a bit from now on." Tom moved up a few more feet. He was trying not to cough, but the smoke was beginning to have an acrid odor. "Cover your faces when you can. This stuff is getting nasty."

"We hear you, lad."

Tom moved up a few feet more, but still told Zoul to hold his position. "I think I hear someone coming," he whispered. "Everyone, hold your positions and keep your sets on." Tom tried to send the beam from his flashlight down the passage. It sounded as if light footsteps were approaching from the adjacent hallway. All of a sudden, the light steps became more of a thunderous sprint. Tom again flashed his beam into the expanse of the hall. Through the dust, he could make out a figure diving through the air, and then quickly disappearing. Tom's light had caught a glimpse of what appeared to be a long object in one of the outstretched arms. As the tip of the object glistened through the dust and the darkness, Tom's eyes opened wide as he leapt to his feet and began to run. "It's Jones! Yarders, follow me forward!" he barked.

Razoul Terrant had seen it all clearly in his NVG's, and knew Tom was correct. He'd made out the body and the sword, but he also saw the other arm pitch something. His instincts made him freeze. He began to hear what Tom had not, a heavy, clunking sound, bounding down the buckled floorboards. Zoul started to make out what it was, and as he did, he shot up and began backpedaling towards an open doorway. "Grenade! It's a grenade! Clear the hallway!" he bellowed as he jumped through the opening.

John Boyle did not flinch. He grabbed Jenn and used his body like a shield. He jumped backwards as he put all the weight of his bull-like frame into breaking down the door behind them. He fell in and rolled on top of the young Sergeant, using the mass of his body to take the brunt of whatever had followed them in.

Tom Miller would not be so lucky. In all the commotion of the chase, he heard Zoul's voice at the last moment. As he dove into the same hallway Jones had come from, the concussion of the blast caught him. As pieces of broken wood and plaster fell around him, Tom Miller lay motionless.

CHAPTER 24

Down the other hall, Zoul began to throw debris from out of the doorway. He had luckily remained unscathed from the blast. He made his way from the room and was able to survey the damage. He saw rusty water spraying from the old, copper pipes, overhead. He also saw parts of the buckled floorboards underfoot were now totally missing, leaving him able to peer into the levels below.

He then peered towards where he had last seen John Boyle and Jenn Gates, prior to the explosion. The floors in that direction also seemed obliterated. Where there was any flooring left, huge wood beams, piping, plaster, and sections of broken furniture from the old offices above them filled the area. It was virtually impossible for Zoul to get near his two friends.

Where he'd last seen Tom was much of the same situation. Zoul felt trapped. His nerve endings were tingling and he felt as if he would pass out. Keep your wits about you, boy. He thought back to the days of when his father worked in the mill. His father had been involved in an ore pellet collapse that had nearly taken the whole crew out in one shot. For hours, his father and his friends dug through the mess came out alive. "Just pray, when things like that happen, son, that you keep your wits about you," his father told him when he made it home. "Just pray." As he began to pray to himself, he could feel himself pick up his headset. "Tom! Chief Miller! Trooper John Boyle! Sergeant Jenn Gates! If any of you read me, please reply! Over!"

"Tom! Chief Tom Miller! Trooper John Boyle.." The bellowing sound of Zoul's voice brought a smile to the Irishman's face. He and Jenn were filthy from head to toe, but otherwise, no worse for the wear. John rolled himself from being over Jenn and started to flick the bits of plaster from his clothing. He grabbed his flashlight and pointed the beam to where Jenn was now sitting upright.

"Are ya' alright, young one?" She began to knock the dust from her clothes and looked at John. "Fine..just fine. Thank you for grabbing me out of there."

"Nothing to it, lass. You'd of done the same." John picked up his headset and began to reply. "Zoul, it's John and Jenn. We're okay, lad. How about you and Tom?"

"I'm fine, Troop, but the Chief was separated from me in the blast. He started running down the hall when he saw Jones. I still haven't heard from him."

John felt the color drain from his face. First Luke and then Al. They'd lost two already tonight, and now, his best buddy was missing. "Come on, Gates! We've got some diggin' to do. Tom is missing, and we've got to find him."

The young Sergeant sprang to her feet. "Oh my God!"

"Whoa, Troop! Hold your horses, you two! Yins have to clear the area! You're in the middle of a full blown collapse. I'll try and get to Tom."

John threw up his arms in disbelief. "Dammit! Zoul, are you sure?"

"Troop, you've got nothing but air in front of that pile of rubble. Find another way, John. I promise, I'll get to Tom."

"Okay, Zoul. Will do," John replied while spitting on the floor in disgust. For the first time, in a long time, he felt completely helpless. He knew Zoul was right. They couldn't risk having any more officers hurt, but it didn't make John feel any better. *To hell with Jerome Jones, I'm getting' tired of losing friends. I just want to know Tom is fine.* "H and Z's, Capitol Gang, you've heard our situation, boys?"

"Affirmative, John," Towny replied. "We'll meet you in the back of the building." Townsend and Tunney's group were already in full stride when they heard the explosion. The two old war horses gave each other a quick glance as they ran together. In both of their minds, catching Jones had taken a back seat. The search and rescue of Razoul Terrant and Tom Miller had become tantamount.

"Chief Miller! It's Zoul! Can you hear me?" The distant voice was getting closer. Through the dust and the haze, a beam of light appeared in the dark. He slowly crawled on his hands and knees through the debris. He grabbed for the beam and shined the light over his body. It looked as if he'd received a few minor cuts from the blast. Otherwise, he seemed fine. He looked up and thanked God for giving him another chance. Tom Miller was alive.

He stood up and began to search for his headset. He couldn't see it, but he could hear the constant chattering of voices from it. He shined the light to where he thought he heard the noise. It was then he saw what had missed him by only a few feet. A pile of mangled wooden beams, furniture, and other rubble standing taller than him, lay in the hallway from which he had jumped.

Tom began to hear the voice again. It was Zoul, and he was getting closer. "Zoul! Zoul! It's Tom! Can you hear me?" He was so happy to hear the young man's voice. He'd thought for sure the blast had taken his young friends life.

Zoul began to hear the muffled sounds of his friend. "It's Tom! Team members, Chief Miller is alive! Repeat, Tom is alive! I'm making my way to his voice!"

John Boyle heard the good news as he and Jenn made their way from the building. "We copy, Zoul! Be careful, lad!"

"Will do, Troop!"

The burly trooper said a silent prayer of thanks, and smiled at Jenn. "The Lord is shining down on my friend today, lass. Tom is alive, now let's go get Jones."

"I'm with you there, John."

Back in the hallway, Zoul carefully made his way to the pile. "Hang in Tom, I'm coming!"

"I hear you, Zoul!" Zoul's NVG's picked up the task ahead of him as he surveyed the pile. "Damn it!" he snarled in frustration. "Tom, can you hear me pretty clearly?"

"Yeah, I hear you, Zoul. The debris field must not be so thick between us. Somewhere in it is my headset."

"I'm going to start digging out, okay?"

"That's fine, Zoul. Listen, I know Jones is still in here, somewhere. Let me get going. Catch up with me soon, okay?"

"Chief, you don't even have your set with you! Can't you please wait a few minutes?" Zoul knew he could plead his case until tomorrow, but he already knew Tom Miller's reply. "A few minutes more and Jones will disappear again. Catch up with me soon, buddy."

"Okay, Tom." Zoul tackled the pile like a man possessed, throwing objects to and fro. He was determined to get Tom, and then catch Jones. "All units, Tom Miller is on the move. I will be backing him up shortly."

Tom felt for his revolver and unholstered the weapon. He knew Jones hadn't gone too far. Tom had read enough of the man's file to know what a cocky disposition Jones possessed. After all the mayhem he'd caused tonight, Jones was playing his games and loving the outcome.

Tom made his way cautiously into the even longer corridor, approached the first doorway, and snaked his way inside. The room was in a typical, ramshackle state of affair. Spent hypodermics and crack vials littered the floor. A small, filthy cot lay in one corner of the room, and the smell of urine and semen was enough to make Tom feel nauseous. As expected, the wall between this room and the next had been blown out. Tom was trying to make sense of why Jones would splendor himself in such squalor.

While he walked through the next few rooms, it was much of the same. He saw dirty diapers, and the smell of fecal odor pervaded the room into which he now stepped. Great, they even bring their kids here. It was hard for Tom to imagine a man such as Jones, who had impeccable taste for high-end men's garments, and such sensual taste in women's gear, walking these scum infested halls.

It was even harder to fathom Jones, who seemed to place such high regard on vanity, especially his hair and facial appearance, performing his twisted, sexual activities with the strung out, unwashed, and possibly diseased clientele wallowing in the muck of these buildings. Tom had put in enough years doing this line of work to try and understand the fine line separating the cross-over from Jones' insane behavior from the more normal behavior of your average working stiff who pays the mortgage, cares for their family, and on occasion, pays a visit to the local 'bump-and-grind' to arouse the sex drive for a night at home with the old lady.

Tom walked for a while more, but there was still no trace of Jones. There wasn't even a fresh shoeprint on these dusty floors. He had the sixth sense to realize Jones' disappearing act wouldn't last for long.

Tom shined his light through the hole and into the next room. It looked as if the room had recently been disturbed. Small dust particles moved rapidly in the air. As he silently approached the gaping hole, his light hit something glistening on the floor. Could it possibly be the edge of Jones' infamous sword? He turned the light away from the room. He could shoot through the wall and try to injure Jones, but he risked the chance of hitting a vital organ. As much as he hated to admit it, he needed Jones alive.

Tom readied himself for what he had to do. Diving in was a risky maneuver, but it was his only choice. Tom breathed deep and began running. The plan was to dive in, roll over, blind Jones with the light in Tom's one hand, and hold the killer to his mark with the revolver in his other. He took flight and prayed his plan would work.

Jerome Jones would have an alternative plan. He saw Tom leaping in and quickly tackled him. The force of Jones' muscular body sent them both hurtling into the back wall of the room. Tom felt the full impact of crashing into the plaster and the beams behind it. He moaned loudly. It felt as if his air supply had been cut off.

While Tom fell to the floor, Jones scrambled to retrieve his sword. Tom held onto the flashlight, but his gun had fallen somewhere. He turned to locate it by the hole and stumbled for it. In a valiant effort, he tried to stretch for its handle, but a swift kick from Jones' boot made it all for naught. Without hesitating, Tom shined the flashlight into the killers face. "Damn you!" Jones snarled as he blindly flailed the sword in Tom's direction. Tom could hear the wind from the swords blade overhead. It was way too close for comfort.

Tom took a page from Jones' book and bull-rushed the big man. As they tumbled to the floor, so did the sword. Tom quickly set to punching Jones' face. His hard fists sounded like a hammer hitting nails. Two hard hits to the face and he could hear him breathing heavy, but he could still not finish him. Tom hit him again, but Jones broke free one of his muscular arms from under Tom's body and squarely connected with the Chief's jaw.

It felt like an anvil had hit him and he collapsed to the floor. He knew he had a good twenty years of age on the well-built Jones, but Tom was far from weak. Tom wondered if Jones was on something, like PCP. If he was, it would be like waging war with a tank.

Jones cockily strode off to retrieve his sword, but Tom found the energy to spring to his feet. He made a mad dash to rush him again, but the big man was waiting for him. He quickly moved to the side and firmly placed his boot into the side of Tom's head. He then picked up the dazed lawman and hurled his limp body into the hallway. Tom's body made a thunderous sound as he hit the wall. He crumpled to the ground and was motionless. He was still conscious, but he was badly beaten. He tried to lift his head, when he could hear Jones slowly approaching. The madman twirled the big sword effortlessly and began to laugh. He was soon standing over the Chief. His grin looked maniacal and his eyes looked glazed. "Well, if it isn't Tom Miller! The hunter of hunter's!" Jones chuckled again. "To what do I owe such a great honor, having been pursued by the best?"

"You won't get out of here, Jerome. They've got you cornered," Tom moaned.

Jones erupted into laughter again. "I think you have it wrong, Tom. From where I'm standing, they are the ones cut off, and I've got you cornered." Jones' eyes narrowed, and his smile was soon erased. "I am impressed, old man. You are smart, and you are strong, but now you need to go. I have other more pressing issues to which to attend." He opened up his leather trench to reveal four long throwing knives. "I could do you with one of these, but I always did enjoy the more dramatic better." Jones let go of the jacket and began to lift the sword over his head.

Tom propped himself up, but he was still incapacitated. He was trying so hard to fight. Lord, I will not leave this world without a fighting chance.

As Jones began his downward swipe, a blast of light flashed from the top of the sword. The shock to the steel blade reverberated through its handle and into Jones' hands. "Fuck!" Jones bellowed as the sword fell away from him.

Razoul Terrant was still a distance from the two men, but with the aid of the NVG's, his shot remained tried and true. "Stay where you are, Jerome! Don't even think of moving!"

Jones had fallen away from Tom, and he remained in a kneeling position. But, he was far from through. Tom could barely make out the hand reaching into the trenchcoat, but when he heard the pin hit the floor, Tom yelled for all he was worth.

"Zoul! Grenade! Get down, now!" Tom tried valiantly to lunge for Jones, but his legs were still too wobbly. He fell down, and the dark figure again made his escape.

Zoul got into one of the rooms and quickly hit the ground. Jones had overthrown his position, so the blast occurred far behind Zoul. He righted himself and made haste to Tom's position. "Tom, are you okay, man?" Zoul asked while he balanced the staggering Chief.

"I'll be alright, kid. Thanks for saving my butt."

"No problem, Chief. You've done the same for many others. Stay here, Tom. I'll go after him," Zoul said as he began to move forward.

Tom retrieved his revolver and put up his hand. "Hold on, Zoul. We're not splitting up again." Tom was mad, and he was utilizing his anger to regain his strength. "Let's go, kid!" he exclaimed, and the two men took off running.

"Zoul, what the hell is going on? Get back to me!" John Boyle heard the last explosion and was starting to become exasperated. He hated knowing he was helpless to aid the trapped officers. "Zoul, do you read me?"

"I hear you, Troop."

"Are you okay?

"Yes, Troop. Tom and I are in pursuit of Jones. Tom slowed him down a bit."

"That's my boys! What's your position?"

"Hard to tell, Troop! It feels like we're in a maze. Where are you?"

"We're assembled in the field behind the factory."

"Okay, we're on it! I'll be in touch!"

"Right, lad! Be careful! Troop out!" John turned to face the group. "Okay, people, you heard it. They are in pursuit. Artis, do you want to hold position until Zoul replies?"

"I think it would be the prudent thing to do, John boy. We've lost two already."

"How's about positioning a few of yer' uniforms by the door the Yarders initially breached?"

"Good idea. I'll get on it."

Sam Tunney walked to where John was standing. He lit a cigarette and looked at the Irishman. "Now comes the hardest part for lawmen like us, John Boyle, the waiting game."

"Yes Sam, it is. It always has been."

Zoul was darting through the halls of the factories offices, and Tom was doing a great job of keeping up the pace. His lungs were burning like a blowtorch, but his body was bursting with adrenaline. Zoul was trying his best to follow the heavy, thudding sounds of Jones' boots. He catapulted up a narrow flight of stairs. "Tom, I wonder if these are the steps Towny said led to the other side of the catwalk!" he yelled as he ran.

"I don't know!" Tom blurted. His breathing was becoming labored, still, he'd be damned if he would give up the chase. "It's so hard to tell! Everything seems out of whack in here!"

"Let's keep going! His footsteps are getting louder!"

"Keep going, Zoul! I'm with you!"

The men soon entered a smaller hallway. Zoul could still make out where he was going. Tom was not having as much luck and his flashlight began to flicker and get dim. He could now only feel what was underfoot as they sloshed through the wet corridor. Huge rats squealed and scattered in every direction as Tom and John scampered by. They rounded another corner and hit dry land. They were soon bounding up another rickety flight of narrow steps. The two men were gaining on the booming footsteps. It was the sound of Jones' boot heels clanging against metal that assured Zoul of where he and Tom were now located.

"We're on the catwalk, Troop! Head for the catwalk!" Zoul's voice was raising in anticipation of again seeing Jones. "Go Troop, go!"

"Sweet Jesus! Hop on your horses, folks! The bastard's headed them back to the catwalk!" John took off running as the rest followed behind. Towny soon caught up to him. "I'll call my uniforms and tell them to be waiting by the door you breached, John. We're gonna' get him, Irish! We're gonna' get him!" John started to pick up his pace, and so did Towny. "By God, man, I hope you're right."

Inside the factory, Jones could hear the commotion being raised behind him growing louder. He sprinted to the end of the catwalk and bounded down the steps. He saw the outline of the door straight ahead and put both hands inside his trench.

Towny had just informed his two uniformed officers to stand ready. Both of them had their guns drawn at the steel door. In a cataclysmic burst, the door flew open, and two lightening bolts of honed steel screamed towards their targets and connected. Before they knew what had hit them, the two officers lay mortally wounded. They were to be the latest victims of Jones' deadly accurate throwing knives.

Zoul and Tom neared the door, and upon hearing no uproar or gunshots, they expected the worst. They were in full stride, and as they hit the last step, Tom stopped to see if he could aid his fallen brothers. Zoul slowed just for a moment, but Tom yelled for him to get Jones.

Zoul could see the long coat and the dreadlocks flying in every direction while Jones was darting across the debris ridden field. He was still to far away to try a shot, so he began to run. When he felt he could reach the fleeing assailant, he stopped, looked through his NVG's, and aimed steady. He furiously unloaded his clip while placing his fire from Jones' kneecaps to his ankles. Zoul could see the dirt kick up on all but possibly his last shot. If he'd hit Jerome Jones, the powerfully evil man was not showing any ill effects. Zoul disgustedly popped out the spent clip, and began to run again while he reloaded. By the time he would look up to aim, everything would become a blur.

From out of the darkness came two beams of light, and the squealing of tires. An older model Cadillac came to a screeching halt only inches from Jones. The passenger side door flew open, and Jones dove in. Tom and the rest of the officers from the raid had reached Zoul's position just long enough to witness the mind-blowing spectacle. Tom, John and Zoul began to empty their clips, with a vengeance, into the cold, night air, as the

Cadillac's taillights became an infinitesimal blip on the radar screen of their vision. Two of Towny's units bound through the field and proceeded to give chase, but everyone involved knew what was to be the outcome. Jerome Jones, the man who'd caused so much death and despair, had again disappeared into the bowels of the city's underworld.

The officers looked at each other with disbelief and despair. Tom, Sam, and John had been through times like this, but even they were blown away by the setback. Tom knew he'd have to put on the quick, game face, and kick everyone into gear. "Guys, I know this is a hard time. We lost two good men, and may lose two more before the nights out. With what we were hit with, we could have lost many more. We will regroup, and we will catch both killers. Remember, we did not catch Kane in a day."

"Chief, I think I may have hit him," Zoul piped up. "The last shot I made, while he was running, did not kick up any dirt."

"Well folks, let's go see if we can find a blood trail." Tom began striding to where Jones had escaped. It didn't take long for them to find what they needed.

"Ah, my boys. Trooper Terrant, fine shot he is, hit Jerome Jones," John crowed. He pointed to the small, spattering of blood that was located behind what looked to be one of Jones' boot prints.

Jenn bent down next to the blood trail. "We have an entrance, but not an exit."

"You lodged it in there, Razoul. Good shot, young man."

Zoul nodded. "It's just too bad it didn't take him down, Agent Tunney," he moaned. Tunney put his arm around the trooper. "Son, you are the first person to successfully shoot Jerome Jones. If anything, you pissed him off. He'll be back on the prowl soon."

"I think you are absolutely correct. There is no way, after being shot, a maniac like Jones lies low," Tom added.

Chief Townsend hastily reentered the scene. "Listen folks, I hate to break up the party, but my boys are saying the local press is on the way."

"I'd take it we'd better get out of Trenton."

"Yeah, Tommy, it's time to get outta' Dodge. This was strictly our call to have you, Sam, and John here. The Governor will have our butts for lunch, if it's found out through the press, out of state cops were in on this. Get going, guys. I'll handle the damage control."

Tom holstered his revolver. "You heard the Chief, let's roll. Artis, keep us informed on the getaway car."

"You got it, brother." He may have looked beaten and battle weary from tonight's debacle, but anyone who met Chief Artis Townsend knew he was a fighter. He would be back.

The two groups dashed to their vehicles and were on the road and out of the city limits in a heartbeat. No one uttered a word for quite a few minutes, but when they reached the wooded stretch of Route 29, the silence was broken by the ringing of Tom's cell phone. "Hello, Chief Miller."

"Tom, it's Sam."

"What's going on, Sam?"

"Listen, I wanted to inform you Artis just called. He said the units already found the Cadillac ditched and no signs of Jones, or the driver."

"Did they run the plates?"

"Yes, they did Tom. Unfortunately.."

"Let me guess. The car was stolen."

"Yes, it was, Tom. It was reported two weeks ago."

"It figures."

"Tom, we've got something else." Sam's voice seemed heavy with concern, almost unnerved. "I just got on my laptop, and I've received another downloaded picture of Jones, Pond, and another individual from the boys in D.C."

"Go on, Sam," Tom replied nervously.

"I think you may want to pull over to the shoulder, Tom. I want you to see who the other individual is with your own two eyes."

<u>CHAPTER 25</u>

A solitary light burnt through the darkness inside the New Hope Borough Municipal Building. Everyone else had left hours ago, but on December 29th, at one o'clock in the morning, Mayor Jerry Ward sat despondently at his ornate desk. His eyes took in all the grandeur of the room while his mind wandered aimlessly. He'd slowly been draining a bottle of Smirnoff.

He began looking at a photograph of the President and himself at the 1996 Democratic Convention. He parted his lips to take another swallow. "How promising a future I had!" he said aloud. He slammed some more of the vodka down his throat, and rocketed the glass towards the door. While it shattered into many pieces upon impact, Jerry leaned back in his leather chair, and began to chuckle sarcastically. "Now, it's all shit."

He lurched forward in the chair long enough to glimpse a picture of his father and him, which was taken at Jerry's college graduation. Well, pop, I guess you were right. I never would amount to anything in your eyes. Jerry began to think about the mess he'd made of his life. He had always been a big spender. The more extravagant the item, the more Jerry Ward wanted to obtain it. He had an innumerable amount of trust funds to choose from while growing up, so money was never an issue. Besides, his parents were very wealthy to begin with, and his mother, no matter how distant she could be from time to time, would never let her "little Jerry," go to the poor house.

His mother may have added to his lavish spending habits during his college years, but when she passed on a few years after he'd graduated, his father made sure Jerry knew fun time was over. The iron fist of Amos Ward was about to hit Jerry with the bitter taste of reality.

Amos had told Jerry to meet him at his spacious office, located in Center City, Philadelphia. Metropolis Steel's headquarters was Amos Ward's baby. He'd always dreamed of a having a building to dwarf the city's skyline. However, an archaic law prohibiting anything being built higher than the statue of William Penn, which rested at the pinnacle of City Hall's tower, had thwarted his ambitions for years.

After decades of legal wrangling from the elder Ward and other developers, the ordinance was finally lifted. In a move of absolute arrogance, Amos would build Metropolis One, a beautifully ornate steel and glass structure which, even now, commanded the Philadelphia skyline. He'd made sure his top floor office had its desk strategically placed towards the view of the Mayor of Philadelphia's office, which now lie hundreds of feet below his structure.

It was into this impressive and imposing power that the newly elected Mayor of New Hope was called. Jerry grabbed the brushed steel handles that were attached to the monstrous twelve foot steel doors leading into his father's lair. The inlays of both doors held some captivating artwork which was personally crafted by the best metalwork artisans Amos Ward could find. Each door contained sculptures of a massive steel plant billowing smoke through its massive stacks. Other figures were depictions of steelworkers pouring a glistening stream of molten steel from the giant ladles into an equally gargantuan casting machine. It was the kind of rough and tumble life Amos grew up around.

A steelman from his teens, he labored at every job in the plant, until his father felt he was ready to succeed him at the helm. The way the molten, liquid steel flowed through the old, open hearth furnaces in which he first worked, was the same way the blood coursed through his veins, hot and fast. It was his kind of work, and the steelworkers were his kind of people. They were a no-nonsense, hard working, tough as nails group of individuals, just like Amos. How he loved this way of life, and how much Jerry despised it.

When the doors closed, Jerry saw the black leather chair facing out to the skyline of the city. "Have a seat, Jerry," the voice beckoned from behind the seatback. As always, his father's tone was very businesslike towards his son. Amos slowly swung the chair around to face the young man. The elder Ward was wearing his usual Brooks Brother's, navy blue suit, with a starched, white shirt, and a mustard colored tie. His salt-and-pepper hair was neatly cropped, and his face still displayed a healthy tan from his annual pre-Christmas trip to the islands.

He's so damn predictable, right down to his socks and shoes. "So, I'm assuming I haven't been sent here to be congratulated on becoming Mayor?" he haughtily asked.

"Mayor of New Hope? Hell, if I'd known those were the small potatoes you were after, I could have sent you to Bucks County Community College. It would have saved me a mint on your college education."

"Thanks, dad. I'll take that as my congratulatory speech from you."

Amos began to laugh. "Ah, Jerry, you always were quick witted. That's what I think your mother referred to it as. I referred to it with a much more, horticultural term. Well, anyway, the reason I asked you here is to inquire about your new residence."

"Yes dad, I bought a house," Jerry sighed.

"A house? Oh no, son. I think from what I witnessed, it was more of a mini-mansion." Jerry was beginning to sweat. "You were by my house?"

"Yes, I was, Jerry, long enough to see what your trust fund was now being siphoned to."

"What I do with that money is my prerogative," Jerry replied in a harsh tone.

"You are correct in your assumption, son. You do realize, however, with what splendid taste you have, and how you've lavished your, shall we call them acquaintances, over the past few years with gifts, the money from the trusts are nearly gone?"

You dirty, old rat. Still nosing into my private affairs, are you? "Who gave you the right to look into my finances, father?"

"Why, Jerry, that would have been your grandfather who gave me such a right," Amos replied indignantly. "You see, son, he'd also noted you were a slight bit, shall we say, eccentric in your behavior. He'd informed his accountant to have me notified immediately if any large sums of money were extracted from the trust."

Jerry's feet began to shuffle as he sunk further into the chair. Oh, father. How you do so love the feel of power. If you only knew how much your son loved it too, albeit, my love for differs slightly from yours. In the end, it all has the same result. "Where is this leading to, father?" the younger Ward asked while he straightened his posture.

"Jerry, you have nearly tapped out a three and a half million dollar trust. You have traveled to exquisite lands, purchased expensive automobiles, spoiled your odd associates, and now, for the coup de' grace! You have constructed a seven hundred fifty thousand dollar estate, and spent another two hundred eighty thousand dollars to furnish and landscape the place."

Jerry was livid. "It is, if your memory has not failed you, my money. I can do with it what I please," he responded through his clenched teeth.

"True, son. Let me inquire this of you, when the money ran out, how did you intend to live?"

"Well, to be honest, I do make a wage, father, lest you have forgotten."

"Sixty thousand a year!" his father howled with laughter. "Son, you've been known to spend that amount in a week!"

"I'm pleased you're enjoying this so much, father, but there is the matter of the trust from mother. I have it, on good authority, she has left me almost seven million dollars." Jerry looked at the old man with a smug expression. Choke on those figures, father.

"Ah, yes, mother's trust. It was to be distributed to you at the end of this year. Did your good authority happen to mention the stipulation of the trust?"

Jerry's jaw began to drop. The beads of sweat began to reappear. "What stipulation?" he stammered.

"The stipulation was, in the event of your deficit spending continuing unabashedly, I, through the power given to me by your late mother, and our attorney, could dissolve the trust." The sledgehammer effect of these words hit Jerry with all of its weight. "Dissolve the trust?" The words just kept echoing through his skull. "What would become of the money?" he asked his father in a low, guttural tone.

Amos smiled ever so slightly at the question. "Why, it would go to the men and women who toil in the mills, Jerry. I'd say they'd enjoy an extra Christmas bonus, wouldn't you?" The chair underneath the young man tumbled backwards as he leapt towards the huge steel and glass desk separating the two men. "What gives you the right?" Jerry exploded.

"What gives me the right," Amos responded nonchalantly, "is it was my money from the start. Your great-grandfather started this company in a minuscule brick foundry located in North Philadelphia. When his son, your grandfather, was old enough to work, which, may I remind you, was pre-teenager in those days, he taught him every job in the plant.

My father relocated to a more spacious plant past Fishtown, along the banks of the Delaware River. He taught me, just as his father had. I worked every job in that mill, through the Great Depression, fought in the war, and came right back to Metropolis. By the time I was thirty, my father basically left control of the everyday operations to me. I ran it from my father's know-how. The monetary end, well, I always had the knack for making a dollar. I didn't graduate from college until I was nearly forty-one. My father could care less about college, but I knew it would make me an even better boss. I graduated from the University of Pennsylvania's, Wharton School of Business.."

"Top of your class. Yes, I know all of this, father, but thanks anyway for the history lesson," Jerry snapped. "Where the hell is this leading to?"

Amos walked to the windows and looked out to his empire in the distance. "In the late forties, U.S. Steel bought up forty six hundred acres of farms and rose fields, in what is now called Fairless Hills. I always told your grandfather we should have built another plant and located it in Bucks County, but damn it if old Ben Fairless didn't beat us to the punch. Fairless Works was going to be a huge plant, so I decided to enlarge Metropolis. Steel was in its heyday. Everyone was using it in some type of application. I built three more blast furnaces, two more rolling divisions, a pipe mill, and more. Hell, I was one of the first U.S. companies to have a continuous slab caster.

We were riding on high times. I was employing over eight thousand blue-collar men and women. Metropolis was helping to build America from coast to coast. I knew, though, that our heady times were about to end. Foreign steel was gutting us all. It was the hardest day of my life when I went to the Union and had to tell them three thousand workers had to go to keep us afloat, but I did it, and the ones who stuck with me were able to weather the storm. I've had to streamline this business. Computers now run some of the operations now. I demolished the outmoded operations, and built other, more modern ones in their place. I took over two failing steel plants in Delaware, modernized them also, and now, all my plants are profitable. Bethlehem and U.S. Steel are sifting through the ashes, and they may die out, but we are still doing well.

Through all of the hard times, I've been able to keep a good relationship with the Union. This company has never had a labor strike in its history, and with all the plants remaining profitable, this will be the third year in a row my hard working folks receive a raise and a big profit share bonus."

Enough of the crap, father. Jerry sighed loudly. "Good for you, father. Again, where is this leading?"

"Where it is leading is to something called responsibility, Jerry. I have responsibility over the livelihood of almost six thousand Metropolis Steel employees. I also have a responsibility to hundreds of thousands of shareholders who expect me to turn a substantial profit on their hard earned money.

Son, you can't even take care of yourself. How you expect to take care of the townspeople of New Hope is a mystery to me. I told your mother a long time ago that I should have molded you like my father had done with me, but she wanted something different for your life. I knew you would be our only child. Your mom just about died giving birth to you, so I digressed and let her have her way when it came to your upbringing. I knew, from a long time back, the Ward blood legacy at Metropolis Steel would die.

We sent you away to the best schools possible, and I always kept alive a false hope that you would eventually see the light. Maybe, you would even want the old man's job someday. I saw from early on you had your own peculiar ways. You always had a propensity for carousing with odd characters who led such odd lives."

"Do you mean gay, father?" Jerry started to laugh. "You can't even say it, can you?"

Amos Ward didn't see the humorous side of Jerry's question. "I don't want to say it. Personally, Jerry, it makes me sick to think that you are.

I let your mother spoil you, and I let you lead your odd lifestyle while she was alive. Your mother is gone now, Jerry, and so I'm afraid, is the money. Now, you can try and get a lawyer and try to sue me, but you won't win. I know every top attorney on the east coast and they will not help you."

"You son of a bitch!" Jerry snarled.

"Yes, Jerry, I'm sure in your eyes I am. In my eyes, though, you are an irresponsible young man who needs desperately to grow up." Amos leaned forward and pressed a silver button on his desk. The gargantuan steel doors opened behind Jerry, and a uniformed guard stepped inside. "Now, Jerry, if you could please leave. I have some pressing business needing my utmost attention. My guards will escort you out, son. Good day."

I could kill you, old man. Jerry wanted so badly to follow through with that thought. "So, that's it, father? Mother is gone, and now, so is your strange son?"

"It's all for the better, Jerry."

"Fine, I don't need you anyway, you conniving old shit!" Jerry exploded.

Upon hearing the commotion, a second guard appeared and they both approached Jerry. "Mister Ward, please follow us out, sir," the second guard replied.

"It's Mayor Ward to you, dickhead!" Jerry snarled.

"Jerry, please show some sense of decorum while you're in my office. This is a place of business, lest you have forgotten." Even now, Amos Ward took such pleasure in scolding his son in front of others.

Fine father, you've won your little battle, Jerry said to himself. "I'm gone, father. You have yourself a good life."

"Good day," his father replied again as the doors closed between them.

When Jerry reached street level of the building, he began to realize his lavish lifestyle had just come to a disastrous halt. It was a devastating blow to the spoiled young Mayor of New Hope. As time went on, Jerry would quickly adapt to being a lecherous individual. Friends and acquaintances were lulled by the young man's charms. They found it very appealing to fuel his sumptuous appetite for the good things in life. In the realm of politics, Jerry hurriedly learned how easy it was to become someone's "whore", or to have them become yours.

In the past year or so, Jerry relied less and less on these individuals, but his clamoring for the good life grew even more ravenous. It led to the speculation that maybe other sources of income had taken their place.

The club scene in the late 90's had really picked up in New Hope, and so had the use of illicit narcotics. The club drug, Ecstasy, had become a big part of the scene, and it was not about to leave. Tom Miller and John Boyle had tried valiantly to arrest the users and shut down the dealers, but as fast as they got rid of one set of them, another group eagerly took their place. It was like a higher authority gave these dealers an open door policy of dealing inside the confines of the Borough.

Although he said all the right words in public, behind the scenes many residents, including Miller and Boyle, were starting to pay attention to a certain individual. The only problem was they couldn't find enough evidence to nail him, and it made this already cocky gentleman feel invincible, almost bulletproof.

All the cockiness in the world could not help him shake the feeling the end of the road was near. While he sat in the low lamplight of the room, his complexion became increasingly ashen. He quickly turned away from the mirror he'd been staring into. Jerry began to feel the rich paneled walls closing in around him. The room, so lavishly appointed, was not an oasis anymore. It had become his tomb.

He slowly opened the top drawer of his desk and produced a snub-nosed revolver. He held it in his hand while he again looked at the picture of himself and his father. "What a shambles my life has become," he said to the picture. "I'll see you in hell, father." He began to turn the gun on himself. Mayor Jerry Ward, even in his final moments, could not take responsibility for his life's actions.

Jerry's swan song would have to wait, for as he cocked backed the hammer of the revolver, the door of his office came crashing open, and two more shiny barrels were also aimed in his direction.

"Och, no! Yer' not going out that easy!" one voice said.

"Put the gun down, Mayor, and slide it towards me!" beckoned the other one. As Ward peered through the glare of the lamp and his drunken haze, he saw them. Here stood the two men who were always trying to ruin his life. He kept the gun pointed at his temple. "Put the gun down, now! Yer' not going out that easy!" the Irish brogue now snarled.

Jerry began to smile. How easy it would be to turn the revolver on them. It would give him such pleasure. He began to think about how the papers would carry the story. "Mad Mayor Sought In Slaying Of Two Local

Heroes." Initially, it had a nice ring to it, but going from Mayor to Death Row was too much for Jerry to swallow. He began to lower the weapon. His senses, earlier drowned away in a sea of alcoholic sorrows, quickly began to surface. Life's consequences have a way of doing that to you, he thought.

"Good move, Jerry. Now, slowly drop the gun and push it to me," Tom said in a relaxing tone.

"Good choice, Jerry," John snorted while he made his way towards the Mayor. "Why don't you sit down, Jerry? Let's have a talk amongst friends." Jerry stared hard into John's eyes while the trooper approached him. His mind kicked into high gear when John stepped behind him. It's not going to end on their terms. I don't know how it will end, but this low class rabble is not about to be the cause of my undoing. The Mayor slyly glanced behind him, and with all of his might, barreled his leather chair into John's body. The burly Irishman was taken off guard and lost his breath from the impact. Jerry saw this, and quickly grabbed John's arm. He hurtled the trooper in the direction of his bookshelves. The impact from the weight of John's frame caused the shelves to collapse, thus spilling their contents onto the dazed lawman.

Tom tried to react quickly in aiding his fallen comrade, but the Mayor was even faster. Ward, seeing his apprehender approaching, grabbed the chair again and pushed it towards Tom who was already hurtling the desk separating them. Tom was hit immediately after clearing the desktop, and became entangled with the chair. Jerry saw Tom crash to the floor, and realized he had ample time to see his escape route. He began sprinting to the eastern point of the room while Tom and John righted themselves.

"Ward!" John bellowed as the Mayor took literally took flight.

The outside air was brisk, the town, in its usual state of peacefulness tonight. Recent days had proved, though, peace could dissolve in the blink of an eye. A disharmonious sound of breaking glass filled the air. Wood, shards of thick, stained glass and the body which demolished them, soon found their way into the holly bushes below. Bruised and bleeding, Mayor Jerry Ward, jumped to his feet, unleashed a horrific yawp, and began to run away. For however long it was to last, Jerry was free from his nemesis.

"Sweet Jesus, Tommy, do you believe this shit?" Boyle asked with exasperation.

"After tonight, buddy, I'd believe anything," Tom replied while he hopped through the remnants of the windowsill and hit the ground.

"Great!" Boyle snarled. "All hell is breakin' loose round here, and now we gotta' deal with this fuckin' idjit." Boyle was soon down next to his friend. "Let's do this, lad. I'm gettn' tired of chasing ghosts tonight."

"My sentiments, precisely," Tom replied as they broke into a jog. He soon reached down and grabbed his two-way. "Sam, if you can hear me, the bird is in flight."

"Hear you fine, Thomas. What's his heading?"

"He's canal bound."

"On my way."

The Delaware Canal had been used for over a century to transport goods from town to town. It was inoperable for quite some time, only being used now for a tourist attraction. Tonight, it would witness a rebirth of sorts, carrying what could be its most dangerous cargo.

Jerry fell into the shallow water, and any pain his body had suffered from the window was soon overtaken by the discomfort of the canal's freezing temperatures. Jerry could hear Tom and John entering the water and bellowing for him to stop running while he was making his way to the opposite end of the canal. He began to climb out, and proceeded to run into the new office and shopping complex being built near the New Hope-Ivyland rail station.

Jerry's body was soaking wet and aching ferociously, but there was no way he was going down peacefully. He wasn't about to give in to those two cops who were ruining his life. Damn them. Damn that old, Fed agent Tunney, too. It figures, I have to get the first asshole in the Bureau who actually does his job. Aggravated as he was, Jerry was still ahead of his pursuers.

Tom and John scurried up the canal's banking. When they reached flat land, the fleeing Mayor came into full view. "I'll kill 'em when I catch 'im, Miller!" John exploded as they again started to run.

"Agreed!" Tom yelled while picking up the pace. His lungs felt like a forest fire, but he wasn't about to let Ward escape. One failed apprehension in a night was enough for Tom Miller. He picked up the two-way again. "Sam, where are you?"

"I'm heading for that shopping center," he replied quickly.

"Negative on that, Sam! Go to the next street. It runs adjacent to the rail yard. Take the first cut in, and then head back to the center. We'll..."

"Put the squeeze on him! Good thought, Thomas," Sam said as he gunned the car back onto West Bridge Street. "I'm coming, gentlemen."

"We'll be there," Tom replied. The two officers hit into a stride neither one of them had probably utilized in years. They were closing in on the Mayor, who had just ducked behind the old rail station.

Their pace became even quicker and John looked over to Tom. "Don't worry, lad, this one we're gonna' get." No sooner had Boyle uttered the words, the officers heard Ward yell, and it was followed by a thud. They drew their weapons and began to round the corner of the station. Their eyes soon fell upon Ward, who was writhing on the ground in agony, and then to the shadowy figure standing above him.

"You won't have any need for those, guys. He's not going to move anytime soon," Sergeant Jenn Gates offered. She'd taken Ward out by the knees with what appeared to be one of the many sturdy pieces of lumber lying about the construction site.

"Gates, what in the hell?"

"Hello, Trooper Boyle. Are you surprised?" she asked with a smile.

"I know I am, and quite pleasantly, I might add, Sergeant."

"Well, Tom, I knew you boys were up to something good when we split up at the station, so I kept my radio on. When I heard this idiot was canal bound, I had a hunch he'd come here. I waited a few minutes and spotted him coming this way, so I just grabbed the lumber. He went down like a ton of bricks." Ward was beginning to come around and when the pain from the blow registered, he let out a shriek.

"Good work, lass. You really waylaid him!" John exclaimed as he winked. As they approached the Mayor, Sam's car lurched into the lot, and stopped within a few feet of the officer's vantage point.

"Well, I see our young lady has beaten us to the punch. Good work, Sergeant Gates." The young officer replied with a nod.

John stooped over the Mayor, who was still moaning from the blow Gates unleashed. "Are you feeling any better, Mayor?" Boyle asked as he grabbed Ward's shoulders. The Mayor could only reply with a slight groan. "Good," John replied as he lifted Ward up and summarily slammed him on the hood of Tunney's car. "Let's talk."

"I've got nothing to say," Ward whined out. "Unhand me you animal. Do you know who I am?"

"You're not the Mayor anymore, asshole!" Tom snapped as he stood next to John. "We have pictures of you consorting with a drug dealer and known murderer, who is wanted by the FBI. He killed two officers tonight, Ward! He left two more hanging on for their lives, and they may die too! He escaped and left a city block in ruins! Needless to say, jerk off, my temperament sucks. Now, talk!"

"Fuck you!" Ward snapped.

John slammed Ward's head onto the hood again. "Wrong answer, shithead! Now, tell us why you were seen in the company of Jerome Jones?"

Ward began to squeal as John tightened the grip on his neck. "My career will be ruined."

"Hey numbnut, if you haven't figured it out, its toast right now. Consorting with a drug dealer and cop killer, abuse of your authority to have drug distribution through the town, while at the same time, hampering the efforts of law enforcement to stop it. You also resisted arrest and assaulted two police officers tonight. Your so-called career is done, but if you talk, your time to serve may be lessoned, boy. It's up to you."

"Will you see to that?" Ward groaned as he looked to Tunney.

"I'll see what I can do, but I have to hear something right here, right now, to make that happen, Mayor Ward," the agent replied.

"Fine," Ward said hoarsely while John loosened his grip. "I started to meet with Jones back in the spring." He sat up and tried to regain his voice. "I knew Bobby Pond, and he introduced me to Jones. You see, Bobby was letting Jones' Ecstasy be funneled through his club. He was making a killing. Bobby and I had oft spoken about my poor financial situation since my father had closed out my trust funds. He fathomed this could be a quick fix to the problem."

"It would also pave the way for Jones having a stronghold in the Borough," Tom snorted.

"Yes, it would. He knew how tough the laws were in town, so he figured if he had me hold you and Boyle in check, he'd have smooth sailing."

"So, you took a chance on morally disregarding your oath to the safety of the people of New Hope for your monetary gain? What the hell were you thinking, Ward?" Sergeant Gates pleaded.

"Money was not the only reason. I couldn't dare have him railroad my shot at becoming Governor."

"How would he have accomplished that, Ward?" Boyle asked.

"He knew all about my private life and who I associated with. It would have been virtually impossible for a chance at the State House if I'd refused."

Tom's eyes widened. "So, the rumors were true. Jones had the cold, hard evidence to "out" you. He knew he had the noose tightly around your neck. If you say yes to his demands and stay quiet, he makes a fortune and gives you a handsome reward to keep your lifestyle going. You say no, he forces your acquaintances to speak publicly about your lifestyle. He knew damn well the conservative Commonwealth of Pennsylvania would never give their support to a gay man who was running for the Governorship." Ward could only nod his head in reply.

"What a preposterous waste, Mayor Ward! All of your brains and talents wasted on greed and power hungry aspirations," Agent Tunney lamented. "How about helping us understand where the female jogger pictured in other shots of Pond and Jones fits into the case?"

"Female jogger?" Ward's face suddenly turned very pale.

"Yes, Ward, the female jogger. Who is she?"

"You do know who it is, don't you?" John asked while he again began to put the squeeze on Ward.

"No, n..nn.no, I don't know. I, I mean, I know you are looking for this particular individual, but I don't know who it is. Jones or Bobby never mentioned her acquaintance to them."

"Then why, Mayor, did you look like you had the fear of God in you when I brought her up?"

"Did I look like that, Agent Tunney? I..I don't know why. Maybe you mistook my expression. You know, I am still reeling from the assault on my person by Gates."

"Apprehension!" Gates snapped.

"Smarting are we, Ward? Let me tell ya' lad, I don't believe ya', nor does anyone else." John's grip was getting tighter. "Now, talk," he whispered. "The truth'll set you free."

"Okay..o.o.okay! I know they've seen the jogger. They said her name was Sandy Jones!" Ward was starting to turn a fierce shade of purple from John's grip. "I swear to you Boyle, that's all I know," he squeaked out.

"I'm not so sure I believe ya'. Maybe a night in jail will jog his memory, ay' Thomas?"

"Troop, I think I have a much better idea, if you and Sam are game."

"Go on, Tommy boy."

"If we arrest the Mayor during the fragile state of mind our town's presently in, I think it would blow up like a powderkeg on us. How about this for an alternative? Sam, if I could utilize your two boys, I could secretly place Ward on house arrest. This way, they could appear to be assisting the Mayor in some sort of operation. They could also appear at the next few days events as a special government detail."

"Why Tom, I think it's a great idea. I could expedite the order tonight."

"Thanks, Sam. I think if we could do this for a few days, then, we could calmly and quietly have him jailed. It would give us a chance to get through the Millennium celebration without any big headaches."

"Good idea, lad. But, ya' know people will be sniffin' around as to why the two Fed boys are escorting the Mayor. How's jabber jaws over there gonna' handle the questions?"

"Well, John," Tom said as he leaned over the Mayor's shoulder. "Our illustrious official here will tell any curious individual the agents are along to assist him in the procurement of any files he has between his home and his office that he thinks may help in the location of our suspects. He feels it's his civic duty, as a public official, to assist the Bureau and exhaust every avenue to apprehend the murderer."

Tom stopped and peered deeply into the Mayor's eyes. The look made Ward begin to shake. "If the Mayor feels he needs to take liberty and stray from these public comments, the agents will bring him to me, and then I'll deal with him." He patted the Mayor's shoulder and leaned closely to his ear. "After losing two of my good friends, and then losing two brothers in the line of duty tonight, it would be a great mistake to do otherwise." Jerry, despite being frigid from the canal chase, began to sweat profusely.

"Shall I take him now, Tom?"

"Yes, Sam, please do. John, would you kindly support Sam?"

"Why, I'd be more than happy to help," John said with a Cheshire cat grin. "C'mon Ward, get in!" he bellowed as he led Ward to the back of Sam's car.

"Well, Chief, I guess I'll be on my way, too."

"Okay, Sergeant. Thank you, again, for all your work tonight. You were all stupendous. Everyone! I don't think I have to remind you, warm up and get some good sleep tonight!" While he lit the last Marlboro in his pack, he quickly closed his eyes, and thought of the upcoming Millennium.

When he reopened them, he had the look of a hardened soul who'd witnessed Kane's prophecy come to fruition. He took another drag, and looked at the clear, night sky. "Lord, I know tonight was tough, but I have a fleeting suspicion, after the Eve, we'll wish for tonight again."

CHAPTER 26

Tom awakened only a few hours after dragging his bruised body home. He used the shower downstairs so he wouldn't wake Debbie. She'd been asleep when he'd arrived home this morning, but was up quickly when she saw Tom's figure in the doorway. She asked him how everything had gone, but when he said he'd talk later in the day, she knew better than to pursue the conversation.

Once she heard the water running, she was up instinctively. She would have arisen soon enough anyway, as the phone was ringing at five-thirty. It was the same time Al used to call, but with Al no longer here, it gave Debbie an eerie feeling to even answer it. She met Tom by the bathroom door with the handset. "It's your new Sergeant," she chirped while giving her husband a quick peck on the cheek. "Not that it's any of my business, but I think you made a great choice."

"You knew already?" he asked only half-surprised.

"I knew it before you probably even stepped foot into Trenton last night. You know how fast news travels in a small town." Tom rolled his eyes, smiled, and playfully asked if anything was secret from the nosybodies in town. "No, not really," she replied with a smirk.

"Good morning, Chief. I hope I didn't wake the two of you."

"Good morning to you, Sergeant. No need to worry, we were already up."

"Listen, Chief, I know Al used to confer with you at this time, but I'm not trying to duplicate his actions. I just.."

Tom cut her short. "Jenn, sorry to interrupt, but I'm sure you had a good reason to call me now. I'm not expecting you to be a duplication of Al Jeaneau. I want you to do the job the best way you know how. Don't give a second thought to how others perceive your actions. Your actions last night alone helped save a young ladies life, and you helped capture the Mayor."

Jenn sounded relieved by Tom's soothing comments. "Thanks for the words, Chief. I just called to see if you'd read the Gazette today."

Tom sighed. It begins, Lord. I told you I'd want yesterday back. "No, Jenn, I haven't seen it yet. What does it say?"

"I think you may want to read it for yourself. It's quite unbelievable."

Tom heard footsteps hastily approaching the hallway in which he now stood while he changed into his uniform. "Did we get the paper yet, hon'?"

"Yes we did," Debbie answered coldly. "You are not going to like it one bit." She handed it to him, and Tom unfolded it to the front page. "WELL KNOWN, GRIEVING MATE SPEAKS OUT," the headline exploded. In smaller print, the caption continued. "Police Are Not Telling Us Everything We Need To Know." Under this, was a picture of an extremely disturbed looking Phil Antos. "How could he do this to you?" Debbie asked angrily. Not wanting to hear an answer, she turned and stormed away.

"I'm assuming you just saw it, Chief."

Tom's could feel the knife twisting in his back. "Yes I did, Jenn."

"How could he say such things about our department? We've been more than forthcoming. We couldn't tell the townspeople everything! They'd be on the verge of creating a lynch mob!" Tom could hear the despair and anger in his young Sergeant's voice. Better to let her vent. She needs to blow off some steam. "I know, you are right, Jenn. They would be ready to hurt someone. That is why cooler heads will prevail."

Jenn started to calm herself down. "Do you think we should pay a visit to the Antos residence today, Chief?"

"Yes, I think it would be a good idea," he replied while he finished dressing. "I'm curious. Phil knows my door is always open. Why not come and see me to air his grievances? Why not see me? Why complain publicly?" Damn, from a stranger I'd expect this, but not from Phil.

"He's too smart for this. He knows the Pandora's Box this could open, the unrest it could cause in a town with such a delicate semblance of order to it."

"Maybe that's what he wants."

"You may be right, Jenn, but what would he ultimately have to gain from this. He's a prominent member of this community. If he stirs the pot, and his criticisms are unfounded, it could tarnish his reputation and damage his business relationships."

"Makes you wonder what his motives are, for sure. Well, what do we do now?"

"Get on the horn to Pags. Tell him to round up Drew and some of the other guys. I want the uniform presence to be noticed at the start of the business day. I'll call John and see if he could spare some of his Troopers.

Hopefully, for the next few days, at least, it will deter the fringe elements from in or outside of town from launching any protests."

"I'll get working from my end, Chief," she said in the usual no-nonsense tone that made her mature beyond her years.

"Thank you Sergeant. Make yourself available to meet John and I at the Logan for breakfast. If anything, it'll show folks we are business as usual, and that we're not going to hide from the criticism."

"Good idea. Besides, it will give us a good feel on how the townspeople are reacting to us. You know, feedback from the masses, so to speak."

"A point well taken, Jenn. Shall we say eight o' clock, then?"

"It's a date."

"Fine, and then later on we'll pay a visit to Phil. He has some explaining to do." Tom hung up the phone and finished combing his hair. He grabbed his notes on last nights' fiasco, and stuffed them into his portfolio. He went into the kitchen and kissed Debbie lightly on the forehead. She had calmed down considerably, but she still had some venom left in her. "I guess you'll be seeing Phil later to find out about this mess."

"Yes, hon', I will be."

"Good, then you pass on this little bit of advice to him. Tell him to get his head out of his ass before he goes making accusations without checking the facts."

Tom smirked as he kissed her again. "I'll make a note of it."

"I'm sure you will," Debbie smiled confidently.

Tom was in the Borough like a flash of light. He stopped at the station to check on the troops morale. Someone had already placed the front page article onto the community bulletin board. "BULLSHIT!" was written boldly in red marker. Tom wanted to keep it up, but his sensible side removed it from view. He did, however, tack it to the board in his office, causing the day officers to send up a small cheer. He spent the next hour or so making some phone calls to Trenton. He talked to Towny, briefly. There was nothing new to report on Jones' disappearance, but he did say the officers who were hit with the throwing knives were making a slow recovery. He also called Mayor Palmer to offer his apologies for not bringing in Jones and creating such a mess in his city.

"Nonsense!" the Mayor replied loudly. "Your men and that young lady handled themselves admirably, especially considering what you were up against. I grieve for the officers and the families they left behind, Tom, but I thanked God when I saw the aftermath this morning. You all could have died last night."

Tom thanked the Mayor for his kind words. "Don't worry Mayor Palmer. Jerome Jones will never pollute your streets again. You have my word."

"Tom, you'd make me one happy man when that happens."

Tom left the station and walked down Main Street. Pags, Drew, and two other uniformed officers were walking the beat. John Boyle had added two Troopers on foot patrol with Zoul, and two more in cars. Tom made a sharp turn into the Logan, and stopped at the front desk. He asked the hostess to please call Agent Tunney and have him join the officers for breakfast. "Officer..I mean, Sergeant Gates already took the initiative and had him paged. By the way Tom, she's a great choice for Sergeant."

Tom smiled in response, and began walking to their usual spot. Along the way, the local's nodded and greeted him in a quick fashion. By the tentative nature of their voices, Tom surmised many of them had read Phil Antos' story. He remained quite unfazed by their reactions. He needed to keep a strong attachment to the populous, so he remained his usually, cheerful self. If he ended up losing their faith, finding the killer could become an uphill climb.

"Good morning, Thomas. We took the liberty of ordering you coffee."

"Thanks, Sam. I see my Sergeant has beaten me to the punch, and invited you to our meeting."

"Ah, yes she did. She is certainly a quick study in détente."

"As well she should be, Sam," he replied jovially.

Tom settled himself into the plush, dining chair. "Well folks, I know we've all been privy to this morning's article. How about some feedback?"

"I'd like to know what the hell he's thinkin' with that head of his, Tommy. I mean, Christ man, he's far from stupid. He, over anyone at this table, knows what's at stake when you develop poor public relations within the community."

"I agree wholeheartedly, John. I said as much to Debbie when I read it this morning. I know he's grieving, but I'd wished he'd shared his concerns with us privately, before going public with them."

Jenn pushed her curls from her face, and looked up from her tea. "Tom, could I add my two cents here?"

"The floor is yours, Jenn."

"Do you think there's a remote possibility he may be doing this for our good?"

"How so?"

"Maybe he feels he could help us by spinning some negative vibes out there. Practically everyone who's lived in this town for years knows how tight we all are with Phil. Maybe he feels if he lashes out at the one's he loves, it will cause an overwhelming sympathy for Luke and Al's deaths. You know, someone may be more willing to come to his door with information concerning things they'd overheard, than to come to the police. It could be there is an angle like that working here."

"Aye, it is a good point, young one. He still shoulda' run it by his friends before causing such a public outcry. Either way, I don't like what he did."

"From my experience, I'd have to agree with you, John," Sam replied. "There are very few times when the grieving victim is as close with the authorities, as Phil is to you. This could very well involve more damage control than it could help us. Still, all in all, it's not a bad theory, Jenn."

"Aye, I thought McGuigan was in our corner with this case. I'd like ta' have a talkin' with that girl."

"You may have your wish sooner than you expected," a light voice said from behind them. "Is it all right for the enemy to sit here?" Mary asked as she shuffled on her heels.

"Come and sit, Mary," Jenn replied while she pulled over a chair from another table.

"Thank you, Jenn. Congratulations on becoming Sergeant. I know it must be a hard time to take it over, but you'll do great."

"Thanks, Mary."

"Look, McGuigan, now that all the niceties are aside, why girl? Why would you let Phil spew his guts out and cause more friction than what already exists here?" John was trying to keep his voice and his temper in control, but it was getting very hard.

She tried to be strong, but a tear rolled down her cheek. Damn him. I didn't want him, of all people, to see me be weak. "John, please, you have to believe me. I wanted to pull back, but when the Times said they'd go with Phil's story and make it front page headlines in New York and the nation, I had no choice but to write it. Listen, you all know Jason is a good and fair editor. He, by no means, wanted to hinder your case, but if we weren't first to press with this, how much credibility would we have left with the locals? They'd see it as us hiding information from the public, and pledging our allegiance with the police."

Mary was starting to get her edge back, little by little. "Now, officers, would that be fair to the public? If they felt that way, would it make it easier or harder for me to write a story on how diligently you are working to crack this case? By the way, as soon as I leave here, I will be busy writing just such a story about your department. A story, John Boyle, I had every intention of writing before the Antos incident came up."

John looked into her intense, green eyes, and tried to search for a reply. The lady's got you, Boyle. She made a good case, but..

"I apologize for being hard, Mary. You are right, Jason Jamison is a fair man, and you have been true to your word. Wasn't there any way though, ya' could've given us a heads up this was coming?"

"I tried. Believe me, I tried. You guys were nowhere to be found last night, after Jenn's press conference. I even tried Tom's cell, and yours, but they were busy. Where were you?"

"We had to take care of some business," Tom jumped in.

"Some business, huh? You were in the insanity over in Trenton last night, weren't you? They were showing shots of the buildings on this mornings news. It looked like a war zone."

"I guess it was."

"Oh, you guess it was. I see," she said with a smirk while she pulled back her long, auburn hair. "Off the record, Tom?"

"Okay Mary, okay," he chuckled. "Off the record, it was hell. We were very lucky more people weren't hurt, and we are all feeling the physical beating of last night. Let me add, though, the walls will soon close in on Jones. He was injured last night, and for that reason alone, I think he'll surface very soon."

She then turned her radiant face in the direction of the elder statesman of the group. "May I ask the distinguished Agent Tunney why I saw his agents escorting our mayor to his office early this morning?"

"You certainly may, Miss McGuigan. The Mayor is helping us try to find some documents he thinks may aid our case. Other than this.."

"I know, you are not at liberty to discuss any cases presently under investigation. It's okay, Agent Tunney. These two old timers already have me used to the routine."

"Old timers, ay? We're not that old, McGuigan," John replied.

"He's right, Mary," John chimed in as he smirked. "Age is just a state of mind, you know."

"Well, if we're talking about you two, I guess it's the presses turn to say I have no further comments."

Jenn started to giggle. "Good one, Mary. I tell them all the time they're acting like two teenage boys." John glanced at the two women while polishing off his plate. "Ahem. Not meanin' to interrupt you two schoolgirls, but if yer' done, we need to go see Phil, Gates."

"Okay, John, okay," Jenn said as she gulped down her last spot of tea.

"Sam, if you're not too busy dealing with your boys, would you like to accompany us?"

"Certainly, Tom, if you think I'd be of any help to you."

"I do."

The group departed, and Mary gathered her things and headed for the door. "McGuigan," a familiar voice said from behind. "Might I see you for a moment?"

"Sure, John, what's up?"

"Look, Mary," John said in a mild tone while some customers passed by. "I know we've been at each other like battering rams sometimes, but I do apologize for questioning yer' loyalty. It was..wrong."

Mary's face began to blush. "To my ears, did I just hear John Boyle apologize to me? Well, John, you do have a heart after all."

"Now, see McGuigan, why do you hafta' be.."

"I accept your apology, John, thanks," she said with an understanding smile.

He began to move closer to Mary, their bodies almost touching. "Say, Mary, after we put this case to rest, I was wondering if perchance, we could get together for dinner. You know, like a peace offering for being such a hard-head for so long?"

"Why, John Boyle, did you just ask me out for a date?" she questioned aloud.

Now, it would be the Irishman's turn to blush. "Semantics, McGuigan, semantics! Must everythin' have to have a title with you women?"

Mary began to smile and laugh softly. "Alright, John, I'll take you up on your peace offering."

"Very well, then."

"You know where I work," she replied coyly while opening the door. "Just call on me when you're ready to do this."

"I will."

John followed her out and when they reached the sidewalk, she turned to him. She moved in close to his thick, strong chest, and looked up at his handsome face with a smile. "You know," she said while twirling a long length of her sparkling hair, "you don't have to wait until the case is done. It's just a thought."

"I'll keep it under consideration," John replied softly. He was mesmerized by her raw beauty. He'd always known how pretty she was, but seeing her act like this brought it even more to the forefront.

Mary winked in reply and began walking to her office. When she had crossed Ferry Street, she looked back to see John still watching her. "Please, be careful out there today!" she yelled over the traffic noise.

"I will, Mary McGuigan! You do the same, lass!" While he watched her walk away, he began to whistle a tune from his childhood days in

County Cork. His leprechauns grin and happy tune came to an abrupt halt when he noticed the three smiling lawmen staring in his direction. "Well, what in the blazes is this? All of you standing 'round grinning like a bunch of organ grinders monkeys?"

"I'll see you two and loverboy at the Antos residence," Sam replied as he walked away shaking his head.

"I'm right behind you," Tom said. He looked back to John and began to grin.

Meanwhile, Jenn Gates could only stare at the trooper. "Say what's on your mind, Gates. God knows, you'll tell me anyway," John crowed.

"I know this is not protocol, but heck, I'm gonna' do it anyway." She reached up, and gave the Irishman a quick peck on the cheek. "I knew it. I told you, John, I knew it! I knew somewhere inside your hard-boiled Irish body, you had a heart."

Boyle tried hard to quickly disarm the Sergeant's glee by showing an air of authority, but he knew it was to no avail. "Will that be all, Sergeant Gates?"

"No, not really, but I do have to catch up with the Chief. See you at Phil's!" She began to jog down Main to get in Tom's vehicle. "Now Gates, don't go makin' a big fuss out of all this, lass!" John shouted to her, but she was already too far along to hear him. John, likewise, made haste to his patrol car, and again, he began whistling the childhood tune. Not a bad morning after all, he thought. Made a date with Mary, got a kiss for doing so from Gates. Hell, finally a happy morning 'round here. "I'll be needing it," he said as he cranked up the engine. "God knows, we all will, 'cause it'll be days like no other here. I just know they will be days like no other."

CHAPTER 27

Phil Antos looked from his living room windows long enough to see the funeral like procession of police vehicles descending upon his property. "The inquisition has arrived," he said to the empty room. He decided it was best to meet them at the door. Where the ensuing conversation was going to lead was anyone's guess. He'd told the papers what he felt was appropriate, and that was it.

Tom led the group up the path. He noticed Phil opening the door for them to enter. "Do come in," Phil said nervously. He received a few light responses of thank you. The officer's tensely shuffled about in the grand hallway while Phil closed the door. He tried to force a smile. "Look, I know why you are here. Please, come in the sitting room and we can talk." He led them in to sit and then hastily went to the kitchen. He soon returned with a serving tray filled with cups of coffee. After placing the tray on the ornate, ball and claw coffee table, he retreated to the comfort of the plush, Queen Anne wing chair near the fireplace.

Tom took a sip from the china cup, and narrowed his eyes onto Phil's. Phil knew they were all staring at him, but Tom's gaze made him restless. He'd known Tom to have a stern presence, but he'd never had the displeasure of having this presence focused onto himself. Tom began to speak as he put down the cup. Keep your temper in hold, Miller, it won't do any good to blow, or at least, not yet. "I'm trying Phil, believe me, I am trying to take into consideration, your anger. You are still grieving. I can understand your right to speak with the press and tell them your viewpoint." He started to stand and pace the room. The color of blood red rushed up his neck with the intensity of the heat from the fire. Nobody could tell if this was caused by the fireplace, or by his temper. Damned if anyone was about to ask him, either. "What I can't understand, Phil, is why the hatchet job on my force and John's?"

"I don't know what you are implying." Phil began to shift about in the wing chair.

"What I mean is, you, of all people, know how many dedicated members of the force took Luke's loss as a personal one. To have them pick up today's paper and read that you don't think we're being forthcoming to the public about releasing all the evidence is like a slap in the face! I have to question your motives, Phil!" Tom had enough of being calm. He lit a cigarette and took a deep inhale.

"Well, have you been totally forthcoming, Tom?"

"As much as we can ever be, Phil. Do you expect me to publicly divulge every piece of information we've found?"

"It would be nice!" Phil snapped.

"It would also put holes in our case a tank could drive through! Come on, Phil. You've been around us all long enough to know better. We try and tell the public what we can, but sometimes there are things they just can't know. We need to protect our case while at the same time, do our best to protect and serve the public." Tom was starting to calm down, but the cigarette was already spent.

"And you think it's worth the risk of the town losing confidence that everything is being done to protect us?"

Sam stood up at this point. "Excuse me for interrupting, Tom. Mister Antos, I am an outsider in your town. From what I've observed, things here are staying fairly normal, especially considering the tragedies of the past few days. Believe me when I say this, I've been in towns where the police have made tragic blunders in being forthcoming, so there is no bias on my part saying this town is lucky. I attribute the success here, so far, to calm voices from the religious and homosexual communities, and especially from the police and troopers. I guess I am in much of the same boat as Chief Miller, Mister Antos. I have to question your motives."

"What motive would I have, Tom, to cause unrest? To screw up your case, and then you'd never catch Luke or Al's killer?"

"That's why I asked what were you out to prove?"

Phil began to pound on one of the end tables. "I wasn't out to prove anything, damn it! I want answers!" The force of the contact sent some of the antique ornaments displayed on the table tumbling to the area rug below. Jenn went to retrieve them, but Phil sternly held out his hand. "I'll get them," he said tersely.

"Now, Phil, lad, I understand you're angry. Realize though, if we divulged every ounce of information to the press, this person could flee, never to be seen again. I have to agree with Tommy. I believe we've been quite forthcoming."

"And never the two roads shall meet, ay' John?" Phil asked as he parted his hands and breathed in deep. "Look, I understand your job better than most. I understand you can't say everything. What I don't understand is why I can't know how things are progressing? Jesus, I mean, I'm like family to you guys, right?"

"Yes, you are Phil, and this is going to sound callous, but if I do it for you, I have to do it for everybody. Right now, there are certain things we need to keep under wraps."

"Even from me?"

"Even from you, Phil. I am sorry."

He took another sip of coffee and arose nonchalantly. "I see. So this is how it has to be?"

"For now, yes it does, Phil."

""I can't say I like it very much."

"I know you don't, but maybe you could help next time by venting your frustrations to me before you go public. I would have listened to your concerns."

"Yes, Tom, you would have listened to them, but would you have really addressed them?

Son of a bitch! You just won't give up, will you? Well, I tried, Lord, but now it's my turn. "You were pretty tight with Rob, weren't you?"

Phil's eyes began to widen. "Where is this question coming from?"

"Let's just say I'm curious. I mean, you and Luke basically groomed him. You also both helped him get financial backing for his club. Hell, you personally designed his club."

"Yes, so I did. What is this all about?" His temper was starting to show.

Jenn decided to deflect some of Phil's anger from Tom. "Phil, didn't you guys ever talk shop? You know, was he having any problems with vendors or getting the right type of clientele to come to his place? You did, after all, have a type of vested interest in how well his place was run. You also had to take an interest in anyone making static on his premises right?"

"Yes, we did Jenn. Why?"

Tom flipped the questioning back to his vantage. "Did Pond ever bother to inform either of you he was entertaining someone you'd kicked to the curb this past summer?"

"Who would that be, Tom?"

Tom walked to where Phil was sitting, and produced three photographs from his jacket pocket. He then proceeded to lay them out on the end table. "Why don't you tell me, Phil?"

Phil peered at the photos and quickly turned to Tom. "It seems to be Rob with two ladies. Why would this be of concern to me?"

"Look closely at the African American individual. Quite muscular for a woman, wouldn't you say? Look at the hair. Look at the face."

Phil was getting annoyed. "Okay," he sighed, "I'll look again. I don't know what this is all about?" He looked again, and for a moment, everything was still. He kept his gaze on the face. As he did so, he could feel a bead of sweat trickling down from his forehead. He sat back and sank into the expanse of the chair. He tried to avert his eyes from Tom's. "Jones," he pushed out.

"Interesting bedfellows your boy chose to have."

"Tom, you have to believe me, I had no idea he was cavorting with the likes of him."

"Never came up in conversation?"

"No, never."

"Interesting thing is, he looks to also be making time with our jogger." Tom pointed again to the pictures. "Take a look, Phil."

Phil slowly edged his way to the end of the chair and studied the woman in question this time. "This is the one you thought had something to do with Al's demise?"

Tom nodded. "Look familiar?"

Phil looked again as he wiped another bead of sweat from his forehead.

"Fire's really hot today, ay' Phil?" John Boyle asked with a grin.

"Y..Yes it is, John." Phil looked at Tom again. "I..I am sorry, Tom. I can't say I've seen her before."

"Or him."

"Him? You mean, you think.."

"We think our jogger is a cross-dresser."

"My God, that's horrible! Rob associated with the people who've killed my friend and my love? After all we did for him!" Phil sank back into the chair slowly. He looked as if his whole world was crumbling right before his eyes.

"Phil, you know some of the more prominent cross-dressers in the community. I know a few of them also. I don't know if they fit the bill, how about you? Do you think any of them would?"

"Am I seeing a side of Tom I didn't think existed? This almost sounds like a blanket accusation against anyone who is homosexual. I thought you would be more understanding considering who your father was." The thought of Tom pointing fingers drained Phil even more.

Tom's neck started to flush with redness. This man, whom I've known for years and treated like family, now thinks I'm targeting homosexuals. The thought of it made Tom so mad he flattened his cigarette into the ashtray. Some of the cherry red embers hit his fingertips, but the hardened detective didn't even flinch. "I'm going to ignore the accusatory tone you used because I know in your heart you'd never believe me to be prejudicial towards the community of fine people here. Now, I'll ask again. Do you think any of the cross-dressers who I do not personally know fit the profile or body frame of the jogger?"

"No, I don't think any of them fit the description," he replied snidely. "It could just be one of Jones' little Ecstasy sluts, you know. Maybe, she's one of those PCP freaks. You know that garbage can make you strong as a bull, and that jerk deals it too from what I've heard."

"You may be right, Phil, and yes, you are correct about PCP. You seem to know some things about Jones. Are you sure you don't know anything more than what you've told me previously?"

"No."

"Nothing that may have slipped your mind from the day you encountered him at the Train."

"No, absolutely not." He dabbed a handkerchief at his forehead vigorously. "Look, am I being questioned for your case, or is there something to all of this?"

The voice of calm entered the discussion. "All we're curious about, Mister Antos, is your contact with Jones. If you say it was just the one time, fine. If there were any further communications, we'd like to know when it occurred, nothing more, nothing less." The reasoning tone made Phil crack a slight smile.

"Agent Tunney, I honestly never had any more contact with Jones. Whenever I visited Robert at his club, I never saw the jogger or Jones in his presence. I hope this answer satisfies you all."

"Yes, I think it does, Mister Antos, thank you."

Phil surveyed the quiet room. All eyes were upon him now. "Will there be anything else?"

"No more questions, Phil." Tom stepped towards Phil. "I do, however, want to say something before we leave. I have always known you have a right to your opinion. I know you always freely say what's on your mind, and it is, at times, refreshing. We have been good friends, hell, we've been like family for many years. You've always known my door to be open to you, or anyone else in town, on either a professional or personal basis. You had concerns, but instead of doing what you've always done, for whatever reason, you decided not to address them personally with me. In this regard, Phil, as a close friend, I am disappointed in you."

Phil's expression was varied. Initially, he looked angry, but his piercing green eyes grew softer. "Tom, I know we are both very emotional individuals. I am, unfortunately, impulsive." He dabbed the sweat again. "You all know this. I let my anger get the best of me with the article. I know I can't take back what I had them print, but I do hope this will not affect our long standing friendship." Phil then quickly extended his hand towards Tom.

Tom accepted, shook Phil's hand, and stared sternly into his eyes. "I hope not Phil, but I guess only time will tell."

"I guess so," Phil responded quietly. "If there is nothing else Tom, I really must get back to what I was doing."

"No, Phil. I can't think of anything else," Tom replied while heading to the door. "We'll see ourselves out. Goodbye." The rest of the officers exchanged pleasantries with Phil and headed outside. The crisp December air was a much needed diversion from the overwhelming stuffiness of the Antos residence. Whether it was imagined or not, Phil's house had turned from its usual charm and cozy feel, into Dante's "Inferno."

Tom was already by his car and lighting a cigarette when the entourage began to approach him. "Folks, there is more of story here than what Phil is revealing."

"Aye, Tom. I know I picked up on it early on, myself."

"Well, gentlemen, I can say this much. I've never seen Phil Antos sweat like that before."

"Good read there, lass. You picked up on it too." The young Sergeant pushed her curls back from her eyes before she spoke. "Oh, absolutely Troop. I mean we've all seen him do work on club and gallery interiors in the July and August periods. Most of those places have been gutted and many had no air conditioning in them yet. You know how hot and incredibly humid this valley gets in those months, and I've never seen the man perspire."

Tom acknowledged Jenn's clever observation with a nod of his head and took another drag of his cigarette. "I think I'd also like to know what kind of a relationship really existed between Phil and Pond."

"You're thinking it's something more than financially assisting an acquaintance, Tom?"

Tom had a pained expression. He did not want to believe his friend of many years had become involved in some sort of indiscretion against Luke, but he needed to keep his personal feelings away from the task at hand. "I detest the thought of what I'm feeling, but yes, Jenn, I feel it's something more. I feel we should also have a glance at Phil's finances to see if any large amounts of money have been changing hands."

"Tommy, you realize what you're implicating here."

"Yes I do, John."

The Irishman sighed heavily. It hurt him to see it had come to this, but he knew Tom was right. "I'll get in touch with my D.A. buddy in Doylestown and have him write up a warrant to expunge his bank records and such."

"John, I don't like it anymore than you do, but thanks just the same."

He then looked in Sam's direction. "An outside opinion by the groups' elder statesman may be useful, if you don't mind."

"Tom, I'd be glad to give you my observations if your keen people had not already stated them. I do think we need to dig deeper into Pond's involvement with Jones. Somehow, I think it will blow open the case. Tom, why don't you see if Artis' boys dug up any more tidbits from Pond's rowhouse?"

"I think it would be a good idea, Sam." Tom put the thick sole of his shoe over the spent smoke. The tobacco underfoot pressed into the ground as he moved his foot to and fro. Sometimes, when he was outside he'd pull just beneath the cherry flame to extinguish the smoke and throw the harmless butt into a trash bin. Two different methods but in the end it fostered the same result. He looked at the ground and paused.

"What are ya' thinking about, Thomas? Whenever ya' get that look, your cooking up something good in that brain o' yours."

"Humor me here for a second, John. Has it crossed anybody's mind that we could really have just one killer?"

A sledgehammer to the head couldn't have described the feeling the officers' had. "Wait a sec', lad. You're thinking Jones is behind all the crimes, just doin' them in different fashions to throw us off?"

"The knives from Luke and Al were made at a place in Newark. Jones and Pond were cozy. Pond and Phil were tight. The Mayor seemed to know them all. Is it out of the realm of possibility?"

"No Tommy, it isn't."

"You know, it isn't out of the realm, Tom, but he definitely would need an accomplice to throw things off," Sam added.

"Yeah, like having a footprint the size of the joggers to throw us off in Al's investigation. This way we would think it was another killer, but he'd really committed the crime. I don't know, Tom. The more I'm thinking, it's not completely out of the question."

"Well, look, it's just a thought, Jenn. I mean, we may still very well have two distinct killers, but it does give us food for thought. Well folks, it's been quite a day, hasn't it? Let's go our ways and look over what we've come up with. John, get Zoul looking into the local files and see if he can come up with anything else on Pond or Jones."

"You got it, Tom."

"Sam, I'm sure you can aid our illustrious Trooper in his efforts. Anything the D.C. boys can give us to figure out if we might have just stumbled onto something would be greatly appreciated."

"I'm at your service, Tom, and willing to oblige."

"Thank you, gentlemen. Now, young lady, I need you to make sure the peace stays on the street. Anything out of the ordinary happens you call John, myself, or Sam for that matter. Make sure Pagano, Rose, and the others keep their ears to the pavement."

"You've got it, Chief."

"Good, I'll get you to the station house."

"If you don't my inquiring, what are you planning on doing, my good friend?"

"I'm going to dig out my old documents on the Village murders, John. I don't know if it will help me see a pattern to the new murders, but it's worth a try."

As the day wore on, everyone diligently went about their business. The lawmen tirelessly went through file after file, paper upon paper, and placed called until their fingers were raw. At the end of the day, they were no further than from where they'd started. They did, however, have a renewed feeling of optimism. The past few days had been harrowing ones. Any, or all of them, could have perished from the perils they'd encountered. Undaunted by no new discoveries, Tom decided to stay at the office, late into the night, burning the midnight oil. He looked to the heavens and prayed to God all their searching was not in vain. He prayed that in the end, he would again conquer evil and bring justice back to its rightful place.

CHAPTER 28

The morning of December 30th took off in as frantic a pace as Tom Miller left it in only a few hours ago. His eyes were burning from the lack of sleep. He hadn't even managed to make it home. He'd called Debbie hours earlier to tell her coming home would be an effort in futility. She'd remembered how the nights in New York were without Tom. She hated them then, and even more so now. She did, however, understand the reasons behind the long nights. She wished Tom luck, and said she'd check on him later in the day. Tom was glad Debbie did not stop by yet. The wounds suffered a few nights back were throbbing and aching. His eyes were burning and red-rimmed from searching the endless streams of notes the Kane murders and the present ones contained.

He thought back to the conversation he had with Sam and John while they were walking across the bridge. He tried to remember all the optimism before the debacle in Trenton. He was trying to forget the physical and mental pains and let his focus remain sharp. It was about this time he received a call from the 'Inkman.' "New York, it's Ink," the young man said with a despondent tone.

"Hey Ink, what's up? You sound downtrodden."

"Nah', not down, Tom, I'm just thinking. Can you make it to the 'Den'? If you can, bring Irish and Italy. I already dialed the Fed man, and he's on his way."

"I'll be there, Ink. This is sounding quite important."

"It could be a big help, or a dead end, but I'd like you to hear it from me, one way or the other."

"Okay Ink, you've got my attention. I'll corral the troops and be there within a half hour."

"I'll be here waiting for you."

The morning sun burnt through Tom's eyelids. God, I remember when "all-nighter's" were part of the job requirement. He quickly put on his sunglasses and headed for the police unit. He then put in calls for John and Jenn to meet him at the Den. While he drove, he surveyed the human landscape. Everyone seemed to be going about their business, as usual. Still, it felt like an eerie calm to Tom. It was as if people were on pins and needles, waiting for hell to unleash its fury on this town, or the world, for that matter. Killers on the loose, predictions of impending doom from a world which couldn't control the computers it invented. It almost sounded like a directorial recipe for the bad "B" movies Tom viewed in his youth at the Village cinemas.

Tom turned onto Mechanic Street and parked along the pathway leading to Nob Alley. John and Jenn were already there and Sam had just pulled in behind Tom's unit. "Good morning, all."

"Aye, and a top o' the morning to you, lad. Misses Miller tells me we pulled an all nighter, huh?"

Tom chuckled. "I knew my guardian angel would be checking up on me. Yes, John Boyle, I did. I'm not too proud to say I'm paying for doing it at the present time, either."

"Ah Thomas, I think we're all quite a few years removed from the way we've had to work recently," Sam replied. "Well, all of us, except for our young Sergeant, I presume. I'm thinking she's able to stay energetic for days on end."

"My God, you think you all had one foot in the grave," Jenn laughed. "I can only hope to have the energy I've seen you three display the past few days when I get older." Jenn reached for the doorknob to the Den, and pulled it open. They followed the aromatic splendor of Ink's cigar smoke straight past the waiting area, the display cases, and back towards the tattoo parlor. There, they found Ink sitting on his round, leather topped stool. He stopped running his hand through his thick, dark hair long enough to see the group approaching. "Hello, my friends," he said in his gravel-toned voice. "Have a seat wherever."

John pulled up another stool and located it next to the young man. "Ink, I don't think I've ever seen ya' look so serious before."

"I don't think I've ever had occasion to be this serious before, Irish."

"Ink, what's going on?"

"I've heard some pretty serious scuttle going around about our friend, Jerome Jones, Tom."

"What kind of scuttle, Ink?"

"The kind of scuttle saying he's behind all of the murders, the ones in Trenton and the ones here. I'm not hearing this through idle chit-chat either.

These are some heavy hitters saying he had something or everything to do with the killings."

"Do you mind if I ask who is telling you this, young Ink?"

"The Brethren and the Warlock camps are two groups, Sam. I also got a call from a buddy at a parlor in Trenton who says he heard a guy who peddled for Jones saying the man is ready to strike again. The peddler says Jones is even crazier than before, because you boys shot him."

So, Zoul definitely hit Jones. "This is some amazing news," Tom replied as he inhaled deeply on the Marlboro perched between his lips. "I have a feeling there is more to this story."

"Yes there is, Tom. My boys in the Brethren say they heard the splinter group in Allentown of the World Church is moving some heavy artillery into their compound. They sound like they're readying themselves for a little prophecy making."

The group all grew wide-eyed at this last bit of information. "Are they sure of this?" Sam asked worriedly.

"They're so sure they said I better let you Fed boys know. Of course, they said they'd be glad to give you some extra muscle in exchange for two of their henchmen serving a smaller sentence up at the State Pen."

"I don't think I'll need their muscle, but I'll take it into consideration. Well folks, I better go make some calls and get some agents and firepower to the Allentown compound. Thank you, young Ink."

"You're welcome, Poppa Fed."

While Sam departed to phone the Bureau, Tom looked at Ink again. "Somehow, I have a feeling we're not finished here."

"I wish I could say yes, Tom. You may want to call Towny and tell him to get his cops and the Feds ready in Trenton. The World Church has a small militia group called The Brotherhood working with them. They're a small, but formidable group of thugs from Jones' ranks who want to take over the daily operation of the city. They have a small, decrepit building across from the Battle Monument. From what I've been told, they have an arsenal ranging from automatic weapons to RPG launchers."

John Boyle almost fell from the stool. "Christ almighty, it's Armegeddon! I'd better call the Jersey State Barracks, Towny, hell, the Guard, for that matter! I better get some guys from our barracks over to help out Sam too. Tom, I'll get Zoul down to your office and have im' start to call folks too." Ink grabbed John's hand before he could dial his cell phone.

"Irish, make sure you tell them this is all supposed to go down tomorrow night. It's supposed to happen in Allentown tomorrow night also. We don't know where else in the country this may take place, but my source says this is all to divert attention from Jones. Nobody knows where he disappeared to, but the story is he's planning to fulfill the prophecy in a way people will always remember."

"I'll let them know, lad. Thank you."

"Hey, anything to save the human race," Ink replied as his trademark dark humor began to make its return. "Tom, I don't know if you want your warden friend upstate to squeeze the man, but I've been told much of this was orchestrated by the master himself."

Kane, that bastard. Tom could believe it. Kane was so evil, it was not impossibile to think Kane would cause chaos before his demise. "I don't know how you found all of this out, but I appreciate it, Ink. I'll give Smith a call and see what he can do."

"Don't worry, Tom. My sources want to see Jones perish. If you make it happen, they'll call in their marker someday soon." He quickly turned to Jenn. "Now, Sergeant Italy, the pendulum swings to you."

"What am I here for, Georgie?"

"Well, besides giving me someone pretty to admire in this motley crew, I've had you come here to tell you to bolster up your street forces tomorrow night. There is word of a Jones accomplice causing mayhem at the celebration on Main Street. It's not a great source, but I'd take heed, nonetheless. I figured I'd tell you this because I know Tom and John will probably be busy making sure the World Church cells are taken care of."

"Thanks for the tip, Georgie. I'd better get back to the station and get the troops prepped for the next few days. I think they'll never be witness to anything like it again."

"I hate to say it, but you're probably correct in your assumption, Jenn. Ink, thanks again for the word. We'll be in touch."

"No prob, Chief. Listen, do you have a message service for your cell phone?"

"Sure do, Ink."

"Good, it'll be easier for me to contact you then."

John returned to Ink's backroom lair. "Well, the Staties over in Jersey are dispatching units to Trenton as we speak. Towny is also adding more of his Strikers to the mix."

"Good deal, thanks John."

"No problem, Tommy."

"Well folks, we'd better start hitting the phone lines with Sam, and make sure we nip this chaos in the bud." Tom and Jenn again thanked the young artist and saw themselves out.

John patted Ink on the back. "Good work, young Ink. We'll be in your debt," he said before he left the room. Ink stared around his lair at the photos of the bands and the paintings of his artwork. It all seemed so trivial anymore. The world sounded like it was turning towards anarchy instead of civility. All the music he'd listened to, with its harsh, hateful lyrics of the "real world," these guys didn't have a damn clue. The real world was happening right in Ink's backyard, and it was scaring the hell out of him.

The day moved like a flash for Tom and the others. Tom had quickly revamped his office into a makeshift "war room," and reports from many areas were soon flooding the phone lines. Sam was the first to report news from the front. The FBI, officers from the ATF, and a handful of State Troopers had swiftly stormed the Allentown compound and secured the area with no loss of life and minimal injuries.

John and Tom were keeping in touch with the Jersey side to see how things developed in Trenton. Within a few hours, they would happily report the raid of the Brotherhood's Battle Monument hideout. Towny's Strikers, along with members of the Jersey State Police, FBI and ATF officers quickly penetrated the groups beaten and depleted forces. The only loss of life and injuries were incurred by the Brotherhood, and even they were minimal, considering the fast and frenzied firefight occurring there. After losing officers the day before, plus watching Jones escape, it was a much needed report of success.

The four officers decided to blow off some steam at the Logan that night. John also placed a call for Zoul to meet them there, since he'd been a very helpful member of the team. The warm atmosphere of the festively decorated room, along with the warm food, was a welcome enjoyment for the ragged warriors. After dessert, John ordered a bottle of Bailey's and a bottle of Irish whiskey. He hoisted his shot glass into the air. "Gentlemen..and young lady! A toast, to a fine group of officers who never gave up, and won't give up 'til justice is served!"

"Here, here!" they emphatically replied. The cacophony of glasses touching filled the air of the dining room. The group moved to seats in front of the roaring fireplace. John refilled the glasses, and grabbed a poker to move the crackling logs. They spoke philosophically of the triumphs and tragedies they'd witnessed the past few days. They also wondered what tomorrow would bring to their doorstep. It was a thought which made them shudder, even in the warmth and safety of this glorious room. Sam wondered aloud if he'd rushed too expeditiously to seize Jones the other night. "Good men were lost," he lamented.

"Good men are always lost battling for what is right, Sam." Tom slowly dragged on his cigarette. "It was the right call to make." The rest of them nodded in approval.

"Wouldn't have done it any other way," John added.

Zoul took a quick shot of whiskey and wiped a drop from his lips. "Sam, I heard about the meeting with Phil. We all know him, but have you developed any opinions about him since yesterday."

"I think we should more look into his friends past. I think Pond was no altar boy, and I think Phil may have known what type of personal he'd become friendly with. Speaking of Phil, how did your call to the D.A. go, John?"

"We're making progress. He should have the warrant served tomorrow. We'll know more then."

"Good. If you need assistance, my office will give any you ask for."

"Good to know, Sam."

Jenn interrupted the men for a moment. "Guys, I hate to keep bringing Phil back up, but if he's involved deeper with something illegal, don't you think he'd want to come clean, especially when some of his best friends are in law enforcement? He knows we could probably help him out of whatever jam he's in."

"I truly don't know, Jenn. Maybe.." The sound of Sam's cell phone cut into the conversation. "Please, if you'd excuse me." Sam spoke for a few minutes and then hung up.

Tom viewed the agents varied expressions. "Good news or bad news, Sam?"

"My good friends, we'll have to discuss my opinions at a more opportune time. Tom, we'll have many things to discuss on our ride tomorrow morning."

Tom held his breath for a moment. "Ride to where, Sam?"

"The Manhattan brass requests our presence. They may have located Jones."

CHAPTER 29

The last items were being placed into the small backpack he'd laid on the living room sofa. Tom had expected this day to come and told Debbie as much just the other night. He'd spoken with John Boyle earlier, and was now going over the details with his new Sergeant. The battle plans were being devised and Tom started to feel jumpy. The thrill of the chase always managed to do this to him and Jenn was taking notice of his rapid actions. "Jenn, John will be patrolling the Bowman's Tower area during the festivities tonight. He knows as soon as you contact him, the killer has resurfaced."

"Do you really think we still have two killers, Chief?"

"It's hard to say, Jenn. The forensics we've obtained so far are so sketchy, but we need to be on guard if there are two killers. Tonight will be the night to fulfill Kane's sick wishes."

"So, I assume I'll be out in the crowds on Main Street looking for our man, or woman?"

"No, let the uniforms handle the crowds tonight. John is bringing ten troopers to aid our cause."

"Chief, do you really think many people will show up tonight?"

"I think the people of this town need a reason to celebrate. They need something to take their minds from the recent days events. Besides, our soon to be jailed Mayor is pressing a lot of flesh, so as to ensure a large turnout."

"I assume he'll be traveling with his escorts?" Jenn asked with a smile.

"My good Sergeant, do you think Agent Tunney and I would have it any other way?

Jenn flashed her radiant smile. "I guess not, Chief. So, what do we have in mind for me?"

Tom put the last of his files in the pack. "Actually Jenn, I need you to stay here and keep a watch over Debbie. You'll have Rob and Drew with you."

"Are you expecting the killer to harm her in some way? It doesn't fit the plan."

"Ah, but it does, my young charge. Kane's plan was not only to hurt homosexuals, but it was also to attack the like-minded individuals protecting them," he said while rapidly loading his backup piece. He also put a box of ammunition in the front pouch of the pack. Lord, I hope it doesn't come to this much shooting, but if it needs to, so be it.

"Why doesn't she go away for the night, Tom? Isn't she worried about something happening?"

"I'll answer that question, honey," a low voice replied from the kitchen. Debbie slowly entered the living room. She put the steaming mug of cocoa to her lips and swallowed lightly. She sat down next to the young Sergeant and smiled. "Jenn, it would be exactly what these animals would expect. If I run, they win. Besides, if the possible second killer is cunning like Kane, they'll know I'm here, or anywhere else without Tom."

Jenn's eyes widened. "You're using yourself as bait?"

"No, Jenn, I wouldn't say bait, but if this person wants to hurt Tom again.."

"What better way to do it?" Jenn asked quietly. "It's quite a risky move, guys."

"Everything involved with this case is risky. I'm not afraid, Jenn. I'll have good protection. This individual may not even surface."

"You're okay with this, Tom?"

Tom smirked in Jenn's direction. "Jenn, like I could ever change Debbie's mind? I had to fight to get her to agree to the protection."

Jenn knowingly smiled. "Well, I'm going to let myself out, Miller's. I want to go over strategy with the uniformed officers. I need to make sure everyone in this department knows their responsibilities tonight."

"Thanks Jenn, I'll be in touch with you as the day goes on."

"As will I, Chief. Good luck and be careful."

"I will Jenn, you too."

"Debbie, I'll see you later."

Debbie grabbed Jenn's arm reassuringly. "Jenn, don't worry. We'll make the best of it." Jenn smirked slightly, and turned to leave. They heard the front door shut while Debbie looked at Tom. "She's nervous about tonight."

"I think it's a mix of nerves over not knowing what to expect and wanting to make sure everything runs perfectly in my absence."

Debbie poked at the remaining wood in the fireplace and lit them. "You mean like Al would have?"

"I think it's the main reason she expects perfection." Tom zipped shut the bag, and reached over to give Debbie a long hug and kiss. It felt, to her, as if things had never changed. The two of them, and their love for each other, could conquer anything this cruel world tried to throw their way. When their lips parted, she stared lovingly at her husband.

"No goodbyes, Tom Miller."

"No, Deb, no goodbyes." He grabbed the backpack and slung the straps over his shoulder. "I have to go. Sam's waiting to be picked up. I'll be home tonight, baby," he said with a knowing smile. "This will all end soon."

Debbie heard the front door shut. She heard the low throated growl of Tom's SUV as he departed the driveway. She walked slowly into the den and peacefully viewed their wedding picture over the fireplaces mantle. She started to cry when she thought of how close she came to losing him the other night. The beast had become much stronger since his run-in with Kane, but Tom still held his ground. The question bothering Debbie was how much longer he'd be able to hold it. She felt the crucifix around her neck and began to sob. "God, keep him safe tonight. I can't bear to live without him."

Tom was driving at a good rate when he spotted his passenger on the corner of Main of Bridge Street. "May I offer you a ride, sir?"

"Ah, don't mind if I do, young man," Sam chuckled while hopping in the passenger's side. "While I was waiting for you, I stopped in this 60's and 70'store on the corner. My one granddaughter loves this, what do they call it, retro stuff. You know teenagers, the stuff we thought was garbage growing up, they purchase it like they are some priceless antique."

"Oh, I know it well, Sam. I see them in there every day. Hell, my friend, they think we're antiques after we hit our forties."

"True, so true, Thomas," Sam said with a smile. "Well, enough about our becoming fossilized in the eyes of youth. Are all the plans in place here for tonight?"

"We're as ready as we'll ever be, Sam."

Sam pointed skywards. "Well, we'll just leave the rest in his hands."

"Yes, it's best to leave it up to him, isn't it?"

They continued driving while Sam shuffled through some papers in his briefcase. "Giuliani is planning to meet with us upon our arrival."

Tom's eyes widened. "They are making this a big deal? He has enough to worry about in the city tonight!"

"You, of all people, should know how the Mayor of New York operates. I believe you two are quite similar in your attention to detail."

"I will take that as quite the compliment, Agent Tunney."

"Please do," Sam replied with a gleam in his eye. Their conversation remained rather animated during the two hour excursion. They discussed the big cases that had brought them to this point. They spoke about their tragedies and also the triumphs. They talked about the important roles family had played in their lives and many other things. Tom felt as if he'd known Sam for years. At least once, during pause in the discussion, he quietly thanked God for sending this man to New Hope and not someone who would have bulldozed the case and caused problems.

Sam looked over from the Jersey Turnpike and stared at the imposing skyline of Manhattan. He marveled at how the Trade Center and Empire State Building held court over this already teeming metropolis. It seemed as if you could touch the heavens from their peaks. Mountains, crafted by human hands. He pointed towards them. "Thomas, I pity anyone not able to view this sight in person. Bar none, the greatest city in the world lies before us."

"This coming from a man working in the most important city in the world," Tom chortled. "I beg to differ, Tom. Washington wreaks of the stench which must have invaded the Roman Empire during its inauspicious demise. There is too much corruption and deceit in D.C., much more than what exists here. No, this city is the real deal. Its inhabitants tell it like it is. People in Washington smile, stab you in the back, and step over you to grab another rung on the proverbial bureaucratic ladder."

Tom laughed loudly. "No wonder the Bureau views you as public enemy number one!"

"At your service," the agent replied with a twinkle in his eyes.

They arrived in Manhattan, and made their way to the Port Authority Headquarters. The Mayor, Stan Tilden, and some of the other high-ups were meeting them at the Port Authority Command Center. The mayor had built this facility after the subway was bombed under the Trade Center. Its main goal was to bring all the city's emergency management teams to a central location in the event of a natural or man-made disaster. Because of numerous threats made against the well being of the metropolis during the Millennium celebration, the center, especially today, was a hive of activity.

Mayor Giuliani studied the contingency plan for a possible Times Square evacuation, heaven forbid some madman actually followed through on their promises. What the world has come to, when you can't even celebrate what should be a momentous occasion, without worrying about deranged individuals injuring or killing innocent people. The thought was soon a memory. He wanted citizens and tourists alike to feel safe celebrating in the city tonight. This was Mayor Rudolph Giuliani's city, and he'd be damned if some lunatic who hated America, or whatever they were hating these days, was going to spoil the days events.

It was also the reason for him to be involved in the Jones proceedings. He'd heard about the debacle that took place in Trenton a few nights back. He knew all the parties involved valiantly tried to capture Jones, but no one expected the resistance they'd faced. The Mayor did not want Jones to be so lucky this time. He looked up long enough from some documents to see Tom, Stan and Agent Tunney being led over by a uniformed officer. A big smile creased his weary face as he gripped the Chief's hand. "Tom Miller, it's been too long."

"Mister Mayor, as always, it's a pleasure to see you. I want to thank you for our involvement here."

The Mayor then put his hand on Stan's shoulder. "No thanks necessary, Tom. I would never miss an opportunity to have Tilden and Miller together again."

Tom smiled and turned his head towards Sam's direction. "Mayor Giuliani, I would like to introduce you to Federal Agent, Sam Tunney."

"Mister Mayor, it is a pleasure to assist you today."

"Agent Tunney, the pleasure is mine. I know how close you were a few nights back to getting your man. I'm confident that the three of you, along with my fine officers will bring Jerome Jones to justice. Hopefully, it will lead you to a quick apprehension of your New Hope killer. Maybe then, we'll never have to speak of the World Church or its atrocities again."

"Ah, thank you for the vote of confidence, sir. We're pretty sure we slowed down his escape capabilities. Young Trooper Terrant quite possibly shot him in the leg."

Stan grinned. "So the information I received is true that he was plunked," he replied in his thick, Brooklyn accent.

The Mayor began to shuffle through some more paperwork and began to speak. "Gentlemen, I must say goodbye for now. I hope to hear good news from you tonight. Stan, take good care of my uniformed officers."

"I will, Mayor Giuliani. Don't worry sir, we'll get dis' guy."

The Mayor began to laugh quietly. "I've never worried when Tilden and Miller are on the job. If anything, I feel sorry for Jones, because he doesn't know what he's in for with you two on his trail." The Mayor said goodbye again as he disappeared into a throng of aides who were finalizing plans for the celebration in the city.

"Well guys, shall we go over our plan of attack?"

"Sounds good to us, Stan." Tilden hastily led them to a table stacked with papers. Two uniformed officers were already seated there.

"Agent Tunney, Chief Miller, these are Sergeant's White and Ortiz. They, along with a few of their officers will be assisting us tonight."

"Good to be working with you, gentlemen. Well, I finally get to meet the man Tilden's been bragging about for years. I get to meet the man who caught Kane," Ortiz said as he shook Tom's hand.

"Stan gives me too much credit, Sergeant Ortiz," Tom replied with a grin.

"Oh, that ain't what we hear, Chief Miller," Sergeant White responded. "Til' says if it wasn't for you, he'd been in the ground and Kane mighta' still been out there, instead of bein' juiced tonight."

Tom smiled again. "Well, thankfully we don't have to worry about such a daunting scenario. I think Agent Tunney has a few comments to make, if you gentlemen don't mind?"

"Not at all, Chief. Please, go ahead Agent Tunney."

Sam stood in front of the table that now seated the main group. "Thank you, Sergeant Ortiz. Gentlemen, I'll keep my expectations about this operation simple. Whatever you need from me I'll try hard to give you. I have two operatives in New Hope who can gather any information you think you may still need. The only thing I ask of you is what I asked of the officers in Trenton. Please, keep Jones alive. We're sure he knows who the New Hope killer is. He, quite possibly, did those murders also. Nonetheless, there is another individual who is aiding him in one way or another. Chief Miller, anything to add?"

"Thanks Sam, yes I do. Guys, even if we corner him, he's not going down easily. Believe me, he's a bull. He's probably going to be loaded up on some type of synthetics. Do not try to take him alone, get backup. He threw everything from knives to grenades at us in Trenton, so be alert to his actions, he moves swiftly. Let's start this Millennium with a positive feel tonight, gentlemen. Let's bring Jones and his New Hope accomplice to justice." Tom swung his arm in Stan's direction. "Well, old partner, it's your show. Fill us in on the details."

Stan began to pace the floor and started rubbing his fingers through his crew cut. "Thanks, Tom. Well, here's the skinny. Jones has been spotted by one of our informants. He's been seen coming and going from the nightclub, 'Echo', which is located on West Fourth, in the Village. Apparently, he has a lucrative silent partnership in the place. He also says Jones seems to be favoring his left leg a bit, thanks to Trooper Terrant. Give him our thanks, Tom. He may have aided us immensely."

"I'll be sure to pass it on," Tom replied with a smile.

"Good. Our informant says he's heard Jones will be at Echo tonight, around ten or so. We'll have two undercover officers inside as part of the, um, "beautiful people" crowd who go there. Tommy, I know you can access any door, so you and Sam will take the rear exit of 'Echo.' White, Ortiz, our uniforms, and myself will lead the frontal assault. Our group will only be moving when our undercover team sees Jones leaving. Tom, move whenever you feel it's necessary."

"So, we're going to try and squeeze him."

"It's our hope to do so, Tom. I don't even care if he sees you. It'll only hasten his pace to the street. Now, once he hits the street, we gotta' pounce on this dickhead. I don't want him gettn' loose in the crowds. If he escapes or takes a hostage to shield himself, we're screwed."

"Tonight's going to be quite the conundrum, Til'. We won't be able to draw our weapons until the last minute. The pedestrian traffic will be in a panic if we go in with ours guns blazing like a cavalry charge."

"Don't I know it, Tommy! This Y2K panic's got our shorts in a knot. All we need is that scenario and people will go running everywhere thinking we got a terrorist on the loose. Jones will disappear into thin air."

"Advantage, Jones."

"Oh, most definitely, Sam, but I know there are enough smart people around this table to figure out ways to compensate for Jones' advantages."

"Sounds as if we'll be striking hard and fast, like what we tried in Trenton. The only difference is we won't be holed up in a deathtrap building. Hopefully, it will work this time, Til'."

"I hope so, Tom."

Ortiz caught Stan's attention. "Til', if that's all, me and Whitey want to fill in the troops about the game plan for tonight."

"Go ahead, boys."

"Agent Tunney, Chief Miller, we'll see you tonight," White said while he and Ortiz picked up their paperwork.

"Until then, Sergeants," Tom replied as the young men walked away.

"Sam, Tom, how would you two like to join me for a quick lunch and then I'll take you to Times Square? I'd love to show you what we've implemented to assure the public's safety down there tonight."

"Ah, it sounds terrific," Sam replied. "Later tonight, say about seven, please join Tom and myself for an exemplary dinner at Delmonico's."

"Delmonico's?" Stan asked in amazement. "Man, now that's what I call a treat!"

"I'm assuming this meal will be put on the Bureau's expense account?" Tom playfully inquired.

"Why of course it will, Thomas," Sam said with a gleam in his eyes. "Let's just say, it's their early retirement dinner for a good and faithful employee."

CHAPTER 30

At a private office, in back of the trendy club, 'Echo', Jerome Jones sat and festered. The bullet from Razoul Terrant's firearm was still lodged into his left calf muscle. It appeared to have stopped bleeding, but a layer of pus was now discharging from the entry wound. It was getting hard for him to tell whether it was the knowledge of being shot, or if the bullet fragments were starting to make his blood toxic; nevertheless, Jerome was acting more erratic than usual.

He'd already alarmed his bouncers to the potential of undercover police or agents being in the club tonight. He knew they would be there, but he didn't care at times. Other moments, it made his paranoia increase. Still, here he was, almost daring them to come and get him.

Jones turned his attention to the chrome clock on the wall. "Nine forty-five," he muttered aloud. He walked to the dark glass masking his office from the view of the club's patrons. He peered out to the dance floor. It was already filled with an array of people. It still mainly catered to gays, lesbians, or bisexuals, but anyone with an excess of cash was more than welcome.

He went back his black leather recliner and began to view the multiple video screens he had access to. He'd already spotted the objects of his desire and quickly had his bodyguards escort them to his soundproofed, private room next door. Two female couples appeared on the screen. The club music had been pumped in for their dancing pleasure. They were all blonde haired, either dyed or natural. The younger couple was white and appeared to be in their early twenties. They were both in very tight and revealing black minidresses and both had stiletto heels on. The older couple must have been in their mid-forties. One was white, the other black, and they also were in very short dresses, silver, not black, and stiletto heels. The older ones got up from the couch they'd all been sitting on and began to dance erotically with one another. The younger ones followed suit, and soon they were all gyrating and caressing each other provocatively.

Jones began to pant heavily. More than anyone else in the club tonight, these four women seemed to catapult his desires into a bloodthirsty frenzy. He stopped viewing the screen and stepped in front of a lit, glass display case, which contained a jewel-encrusted sword. Its forged steel blade, so bright from never being used seemed to light up the whole room. Tonight will be your debut. He began to grin with delight as he grabbed the ornate handle and effortlessly sliced the blade through the air. Tonight, you'll pay with your lives for what you've turned me into. You'll pay for the sodomizing I'd received at the hands of my dope addict father. You'll pay for the drunken mother who'd molested me from the time I was a young boy. You'll pay for making me into the freak I've become. "Kane's prophecy will be done!" The sword began to move faster through the darkness.

The women had stopped dancing and found their way back to the black sofa. They began to look around the private room. It was painted black, but colored neon lights lit it adequately. They began to notice the pleasure toys put there for them to use however they desired. The older women began to talk about how they'd heard of this room. The younger ones spoke of Ecstasy and cocaine orgies they'd heard of taking place in here.

The door slowly opened, and a hulking figure stood in their midst. His cocky swagger was in evidence as he stopped in the lights path. They could see he wore black boots, black jeans and a black muscle shirt. His dreadlocks were pulled back in a ponytail, revealing his chiseled, handsome features. "Ladies, welcome to my private lair. I've seen all of you in my club before. I must admit, your attractiveness has left quite an impression." He walked over to the mature women and smiled. He slowly started to dance and the women started to move around him. After he felt and groped his way around both of them, he reached into his pocket and produced a small bottle containing his beloved Ecstasy. Upon seeing the bottle, the younger blondes decided to join the party.

The women ingested the drug and Jones decided to speed up the sexual frenzy by offering some cocaine and champagne. "Drink up, snort up, ladies. The more you do, the sooner you'll reach sexual nirvana," he said with a grin. He stood and watched them begin to dance with each other in a stimulating manner. "Ladies, please enjoy each others company. Avail yourselves to anything in this room your heart desires. I shall return shortly."

He hobbled back into his office and viewed their goings-on from the television screen. He watched their actions become increasingly sexual towards one another. The drugs and alcohol were achieving the required effects Jerome wished for. More pus began to trickle down his leg. Jerome pounded his thick hands on the desk in frustration. His face was beginning to flush and his anger was building to a crescendo. He'd soon revisit the ladies.

It was like playing a chess game when you were on these stakeouts. You knew what your next move would be, but you still had to wait your turn. Tom, Sam and a few young officers perched themselves on the back stairway, ready to strike at any time. "Sam, this cat and mouse game with Jones is wearing me out."

"I know, Tom. Maybe tonight we'll have the results we expected in Trenton."

"Hope you're right, Sam."

"So, have we heard anymore about developments in New Hope? I saw you on your cell phone while Stan and I conversed outside Delmonico's."

"Jenn said Phil received the paperwork to show his financial dealings, et al. She said he came into the station yelling and asking for me. She told him I was out in the field, so she said he starting yelling to her about lawsuits against the department and something about what kind of friends we turned out to be."

"Ah, the loyalty ploy."

"That's what I thought. Jenn tried telling him things like this are very routine matters in cases that are so complex, but he just stormed out of the office still yelling about us being traitors to Luke and himself."

Sam shook his head. How quick they try to hit you with guilt to take the pressure off their backs. "Anything else?"

"Yes, she also said the town will be turning out in a big way for tonight's Main Street celebration. John added some troopers to her already good-sized police presence. We should be in good shape."

"Speaking of John, where are he and young Zoul going to be tonight?"

"John will be at the Bowman's Tower celebration, and Zoul will be at the Magill's Hill Park festivities."

"So, they're both within a stones throw of New Hope if the killer graces your town with his presence."

"Yes they are, Sam." Tom adjusted his headset and took a sip of much needed coffee. "Stan, what's going on my friend?"

"Nothin' up here, Tom. Our undercover officers are on the floor of the club. So far, we have no Jones sightings. They did see four women being escorted to a walkway above the floor. They tried acting like they were looking for the restrooms, but the security goons told 'em it's a no admittance area."

"So, it's a stalemate, for now."

"You got it, Tommy."

"We're waiting patiently back here. He'll emerge eventually. How are your guys up front?"

"Just hanging in, like you are. They're mixing in with the crowds. This freakin' Millennium! The amount of people out here is nuts!"

Tom chuckled to himself. Stan hadn't changed a bit. His impatience was legendary. You almost lost your life to Kane because of it, Tom thought. Don't let it happen again tonight, buddy. "Hang in there, friend. Give us a yell when we're moving."

"You got it, Tommy."

Tom lit a Marlboro and rested himself against the brick wall behind him. He looked at Sam and the agent nodded. "And, so we wait," Sam replied while checking his watch.

Jerome Jones ceased viewing the action in the next room long enough to glance at his gold watch. Ten-thirty, and they're still going strong. He increased the volume of the sound system. Two speakers pumped out the music playing in the club, the other two churned out the sensual moaning of the women in Jones' playroom. He again viewed the monitor. The drugs and alcohol had done their work. The women were well into the throes of sexual bliss. Their bare bodies writhed and tumbled back and forth, and the room became their private orgy palace.

He became increasingly aroused when he again turned his attention to the monitor, but it would be short lived. The small scab covering the gunshot wound had split open, sending a torrent of muddy colored fluid down his leg. He grabbed for his sword, and as he did, a sound erupted from his lungs of pure evil. Jones felt like he was going in and out of consciousness as he flailed wildly around the room with his weapon of destruction. When he was finished, the room was demolished. He looked again to the screen and stared deeply. No erotic image entered his mind. He was now repulsed by what he saw. It drove him into a rage beyond his wildest dreams. Jerome Jones had been hurt by man's steel, which had pierced his skin and poisoned his blood. Now, man would pay dearly.

The door behind the women swung open, and they pulled away from each other long enough to see the dark, hulking figure holding a luminous object. In the haze of their drug induced climax, it was beautiful to behold. Jerome began to lure the four serpents. "Come, come to the master, my lovelies. Kneel in front of me."

As they seductively slithered towards him, the youngest blonde approached the gleaming steel and clasped it between her hands. The rest of them followed suit and caressed the blade as if it were heaven sent to fulfill their own selfish indulgences. The youngest one stared at the master seductively while she worked her perverse actions on the blade, but it would not achieve the expected results.

The master recoiled the blade with lightening speed, thus slitting the women's hands. Jones began to boil over with hate. "This is how you show love to the master? Die, you Delilah!" He plunged the sword deeply into the youngest ones abdomen. He recoiled again and while she lay on the floor, trying to slow the blood from flowing, he dislodged her head from her neck with one fluid motion. The three remaining women stumbled backwards as they tried to comprehend what just happened but the drugs and alcohol had basically paralyzed them.

The sounds of screams and music collided in the soundproofed room while Jones swung the sword with reckless abandon. The screams lessened and the forceful swoosh of the blade increased. He slashed indiscriminately through flesh and fabric. Blood splattered the room as if it had been released from the fine hairs of a paintbrush. The master, in his furious pace, had cornered the final object of his rage. He hurriedly drove the sword through her while she fell over some toppled furniture.

He began to view the carnage in the room. You've not yet paid, but you will. You will pay for making me what I've become! Within a matter of minutes, Jerome Jones had mutilated and dismembered the helpless women in a fit of unholy terror not seen since the times of Jack the Ripper. While slipping further into insanity, he picked up his sword and licked the flowing blood from its blade. "Kane, you may be famous tonight, but they'll remember me forever!" The thought of this broke Jones into a fit of laughter.

Jones stood up, walked to the other room, and picked up a towel from the offices lavatory. He was coated in blood and he did his best to clean off. When he was through, the towel and the sink had an unsettling red hue. Jones quickly changed into new clothes that were neatly hung in his wardrobe. He put on his trademark, leather trench and then went to his desk drawer. He opened it, reached inside, and removed two glistening throwing knives. They would replace the ones he adeptly utilized in Trenton. "I know I'll have to run the gauntlet, Lord, but my escape to salvation will not be impeded by man." He next paged his security force to block off attempts made by anyone to impede his progress to the street.

Jones opened his office door, and was met by one of his yellow shirted security men. "Will the women be joining you, sir?" the young man with the shaved head asked.

Jones grinned and started to chuckle. It was the type of response making many in the club, the shaved headed youngster included, wonder if Jones was truly a mental case. "No, they won't be. Leave them to play with each other a while longer." Jones began to chuckle again at the thought of the shaved head coming back up to escort the ladies out of the back room. Happy New Year, kid.

Jones slowed his pace long enough to view the club floor beneath him. The band had come back on stage, and their hard and heavy sounds were deafening. Jones put his arms around the shaved head's muscular shoulders. "Get two more of your boys to walk me out. I'm expecting resistance when I leave here tonight."

"Cops again, sir?"

"As always."

The female undercover, Turner, spotted him first. "Til', Jones is on the platform!" The music was ear splitting by this point. Stan was yelling in desperation for her to move to a better vantage point, but he wasn't sure she heard him on her earpiece. He nervously chewed on his fingernails. Not even a minute into the encounter, and already things are going to shit.

Turner and her male partner, Phillips, tried to advance slowly. She'd vaguely heard Stan, but she was savvy to the drill. "Til', this place is jammed! We're trying to get close but it's gonna' be tough without causing a commotion! He's got his personal goon squad leading him to the floor level!"

Stan kicked the ground in frustration. Shit, he knows my people are in there.

Jones stopped halfway down, and perused the landscape again. The band was cranking out a ferocious set and the crowd seemed duly revved up to usher this new year in loudly. Jones smiled at the scene while he resumed his descent. Here's to the Millennium, and all of its decadence.

Turner and Phillips started to cross the front of the stage. They tried to line themselves up with Jones and his men and push them into the waiting arms of Tilden. Turner decided it was the right time to play her trump card. "Chief Miller, it's time!"

Tom barely heard the call and alerted the troops. "Let's get a move on, gents." Tom picked the lock, opened the back door slowly, and they slid in with no resistance. "We're in and coming fast, Turner!" Tom was hurrying through the brightly lit corridor, until he viewed the scene ahead. "We've got some bloody boot prints here!" The rest of the team came to a halt by the bloody prints. Tom got back on his microphone. "Turner, where did the security take those girls?"

"Down a hallway located behind the platform!"

"Make your way to Jones, we're going to be a minute!"

"I heard you, Chief! Til', get ready, we're moving!"

"Okay, Turner! Tom, what's up back there?"

Tom opened the door, and the SWAT duo rapidly entered the room with their rifles aimed ahead and searchlights on. The four men viewed the overturned office and Sam's light picked up a door in the back and the carpet in front of it seemed to be soaked. "Til', we may have found the girls. I'll get back to you." Tom moved slowly to the door. He gave the nod, and the SWAT members kicked in the door and entered the room. Their lights would very soon reveal the horror inside. It was worse than anything they'd ever seen before. "Jesus, Sam! This is beyond the sacrifice stage, he's gone berserk!" Sam bent down next to the remains of the women and picked up an empty pill bottle. These poor girls probably never knew how precarious the situation was until it was too late.

"Til', get to Jones! He mutilated all four women!"

Stan looked at the ground and spit. This dick is gettn' on my last nerve. "Turner, move in on him, now!"

Turner and Phillips were within arms reach of pressing Jones and his men, but it would not be close enough. Both officers were hit from behind and knocked to the floor. The bands chaotic sound had provoked a large portion of the revelers into starting a mosh pit by the stage. Turner tried to stand up, but she was knocked over again. She was separated from Phillips, who was being squeezed against the stage. "Chief, we need help now!" Turner screamed in pain. Jones saw the fracas below and smiled broadly. He gave the band a quick 'thumbs up' and proceeded to the entrance.

Tom heard the pleas from Turner and the men began a full sprint down the hall. They made it to the balcony and saw the melee. "There's no damn way we're getting through this! They see the rifles and these people are going to trample each other to get out! Sam, take the guys and turn around, I'll get these two!" Sam and the two officers disappeared back down the hall. "Til', get ready! Sam and the SWAT guys are coming to stabilize your position! I'm going to get Turner and Phillips! Jones must be headed your way!"

Tom ran down the stairs and into the fray. He saw Phillips getting kicked by a young tough, sporting a mowhawk. Tom kicked the punk in the knees, and as he buckled from the force, Tom connected with the kid's jaw for good measure. Once Tom got Phillips to his feet, they bulled their way to Turner's position. The two punks knocking her around went crashing to the floor, courtesy of some quick punches from Miller and Phillips. Tom grabbed Turner's hand and pulled her up. "Come on, we're out of here!"

Stan started running towards Echo's entrance with his men. Within the throng of pedestrian traffic, he identified three yellow shirts followed by the dreadlocked menace. Stan drew his gun, and pointed it skyward while he bumped through the crowd. "Jones, Jones!" He yelled the name again and again. He could hear his officers yelling for people to clear the way. Jones and men spotted Tilden and began to run. The crowd gave Jones the window of opportunity he needed to flee, but his henchmen were not so lucky.

Stan bumped into a few more people and began to chase Jones up West Fourth. Tom reached the entrance long enough to see this and decided to join his old partner in the pursuit. His legs were under strain from the running and beatings of the past few days, but the adrenaline rush made him catch and pass Stan.

Jones darted from West Fourth and onto Broadway. He'd nearly navigated the wide street when he was slightly clipped by a passing motorcycle. He tumbled onto the ground, as did the biker and his machine. The bewildered biker bounced up quickly and ran to see if Jones was hurt badly. Jones quickly jumped to his feet and delivered his reply with two quick motions into his coat. The silver streaks of lightening hit the biker, who fell to the ground writhing in pain. The shocked pedestrian traffic watched Jones pull up the motorcycle and get it started. He began to lurch forward and made a sharp, deliberate turn, which sent his pursuers sprawling to the pavement.

The two men regained their footing and watched Jerome Jones race deeper into the West Side of Manhattan. Stan's foot connected with a wire trash receptacle nearby, sending trash blowing in every direction on this mild, but windy night. As they caught their breath, Tom's Explorer hurtled into view. "Get in you two," Sam yelled from the open window. "We already have units in pursuit."

The men jumped in, and Sam adeptly jockeyed the vehicle through the traffic. Frantic reports came in from the other units about Jones wildly taking the cycle from the streets and onto the sidewalks. After a small break of silence, the next report in said they'd lost Jones somewhere around Wall Street. "Not again! This asshole can't get away again!" Stan was about to blow harder, when Tom calmly put up his hand. "I don't think he wants to, gents."

"You think he has plans for us, Thomas?"

"Yes I do, Sam." Tom thought back to Kane's words in prison. He'll die a glorious death, because all he knows is notoriety. "Gents, hear me out. If you were Jones, where, in a city full of such largesse, would you make your last stand?" All three men looked skyward to the mammoth monoliths they were approaching. One hundred and ten stories of last stands would make for great print. I remember when Stan and I were there to handcuff that Frenchman after he'd walked a tightrope between them. Now, on the eve of an already insane night, he's going to lead us on a two thousand foot manhunt. Tom grabbed the two-way. "Turner, get those units to the World Trade Center. We'll find Jones there."

"Say again, Chief?"

"You heard the man, Turner," Stan replied. "Get our people to da' Trade Center, now!"

"Christ! Til', where do we begin to look?"

Good question. The Explorer came to a screeching halt on the pavilion leading to the North Tower. Stan looked up at the massive structure and shook his head. Damn good question. The three men disembarked, and quickly met White and Ortiz's group in full stride. "We passed the cycle on the way up here. Where do ya' need us, Til'?"

Ortiz's reply would come in the form of a push. Tom and Stan had looked into the clear night sky long enough to see it coming. What 'it' was wouldn't be known until the pavement shook from the impact, followed by the sounds of glass breaking with deafening force. The two men had pushed everyone out of harms way. Now, they went to view what nearly ended their lives. Fragments of wood littered the impact point. "This guy's got a real problem with office furniture," Tom said quietly. His old partner gave him a rather perplexed stare. "Nothing, Til', I'm just thinking out loud."

Tom quickly got his focus back on the task at hand and started jogging. "Let's get to the security desk on the main floor. Someone has to be chasing him." Tom came to the doors first and saw the glass was blown out. Tom drew his sidearm and the group quickly followed suit. Ortiz carefully approached the desk and stopped cold. "No pursuit here, mi amigos," he said quietly. Two more of Jones' honed instruments of destruction had found their targets.

Tom got behind the desk and rifled the dead officer's pockets. He pulled out a ring of keys and proceeded to the main board. "Til', remember when we investigated the Morrow murder here in eighty-three?"

"Yeah, I do, Tom. They thought Morrow killed himself, but.."

"But, they found out someone entered the building after him that night by checking the elevator board. Remember, it kept track of the last movements in each elevator?" Tom put the fat, round key into the lock on the board, and turned it. "It's showing recent movement on the express elevators." Tom turned to look at the group. "Our man would be on the observation level, folks. Til', I think it should be just you, Sam, and me up there. I don't think bringing an army is going to do us any good."

"I agree, Tommy. Ortiz, White, get your guys outside and cordon off the area."

"You got it, Til'," Ortiz replied. Tilden's radio began to crackle. "Til', it's Turner. We're outside the Towers. What now?"

"Turner, stay out there. Ortiz and White are coming out with their guys. Jones is topside. Call in reinforcements and block the street. Nobody, unless it's the Mayor, is to get access up to the pavilion. Am I clear, Turner?"

"Got it, Til', you can count on us." Stan looked at the express elevator doors, and then to Tom and Sam. "Well, are we ready to do this?"

Sam checked his firearm and nodded. Tom gave him a quick smile. "You know me, Til', it's why I get paid the big bucks." The doors closed behind them and the quick ascension to the heavens began. "Do they still keep a guard up top, Stan?"

"Think so, Tommy."

"Then I'll assume he's met the same fate as his counterparts downstairs," Sam sighed heavily. All of this damn death is really getting to me. The three men kept their weapons out and watched the floors whip by on the digital counter. Not a word was spoken between them. They'd all been down this strange road before and they knew what had to be accomplished tonight.

When they reached the last floor, the doors opened wide to reveal a blood-stained floor. The dead officer lay a few feet to their left. They quickly felt the breeze behind them and heard the heavy panting from around the corner. They slowly approached the sounds, and soon viewed their madman. He was straddling the safety bar between the observation point and the large window he'd broken. The wind, at this height was strong, and Jones was gripping the bar with both hands. He turned to face his confronters and grinned wildly. Tom approached Jones slowly, but kept a good measure of distance between the two of them.

"So, we meet again, Tom Miller," Jones chuckled. The lunatic grin was still pasted across his face. "Yes, we do Jerome. I know asking you to come away from the window is pointless right now, so would you mind if we talked?"

Jones chuckled again. "Go ahead, Miller. I'm sure you, and Sam Tunney, and Stan Tilden will all be asking me questions." Tom lost his serious demeanor and broke a quick smile. "So, you know all of us here, Jerome?"

"Wouldn't you want to know the names of your pursuers, Thomas? I know Tilden. He's been trying to get my clubs shut down for years in this city. Sam Tunney, I knew his bio before you gents attacked my compound in Trenton. By the way, you lost men that night because I have good contacts in Townsend's department. I pay them well to keep me informed. Miller, I've known of you the longest. I read your book, I've kept tabs on what you've done since you caught Kane. I made it a point to try and make inroads with my drugs into your town just so I could keep an eye on you."

"So, has it always been about the drugs, even the killings? Was it all that simple?" Tom had struck a nerve with his question. Jones stopped grinning and glowered at the lawman. "No, it hasn't been that simple! I tried to use faggots to peddle my wares out of their clubs for two reasons. One, I knew with their high-end clubs, I could make a killing with profits. Two, if they denied me access to their clubs, I'd kill them, Kane style. In a perfect world, it took pressure from my drug operations and made you all look for a Kane copycat. It also gave me a sense of pleasure to do away with the people who made me this way."

"Homosexuals made you this way? I think that's quite a ridiculous statement." Tom was trying hard to get under Jones' skin and get some answers before the man snapped and tried making the three officers his next victims. "It's not ridiculous at all," Jones replied snidely. "When you're molested at a young age by people you trusted, tell me you wouldn't hate these people. I had a bisexual father who raped me at the drop of a dimebag, Miller."

"So killing these homosexuals is your revenge?"

"Partially, yes."

"Partially, I see. So, the other reason was to be profitable at their expense." Tom moved slightly closer to Jones. He could see the blood running around Jones' boot. The gun wound must have opened again. "May I ask you something else, Jerome?"

Jones reached into his pocket while he watched Tom approach him. "Sure, Miller, ask away."

"Did you kill Stone and Jeaneau, also?"

Jones eased his hand from the throwing knife's handle. "You want answers for New Hope, Thomas? Fine, let's talk about New Hope. Yes, I was there when Stone was murdered. I was there to see Jeaneau get his too. I dragged his ass all around the house, and I hung him on that pole. Stone, I dumped his body in your town and then I got driven into Trenton. I was there, but I didn't kill them. I left that go to a person who wanted them dead even more than I did."

Bastard, you were there to watch it all. Tom locked his eyes onto Jones'. His stare was almost as wild as Jerome's. "Did the jogger drive you to Trenton?"

"The jogger?"

"Yes, the female, well, if she is female, jogger. Did she take you to Trenton in Stone's Lexus?"

"That's a good guess, Thomas. It's why I admire you, Tilden, and you also Agent Tunney. You are all so perceptive."

"Who is the jogger?"

"Oh, Thomas, I can't make it that easy for you."

"Why can't you, Jerome? Look at where you are right now. What do you gain by keeping the identity a secret?"

"What do I gain? I keep evil alive, that's what I gain." He started to grin again. "Hell, that's worth the price of admission alone. Besides, if I keep this person alive, your pain will continue. Yes, heroic, do-gooder Thomas, your pain continues." Jones put his hand back into his pocket and grabbed the knife handle hard.

After all these years, I have my answer. Tom swallowed hard. "Who is the jogger, Jerome?"

"The killer of your father, Thomas," Jones replied with a chuckle. Jones slid from the bar and now stood by the opening. How beautiful the city looks. How different it will all be when Kane's prophecy comes to fruition.

"What's the name, Jerome?" Tom lifted his revolver and took aim. If he's throwing the knife, I'm taking him out. Nobody up here will die except him. "What is the name of the jogger, Jerome?"

"You'll know it soon enough, and your pain will continue."

"Damn it, Jones! Who is it?"

Jerome smiled and took his hand away from the trench. "Your pain will continue, Thomas, and you are a long way from home."

Before any one of the lawmen could say a word, they stared blankly into the vacuum before them. When the reality of what happened sunk in, Tom reached the safety bar first and realized all he could do was look below to the sparkling lights.

It seemed like forever, this flight of fancy, but the deed was accomplished in an instant. Nobody would ever know for sure if he'd achieved some type of salvation or damnation, but for now, Jerome Jones had assured himself of a well-documented and glorious demise.

CHAPTER 31

The three men said nothing during the ride down. They all looked mentally and physically drained, Tom more than anyone. When they departed the elevator, he lit a Marlboro. What a blur this week has been. Between the murders, the battle in Trenton, the club, and now this, Kane's approaching death will almost seem anticlimactic. The chirp of his cell phone snapped Tom back to the present. He'd received a message, so he contacted his voice mail, and waited.

"Tommy, it's Ink." Tom noticed Ink's voice sounded nervous. "Tommy, call me back, bro'. It's around ten-thirty, and I'm alone at the Den. Remember when Al was killed, you told me about the note you found? I know who the wolf in sheep's clothing is. It's…" Tom heard nothing more. The message had been cut off.

"What's wrong, Tom? Your face looks drained."

"It was Ink, Sam. He said he knew who the wolf in sheep's clothing was, and then the line went dead."

"Ya' think the wolf found him, Tommy?"

"Only one way to find out, Stan. I'm calling Gates and having her send Pagano and Rose to check on Ink. I redialed his number and I'm getting no answer."

"The satellite transmission may be jamming, Thomas. It could be nothing more than that." Tom looked even more nervous. "I hope you're right, Sam, because I can't get Gate's cell either, and my house phone just keeps ringing."

"Keep trying, Tommy, you'll reach them," Stan replied as the men started to walk towards the pavilion. Turner's group had already surrounded Jones' disfigured body and the reinforcements started pushing away the press contingent. John Royce, from the Reporter, saw the lawmen approaching. "Chief Miller, Agent Tunney, Detective Tilden, what happened up there?" he asked in a bellowing voice. Tom decided to field the question. "We really have nothing to say except, Jerome Jones fell to his death from the Trade Center."

"Was it suicide?" another reporter asked.

"Yes, it was."

"Tom, was he the copycat killer?"

"John, all I can tell you is that he confessed to some of the murders. He knew who committed the others, but he divulged nothing more." Tom jumped when he heard the cell phone ring. Thank God, someone is calling me. "That's all the questions I can answer now." Stan Tilden came to the forefront. "Okay guys, give my people some room to work here, and I promise we'll answer everything in due time." Stan grabbed Tom and Sam while Tom tried to answer the phone. "Guys, lets get back to the P.A. Command Center and away from this mess."

Tom was still trying to make out the noise coming from the earpiece. It almost sounded like music. It became crisp and clear while they moved further away from the noise of the crowds. It was a hauntingly familiar sound and Tom began to realize what it was when they entered the command center. "It's 'Symphony Fantastique'," he murmured.

"What did you say, Thomas?"

"Someone is playing 'Symphony Fantastique' over the phone. Kane said it was what he used to roll through his head while he was killing." Stan's face drained of its color now. He remembered the conversation at Clinton Correctional. "Tommy, slide the phone into this holder, and start talking. We'll put it on speaker and try to trace it."

Tom followed Stan's lead and the music began to reverberate through the room's speakers. "Hello? Who is this?" He received no reply. "Hello, could we stop playing games here?" Again, no answer came. "Damn it! Who is this?"

"Now, is that any way to act while such good music is being played?" the familiar voice asked.

Tom's eyes grew wide. It couldn't be. There's no way it could be. He took a deep breath and looked at Sam and Stan. They too could not believe their ears. "Is there any reason you're calling? I need to keep this line open."

"Oh, I think you know the reason I'm on. I just saw the news break in to announce Jones' demise. What a way to die, jumping from the Trade Center. It's such a shame, he was a disturbed, but quite capable accomplice."

"So, you're the wolf in sheep's clothing?"

"Oh, I see you received Ink's message. He'll be out of commission for some time. Pity how hard I had to hit him, but I wanted you to know when I was ready. Yes Tom, guilty as charged, I am the wolf." Everyone in the command room now knew who the killer was. Stan and Sam looked beside themselves, but it was Tom whose heart had sunk.

He sat on the edge of the table and lit another Marlboro while his mind raced feverishly. Was it ever really a friendship? Was the moment right, after all these years to implement whatever sick plan was rolling through your mind? Did you kill my father?

The silence was soon broken by the voice on the cell phone. "Are you surprised, Tom? Disappointed? Oh, my little Keystone cop, I bet you feel like you've been taken for the fool."

"Why did you do the killings, Phil?"

"Are we talking now, or fifteen years ago, Tom? It will all come to the same conclusion, if I don't get what I want, people pay dearly."

Tom took another drag from the cigarette. "It was you who killed my father."

"Yes it was, Tom."

"What could my father possibly have that you'd wanted, Phil, money, notoriety? Hell, you ended up with all of that anyway!"

"No, Tom, it was much easier than that, your father had Gary. I was one of his students in the Village. I fell in love with Gary. He was the only person who'd ever treated me with respect. I will admit to being captivated by his talent. One day, when I got the nerve, I told him my true feelings."

"What did he tell you, as if I didn't already know?"

"He said he was flattered, but Edgar would always be his soul mate. He didn't think anything of it, but I was so downhearted by the whole matter. I yelled to Gary that I wasn't one to take no for an answer, but Gary told me to stop being irrational and to please leave his studio."

"Well, I know you didn't kill Gary, but you were planning to do the deed?" Phil began to chuckle. Tom never paid attention to it before, but Phil's chuckle sounded very similar to Kane's. Could they have been accomplices?

Phil spoke again. "I had planned Gary's demise perfectly. I climbed up the fire escape of the studio, opened the storeroom window, and crept in. I opened the door of the room a crack and saw Gary. I took out a knife similar to the type Kane was using, and was ready to make my move. That's when I saw him coming in the studio door behind Gary. I guess killing was becoming so easy for Kane, he didn't even take the time to be inconspicuous. I could've startled him, maybe even stabbed him and spared Gary's life, but I was awestruck by Kane's abilities. I was filled with such hatred of Gary, I was actually excited to view his last moments."

Tom squashed the butt into an ashtray and quickly lit another one. This filthy prick was turned on by Gary's death. He looked to Stan and Sam to see how the trace was coming. Sam quickly passed him a note. "We're having problems. It's a cell phone but the system's so flooded with calls, we're having troubles making the trace." Tom turned his attention back to the conversation. "So you saw the whole thing and did nothing."

"I didn't want to stop him. I viewed his handiwork from behind the door. It created such a bloodlust in me. I needed to get away, but the animal instincts inside Kane must have sensed someone else there with him. I tried to turn and run, but his eyes caught mine. He came to the door and I froze, it was like I was mesmerized. Before I knew it, he was in front of me. His eyes pierced through mine, and he looked down long enough to see the knife in my hand."

"Did he say anything to you?"

"Yes, he said if he were a rational man, he'd have thought the knife to be for him. He said he sensed my hate, and that now I would hate even more because he'd killed what I'd wanted to destroy myself. He said I'd continue his work because I hated being homosexual, and I hated what people had done to me for being one. He said he spared me because I would not spare the rest."

"How did my father's demise come about?"

"I saw your father the next day. He'd known I'd made advances towards Gary. I was still lusting for Gary's blood. I told him Gary got what he deserved. I thought your old man would kill me when I initially looked into his eyes, but he just grabbed me and hugged me. He said I was a confused, angry young man, but my anger would pass as I matured. Edgar said I'd come to know that two wrongs don't make it right."

"Two wrongs don't make it right. Sounds like what Al told you just a few days ago."

"Yes it was, and I didn't need to hear it from him either. It's why I used the knife I'd planned for Gary on your father. The bloodlust in me was satisfied, at least, until recently."

"So, you killed my father and Al because they admonished your outrageous behavior?"

Phil's voice grew bone chilling cold. "I told you before, Thomas, people pay dearly when I don't get what I want."

Tom ground out the Marlboro, and again immediately lit another. "Is that why Luke met his untimely death?"

"Ah, Lucas, my love. He was a great man, but he was too honest. You see I was much like my friend, Jerry Ward. I like my taste for the good life, which is why when he introduced me to Jerome Jones and Robby Pond, I immediately enjoyed their lifestyles."

"So, you'd already met Jones before he pulled his appearance at the 'Train'?"

"Yes, I had. We wanted to get Lucas on board, so we staged the 'meeting' to see if he'd bite. We expected it to go sour, but Jerome thought I could charm him into seeing things our way."

"Of course, we've seen the results of your charms. So, you couldn't get your way with Luke and you killed him?"

"I tried talking Luke into using the 'Train' as a peddling spot. I tried to let him see what a lucrative side business it could become for us. He naturally became upset. He said I'd been spending too much time around Ward. He said Jerry's sliminess was starting to rub off. He told me to end my association with Jerry, or he'd make sure Jerry's little affair with Rob Pond would become public."

"So, you pushed the man you'd been with for years into blackmail, just so you'd cease in your plans? You'd become so obsessed with the money you'd receive from selling the Ecstasy?"

"No, Tom," he hissed. "My obsession is power. The type of power Jones had over people. The kind of power putting fear into the hearts of the weak. You see, when I told Ward and Jones about Luke's plan, they were the one's who panicked. That's when I told them about my plan for the Kane prophecy. We could use Kane's insane prophecy to scare off anyone who would not fit into our plans."

"Such as Luke and Al? Were they getting too close to discovering the master plan, Phil?"

"They would have eventually known everything. It's why they needed to be dealt with. Kane's prophecy was the perfect vehicle to put our plans in motion."

"Rob Pond, he didn't fit into your plans anymore?"

"Rob was getting careless and greedy, a bad combination in any business. I told Jones to make an example of him. I think it set the wheels in motion very well. Jones unwittingly put the pressure on himself with his sloppy, brutal, murderous style. I knew he'd leave his prints everywhere. He'd be the easier target for you and the Feds to get."

Tom looked to Stan and Sam, and there were still no results on the trace. Sam tried again to get Tom's house number, but was getting no answer. "I think I'd better get Boyle involved," he whispered to Stan, who nodded in agreement. "I guess Ward came up with the idea of getting the FBI involved because he thought they'd come in and muddle the process up immensely. Until, they sent him Sam Tunney."

"Yes, Tunney fucked things up royally for us. It figured we'd have to get the only conscientious agent in the Western hemisphere sent to New Hope."

"Were you alone when you committed the murders or was Jones your strongman?"

"Thomas, how perceptive you are. Yes, he was my muscle with Luke. He'd hit him from behind when I confronted Luke at the 'Train' that night. I took care of the ritual process. He dumped the body, and one of his ruffians took him back to Trenton after the deed was done. I dumped the car at the Holly Edge and laid the trap in the woods."

There was a pause in their conversation. Slim body, piercing eyes, it was all starting to come together. "You were the jogger, weren't you? It's why you started sweating the other day when I asked you about the possibility of the jogger being a cross-dresser."

Phil started to chuckle again. "Thomas, I knew you, Boyle and Tunney would be hard to shake. It's why I'd hoped Jones would have seen to your untimely deaths in Trenton. Yes, I was the jogger. I was the one who attacked Al, and Jones beat him and dragged him through the house while I made the cuts. Jones also put him on the pole. The best part about having Jones around was he dumped all my bloody clothes from both murders in some lot by the World Church. He said the cops would never even raise an eyebrow if they found them anyway."

"So, Jones finding his way into New York tonight wasn't a chance occurrence at all. You wanted to split us up."

"Yes, it would have worked so well, but I will still get the last laugh, Thomas. You see, when you caught Kane, you made it hard for me to get what I wanted at a young age. It's why I tracked you to New Hope all those years ago. It's why I made it a point to become a part of your inner circle, a part of the family. I wanted to hurt everything you'd ever loved in life, and I've succeeded rather well. Tonight, I will complete the deed."

Tom's felt the sweat pour down from his forehead. He knew why he couldn't get in touch with Jenn now; Sam knew too, and was frantically calling Boyle's cell number again. "Phil, where are Rob and Drew?"

"They would be lying dead in your driveway, Tom. The little trick Jones showed me with the throwing knives worked like a charm. Don't worry, Tom, I don't think they suffered too much."

Tom heard Sam speaking quickly in the background. *God almighty, I hope you reached Boyle.* He focused his attention again to the phone in front of him. "May I ask where Jenn is, Phil?"

"She would be knocked out and tied up in the kitchen, Thomas. I didn't want to kill her just yet. I'd like her to come to and witness my masterpiece, the downfall of your life. I told you I'd take away everything you loved in my note!"

He was shaking terribly. He lit another cigarette and looked at his revolver. *I am an eternity away from helping her. The bastard trapped me here, damn it!* "Where would Debbie be, Phil?"

"Glad you asked, Tom. She would be watching the glorious scene in Times Square with me." He could hear her in the background whimpering. He looked at the screens in the command center. For the first time, he noticed the view of Times Square and the hundreds of thousands of boisterous revelers. *Lord, I have never felt so alone.*

John Boyle received the call from Sam, and was into his vehicle with lightening speed. He grabbed his two-way and called Zoul. "Zoul, Zoul, leave the Hill and get to Tom's house now! The killer is there! It's Antos!"

"Say again, Troop?" the startled young trooper asked.

"It's Phil, godammit! Antos is the killer!"

Tom could still hear Debbie's light sobbing in the background. "How is Debbie, Phil?"

"I'd say she's fine, Thomas. She's just smarting a tad from the way I had to knock her around to get her tied up. She is a fighter, your little lady." Tom looked again at the screen showing Times Square. Many people did not know what to expect of the next few minutes, let alone the aftermath, but Tom knew one thing, his life was hanging in the balance. John Boyle, if I ever needed you more, I couldn't say.

Boyle came screaming down Route 32, slowing only when he reached the Borough. His men had kept one lane of Main Street open, just in case of an emergency. The celebration was in full swing in New Hope, but John had no time to waste on such trivial matters. Debbie needed help, and he and Zoul were the only ones who could get to her. His men waved him through the intersection of Main and Bridge. When he reached the opening, he hit his siren and tore up the asphalt. "Sweet Jesus, help me save a friend tonight."

The straps were put tightly around his scarred arms. The priest asked him if he'd anything to say, but he only smiled and looked ahead with his demonic gaze. His arm was prepped and the order was given to administer the injection. He thought about what he'd told Tom Miller the other day. It made him to think about his prophecy coming true. Jones had never gotten word back to him, through his prison cronies, about who he'd conspired with to cause Miller's downfall, but he had a good guess. My young friend from fifteen years ago; I told you your hate would help me. The priest saw the reaper's grin and mistook it for a man making his peace with the Lord. "It will all be over soon Martin," the priest said as he bent down near his ear. The lethal dose administered had begun to suffocate him, but he still managed to smile. Yes, it will be over soon, but not just for me.

Tom tried to maintain his composure, but it was becoming a hard task to achieve. He kept the chatter going with Phil, but the jovial tone of Phil's voice made him feel nauseous. It was getting close to midnight and Tom had very little energy left for this. "Tom, are you still there?" the gleeful voice asked. "Yes, Phil, I am. Can I ask you something?"

"The time is passing quickly, Tom, but go ahead."

"Phil, why would you want to fulfill this prophecy? I understand your covert use of it to attain riches, but there must be something more for you to be this elaborate. There just must be something more to it."

"There is something more to it, Tom! I hate what I am, and I hate what people have made me into! I want to die, and I want the people that have hurt me to die also."

"You want Debbie to die? She has adored you, just as Luke and Al did. They offered you their love and friendship, and you repay them with death?" Tom didn't know what else to say, and the line became silent for a brief moment. "I'm tiring of this conversation, Tom. The time is quickly winding down on the century and I have to prepare for what I must do."

Red and blue lights flickered through the trees as the white streak lurched through the side streets. It was amazing John Boyle had kept the car from rolling into the ditches because the speed he reached at points was hard to fathom. He'd made the hard turn from Sugan and was now on Chapel. In the distance, he saw lights hurriedly approaching. "Zoul, is that you on Chapel?"

"It's me Troop! I'll be at Tom's house shortly!"

"I'm comin'! Sweet Jesus, I'm comin', Zoul!"

"Tom, would you like to speak with Debbie before I hang up?"

"Yes, I would like that, Phil." He could hear the television over the phone and again he heard Debbie's light sobs. "Don't cry Debbie, this isn't goodbye."

"I..I love you, Tommy. I always will." Her sobs were becoming more labored. Tom slammed the desk. This is not how it will end, Lord! "No, Debbie, this is not goodbye!"

They killed the headlights as they approached the house. Within seconds, they were out of the vehicles, and swiftly moving past the bodies of their fallen comrades. The reached the front door and drew their weapons. "Are ya' ready for this, lad?"

"This is what it's all about, Troop."

Phil began to prance behind Debbie with the knife. He glanced at the jewel-encrusted handle and then again to the television. The countdown from ten had just begun. "Debbie loves you, Tom, and you can't even tell her goodbye? Such impudence!"

He was going to try and plead with Phil, but he heard the cracking of wood over the phone. He heard John Boyle's voice. "Phil, for the love of God, put the knife away from Debbie!" He could hear Zoul say he had a clear shot, and he could also hear the deafening countdown from Times Square. Sam, Stan and a handful of officers in the control room listened helplessly along with Tom.

"Get away, John. Let me finish what needs to be done!"

"Not a chance, Phil. Drop the knife, an' get out from behind Debbie!"

"Troop, he's got it to her neck! Let me take the shot!"

Tom was desperate. He started to think about Debbie and all their years together. He saw it in a flash, and wondered if Debbie was doing the same thing. It meant he'd given up on hope, but he needed to say it. He needed to scream it. "Debbie! Debbie! I love you!"

"Tommy!" she screamed.

"Antos, I'm not tellin' you again. Drop it now! NO!"

Everything became a blur. They all heard Debbie scream, the gunshots that followed and, in between the roar from a very safe Times Square celebration, they heard nothing. The world was now into the first seconds of a new century, but it didn't matter. Tom put his head down and began to cry. Stan walked over to the phone and pulled it from the speaker line. Stan was talking into it, but Tom couldn't hear a thing anymore. Everything was a blur. Sam sat down and put his arm around him. There were no consoling words from the wise, old agent. The best he could muster was an understanding nod.

The buzzing of the meshing noises was starting to clear from his ears, and he began to see the other officers in the room running around. Had the new century not gone off without a hitch? Was it the beginning of the end, after all? He saw Stan slam the phone back into the holder. His old partner quickly approached Tom, and grabbed his face. Tommy was still in a daze but he saw the smile and then he heard the voice fill the room. It boomed like the voice of an angel from the heavens.

"Thomas Miller, if ya' can hear me, lad, there is a pretty young lady here who wants you to come home! She has not received her New Year's kiss yet!"

The room exploded into a celebration of their own, and Tom turned to hug Stan and Sam. After being slapped on the back and congratulated by everyone there, he made his way to the phone, pulled it from the holder and began to speak. "Debbie Miller, I love you! Happy New Year!"

He could hear the sobs again, but this time they were followed by a joyful voice. "Happy New Year, Tom! I love you too! Come home!"

Home. The thought of it sent a warm feeling through his whole body. Even after all the sorrow of the past few days, the beaten, weary warrior would be able to happily retreat to the confines of his domain. More importantly, he'd finally be able to put his arms around Debbie, hold her tight and kiss her for what would seem like an eternity. "I'll be there, Debbie. I'm coming home."

CHAPTER 32

The warm breeze was lazily sweeping through the trees. It was a beautiful day for a parade in New Hope. The lampposts and the storefronts along Main Street were festooned with American flags of all sizes and the flowerboxes overflowed with red, white and blue petunias. This would be a Memorial Day to celebrate, and to remember.

Tom Miller smiled while he watched the festivities from his seat on the dais, and the Veterans Band began to play the National Anthem. A new flagpole now stood on Ferry's Landing, and the Stars and Stripes soon graced its heights. Next to the pole was a cherry tree, dubbed the Liberty Tree by the local high school children who planted it in memory of the fallen victims of the Millennium Murders.

The Millennium Murders, as they were referred to after Mary McGuigan's nationwide bestseller, had produced an even larger tourist increase for the town. People from every corner of the earth wanted to see where these gruesome murders occurred, and except for a few instances of outsiders trying to make a fast profit on the towns tragic events, the strong fabric of the New Hope residents remained solid. Yes, things were getting back to normal, Tom thought, but enough had changed.

It was a given about the grief people still felt over the losses of Andrew Rose, Rob Pagano, Luke Stone, and especially, Al Jeaneau. Phil

Antos' name was very rarely mentioned in town again. All most people knew was he'd been laid to rest, in a nondescript grave, located in a cemetery in New York City. The headstone read Phil Antosky, his original name.

Tom watched the young lady finish her speech and smiled as she sat down next to him. "Very eloquent speech, young lady. It couldn't have been said any better, Chief Gates."

"Thanks, Tom, but I'm sure you'll try your best." Tom looked at her and winked. She had been interviewed on national talk shows, had her face grace the cover of quite a few periodicals, but Tom would forever remember her as the woman who saved Debbie Miller's life. Although John and Zoul had fired rounds that night, it was Jenn Gates, who'd escaped the ropes binding her, and after pulling her secondary piece from her ankle holster, made her way into the living room. It was Jenn who delivered the fatal shot, shattering the back of Phil Antos' skull. Knowing he'd be leaving the town in capable hands, Tom gladly handed her his badge in February, for he had other avenues to venture.

A light that had been turned off for too long in this town would blaze again. On a bright, but chilly April day, Tom and Debbie Miller signed the papers helping to restore this vibrant community back to the days preceding those fateful ones of last December. Tom unlocked the door and found a stool. He opened the case he was carrying, revealing Edgar Miller's saxophone. He put the gleaming instrument to his lips, and the sweet sounds of "Caravan" began to pour forth. A week later, 'The "A" Train' would again open its doors, and everyone would come.

A few more people would speak, and then it was Tom's turn to address the audience. As he stood at the podium, he spotted Debbie and smiled. He looked briefly into the clear, blue sky, and then brought his gaze again to the crowd. "There would have been a time in my tenure, as a law officer, that I would have used this event as a time to mourn the loss of good friends. Today, I think I'd rather rejoice in their lives. They were lives they enjoyed to the fullest. True, some were younger than others, but the vigor with which they lived spanned their true ages. Today, I want to celebrate in the lives of Andrew Rose, Rob Pagano, Lucas Stone, and Al Jeaneau. Three of them protected and served everyone in this community with a commitment to decency, respect, and tolerance. The other gave us the joy of music. They all gave back to this Borough, whether it was talking to our youth, sponsoring charity events, whatever it was these men were involved.

I also want to celebrate the vibrancy of two individuals, especially. Al and Luke knew the consequences of being open and opinionated about their lifestyles. They handled themselves with dignity, grace, and many times calmed the voices of anger with their incredible wit and humor. No matter how their tragic deaths tried to pull the fabric of this town apart during those waning, dark days of December, their love of life kept us all hopeful that time would heal the wounds, and it has."

Tom began to chuckle. "I know, somewhere out in the blue skies overhead, Al Jeaneau is yelling, as he did in our many spirited conversations. Miller, is there a point to all of your babbling, and if there is, could you please get to it?" Many in the crowd began to laugh. "Well, Al Jeaneau," he said again with a grin, "here it is. On this Memorial Day, I dedicate the Liberty Tree to you and Lucas Stone for their lifelong struggle to lead their way of life in freedom. I also dedicate this tree in the memory of Andrew Rose, Rob Pagano, and again, Al Jeaneau. Your love and dedication to the well being of New Hope's inhabitants and the freedom of choice they enjoy will never be forgotten."

Tom and Debbie remained in the Borough for the rest of the afternoon, and then she departed to 'Train' to catch up on some talk with friends. As the blue and pink hues of the sunset sky mixed together over the Delaware, Tom turned to see two familiar faces on the corner by the Logan Inn.

"Mister Mayor, would you happen to have time for an old friend?" he asked loudly as he approached. "Your friend, Mister Mayor, he looks quite familiar. I knew a gentlemen like him, but he always dressed in suits and not in civilian fare."

The two men began to laugh mightily. "Aye' now, Tom Miller, I am not the Mayor yet. The swearing in doesn't take place until next month!"

"Details, Mayor Boyle, mere details. If you talk to your fiancée, Miss McGuigan, she has everybody believing you are the man."

"Well, that's my lass. Why do you think I had her be my campaign manager when she left the paper?"

"A very good choice, indeed, my friend," Tom replied with a grin. "And, what may I ask brings you back here, my esteemed elder statesmen?"

"Ah, tact was always one of your strong points, Thomas. I wouldn't dare miss the ceremonies," he said as he winked.

"Well, it's good to have you back here, Sam Tunney, for whatever reason."

"It's a pleasure being here, Thomas. Of course, now that I'm no longer with the Agency, I can't get them to foot the bill for the Logan, but I think the old man can manage."

"I'm sure you can," Tom grinned.

"Well, if you gentlemen will excuse me, I'm going to my room to get changed. I hear there's a great new place in town to hear jazz, and it so happens, I know the owner."

"We'll see you later, my friend."

"I'm looking forward to it, gentlemen."

As Sam departed, John and Tom walked across Main Street to view the memorial site again. The placid waters of the river created a nice backdrop to the spot. "They put the tree right where Lucas was found."

"I took notice of that, Tommy."

"Such a tranquil spot, for such a brutal act."

"Was thinkin' the same, lad. I was looking here before and wondering how Phil could hate life so much? How could he especially take it away from the people he'd supposedly loved so much?"

"I don't think we'll ever truly know what was going on in his mind. In many ways, he was far more of a menace than Jones could ever have been."

"Yer' right about that, lad. It makes you shudder to think about what they could have accomplished with the murders and the Ecstsay, especially if Ward was still runnin' things."

The wind began to pick up again as Tom looked towards the river. It was not the warm winds of earlier. The pinks of the sky had become gray, and the water was getting choppy. "Well the good thing now is we don't have to worry about Ward, because he's in Bucks County Prison serving a life sentence. Neither of us has to worry about the police end of things anymore, because Zoul is running the local barracks, and Jenn Gates is Chief of New Hope."

"You better get used to calling her Chief Rossini. She and Ink are getting' married in July. Heh, who would of thought of it, Ink and Gates? What a unique pairing."

"I'm sure many an eyebrow was raised when Mary McGuigan and one, John Boyle were engaged also."

"True, so true, Tommy," John chuckled.

The winds began to blow harder as the men zipped their jackets and began to depart the memorial site. When they reached Main Street, the two of them looked towards the site again. "Any regrets on how we handled this case, lad?"

"Only the four names I'm looking at, and the others in Trenton and New York. Otherwise, I think we did the best we could humanly do."

"I agree, Tommy. Wholeheartedly, I agree."

The two men began walking up Main Street, and towards the 'Train'. "So, do you care to join an old soldier and trade some war stories?"

"Aye' lad, I think I'll take ya' up on that. Besides, it looks like a storm's brewin'."

"Isn't there always, John Boyle?" Tom asked when they reached the clubs entrance.

"Aye', I believe you are a wise man, Tom Miller! You're a right wise man, indeed," John laughed as the wind blew the door closed behind them.

Through the hills and valleys, the cold, foreboding waters of the Delaware flows, while up above, gray clouds engage in a fierce, calamitous ascension towards the east. Darkness approaches, with a vengeance.

ABOUT THE AUTHOR

After a brief stint as an English major at the Pennsylvania State University, Richard Cucarese labored at a local steel mill, which, before it closed, was the lifeblood of the local area. It was the interesting and colorful lives of the people he worked around which gave him the impetus to continue his writing. Three years ago, he began writing pages of notes while walking around his favorite spots in New Hope. Those notes became Black River, his first novel.

Born in Brooklyn, New York, he moved to Yardley, Pennsylvania and lived there through most of his youth. He currently resides in Levittown, Pennsylvania, with his wife and baby daughter. He is currently working on his second murder novel, Steel Town.

ISBN 141202262-2

9 781412 022620